Foreword

Don't bother trying to be a writer – there are far too many people at it already.

Well, that's the sort of attitude that some people in the business seem to have. Publishers, agents and magazine editors are very busy people. Sources of encouragement for new writers are as rare as rhinos in Reigate. For this reason alone, the annual Ian St James Awards for short fiction are vital. Each year, sixteen writers who have not yet published a novel see their work appear in the anthology. Another sixty-four runners-up are published in *Acclaim*, the bi-monthly magazine launched so that the Awards could help more new authors into print.

This year, the organizers received four thousand two hundred and twenty-five entries. A vast team of professional readers made a full report on each story and all entrants received a copy. From these critiques, a shortlist of eighty was drawn up and then seven judges, myself included, selected this anthology. The administrators of the Awards are often asked what the criteria are (not least by the judges themselves). Actually, it's very simple. The length of the stories varies from 2,000 to 10,000 words. The subject matter can be anything except work for children; the style ditto. This year's book includes fiction which could be called experimental, romantic, literary or fantastical; often within the confines of one story. Winning tales come from Britain, Ireland, the USA, Canada and Greece. If you want to know what sort of story to write the only real answer is – a good one. It's a subjective judgement, of course, and tastes always vary but, by and large, writing which stands out is sprightly, original, individual and, above all, written from the heart. Whether you love the work in this collection or hate it, they are all stories which impressed us in some way or another.

Thanks are due then to my fellow judges – especially Ian St James for his continued support and Nick Sayers, Deputy Publishing Director, HarperCollins Trade Division. It is never easy for a publisher to justify a book containing work by virtually unknown writers. Harper-Collins' involvement with these Awards is a highly welcome demonstration of their commitment to new and exciting work. This year, the Awards have also benefited from the support of pensions specialists NPI, who printed and distributed thousands of entry forms, and from Elysée, who have presented all shortlisted writers with fountain pens. Looking ahead, the organizers would like to be able to introduce new ideas; reduce the entry fees to widen participation from writers across the world, increase the print run and distribution of *Acclaim* and run short-story workshops around the UK. To do this will require the backing of a major sponsor. At the moment the Awards break even but only just, and the judges and staff are all unpaid.

A special mention is therefore due to the administrator, Merric Davidson, who, as well as directing the Awards, also runs the New Writers' Club which publishes *Acclaim* magazine. His endless enthusiasm and capacity to get by on very little sleep ensure the healthy continuance of these Awards.

In addition, all entrants contribute. Without the writers who send in their stories each year the Awards would not exist. There is a tendency within the industry to be a little snooty about enterprises such as this – to

THE 1994 IAN ST JAMES AWARDS

Judges

RODNEY BURBECK
Book Trade Journalist

LOUISE DOUGHTY
Novelist

ALAN DUNN
Novelist

MAGGIE NOACH
Literary Agent

IAN ST JAMES
Novelist

NICK SAYERS
Publisher

JOHN TRENHAILE
Novelist

BROUGHT TO BOOK

The winners of
the 1994 Ian St James Awards

HarperCollins*Publishers*

HarperCollins*Publishers*
77–85 Fulham Palace Road,
Hammersmith, London W6 8JB

A Paperback Original 1994
1 3 5 7 9 8 6 4 2

A catalogue record for this book
is available from the British Library

ISBN 0 00 649360 2

All royalties from the sale of this book will be paid to
The New Writers' Club and used for the furtherance and expansion of the
Ian St James Awards

Set in Linotron Sabon by
Rowland Phototypesetting Ltd
Bury St Edmunds, Suffolk

Printed in Great Britain by
HarperCollinsManufacturing Glasgow

regard them as somehow amateurish or not terribly serious. This is a gross mistake. The people who enter the Ian St James Awards and the readers who buy this book are the writers and readers who keep publishing alive. Apart from encouraging potential novelists, all those who support awards like these contribute to an important and often undervalued facet of our literary culture – the art form of the short story.

For the authors selected, it is a step forward in a possible writing career. I should know. In 1990, the second year of the Awards, I was one of the winners – and a part-time secretary. This year, the sixth, I am a judge – and a full-time writer. I look forward to the next six successful years, when maybe the person introducing the year 2000 anthology of the Ian St James Awards will be one of the writers you are about to read in *Brought to Book*.

LOUISE DOUGHTY

(Louise Doughty's first novel, *Crazy Paving*, is published in January 1995.)

(For further information on the Ian St James Awards and *Acclaim* write to the New Writers' Club at PO Box 101, Tunbridge Wells, Kent TN4 8YD or telephone 0892 511322. The closing date for the 1995 Awards is 28 February 1995.)

Contents

THE SECRET
OF THE LAKE

Jackie Kohnstamm

Jackie Kohnstamm has always lived in London, apart from student years spent at the University of East Anglia and in France. She has worked as a lecturer, translator and secretary and has been writing for ages – mainly fiction and radio drama. In 1991, the BBC broadcast her first radio play, *The House at Number 9 Rue Fleurie*. This is her first published story.

THE SECRET OF THE LAKE

You could call it a triumph. No more hospital. We're managing at home. It's a relief to know there's nothing more they want to do to you.

Now you have grown weaker, your bed is downstairs. You look straight into the garden, but do you see it? The May tree, roses, the pink busy Lizzie grown into a bush outside the window? Or do you expend so much energy breathing that you see nothing at all? Air has become such an elusive element.

Shall I take you beyond your breathing? Will you come with me to a place you used to know and where you felt happy and safe? 'Listen. Are you listening?'

'Why?'

'I'm going to take you on a journey.'

'Where?'

'In a story. About a young girl. What shall we call her?'

'I don't know.'

'Try. Think of a name.'

'Rosemary.'

'Good. Close your eyes, then.'

'I want to look at you.'

'But you'll see everything more clearly if you don't look. And my voice will be with you all the way. That's better. Are you lying comfortably?'

'Very.'

'Then we'll begin.'

*　　*　　*

Rosemary lived with her parents and older sister and brother in a large flat on the third floor in the heart of the city. When springtime came, the big plane tree outside her bedroom burst into bright green leaf. However, as the city grew hotter, and Rosemary watched dust settle on the broad leaves, she longed to make them shiny again. One early summer's day she could bear it no longer. She fetched a damp cloth from the bathroom, opened the French windows, clambered onto the edge of the balcony, leaned out and wiped as many leaves as she could reach.

'Are you trying to kill yourself, child?' Mother shouted and pulled her away. 'I can't bear to see such a thing!'

'Then don't look,' said Rosemary. 'Why do we have to live in town, anyway?'

'Because your father's work is here, and if he didn't work, you'd have no food on the table.'

But, thought Rosemary, if we lived in the country, then I could gather berries, wild mushrooms and herbs and Father needn't work so hard to feed us all. She announced her idea that night at supper.

'Yes, child, now eat what's on your plate,' said Mother.

For all the world as if I were five, not fifteen, thought Rosemary. Well, fourteen. Almost.

'The country!' scoffed Bella. 'Whoever heard of the latest fashion coming from Little-Wart-on-the-Bum? The country's full of half-wits and everyone's grandparents who didn't manage to get away.'

'And no culture,' yawned Henry, who had just got up. At twenty-five he still lived at home and modelled himself on those great painters who drank late into the night and slept during the day.

'What about you, Father?' asked Rosemary.

'Wouldn't you like to live out of town in a house with a garden? Especially when it gets so hot and the roads melt?'

Father wiped his mouth, freeing crumbs from his moustache and beard. He was a fastidious man. 'It's funny you should say that, Rosemary,' he said at last, 'because I've been thinking along similar lines myself.'

'Father!' Three jaws dropped open. A lock of Henry's long, wavy hair fell forward into his soup spoon. Bella's bangles jangled. Mother set her elbows on the table and forgot to admonish herself. Only one pair of hands clapped with glee.

The house stood on the shore of a lake. Father had rented it for three months from a family spending the summer abroad.

'By the time we return to the city,' he told Rosemary, 'the leaves on the plane tree will be turning yellow, so will not require washing.'

They arrived at dusk when a cool wind was blowing. Rosemary ran round the wooden porch, down steps into the garden, along the crazy paving path beside shadowy clumps of flowers and shrubs to the edge of the lake. A small rowing boat was pulled up onto their tiny beach. The wind stirred up wavelets which slapped against the hull. Rosemary kicked off her sandals and let the water run over her toes and suck at the mud beneath them.

She looked back at the house, at lights going on and off in the different rooms, at the silhouettes of her parents, brother and sister against the windows. Only one remained dark. It was beneath the eaves, an attic window on a level with the treetops. Time to investigate.

'My room's the biggest!' Bella was standing in the doorway, arms crossed.

5

'Mine has windows on two sides,' said Henry, moving his easel around the room. 'And where are you off to?' he asked as Rosemary made for the ladder which led up to the roof.

Rosemary instantly felt at home in her room. She loved the sloping ceilings and dormer window against which the branches of a tree gently tapped. And she loved what lay beyond, the great expanse of shimmering, silver lake.

Late that night she opened the shutters and dragged her bed over to the window. She lay for a long time staring at the dancing shadows cast on the walls by the moon. Strange shapes, ever changing. Eventually she fell asleep. Or did she?

Rosemary's limbs felt lighter. She began to float upwards. Her bedclothes fell from her as she rose in the air and drifted through the window. She brushed past the trees and soared out over the lake. She swooped and skimmed the surface, then, supported by a current of air, rose up and up, higher than the house. She could see all the rooms where her parents, brother and sister slept. She could see her own attic window. Through it were visible the bed and a figure sleeping in it. That's me, she thought. There I am!

How relaxed you look! Each breath is long and even now. Surely you've fallen asleep. But no. Your eyes open. You are looking straight at me. Expectantly. 'Very calming,' you say, 'like a dream.'

'Shall I go on?'

'If you have the strength.'

You are the one with little strength. But it helps you to make out that I am as you are, and so push away what is.

*　　*　　*

Rosemary woke to find that the sun had taken the moon's place. It splashed yellow patches on her wardrobe, chair and table. She jumped out of bed and leaned out of the window. The lake glittered bright blue, the trees hardly stirred. The house was also still. She looked at her watch – only six o'clock. At least the birds were awake. She decided to join them outside.

Rosemary tiptoed through the sleeping house, then ran down the path to the boat. She rowed along the shore, passing house after house, shuttered and silent. She was the first person ever to breathe this fresh air. She drew it deep into her lungs and expelled it with a sigh.

The houses she passed were large and elegant, with imposing terraces and gardens. All except one, which looked out of place. It was stuck between two rambling mansions and seemed to have been constructed out of driftwood. The garden was colourful and wild, the flowers fought amongst themselves to reach the sun.

Here at last was movement. A red and white check curtain was drawn back, the rickety door opened. A white-haired woman stepped outside, waved and beckoned. Before she had time to think, Rosemary rowed to the shore, jumped out of the boat and ran through the garden to greet her new neighbour.

'Been for a swim?' The woman pointed to the towel draped round Rosemary's neck.

'Not yet. I'd like to, if it's not too cold.'

'It'll be fine. There's nothing like an early morning swim, particularly if you have a hot drink immediately afterwards. Would you like chocolate?'

'Oh yes!' cried Rosemary, eager to earn it.

'Off you go, then, and I'll heat the milk to a froth. By the way, what's your name?'

'Rosemary.'

'I'm Olga.'

Rosemary left her clothes in the boat and waded into the lake. Olga. She rolled the word around her mouth. It sounded exotic. It also sounded familiar. Why should that be? She shivered as the cool, silky water reached her waist, took a deep breath and plunged in. Suddenly the shore, trees and houses seemed far away. Her own splashings and the smoke rising from Olga's chimney provided the only movement in the stillness. She dived, felt a rock graze her knee and weeds wrap around her foot. When she looked up, she could see the sun speckling the surface. But the water all around and beneath her was murky. She wondered how deep the lake was.

'So tell me about yourself,' said Olga as her guest sipped at an enormous cup of foaming hot chocolate.

Rosemary looked over the rim in surprise. As the youngest of the family, she was used to being overlooked, not asked about. What was there to tell about her almost fourteen years? Mother, Father, Bella and Henry, of course. The dusty city and washing the plane tree. School. 'The best thing is,' she said as she drained the last of her drink, 'we've got two weeks of term left, and I can be late every day! Because I'm going with Father on the train, which only arrives when school starts, at eight o'clock. Then every afternoon I'll take the train back alone and go for a swim.'

'And come and visit me, if you like,' said Olga.

'Yes, please!'

The family settled into a routine. Rosemary enjoyed the novelty of travelling with Father every morning, even though he was always too busy with his papers to talk to her.

At home Mother was the calm centre of a kitchen tornado. Several pans bubbled on the range. The table

8

sagged under steaming bowls of stewed fruit, jars of jams and jellies. Mother had taken to country life in a big way. Not so Henry and Bella.

On the last day of school, as Rosemary dashed upstairs to put on her swimsuit and celebrate freedom, she found Henry's door wide open. He was dragging his easel from sunny to shady spot, muttering: 'Does here feel any better? No! Let's try here. No!' His brush and palette lay untouched by paint.

Bella held court on the beach. Much to her disgust, she only had one courtier: boring Bernard from next door. Every afternoon he played her Richard Tauber love songs on his wind-up gramophone.

Bella lay on her side, chin cupped in one hand, gazing into Bernard's eyes through half-lowered lids. Today she's Marlene Dietrich, thought Rosemary. They took no notice as she picked her way over records, lemonade glasses and their bodies to reach the boat.

'So how was your last day at school?' asked Olga. And for the first time on that as on every other day, Rosemary felt she had suddenly become visible.

'I had an Aunt Olga,' you say, startling me. I had almost forgotten you were there, so wrapped up was I in the story. 'She wasn't my real aunt. She was married to my uncle. She was beautiful, with jet-black hair, and very vain. As a child I loved playing with the things on her dressing table. It was full of creams and powders and perfumes.' You pause. 'Is it the same one?'

'Possibly. Only in my story she has white hair.'

'Aunt Olga's hair would be white by now, unless she dyed it,' you say with Rosemary's kind of logic. But then, isn't Rosemary based on you? The boundary between real life and story is blurring. 'Knowing her, she'd have dyed it.'

'No!'

'Why not?'

'That's all wrong for the story. This Olga isn't vain.'

'Isn't she?'

'Weren't you listening?'

'Don't be cross with me –'

'I'm not cross!' But I am. Yet how can I be when you're so ill? Now look what I've done! Your frightened look has come back again. Why the hell can't I let Olga dye her hair if that's how you see her? Only I'm also afraid – of losing my grip on the one thing over which I have some control. 'Are you tired? Shall I stop the story?'

'No, please . . . tell me . . . about Olga.'

The name Olga rang a bell with Rosemary. She knew it was Russian. Was that why she connected it with her set of babushka dolls? They had always been her favourite toys. She still enjoyed opening each one and being greeted by a smaller version inside. Come to think of it, the dolls, round and pink-cheeked, resembled her new friend along the lake. 'Mother, who gave me these?' Rosemary asked, bringing them into the kitchen.

'My Russian aunt. She had a soft spot for you because you were born on her birthday – but I've told you this before. They're very old. Don't get flour on them.' Mother was rolling out pastry.

'What was her name?'

'Olga.'

'So she was Olga, too!'

'Who else is Olga?'

Rosemary hesitated. She had not mentioned her visits to the little ramshackle house simply because, here in the country, no one ever asked her where she had been. She relished having a corner of life that was entirely her own. This, she thought, is how grown-ups must feel all the time!

'Did your Aunt Olga die, then?'

'When you were only a year old. But you know all this, Rosemary.'

'I'd forgotten.' *Surely, Rosemary was thinking, someone must have seen me rowing on the lake with Olga. When I waved to Bella yesterday, she seemed to, though she was busy with Bernard and didn't wave back.* 'Mother, have you noticed a small house on the lakeside when you and Father take your evening stroll? A wooden one, different from the grand ones, about sixth on the left?'

'No.'

'Are you sure? It's more like a shed, really. With a wild garden. Lots of flowers.'

'I've seen the wild patch. Overgrown. Very out of place.'

'That's the one. But no house?'

'Of course not! A wooden shed in a nice area like this? Really, Rosemary, you and your stories. Now, mind out of the way. I must get to the oven.'

'What's she baking?' You are agitated again, clutching at something only you can see.

'Er . . . cheesecake.'

'Shortcrust pastry?'

'What else?'

'The oven . . . too hot! Left it too long –'

'Look, the cake isn't important. All right? Now, let's get back to Olga.'

'Must we?' You hold my gaze, as though afraid of what I might say next. 'Olga . . . is she real?'

Do you want her to be? I take your hand. Suddenly I feel so tired. I want to lie down and somebody tell

11

me a story. I want the doorbell to ring and our fairy godmother to arrive. I want her to wave her magic wand and take away your fears. When your fears go, so do mine. Only right now they're rampant; formless shapes growing in my stomach, billowing into my throat, mirrored in your eyes as they plead with me. Don't you understand? I'm not brave and strong and all-knowing. I'm as much in the bloody dark as you are.

You mutter something.

'What was that?'

'Fly . . . '

'Flying?'

'Window . . . '

'You mean Rosemary? When she floats out of bed at night?'

You nod.

'Would you like her to describe it to Olga?'

You nod again.

'Listen to the story, then. Are you listening?' You draw one longer, deeper breath. At last the pattern is broken. For the moment we both feel easier.

Every afternoon Rosemary explored the lake with Olga. They swam from the shore in the warm shallows, or rowed out and dived into the cool depths. One day Olga took her to a tiny island inhabited only by birds and insects. Rosemary paddled and collected pebbles which she put in her swim hat. Then she joined Olga in the shade of the only tree and emptied the contents of her swim hat onto the grass. 'Look at these colours! I bet Henry would have trouble matching them if he tried to paint them.'

Olga examined the pebbles in the dappled light. 'Under water they would look even brighter,' she said.

'Under water? You can't see a thing under water. It's all muddy.'

'It is in daylight,' smiled Olga, 'but I mean at night.'

Rosemary looked at her friend in amazement. Then she thought about her nightly travels. 'You know,' she said, 'every night I have the same dream. At least, it must be a dream, although it feels so real. I float out of bed, fly through the window and over the lake. I swoop and soar and even see myself in bed, asleep!'

Olga didn't seem in the least surprised. 'What kind of feeling does it give you?'

Rosemary hesitated. 'At first it makes my heart kind of jump, as though I shouldn't really be doing this. Then I just take off and feel free and peaceful. I also feel that I'm on the edge of something important, that there's a secret in the lake and that it's only when I'm flying that I come close to finding out what it is. I'm almost there, yet never quite learn it.'

'Would you like to?'

'So there is a secret!' Rosemary stared at Olga. 'Do you know what it is?'

'Yes. I do.'

'Can you tell me?'

'No.'

'Why not?'

'Like everyone else, you have to find out for yourself.' Olga took Rosemary's hand in her own. 'I think you're ready,' she said at last.

'Ready?'

'To learn the secret of the lake. I can't tell you what it is. But I can show it to you.'

'Now?' Rosemary jumped up.

'No, no!' Olga laughed. 'Don't be in such a hurry. Come on, sit down. I can only show you at night. When the lake is empty again. When the people have finished *bathing and sailing and fishing. When the ripples have settled and the surface is smooth. When the reflection of fire from the setting sun has been doused by the silver light from the moon. Only then can you learn the secret. And once you've learned it, you can't unlearn it. The knowledge will change you. Your mother, father, brother and sister will appear different to you. Are you sure you want to?'*

'Yes!' cried Rosemary. 'Staying the same is boring, Bella would say.'

'Then meet me at my beach tonight. We'll row out to the middle of the lake where it's deepest. And, although it will be dark, I promise that, when you dive, you'll be able to see what is closed to you in daylight and what you've come nearest to in your night-time travels. Tonight you'll learn the secret of the lake.'

'No!' You've sat bolt upright. 'Rosemary shouldn't! Suppose the boat floats away! And they can't ... return.' You lie back, exhausted.

'Perhaps Rosemary won't want to return.'

Should I have said it? Too late now. Your face is without expression. You say nothing.

'All right. We'll stop.' I hold your hand again, only this time the gesture is mechanical. A wall has suddenly reared up between us. If you won't let me tell the story, I don't know what else to do. How many stages are there to this dying business, for goodness sake? Which one are we at now? How often I've felt: this is it! Only to find that it wasn't.

Then I see you're lying at a funny angle. I can do something about that. 'Are you uncomfortable?'

'Possibly.'

'Shall I sit you up a bit more?'

I place your arms around my neck, my arms about

your waist, brace myself and lift you up. As your head comes forward, you kiss my neck. That kiss says everything you no longer can. In that instant I know it will have to last me a long time.

'Shall I tell you about Rosemary spending the evening at home, then? A cosy evening with the family?'

'Cosy. Family. I like that.' You close your eyes. You can already see the lakeside house in the evening, with lamps set on low tables. The golden glow from the sitting room spills out onto the porch and the edge of the lawn beyond.

Father was late home that evening, so the family ate without him. Mother grilled trout and called when they were ready.

Henry carried his plate over to the conservatory where he had at last set up his easel. With the plate balanced on his knees, he simultaneously ate, applied paint and spat out fish bones.

Bella was on a diet, so refused food. However, she did allow herself a few pralines from the box given to her by boring Bernard from next door. She draped a towel over Father's footstool and settled in his chair.

Mother ate her trout while standing by the kitchen range testing a simmering saucepan of redcurrant jelly.

Rosemary sat alone at the kitchen table to eat her meal. She had some misgivings. 'I hope I don't swim into any of your family tonight,' she told her fish, and chewed without enthusiasm. Then she went upstairs to prepare.

She put on her woollen swimsuit, her shorts and a blouse. Then into her knapsack she placed, along with a towel, her babushka dolls. I'm all ready, she thought.

Downstairs she left her knapsack on the porch. Father had returned and was hovering over Bella.

'There's no point me moving, Father, you're going to eat in a moment. Anyway, I can't. They're not dry yet.' She indicated her feet stuck out on the footstool in front of her. The toenails glistened blood-red. Wodges of cotton wool prised each toe apart.

'What a waste of good cotton wool!' complained Father. 'I don't work hard to earn money for you to fritter in this way.'

In answer, Bella stuck two large pieces of cotton wool in her ears and began to varnish her fingernails.

Mother came in. 'Two minutes, Father,' she said, licking a wooden spoon. 'Mm, I think this is gelling.' She went into the conservatory. 'Finished, dear?' she asked, put the tops back on ten tubes of paint, then whisked away a pile of dirty plates and glasses.

'Take your own plates out to the kitchen, Henry!' cried Father. 'Mother isn't your servant.'

'She seems to be yours,' muttered Bella.

'And I want you out of my chair now, young lady!' Father kicked the footstool away. Feather-light balls of cotton wool flew into the air and rolled around the floor.

'Now look what you've done, both of you!' cried Mother, and rushed over to pick them all up.

My family, thought Rosemary. She looked at them in turn and saw Father's sense of responsibility, Bella's need for affection, Henry's doomed desire to capture Truth and, most of all, Mother's warmth.

She slipped out to the porch and picked up her knapsack. She left the pool of yellow light and walked down the path to the beach. She pushed the boat into the water and paddled along the shore. A shadow was waiting for her.

'I'll row,' said Olga, clambering into the boat. 'What's this?'

'My knapsack.'

'My dear, you won't need this in the lake.'

'No, but after. It has my towel and . . . '

'And?'

'My babushka dolls.'

Rosemary felt a hand on hers. 'Leave your knapsack here, Rosemary,' said Olga softly. 'Believe me, once you've learned the secret of the lake, you'll find you won't need my babushka dolls.'

The moon shone on Olga's round face. 'Are you,' whispered Rosemary, 'Mother's Aunt Olga?'

We have reached a dangerous point. I have taken you where you didn't want to go. How's your breathing? Shallow, but it's been worse. 'Are you asleep?'

'Me?'

'Of course you.'

'You've been here all the time, haven't you?'

You are looking straight at me but seem to be talking to someone else. Who? There are only the two of us. Yet, while the living shy away, memories of the dead float in to keep us company. Is it they who are nudging you now?

Rosemary trailed her hand in the cool, silvery water as Olga rowed towards the middle of the lake. The moon was almost full. As the shore lights receded, the stars appeared brighter. There was more of a breeze. Rosemary wondered, just for a moment, whether she really did want to know the secret of the lake.

Suddenly Olga shipped the oars and leaned forward to touch her knee. 'Look over there,' she whispered, pointing into the darkness.

At first Rosemary could see nothing. Then she saw what looked like a wave forming below the surface. 'Do we swim now?' she asked.

17

'Not yet.'

The wave grew bigger, the moonlight accentuated the swell until glimmers appeared. 'I can see bubbles,' whispered Rosemary.

At last the surface broke, and she saw what she took to be a fin. Then came a surge, a sudden arc of silver droplets as a dark shape leaped through the air. She saw a long head with a blunt nose and a mouth which seemed to open in a smile as it eyed them sideways, then plunged back into the lake.

'It's a dolphin!' cried Rosemary in delight. 'Are we to swim with a dolphin?'

'You are,' replied Olga.

'What about you?' Rosemary felt another flutter of uncertainty.

'My task was just to bring you here to meet him.' Olga took her hand. 'It's time to get ready,' she said. 'Don't be afraid.'

Rosemary pulled off her blouse and shorts, shivering a little in her swimsuit.

Again the water around them swelled, the boat rocked, the bubbles formed, and the surface broke. The dolphin sprang out of the water, so close that he splashed Rosemary's bare shoulders. She felt the rush of his body before he dived into the lake once more and disappeared.

'Stand up, Rosemary. Catch hold of his flipper next time and jump.'

This wait was the longest, while the water swelled, the boat rocked, and Rosemary fought to keep her balance. Then there he was again. He leaped over the boat, he touched Rosemary, she caught hold –

To her surprise, instead of diving, they kept on soaring, up and up in a wide arc above the lake. Rosemary saw the boat with Olga bobbing far below. Along the *twinkling shoreline she recognized her family's house standing in its golden pool of light. She saw her own attic window with her bed beneath it, and, for the first time, her bed stood empty! There's no need to go back, she realized. I need only go on.*

The dolphin's nose curved downward; the water came up to meet them as they flashed past the little boat.

'Goodbye, my dear, goodbye!' Rosemary heard Olga cry as the water touched and enclosed her.

Now is crucial. I stroke you all the time. I hold your hand, cool and inert, in my own. Everything about you spells effort: pinched nostrils, hollow cheeks, cramped toes. Your eyes are neither open nor closed; I find that hard to bear. Have you been listening to my story? From far away? Has it helped? Does it still? It mustn't get in the way. Yet I can't stop. So I'll continue. Quietly. In an undertone. More to myself than to you. While I hold you. That is all I can do.

Olga had spoken the truth. The world under water was full of colour and light. Rosemary gasped at the beauty of the rocks: fantastic shapes of silvery brown and pink. Weeds, ferns and trees of all shades of yellow and green swayed in the currents. Fish with luminous stripes popped out to eye the newcomer, then flicked their tails and swam away.

The further they plunged, the more the light increased. The dolphin was taking her through a narrow gorge of white rock which gradually widened and fell away until they were speeding along a plateau covered in glistening sand.

'The sea!' cried Rosemary. 'We've reached the sea!'

More dolphins swam towards them from all directions. They circled her and the dolphin guide, nosing, brushing her with their flippers, making soft noises of greeting. They provided an escort leading to the edge of the plateau where the brightest light beckoned.

Rosemary discovered that she was no longer riding on her dolphin's back, but swimming among them as free as they were, guided by their muted calls. Together they entered a brilliant corridor fringed by sea plants which caressed them as they passed. Rosemary felt warm in the underwater sunlight, a part of all that surrounded her.

What a change in you. It happened so quickly. Your breathing is calm and light, but your lips are dry. I wait for the next breath. How long do I watch, not quite knowing? I can't believe it. Surely you'll take another one. Just one more.

I touch your face. I kiss your cheek. I sit on. And on. What else should I do? It's all I've been doing for months. As I watch, I remember – do you? – how Catherine coaxed you to eat my soup. Leek and potato. How Kate played music to ease the night. Was that only yesterday? And I? What did I do? Oh yes. I told you a story.

The professionals busy themselves in a murmuring way. The doctor comes to examine you and fill in forms. She seems awkward. Yet isn't this the moment we've been working towards? The nurse, on the other hand, treats both me and your death as normal. Comforting. She washes and dresses you in a fresh nighty. A gentle ritual.

One by one my friends turn up. You always made them welcome. They want to say goodbye.

Suddenly I notice your pinched look has disappeared.

Your mouth is turning up at the corners. Would you believe it, you are smiling! 'Thank goodness that's over,' your smile says. 'Well, I'll be off, then.'

That's when I see you have gone. No doubt about it. I sense no dawdling, no reluctance, no lingering presence. On the contrary, I can feel your relief. And I realize with a shock that you have left me here, alone.

I am incapable of movement, unconnected to myself, the room and to those around me. Two husks, I think, you and me. But with that thought comes another one, terrifying in its clarity: in time I shall learn to live a new life, a full one, unrestricted by your fears, and this I shall only be able to do because you are no longer here.

I believe you knew that, too.

SHE'S ONLY A DOLL

Stephanie Ellyne

Born in New Orleans, Stephanie Ellyne worked as an actress in Oregon before moving to London. She was a winner of the 1989 London Writers Competition, the 1991 Ian St James Awards for her story *Me and Renate*, and had a short play broadcast on LBC as part of the 1993 New London Playwrights Festival. Stephanie works with bands in London and Düsseldorf as a singer/songwriter, and is currently writing a novel.

SHE'S ONLY A DOLL

How I longed for a sister. Pale child to admire me, pretty fetcher of favours to whom I'd relinquish nothing. Her azure eyes would rake me as I ransacked her dolls' house. Damp crumbs on the pale stones. Whom I could blame for the broken vases, the sound of scuffles from the upper rooms, the limping cat.

My parents had different ideas.

How to encourage their compliance? I yearned for lust to strike their placid suburban lives, a touch of recklessness one stale summer night. They remained, alas, uncompromisingly buttoned and behaviourally correct.

Were they, I wondered, susceptible to bribes? Oh for residence in a sparsely populated totalitarian state, where frequent childbirth was required and enforced! My parents were, if nothing else, good citizens.

I, though, prided myself as manipulation incarnate, restless spirit giggling at the wake of respectability, Pan's boss-eyed baby child. And I wanted a successor, an acolyte to gawp at my tales of mayhem wrought. Something to disturb my parents' pale calm – sheer chaos in a crib.

The most potent act my parents have accomplished to date (my own singular conception aside) was to introduce me to Seraphina. A doll, costly porcelain companion meant to reinforce pallid feminine virtues of dress-up and quiet down. They've yet to realize their error. Together we create a force they'd not reckoned with. No longer do I pour out my girlish woes, each snot-stained confession to dreary Mummy, but seek comfort in the arms of a more elegant companion.

I find it. And more – things you'd never dare to dream.

My sweet Seraphina. The wide shining eyes which close when her head tilts back, popping open to stare through you when least expected. Snowy porcelain skin and vivid scarlet pout, soft raven hair in startling contrast to my own blonde curls when they swim and mingle on the pillow. Her face is always perfect, always quite the same. How I envy that control.

Nothing gives her away.

Her night whispers inspire me. At first, understanding my timidity, she only spoke to me in dreams, filling my nocturnal fancies with suggestions for the morrow. I'd wake to her steady smile, the same immobile innocence I glimpse in my own looking glass. But within the shining blue glass of her eyes I felt a heat, a heart.

In the beginning I was frightened. When she was naughty I knew I should punish her. And she was dreadfully, dramatically naughty, right from the start.

Our first night together Mummy tucked us in cheek to cheek, prim and proper as every Daddy's favourite daughter. But when I woke, flushed, bedclothes in disarray, I found her beneath my nightdress, avid mouth pressed tight to the stickiness beneath my belly.

I was not brought up that way. Here we do not dwell on the delights of the nether regions. We are clean and correct, sweatless and above board. Seraphina's behaviour proved she was not so fortunate in her parentage. All she had in the world was me.

I knew she needed discipline, a firm hand to pull her back from the precipice on which she tottered. But I had so little understanding of her needs, the foul passions which drove her.

To be the more effective, I needed to learn more about them.

NELL

My daughter's becoming more and more disturbed. She talks to herself at night. She can put on trick voices in such a way you'd swear there were two people talking. I wake up at 3.00, 4.00 a.m.; the steady stream of voices from her room continues unabated. When I'm really tired I can spook myself by imagining the voices overlap. I became so sure she was hiding someone in her room that I once burst in, but she was too quick for me. She's nothing if not a consummate actress, my Molly – lying there as if she'd been asleep for a hundred years, golden lashes furled on her cheeks sweet as an angel, her big doll in her arms. In the dim light it looked like two little girls bedded down together.

I've never liked that doll. But it's all she has – the other children won't play with her any more. They don't like her. I tried for a long time to deny that, but there's no point in fooling myself. And I don't know why. She doesn't bully them or boss them around – she saves her temper for me. She has no time for other children. Adults have more uses.

Frederic doesn't understand my fears. He can't see beyond the curls and dimples, the trusting smile as he kisses her good night. His little girl can do no wrong. Lord knows he pays more attention to her than to me! But there's something odd about her – she's just too perfect. She knows the effect she has on people and she gauges it, calculates each action by its effect on her audience.

I'd die for my little girl. But when I see the contempt

27

in those big blue eyes I'm afraid of her. She cares for nothing but that doll.

MOLLY

Seraphina became quite bored with me. How I pondered, fretted on the sibling problem! There was the simple expedient of bringing together Mummy's diaphragm and the point of a pin. An idea I discarded for its lack of originality.

Ingenuity can be claimed for me, imitation never.

In any case, the problem seemed to originate prior to any need for contraception. Control was unnecessary in the night silence of their room. I blamed dear Daddy, much older than her and noticeably grey. A certain dim charm on his part did not improve a dull-normal libido. Adultery was the ideal solution – I had no overwhelming desire for a full-blooded sibling – but sadly my mother, though fair, fertile, and not yet forty, was most unlikely to stray. Her hours were filled more with dubious self-improvement schemes and speculation upon my character than with the manipulation of trouser flies.

Measures had to be taken.

There was a youth that helped around the house. Gardener, window washer, handyman, his precise function as indeterminate as his age. The gaze, open as an infant's, was somewhat complicated by the gold hint of stubble grazing his chin. He was certainly old enough for my purposes, as the nervous tumescence straining his stained trousers too often proved.

I approach him in my protective colouring, hair ribbon firmly in place, a lisping vision in short socks and lacy dress.

'Karl,' I chirp, 'my Mummy asked me to give you this.'

He drops his spade to take the note, carefully forged on her scented notepaper. As he unfolds it I skip about the garden, covertly watching his lips move as he struggles through the polysyllables.

My dearest Karl – I beg you to forgive me for confessing myself to you this way. How devoutly I long to divulge my feelings in the flesh, but fear that under your manly gaze my knees would weaken, my resolve crumble, and I would give myself to you utterly. Did I say fear? Forgive such prevarication, beloved. What I meant was hope. The time has come to reveal all to your compassionate and noble heart. I love you. Only your possession of me can break the bonds of passion that enchain me. You must take me as if by force, with the fury and simplicity of an immense beast. I beg you to ignore any plea, any protest that might issue from my lips as the feeble yappings of a bitch in heat. No matter what I say, continue in your manly duty. And if in my delirium I should strike you, meet violence with violence. For as you might put it, far more directly and winningly than I: I like a bit of rough.

I'll meet you in the summerhouse at noon. Please accept this as a small token of my esteem.

Your Nell

A fifty-pound note, rescued from Daddy's wallet earlier that morning, flutters past his astonished eyes.

'Hey, sweetheart!' Karl shouts. 'Come here a minute.'

I bound over and stand before him, hands clasped demurely behind my back.

'You say your mum give you this? What time was that, then?'

'Right after Daddy went to work. Is something wrong?'

'Everything's fine, love, just fine.' He smirks at me. 'How is your mum these days? Is she all right?'

'Well,' I say hesitantly, 'if anyone asks, Mummy says she's fine. But I don't think she's very happy. She's always sighing and looking out the window.' I lower my voice. 'And – *rubbing* herself. Like she itches.' I dig one toe into the earth, watching the dust besmirch the shiny leather, look up to meet his grin. 'I'm going to go play now. My dolly's waiting.'

He winks as I run off, poking his spade into ground dark with discarded blooms.

'Oh, Karl,' I call back over my shoulder, 'Mummy asked can you please put some blankets into the summerhouse. She might want a nice lie-down later.'

She's already been given her invitation for the puppet show to be presented there at noon.

NELL

The night before it happened I dreamt I was on a stage.

Red velvet curtains part; a spotlight shines into my eyes. I can't see the audience but hear whispering, an occasional giggle. I know they're out there.

A drum rolls and I walk to the centre of the stage. I move awkwardly, limbs jerked and pulled by unseen hands. I smile prettily despite my fear. I have my role to play.

A huge man stalks on, face obscured by his pointed black hood. Somehow I know it's the handyman, Karl. He snaps his fingers and I fall to the ground. He kneels behind me to tie my hands, but when I look back I see

Molly, my Molly, with dead glass eyes that roll and snap shut with every tilt of her head.

I scream for someone to help me. The lights come up with a sinister hum. I crane my head forward only to see, in every seat, Molly's horrid doll. I squeeze my eyes shut, but with my hands tied I can't stop my ears. I hear them laughing, clapping and clicking those tiny porcelain teeth with approval.

While it happens.

MOLLY

I watched my parents and bided my time. I don't know what she said but Daddy knew it wasn't his. As her bruises faded and waist thickened, his attitude cooled. Karl's bulky frame never graced the garden again, but there was no mention of him, no summoning of the police, no hint of a scandal. They were obviously determined to let the matter pass as quietly and unsensationally as they lived out their lives. But for the bulge under Mummy's floral frock it might never have happened.

Save for Seraphina's new attitude towards me.

My darling, so distinctive in other ways, showed the most tedious signs of jealousy over the coming infant. Aloof as an unwilling bride, silent as a nun, she lay immobile while I gripped her, muttering wild words of love and reassurance. I made every effort to assuage her anxieties.

She'll have even more scope once the baby is born, I vow. No one can usurp her power. I'll train the little darling to fulfil whims every bit as malicious, as sweetly malevolent as Seraphina could wish. Both sisters will serve her, her honour doubly acknowledged. And would

I not, I murmur, stroking her chilly thigh, be a far more effective slave to her if I experience for myself the weight of power; the hauteur, the whipcrack of the mistress?

I sense her doubts in the dark.

There's nothing else for it. I lift her in my arms and hold her above me until finally, reluctantly, she's forced to meet my eyes. I tell her my decision and wait patiently for my treasure to relent.

Slowly the tension leaves her. At last she yields, tumbles into my arms, trembles once more to my touch. Reunited we rock together, I crooning my love and relief as her tears pepper my cheeks.

NELL

I lay stiff in the darkness, straining my ears towards Molly's room. The mumbling and giggles – those from Seraphina as deep as a man's – hardly worry me now. What I dread is the silence. They're up to something.

I try not to sleep at night. I fight it as you would the cleverest, most subtle enemy, this previously comforting cloak now threatening to smother me with subterfuge, guile, promises, and lies. It's not even the sleep I dread, but what must come with it. My dreams are filled with tiny coffins.

It's incredible given the circumstances, but I long for the baby to come. Someone new to love, quite pure and untouched, who'll be happy to see me and will need me, really need me. Frederic spends most of his time at the office. My Molly is lost. There's nothing I can do for her in this world. She's gone too far. I content myself with praying for her soul.

Most of the time I feel quite alone. But if you're alone

you can do as you like. Not me. I'm always watched.

They have ways of knowing everything I do. They're biding their time, waiting for something. Sometimes I think I know what it is. I don't bother to tell anyone. They already think I'm half mad.

I know what's real now and it's up to me to protect myself. I rely on my senses, not the comfort of lying tenets passed down through the blood-soaked ages. I've learned to my cost that the bond between mother and daughter is as thin as poisoned water. Dreams are more to be trusted. And mine tell me those two in the nursery are trying to kill my baby.

MOLLY

The plan's almost too simple to satisfy, yet Seraphina reminds me the most elegant things are plain.

We've stretched a thin, very strong twist of cotton at the top of the stairs outside my room. Poetic justice calls for it to be one of my hair ribbons (too bright) or a strand of Seraphina's hair (too short) or, best of all, a length of the fine yarn she's begun knitting baby clothes with. In palest blue – she seems to be pinning her hopes on the babe being of a gender traditionally more drawn to daggers than dolls.

As delicious an irony as this would be, we've abandoned it. We can't be sure the delicate yarn won't break before it's succeeded in trapping her ankle and pitching her headlong down the stairs.

Which is, after all, the point of the exercise.

So, a length of plain cotton. Braided tightly by Seraphina's small skilled fingers, an inky blue so as to be unseen in the night gloom of the hall. One end is knotted firmly about the foot of the right banister, stretched loosely across and looped around the left banister, the end leading to a knot at the side of my bed. As she ascends the stairs in response to my frightened midnight cries it will lay flat and unnoticed on the top stair. But when she leaves after comforting me I shall pull my end of the cord, stretch it tight as a garrotte at the level of Mummy's demure (though at the moment slightly swollen) ankles. Thump thump thump, screams and cries, and in the confusion the cotton is whisked away. One quick tug and voilà! The end of baby – and a satisfied, more sensual Seraphina.

I work on my embroidery and sing to myself as I wait for bedtime to come. Her small back rigid, Seraphina stares at the wall. The suspense must be getting to her.

We have found that the least entertaining part of our diversions is the interminable waiting for the right moment to unleash them.

NELL

Since I lost the baby everything's terribly clear. My marriage is over. Frederic scoffed when I told him what Molly had done. He thinks I'm imagining it. Certainly I was ill during my pregnancy, suffering dreadful delusions, but I've had a long rest and my senses are fully restored. There's something wrong with my daughter and I'm the only one who sees it. I cried and threatened until Frederic agreed to send her away to school. I suspect it's actually meant to protect her from me. He told me I'll have to see a psychiatrist.

I waited until he left. Then I called Molly into my room and confronted her. I told her I knew she had planned my fall. She eyed me coolly, clutching that infernal doll, and said I couldn't prove anything. I admit that

I lost control. I slapped her face as hard as I could and shook her, shouting that she's to be sent away to school and won't be able to harm anyone again.

She went pale but of course she didn't cry. The doll probably won't allow it.

'You know they won't let me take Seraphina,' she said. That was all that concerned her.

I seized her loathsome doll and threw it into the fire. It gave me quite a fright because in my excited state I imagined I felt it twist in my hands.

Molly let out a terrible scream and thrust her arms into the flames. Before I could stop her she dragged the doll from the fire and beat its blazing skirts against the floor. One of its eyes had fallen out and the dress was scorched, but for some reason everything else was intact.

Molly's hands were burned but she didn't seem to feel it. She actually smiled.

'We'll make you sorry you did that,' she said and ran out of the room.

I've locked myself in until Frederic comes home. I don't know what else to do. I'm a terrible mother. My little girl's alone in the house, hurt, probably scared out of her wits. I should go to her, ring for the doctor, bandage her poor burned hands. But as long as she's with Seraphina I don't dare go near her.

So I huddle like a beetle in my cold, dark room. I can't even light another fire because I dread seeing Seraphina's half-melted eye staring up at me.

MOLLY

Daddy seems to have given up this misguided notion of sending me away to school. It's always possible Mummy made it up. He certainly hasn't breathed a word to me about it. Of course, he hasn't been particularly loquacious since the funeral.

We are a bit disappointed in his insistence on a prolonged mourning period. I've always known he was staid, but I had suspected there was a bit of spunk concealed beneath the banality. Evidently not.

It's not as if the fire destroyed the entire house. A man of his means can certainly cope with the expense of having a bedroom refurbished.

I couldn't have lived without Seraphina. She is the heat that fires my brain, the anarchy that invades my nights. All passions are realized within her firm embrace. I long only to know her, to prove my fealty again and again through countless depraved acts.

Mummy's unforgivable error, in its totality more offensive than any actual injury to Seraphina's person, was her continual maddening insistence that my darling was 'only a doll'.

It was this utter lack of respect that had to be paid for. Insulting as well as ludicrous. Her butter-smooth limbs are too hot to the touch. She can't be explained away that easily.

If she's only a doll, then I'm a normal child.

At times Seraphina is gripped by a dreadful ennui. She ceases to respond to my endearments, suffers rigidly my caresses, eye locked unblinking to the shadows on the ceiling.

I know what she's thinking. She fears that I will tire of her, abandon her, as the years pass, to more conventional pursuits, toss her face down in a chest to moulder amongst matted teddies and cry out unheard to other cracked and dusty dolls.

I murmur imprecations against her fear, lick her brittle cheek. I will prove she is my only mistress.

There is nothing I will not do.

THE FOOD
OF LOVE

Sue Camarados

Sue Camarados was born in Cornwall and educated in Crawley and Newcastle. Since graduating in Music, she has moved to Greece, married, brought up two lovely daughters and spent her time learning Greek, gardening, singing in choirs, teaching English and learning to fit in amongst a people who are culturally very different from the British. She discovered a passion for writing two years ago when forced to give up playing the viola. She loves writing about the Greeks and is working hard on a book of short stories about them. This story was written on the island of Andros.

THE FOOD OF LOVE

Stark naked, his skin pitted and shiny like the bark of an old olive after a spring shower, Costa stood dripping water onto the stone flags of the kitchen, straining to hear his son's voice through the crackling phone line from Athens.

'That you, Giorgo?' he shouted. 'How are you, my boy? You'll have to speak up!' His short, wiry body, tightened to the earpiece. 'No, of course I wasn't asleep.'

Water trickled from the few strands of his grey hair onto the sinews of his tanned back. His legs, veined with age, were trousered in the pale skin of the field labourer.

'This weekend? Yes, of course. Your mother'll be delighted.' He had to shout. These damned crossed lines! Women chatting for hours . . . 'What's her name? Na . . . What's that? . . . Natalia!'

There was silence down the line at last.

'That's a fancy name, isn't it? What does her father do? . . . Eh? Well . . . I was only asking!' He had forgotten; you weren't supposed to ask any questions. 'See you both on Saturday then.'

He stamped the water off his legs and put the phone down thoughtfully.

Lola came in from the kitchen garden, her arms laden with spinach. She looked at her husband, rooted to the scullery floor. 'What happened?' she asked.

'Bring me a towel,' he said. 'Our Giorgo phoned and I was in the shower.'

Lola laid the spinach in the white marble sink, her arms trembling with excitement. 'Why didn't you call me?' She hurried to unfold a freshly laundered towel, flapping it in the air, fussing around her husband's gnarled old body with it.

'He's coming down at the weekend, you'll see him. He wants to bring a girl. A Natalia.'

Lola flushed. She brought her husband's clean white underwear and helped him on with his shirt, dancing around him, her fingers shaking. So, Giorgo was bringing a girl home at last. She knew what that meant. He was getting married, he was bringing them his future bride.

'Who is she?'

'I've no idea.'

'Well, what did he say? Is she a local girl?'

'I doubt it, with a name like that!'

'Natalia . . . Natalia . . . Oh Costa, it does sound grand!' She hugged him tearfully.

'Now, for goodness' sake, woman, calm down.'

'What does she look like?'

'How should I know? Good Lord, we were only on the phone for a few seconds.' Then he said, almost to himself, 'A shipowner.'

'What's that?'

'A shipowner. Her father's a shipowner.'

'Oh Costa!'

They looked at each other, hardly knowing what to say.

Lola went to the cooker to pour out his coffee from the tiny briki. 'Saturday. My, that's only two days away. What shall we feed her? We must slaughter a lamb; city people eat lots of meat. And those young cockerels; the ones that hatched last season – they'll be as tender as fresh shoots.' She was talking to herself really, running through the menu in her mind as she bent over the hob. Costa knew he would get no peace till she had it all settled.

He looked out across the valley. 'So, it's Natalia; a shipowner's daughter.' At least she would have a good dowry. He couldn't put his finger on it; but a vague misgiving tickled the back of his mind like a mosquito worrying his sleep. What sort of demands would this Natalia make on a man like Giorgo, brought up in the village? 'Natalia.' He repeated the name, deliberately. 'She may be spoiled. These city girls . . . '

Lola brushed aside his doubts. 'She's Giorgo's bride,' she said, spreading a lace napkin and putting his coffee down in front of him, 'and that's good enough for me. We'll treat her like a queen.'

The next day, before dawn, Costa rode out to the olive grove on his mule. They had grown old together, these two, and fitted snugly like pieces of a jigsaw. They swished through the dried grass, kicking up clouds of buzzing grasshoppers; tiny brown teeth which rained noisily aside as if the mule's trotters were opening a huge zip across the valley. By the time they reached the olive grove the sun was licking red over the mountain, sucking at the sap from their bodies.

His naked torso running with sweat, hat pulled down over his forehead, Costa laboured all morning in the grove side by side with his hired workers.

When the sun was past its highest he sat under the shade of the olive tree and took out a loaf of fresh, crusty bread. With his weathered old hands, knotted and gnarled as the tree he rested under, he broke it into four chunks and passed them around. Then he took out the goat's cheese which Lola had carefully wrapped in aluminium foil and cosseted in a linen napkin. He pulled it apart, leaving earthy fingerprints in its whiteness.

'Here,' he said, offering it round, 'my brother sent it down from Metsovo.'

The corn bread was crisp and nutty. His molars dug deep into the crust and with a twist of his head he tore off a mouthful, chewing at its grittiness. It satisfied him. The feta crumbled like wet chalk in his mouth. He let the comforting taste of goats' milk melt on his tongue. Its briny tang seemed to be carried straight over the hills by the sea breeze.

He wedged a jar of shiny, black olives in the roots of the tree and brought out a tiny bottle of tsipouro. 'My son's getting married,' he announced, tipping the rim to his lips. The burning liquid fumed down his throat. He smacked his lips. 'Here.' He passed the bottle round. They drank in turn, sucking in the fiery liquorice, swilling it round their mouths till the sweat poured off their bodies. Then they lay back in the hot breeze to dry the heat out of them. 'Natalia,' he mused. 'So; there's to be a wedding . . . grandchildren.'

Thirty years of hard work bringing up Giorgo, feeding him, educating him, instilling his own principles of goodness in him. How do you create a sound, honest, hard-working and, most important of all, happy person, he wondered. Giorgo was a marine engineer, successful; he had a good job in a shipping company. But was he happy? Was he at peace with himself? Costa didn't know and he worried.

It hurt him to think that his grandchildren would not have the run of the farm; that they would be cooped up in a high-rise flat, however grand. Battery hens, he thought. He couldn't believe that anyone, much less a child of his, could be happy in the city.

As the tsipouro penetrated his veins, the buzz of thoughts softened, melting into unison with the rasping feet of the cicadas in the branches above him. He let the heat wash over his body and fell into a fitful doze.

Later, when the sun was glinting through the pitted trunks of the olive trees, the men rose. Costa heaved a watermelon out of the water tank. He put the huge green ball on his lap. Then he brought his fist banging down and split it in two. He broke off chunks, handing them out. The men sucked greedily at the cool nectar, filling their mouths with sweetness. Red juice dribbled down their chins as they slurped, their jaws wading in the watery crescents. They spat out the pips, little hard pithy grains which their tongues worked to the front of their mouths and then expelled with a plop.

'Giorgo won't be sitting in the fields,' murmured Costa, shifting his aching bones, wedging them between the sinewy roots of the olive tree.

He ran his palms over the soil, lifting the scent of dry earth to his nostrils. 'Natalia,' he said again. Had she ever touched the soil? She probably had long painted fingernails. He imagined her soft, white hands and was aware of a dull pain clawing at the pit of his stomach. It wasn't the first time. I must cut down on the tsipouro, he thought.

He arrived home at dusk and unsaddled. The warm, rancid smell of animal sweat and leather lured the flies from their dust. He watched the mule jerk, swishing its tail and flicking its head in a weary dance, its ears and flank blackened by the biting droves. Then he busied himself with the saddle, trying to drive away the pain which still nagged at his insides.

Lola was in the kitchen preparing sweetmeats; almond cakes and spicy baklavas, tiny nuggets of walnut and honey wrapped in layers of filo pastry. She had made grape and almond preserve and stored it in dainty glass jars covered in muslin. Costa took a long, appreciative sniff.

'What a heavenly aroma to greet a tired man with,' he sighed, and reached out his hand.

'Here,' said Lola, wrapping the sugary pastry in a paper napkin, 'just one. They're for Saturday.' She sat down. 'I was thinking,' she said, 'I'll marinate the lamb in lemon sauce, with oregano and fresh olives. Then we can roast it on the spit till it's tender and dripping in juices. We'll do Giorgo proud.'

'That we will.'

Costa crossed the stone floor and gave her a hug. There were times when he couldn't get over what a good woman she was. He went out to have his shower; to ease the aching in his legs.

On Saturday they were ready long before the familiar hoot of Giorgo's car was heard at the turning and they rushed out to see the old Toyota bumping up the dirt track.

Giorgo helped Natalia out and then bent down to give his mum a hug. She kissed him on both cheeks, then held him at shoulder length to have a better look at him. 'My,' she said, 'you've grown handsome!' He was even better-looking than she remembered. He seemed to glow. A shy tenderness which she had not seen in him since he was a little boy lit his expression as he indicated the glamorous, gawky girl at his side.

'Mum,' he murmured, 'this is Natalia.' And Lola had to stretch up on tiptoe to kiss the white-faced girl who was all teeth and smile.

When Natalia breezed into their small kitchen-cum-living room, stooping to fit under the doorway, Lola saw it anew. It was small and cramped, with rough whitewashed walls and an uneven stone floor. Glazed clay pots and pans stood in for ornaments and the telly dominated from its podium on the chest of drawers.

The only chairs were upright wicker ones. She realized that theirs was a farmer's house, for sleeping in, and she was ashamed.

This girl, tall and unhealthily thin, in her short skirt and high heels which caught in the flagstones, wouldn't fit. Her hair was swept up into a roll on the top of her head, adding to her height. Fake gold and diamond earrings hung like mini chandeliers above her bare shoulders. She wore a tank top which barely covered her ample breasts. And the smile! It was so overwhelming, so open-toothed, that it added to the effect of bareness. Lola felt the shock in Costa's eyes.

She rushed to brew Greek coffee and put out little glass platters of fig preserve. Natalia fingered the spoon politely.

'Come on, eat,' coaxed Lola. 'It's delicious, I made it myself.'

'I'm on a diet,' the girl apologized and Lola winced. The figs lay there, pithy full stops stranded on the table, cutting off the flow of words between the two women.

'We've roasted a leg of lamb specially,' said Lola proudly. 'I've wrapped it in oregano and basil leaves and it's sweet and tender as anything you've ever tasted.'

Giorgo stole a nervous glance at Natalia and bit his lip. 'That's wonderful, Mama, but Natalia's a vegetarian. I should have told you.'

'Don't worry about me,' laughed the young girl. 'I'll eat salad.'

'Salad!' The incredulous lilt in Costa's voice barely masked his outrage. Lola saw the anger in his eyes glinting as sharp as the carving knife in the tender belly of the lamb on the spit. 'Lola, go and run up a spinach pie,' he said quietly. 'Nobody needs to eat salad in Costa Papariga's house. And warm up some of those stuffed aubergines and the artichoke hearts in lemon and dill.'

'There's no need, really,' the girl protested.

'Dad, she likes eating salad.' Giorgo was laughing.

'Ssh . . . ' Lola chided. The girl was smiling helplessly and there was something endearing about her outright manner. 'There's plenty of food; fresh vegetables just cooked this morning; straight from the garden. You just wait two minutes, now.' And she bustled into the kitchen.

As she heated up the plates, Lola could hear the clink of glasses as Costa poured the retsina. And his voice, rising above the others, above the song of the cicadas and of the breeze whistling through the olive trees.

'All this land, to the horizon on all four sides,' he was saying to this girl who didn't eat meat, 'is farmed by us, and will belong to our children.' A cock crowed into the midday sun. 'Years of hard work; going without. Young Giorgo and his sisters were born right here in the house. See that olive grove over there? Well, in those days . . . '

Lola heard his voice as it rose and fell, warming to the story he had to tell this young wisp of a city girl; about the farm, the olive grove. How they had started from scratch, working day and night in the fields to build up the farm. How Giorgo had grown up and how he and Lola had scrimped and saved to send him to the best schools in Lamia, and later to university. And she found herself nodding, and remembering, as she busied herself with the plates. Yes, that was how it had been.

They had always imagined Giorgo would marry a village girl; take over the farm. But she had known in her heart of hearts that with such a good education it was unlikely. None of the girls had married farmers either.

She could hear Natalia laughing; clear, high-pitched

hoots. And Giorgo, too. They sounded so happy. Well, really, she thought, what more can we ask for?

Soon Costa would be asking Natalia about her family, her religion. Would he ask her how many children she wanted? Would this girl even want children? Some of them didn't these days. She shook her head. Giorgo's voice drifted in from the patio.

'. . . and the old nanny goat?'

'Just fine, two dandy little kids we've got for Easter. Remember that time . . . '

Yes, she remembered. Giorgo running in with an orphaned kid in his arms. Her lifting the bedcovers in the morning to find them huddled together, both fast asleep. How on earth would he spend his life in an Athenian flat, halfway to heaven with regulated air? She carried the tray out to the patio.

Natalia was talking to Costa. '. . . In a flat in Kolonaki. But of course they have an island house as well for the summer.'

'And your father? I hear he's a shipowner.'

'Dad? Oh, he just has a couple of ferry boats; the ones that go back and forth from the islands.' She was laughing. 'He's not a real shipowner.'

'Don't make light of what he does, love.' That was Giorgo; soft yet insistent. He hadn't changed. 'He's one of the most successful owners in that line, Dad. Nice person, too. You'll like him.'

'I'm sure I will.'

Poor Costa! Yet Lola could sense he was beginning to take a liking to this girl with the wide-brimmed smile. She was artless and begged protection.

After dinner they sat outside eating the black, juicy grapes from the vine. Costa felt the pain again. Lola saw it flash across his face, knifing the warm, brown eyes as Giorgo and Natalia were getting up to say goodbye.

And then it was gone and Costa was hugging Natalia, his arm round her bony flesh in a fatherly gesture. 'Natalia,' he said, taking time to pronounce the name with a flourish, rolling it around his tongue, 'you're one of us now.'

Wine had relaxed both him and the girl and she laughed up at him, blushing. To Lola she looked like an exotic bird perched there in his arm; one which had strayed too far from home.

'We must meet your parents,' said Costa. 'We'll invite them over; ask them to stay with us.'

'Dad? He's nearly always away.'

'Away?'

'Yes, abroad. He travels a lot,' explained Giorgo.

'I'll pin him down,' laughed Natalia.

'Good.'

When Natalia and Giorgo had gone, Costa sat outside studying the moon as if it could give him answers; the stutter of the crickets comforted him. The girl was spoiled, that was for sure. She obviously hadn't been brought up properly, but then, if her father was away all the time, what could you expect? She gleamed like that electric strip lighting they had everywhere in the city.

But you couldn't ignore the spark that passed between her and Giorgo. And there was an innocence about her that was attractive. She had displayed genuine interest when he showed her round the olive groves, slipping off her highheels for some of Lola's old sandals. And she was so vulnerable; with that white skin of hers, almost transparent. She reminded Costa of one of those porcelain vases that adorned the shelves of city houses.

'Don't take it too badly,' chided Lola at his side.

'A new generation,' he answered. He looked at her. She was strong and sturdy from years of work in the fields, rosy-cheeked. Like a beautifully glazed earthen-

48

ware pot, he thought, warm and reliable. He took her hand and squeezed it. 'Not like us, eh?'

'No.' She smiled.

'What do you think of her, this Natalia?'

'I never expected . . . ' Her voice trailed off, uncertain.

'Neither did I.' As they sat in the moonlight under the vine, looking out on what they knew was soon to become an abandoned farm, Costa's hand instinctively went to his side. His face was ashen.

'You'll have to go to the doctor, won't you?' chided Lola softly, and the mood was broken.

'Doctors! What do doctors know?' He detested the very word. 'Doctors!' he muttered, swiping at a mosquito which was buzzing in his ear. His health was his own concern. Didn't he always mend his own farm tools these days? All that was required was a proper understanding of their needs. Bodies were the same; machines which worked to a rhythm, responded to a loving hand. Time would mend it and he would help it along by cutting down on the tsipouro. 'Stop fussing, woman, you're always fussing,' he shouted.

'I just thought . . . ' Her voice trailed after him as he stamped indoors and turned on the TV.

During the days that followed the pain got worse. Costa was deeply disturbed. He didn't like his body playing him up and he showed his contempt by ignoring it. He got stiffly on his mule every morning and set out for the fields. His legs were swelling up and his temper was frayed at the edges. He cut down on the tsipouro but that didn't seem to help. He even confided in Petros on the neighbouring farm.

'That'll be a gallstone,' he was cheerfully reassured. 'Old Boutos had one. Doctor told him to drink plenty of water.'

49

So Costa turned to Adam's wine; he downed gallons. He was convinced he could wash the stone out, flush it through his system with torrents of icy cold water. All day long he drank from the fridge and gulped down watermelon and all night long he ran to the loo. 'Just going for a drink,' he would say if Lola happened to stir as he was creeping out of bed. He didn't want her fussing or worrying while they were busy preparing for Natalia's parents.

Neither of them got much sleep. After three weeks the stone still hadn't budged and Costa was at his wits' end. He felt Lola's concerned eyes on him all the time. His nerves were on edge. Every time she mentioned doctors his patience gave out.

'Doctors! Doctors are for the sick,' he dismissed her irritably.

Feminine wiles. She tried a new track; cooking his favourite dishes, mousaka and fasolada, spoiling him till his barriers were down. Then she would softly bring up the subject again. And he just couldn't keep his temper.

'What are you trying to do, woman, get rid of me? I'm not on my deathbed yet.' He felt guilty, sniping at her. He knew he was being illogical. 'Besides,' he argued, 'we've got Natalia's parents coming next week. So much work to do.' This was his ace.

Lola's preparations for Mr and Mrs Vassiliou's visit were majestic. It wasn't every day she had a shipowner for lunch. Waves of apprehension shivered through her from time to time, and then she would busy herself with the preparations. She would show them what village hospitality was like. She didn't need to look in her wardrobe to know that she didn't have anything to wear. Who needs smart clothes on a farm? She went into town and bought a dress; imitation silk, 'polyester' in English. She got Costa a new pair of trousers.

She whitewashed the outside walls and painted the shutters. The bedroom had to be redecorated and Lola put up pretty new curtains. The bathroom was a problem. They would all have to share it and the tiles were cracked. She didn't want to ask Costa to retile it while he was so out of sorts so she hung bunches of dried flowers up to hide the worst parts. Costa limed the trees in the kitchen garden and the joins between the crazy paving.

Lola had scrubbed the house from top to bottom and starched the embroidered linen from her dowry. They had opened the best barrel of wine, carefully filtering it into the crystal jug given to her at her wedding.

All was ready. The day before the Vassilious' arrival Lola squeezed the fresh plump lemons over the taut flesh of the lamb, picking out the pips. She lifted the big keg from under the sink and poured out a jarful of olive oil, bathing the virgin flesh in the rich liquid. Then she sprinkled it with fresh oregano, her fingers working the stalks, filling the room with the tang. She tried to forget about Costa's problem. He would come round. They would go to the doctor, who would tell them there was nothing to worry about; give him some tablets to take and tell him to come back in ten days' time. That's how it always was.

What would the Vassilious be like? The girl was spoiled, that was for sure. Did she even know how to cook? Poor Giorgo, who would look after him? The parents had an au pair, whatever that was. They were not vegetarians like their daughter, Lola had checked. But she made a spinach pie anyway. She emptied the young green shoots onto the kitchen flagstones and sat on a chair cutting off the roots, discarding the stringy leaves, picking out only the softest and freshest. Then she made the filo pastry, kneading the oily dough expertly. Did Natalia know how to make spinach pie? She doubted it. She rolled out the dough into wafer-thin sheets and laid it in her huge baking tray.

As she was brushing each dry sheet with olive oil Costa hobbled in, bent over in pain. He lay down on the couch and pretended to be reading the paper.

'You're home early.'

'I thought I'd come and give you a hand,' he beamed.

'Are you all right?'

'Of course I am. Well, just a bit tired. My legs are a bit heavy.'

'Let's have a look at them.'

'It's nothing, woman, stop fussing.' But he pulled up his trousers and the puffy, swollen legs glinted in the dim light.

'Holy mother of Jesus,' Lola panted. 'I'll get the doctor.'

Costa looked at her. 'It'll go away,' he said. They both knew it wouldn't. 'I'll go to the doctor tomorrow,' he agreed, 'after they've gone.' He had given in.

He lay awake that night, the pain shooting out from under his puffy skin. He climbed out of bed for the umpteenth time and padded along to the bathroom. Try as he might, he couldn't force more than a few drips out of his waterworks. He checked his legs; they were pale and mauve, and watery strips of pink glistened under the light. What the hell was wrong with him? Doctors! Whenever he had taken his farm tools to the workshop in town they had always come back in worse shape. God knows what sort of a mess a doctor would make of him.

In the morning he tugged at his new trousers, straining to do up the top button; his belly had risen like dough.

*　　*　　*

52

Mr and Mrs Vassiliou came down by car, not the Mercedes Lola had imagined, but a navy blue Jeep. As soon as they stepped foot on the path two things struck Lola: one was the very dark colouring of Natalia's father against the white pallor of his wife, the second was their difference in height; he was almost a dwarf. Something else soon became obvious: they had been arguing. Their smiles were a shade too bright.

Nichole, as it turned out she was called, was overdressed and decked with jewellery like a Christmas tree. She glanced around her anxiously, as if she had landed on the moon instead of in the countryside. Her linen skirt had got creased in the car. She pulled at it, smoothing it down as she teetered along the path and stumbled as her heel wedged in the stones.

Lola rushed to her side, blushing in shame. 'We should have had the path paved,' she apologized. 'Are you all right?' She stood brushing and dabbing at the woman's skirt until even Costa looked embarrassed.

'Aren't you going to offer our guests a drink?' he asked.

'Of course ... there now. How silly of me. Do come inside.' She poured tiny glasses of cherry liqueur, sitting them gracefully on a white linen tray cloth; then added a bowl of pistachio nuts, a spoon of fig preserve.

'I made it myself,' she beamed, bending in exaggerated welcome over Nichole.

The woman took it and uttered a polite 'To your health.' She smiled briefly and peremptorily sipped the liquid before putting the glass down as if its very sweetness irritated her.

Lola plied her with fig preserve; kept refilling her brimming liqueur glass. She felt unprepared, almost naked. The girl she could cope with. There was an innocence and directness which brushed their differences out into the open. Besides, she was happy. But this woman's sophistication terrified her.

At lunch time, Costa ushered them all onto the verandah where they sat under the shade of the vine. In the centre of the table Lola placed a huge platter piled high with roughly hewn chunks of steaming lamb. The air filled with the warm, heady fragrance of lamb fat and herbs.

'Mmm . . . that smells good,' beamed Alex.

How funny he looks, in his white suit and white shoes, thought Lola. He wore a thin red tie which flopped over his generous tummy. And he was so dark-skinned; the sort of colour that she associated with Arabs and gypsies, not shipowners.

She took the spoon and dished three huge chunks onto his plate. She wouldn't take no for an answer and he soon gave up protesting. There was little room for anything else. She plied them both with salads and spinach pie, roast potatoes and fresh bread.

Nichole picked at her food, making only a tiny dent in the pile amassed on her plate.

'Eat up,' Lola cajoled, 'there's plenty more.'

She was upset by the way the woman cut the meat into tiny slivers, tugging at the strands with her knife, folding them delicately until the fibres were mashed. Didn't she like the food?

She was worried sick about Costa, too. Not that anybody could have guessed he was ill. Only Lola knew, as she watched him pick up his glass to propose a toast, that his best jacket was buttoned over the place where his trousers would not do up.

'To the health and happiness of our children,' he toasted.

'Hear, hear.' Alex held up his glass in an exaggerated

gesture. 'They're two wonderful youngsters, eh, Costa?' he boomed.

And the women drank to that, happy to find common accord, to avoid for a moment the embarrassing silences and false starts which bedevilled their conversation.

That evening, in the surgery, the doctor was blunt. 'With a prostate like that it's a wonder your kidneys haven't packed up altogether,' he chided. 'Why on earth didn't you come in sooner?' He didn't wait for an answer. 'It's hospital for you, I'm afraid,' he said.

Costa's eyes puckered; unfocused. 'That's impossible! We're in the middle of harvest.'

The doctor looked at his bulging legs. 'You haven't got a choice,' he said.

'How long for?' asked Lola.

'At least a couple of days. We've got to unblock his waterworks. And we'll need to do some tests.'

Another doctor came and examined him; a surgeon. 'We'll have to force it open,' he smiled, and plunged a tube into the most sensitive layers of Costa's masculinity, which made him scream out despite himself. His mind flashed back to the village schoolyard, the roundup by the SS, the floggings, the men lined up against the wall and shot. He didn't like this place at all.

At first they put him on a fold-up bed in the corridor because they were short of space. But then they found him a bed in a ward with five other patients. Next to him was an old man in the terminal stages of cancer, whose relatives had grown weary of the twenty-four-hour vigil around his bedside and hired a series of nurses – three a day on eight-hour shifts. These nurses, young girls, sat by the window chatting to other hired staff, joking, complaining about the wages. Every now and then one would get up and sniff. 'Ugh,' she would say, 'not again!' And go over to the bed with a sigh. 'Come

on, grampers, turn over and let's change your nappy.'
They were pretty, these girls, and they made a fuss of
Costa. He flirted with them when Lola was out of the
ward.

He fretted in the uncomfortable bed for a week while
they carried out tests and took blood samples. Lola
never left his side, except at night. Then he had night-
mares in which great white machines – masses of tubes,
pipes, switches and bleepers – attacked him, sucking his
blood till he was as pale and insipid as Natalia's mother.
He would wake in a cold sweat.

He knew what cancer was; he'd heard the word and
he knew several people who had died of it, not including
old Sam in the next bed, who was at death's door. But
he didn't believe that he had it.

'Doctors!' he muttered contemptuously, when Giorgo
and Natalia came to see him. 'They're out to make a
packet. Stands to reason. If they put the fear of God
into me and say I'll die if I don't have this and that
treatment, this and that operation, they'll make more
money than if they tell me I'm as fit as a fiddle.'

He didn't care if they thought he was wrong. He
knew. These white walls were driving him mad; white
sheets, white bedcovers, white coats, bouquets of
flowers – it was like a mausoleum. And the groans of
old Sam were keeping him awake all night. And the
lights! The paid nurse read women's magazines all night
under Sam's overhead lamp. What did she care if he
was blasted in 150-watt brightness; he'd be dead by
next week. And the food! Where was Lola's home-made
cooking? And the noise! It was unbearable. The relatives
of the man in the bed opposite sat round the clock at
his bedside watching soaps on the portable telly half the
night. And the injections! The pain! He'd had enough.

Costa woke up one morning utterly convinced he

would die if he stayed there a minute longer. Nothing that Lola could say would change his mind. He checked himself out and took her back to the village. They didn't understand, those doctors. Never in a month of Sundays would he get better locked up in a hospital in Athens; not if he swallowed all the pills in the world. He hated the city; its traffic, its smog, its bad-tempered people, always in a rush. He needed the smell of the earth in his nostrils, the taste of early morning dew, time to sit under an olive tree and reflect.

Out here in the countryside nature would heal him. It would put the balance right. And then there was the engagement. It was to be a posh affair, a hundred guests, Alex had said. He would need a suit.

Chemotherapy; a long word. Lola was so desperate for him to have it that he gave in. As long as he didn't have to stay in Athens. He went to the local hospital once every ten days and they pumped pretty coloured tubes of their new-fangled poison into him. It went against everything he believed in.

His days in the fields grew shorter. 'I can't sit around in the olive grove when we've got an engagement party to plan,' he explained. 'Giorgo is going to have everything perfect.'

'What shall we buy Natalia?' asked Lola. The question had been burning in both their minds. It had to be solid gold, expensive enough to be worthy of adorning Giorgo's bride.

'A necklace, it has to be a gold necklace,' decided Lola. 'I'll go to Athens, find something really exquisite. I want everyone to gasp in delight when you put it round her neck.'

'We'll have the engagement here in the village,' Costa announced out of the blue one day.

'What, with you in that condition?' asked Lola gently.

'There's nothing wrong with me that a good party won't cure.'

He laughed and walked over to pick up the phone. His legs were pitifully thin, fragile like the pins of a bird. Lola wondered how they would manage.

'I've booked the Panorama Tavern,' he shouted down the phone to Giorgo. Another crossed line; he swore to himself. 'It'll take a hundred people and they'll team up with your mum on the catering. I reckon there are about forty on our side so tell Natalia to send out the invitations.'

'How are you, Dad?'

'I'm fine.'

'Are you getting out to the fields?'

'Regular as clockwork.'

'And the olives?'

'All in; a real bumper crop.'

He wasn't telling the exact truth. It was the first year that Costa had not been able to pick the olives himself. It was all he could do to get astride his mule and bounce along to the olive grove. He was nearing the end of his chemotherapy. 'I told you those doctors are a load of crooks,' he told Lola. 'Look at me! All I had before they started poisoning me was a minor plumbing problem. Now I hardly have the strength to get out of the chair.'

Lola went to Athens and chose the necklace. It was shaped in wafer-thin gold leaves like the ancient head-dress of Philip of Macedonia. She bought herself a linen suit in a pale shade of apricot. As she admired herself in the mirror her warm, black eyes smiled, imagining Costa's face when he saw her in it, how proud he would be. She had forgotten . . . Ah, well.

She visited the specialist while she was there. He

58

looked up sympathetically as she walked in. 'How is he?'

'Weak.'

'He would be.'

'He won't admit it but he can hardly get out of bed sometimes.'

The doctor lit a cigarette. 'Look, make him comfortable. There's nothing else we can do, I wish there were. He's a tough old bird. Who knows, perhaps he'll fight it?'

She fought back the tears. 'Our son's getting engaged soon,' she said.

The doctor leaned over and took her hand. 'Then make it an occasion to remember.'

She bought Costa a suit. His last suit; he'll wear it at the engagement, she thought, and then...? She wiped her eyes with a tissue. When she got home he tried the suit on. It was grey, cashmere, the very best she could find. She had bought it two sizes smaller than he usually took but it still hung baggily around his waist. He turned this way and that in front of the mirror, plainly unnerved by his dapper appearance. 'I'll wear it around the house a bit. Get used to the feel of it,' he said.

When he got up from his afternoon siesta he took off his pyjamas and donned his suit, shuffling out to the verandah and winking at Lola. 'Get me!' he swaggered. 'Bloomin' uncomfortable. I don't know how they stand these things all day.'

After a while he went back to bed. She sat on the patio, rubbing her eyes which were red and sore.

On the day of the engagement everybody woke up early. Giorgo and Natalia had come down the previous night, bouncing into the tiny kitchen, hugging and kissing

Costa and Lola. Natalia had flopped onto a chair and spilled out her happiness in excited chatter about the arrangements. She was radiant, and Giorgo, as always, stood protectively behind her like a shepherd watching over his prize lamb.

Costa had booked every available room in the local hotel for his Athenian guests. The tavern was decked out in flowers and Lola had ordered an iced cake from the best patisserie in Lamia. Giorgo helped load the wine barrels into the van and Lola loaded huge trays of sweetmeats. She had been cooking for a week.

Morning dawned on a sky of rare pastel blue. The tiny whitewashed cottage looked exactly like a child's painting of home. Standing on the patio, looking out on the fields laced with wild scabious, splashed with clusters of cyclamen, Costa had an overwhelming feeling that life would go on. With or without him. That this was just the beginning. He picked up a handful of carob seeds from the ground.

'God has blessed the day!' he shouted and raised his hands as if to conduct the scene, scattering the seeds over the dry earth.

His new suit hung lovingly pressed in the closet. At exactly five o'clock he took it out and hung it loosely round his haggard body. Then, as if expecting, he paced the floor and kept guard over the clock. 'It's time we were going,' he shouted to Lola. And as she came timidly out of the bedroom he gasped.

Under the pale apricot suit she wore a white lace blouse which ruffled seductively up to meet her black wavy hair. She smiled shyly, and Costa blinked; he could have sworn she was only nineteen again. Fresh as the first sprig of orange blossom in spring she looked, the one he had picked for her when he had asked her to marry him. Heavy with the musk of youth.

'My, Lola, you look a fine sight.' He cast his eyes lovingly over her from head to foot. 'Not since . . . ' His voice trailed off and he took her in both arms and smacked his lips over hers.

By eight o'clock the tavern was packed with guests. The Athenians had come down in sleeveless silk dresses. Bold designs and glistening jewellery trailed their immaculate coiffures. They clung to each other in groups, shivering like greenhouse plants in the chill night air. Nichole, in a satin dress glistening with sequins, wove in and out, introducing them to each other, mingling, threading her nervous laughter amongst them. She reminded Lola of a queen bee flitting from flower to flower.

Costa and Lola's relatives swarmed around each other, laughing and shouting, calling to each other across the tables. They had been looking forward to this celebration. Their plump, rosy cheeks contrasted sharply with the pallor of their city counterparts.

Costa sat at the head of the table with Alex on one side, and willed himself to stay upright.

'You're looking very fit,' remarked Alex.

'Never better,' he nodded. 'Fit as a fiddle.'

The long lines of tables were decked out in white cloths. Lola fluttered down the line, squeezing a hand here, a shoulder there, smiling, encouraging, until she was satisfied everyone was happy. Clusters of grapes hung over the guests and vine leaves latticed the stars.

Five lambs turned slowly on the spit, their fat dripping onto the white-hot charcoal, where it sizzled, filling the air with the aroma of lamb crackling.

The villagers took turns to rotate. Natalia was there, too, on Giorgo's lap, laughing, shielding both their faces from the heat and smoke whipped up by the sudden gusts of wind. Skewers of liver and kidney, parcelled in lily-white intestine, shone black, bursting out of their bonds.

'Taste this,' insisted Costa, raising the fork to Alex's mouth.

'Juicy as a wench!' said the other, slapping Costa on the thigh.

The villagers' enthusiasm overflowed. Brandishing chunks of lamb in the air, they tore the fibres apart with their teeth, grinning, loudly smacking their lips as they chewed the tender threads. Then they swilled it all down with several gulps of wine, emptying their glasses in one. Lola loved them all. She tried to put Nichole's guests at ease, hovering over them, making sure they had everything they wanted.

Costa tore off a hunk of bread, dunking it in the oily juice left in the empty salad bowl, swishing it about.

'Come on, Alex,' he said. 'This one's for you.'

'Don't mind if I do,' the other man said, laughing.

Costa ripped off another, soaked it and pulled it dripping towards his mouth. Tilting his head back, he fed himself like a hungry bird, letting the oiliness seep down his throat before swallowing the soggy bread. He put his arm round Alex and raised his glass with a hand which trembled. 'May they live to be a hundred,' he beamed.

Alex, red-faced, loosened his tie, held up his swaying glass. 'To a bevy of grandchildren,' he slurped.

'Every one of them just like us!' sang Costa.

'I'll drink to that.'

After the meal Costa stood up and motioned for silence. He took a deep breath, puffing up his frail body like a swelling accordion. Then his rich and vibrant voice boomed over the tables, taking even Lola by surprise.

'This is the happiest day of my life.' He smiled at

Giorgo and Natalia, looking round to make sure everyone was listening. His eyes where moist. 'I give you . . . beautiful, sweet, Natalia . . . and my son, Giorgo.' He put an arm round each of them, his voice cracking. 'No man could ask for more. I am very proud.' He stopped, brimming over.

Lola wiped her eyes and went up and kissed each one of them tenderly on the cheek.

'Here's a toast . . . to the happy couple,' shouted Alex. And he raised his glass and drank down half the bubbling liquid. But Costa hadn't finished. He motioned for silence.

'I would like to present the bride-to-be with this little memento of the day,' he announced. Lola, flushed and dewy-eyed, handed him the velvet-lined box. He opened it and held up the beautiful gold necklace for all to see. Then he went behind Natalia and hung it gently around her neck. He kissed her tenderly on both cheeks. 'You will be the jewel in our family,' he promised.

He hugged his son and for a moment the tears spilled over. Lola put her hands on Nichole's shoulders and smiled. The two women looked at each other and their tears mingled as they kissed cheek to cheek.

Then Costa lifted his arms and laughed, breaking the spell. 'Let the music play!' he shouted. The violinist raised his bow, the accordion player opened his deck and the bouzouki and lute players strummed, using their long fingernails as picks. The music was off in a wail of national dances which meandered across the tonalities and the bar lines, the melodies flowing freely across the fields.

Costa ordered the waiter to fill up the glasses. 'Drink up,' he urged his tipsy guests. 'We have to empty the barrel tonight.'

The village ladies jumped to their feet and started

dancing. The Athenians, loosened by wine and fresh air, were not far behind. Soon, long winding snakes of dancers flourished their hankies to the rising moon. Hand on their hips, they stamped their feet and kicked their legs with gusto. Alex even did a belly dance with Lola's sister, picking up a glass from the ground in his mouth and drinking the wine with his arms spread out, circling round and round to the music.

Natalia was first to see Costa get up.

'Look!' She nudged Lola and Giorgo and they watched as Costa walked purposefully towards the dance floor, hankie in hand, and joined the front of the snake. Cheers went up from the tables all around. Costa had always been a good dancer. Now he stood upright, his haggard face proud, and danced with his head in the air.

He bent cautiously down and smacked his heels, rising again with arms aloft to cheers and wolf whistles from the table. And Lola, looking on, didn't see his hollow cheeks, red and glistening with sweat, or his baggy trousers which flopped up and down as his feet wound in and out. She didn't see his eyes raised to the stars or his body wasted as a living scarecrow. What she saw, as he led the dancers through a dignified circle, was a young man, strong as a sapling, running through the orange grove, laughing, holding out a sprig of blossom. She saw his eyes, flashing with fun and vitality, raised to hers.

And then it was over. Costa graciously unlinked his hand and staggered, still upright, to his seat. A roar of approval went along the tables; glasses were held high. 'Long live Costa,' they toasted. He patted Lola on the hand. 'Ah, well . . . ' he said. 'Not as young as I used to be.'

'No,' she said, 'none of us are.'

They got home at three in the morning. Costa lay down on the bed in his grey suit, quite still.

'Lola,' he spluttered, 'Lola.' His voice was faint but teasing. 'Wasn't that just the best engagement party you've ever been to?'

'It was. And the children? Giorgo? Natalia? Aren't they wonderful? Will they always be as happy as that?'

'They'll be different; not like us.' He sighed. 'Other generation; other lives.'

She took off his shoes, helped him undress and put his pyjamas on. 'Under the covers with you and get some sleep,' she whispered. But he was already snoring, a shallow, rattling noise. She turned the light out and crept in beside him.

The next morning Lola woke up late and Costa had already gone. She climbed out of bed and hurried into the kitchen.

'Costa . . . are you there?' she called. There was no reply. 'Costa . . . ' She went bare-footed out onto the patio, squinting in the bright sunlight.

She scanned the valley up and down until she saw him. She could just make out his rake-thin figure as the mule plodded steadily along the scarp on the opposite side. 'Well, I'll be . . . ' she said to herself.

She watched her Costa as he scaled the hillside, getting all the while smaller and smaller. Her eyes hurt in the glare but she never lost sight of him. She watched his silhouette swaying to the rhythm of the mule's shanks, watched till he reached the crest of the hill. For a moment he seemed to pause there.

'Costa . . . ' she called out his name. Then, before she knew it, he had fallen below the horizon, out of sight, and she was walking indoors, wiping away the tears with the back of her hand.

A IS FOR AXE

Mike McCormack

Mike McCormack is twenty-eight years old. He was brought up in Louisburgh, Co. Mayo, and gained his degree in Philosophy and English from University College, Galway. He has been writing for the last three years and was recently shortlisted for the Hennessy Award in Dublin. As a result of this, his story was published in the *Sunday Tribune*. He has also been published in *Ambit*. Mike now has a collection of his short stories and a first novel nearing completion.

A IS FOR AXE

A is for Axe

Six pounds of forged iron hafted to a length of hickory with steel wedges driven in the end. During the autopsy the coroner dug from my father's skull a small triangular chip which was entered as prosecuting evidence by the state. It was passed among the jurors in a sealed plastic bag like the relic of a venerated saint.

More than any detail of my crime it is this axe which has elevated me to a kind of cult heroism in this green and pleasant land of ours. I am not alone in sensing a general awe that at last small-town Ireland has thrown up an axe murderer of its very own. It bespeaks a kind of burgeoning cosmopolitanism. At last our isolated province has birthed a genuine late twentieth-century hero, a B-movie schlock horror character who is now the darling of downmarket newsprint.

As I was led to trial several of my peers had gathered on the steps of the court house. Long-haired goateed wasters to a man, they sported T-shirts emblazoned with my portrait and short lines of script: *Gerard Quirke for President*, they read or, *Gerard Quirke – A Cut Above the Rest*. My favourite: *Gerard Quirke – A Chip Off The Old Block*.

B is for Birthday

I have picked through the co-ordinates of my birth and I find nothing in them which points to the present calamity. I was born on the twentieth of October 1973 under the sign of Libra, the scales. It was the year when the sixth Fianna Fáil administration governed the land, added two pence to the price of a loaf and three on the pint. In human terms it was a year of no real distinction; if there was no special degree of bloodshed in the world of international affairs neither was there any universal meeting of minds, no new dawn bloomed on the horizon.

I have these details from a computer printout which I got from James, a present on my eighteenth birthday. He bought it in one of those New Age shops specializing in tarot readings and incense that are now all the rage in the bohemian quarters of cities.

I was named after St Gerard Majella whom my mother successfully petitioned during her troubled and only pregnancy.

C is for Chance

Chance is at the root of all. 3, 12, 20, 10, 27, 8. My date of birth, my father's date and my mother's also. These are the numbers my father chose on the solitary occasion he entered for that seven-million-pound jackpot, the biggest in the five-year history of our National Lottery. And for the first and only time in his life the God of providence smiled upon him.

D is for Defence

I had no defence. To the dismay of my lawyer, a young gun hoping to make a reputation, I took full responsibility and pleaded guilty. I was determined not to waste anyone's time. I told him that I would have nothing to do with claims of diminished responsibility, self-defence or extreme provocation. Neither would I have anything to do with psychiatric evaluation. I declared that my mind was a disease-free zone and that I was the sanest man on the entire planet. As a result the trial was a foreshortened affair. After the evidence was presented and the judge had summed up, the jury needed only two hours to reach a unanimous verdict. I was complemented for not wasting the court's time.

E is for Election

As a child nothing marked me out from the ordinary except for the fact that I had been hit by lightning. I had been left in the yard one summer's day, sleeping in my high-springed pram when the sky darkened quickly to rain and then thunder. All of a sudden a fork of lightning rent the sky and demolished my carriage. When my parents rushed into the yard they found me lying on the ground between the twin halves of my carriage, charred and blackened like a spoiled fruit. When they picked me up they found that the side of my head had been scorched by such a perfect burn that, were it not for the ear it had carried with it, you could have admired the neatness and tidiness of it. While my mother carried me indoors my father stayed in the downpour, shaking his fist and bawling at the heavens, cursing God and his attendant angels.

In the coverage of my trial much has been made of this incident and the fact of my missing ear. Several column inches have been filled by pop psychologists who have repeatedly drawn parallels between the lightning strike and the axe. All have sought to deliver themselves of fanciful apocalyptic axioms. It surprises me that at no time was a theologian asked to proffer his opinion. I feel sure he would have found in the incident some evidence of a hand reaching out of the sky, a kind of infernal election.

*   *   *

F is for Future

My life sentence stretches ahead of me, each day an identical fragment of clockwork routine piled one upon the other into middle age. I do not care to think about it. Seven months ago, however, after my father came into his fortune, I dreamed of a real future. Hour after hour I spent in my room working out the scope and extent of it, embellishing it with detail. Eventually I polished it to a gleaming prospect of travel in foreign climes, sexual adventure and idle indulgence. I mapped it out as a Dionysian odyssey, a continual annihilation of the present moment with no care for the morrow. It would take me in glorious circumlocution of the earth all the way to my grave, ending in a fabulous blowout where I would announce my departure to the assembled adoring masses, an elegant wasted rake. I was careful enough to leave blank spaces in the fantasy, filling them out during moments of conscience with vague designs of good works and philanthropy. I confess that these were difficult assignments, my mind more often than not drew blanks. My belief is that I had not the heart for these imaginative forays. My cold and cruel adolescent mind was seized mainly by the sensual possibilities and I hungered cravenly for them.

G is for God

My father stayed in the downpour to decry the heavens and my mother pointed out in later years that it was at this moment God set his face against us and withdrew all favour. Whatever about God, it was at this moment that my father turned his back on all religious observance, an apostasy of no small bravery in our devout village and probably the only trait in his personality I took after when I entered my own godless teens. A steady line of self-appointed evangelists beat a path to our door to try and rescue him out of the cocoon of hunkered bitterness into which he had retired. But my father's mind was set. The God of mercy and forgiveness was nothing to him any more and the community of believers were only so many fools. He could be violently eloquent on the subject. In black anger he would wrest me from the cradle and brandish me in their faces.

'There is no God of mercy and forgiveness,' he would roar. 'There is only the God of plague and affliction and justice, and we are all well and truly fucked because of it. This child is the proof of that. More than any of you I believe in Him. I only have to look at this child to know. The only difference is I have no faith in Him.'

These rages would reduce my mother to a sobbing shambles. She would recover, however, and then redouble her observance on his behalf, attending the sacraments twice daily to atone for his pride. Icons flourished in our house and the shelves and sideboards seemed to sprout effigies overnight. My father ground his teeth and reined in his temper.

H is for History

I have admitted my interest in killers at the pre-trial hearings. However, even now, I maintain that it is nothing more than the average male teen infatuation with all things bloody and destructive. Like most young men of my generation I can rhyme off a list of twentieth-century killers quicker than I can the names of the twelve apostles. At school I listened critically to the tales of the great ideological killers. I became convinced that the century was nothing more than a massive fiction, an elaborate snuff movie hugely budgeted and badly edited, ending with an interminable list of credits. I came to believe that beneath this vast panorama of warring nations and heaving atrocities the true identity and history of my time was being written by solitary minds untouched by ideology or political gain, solitary night stalkers prowling alleyways and quiet suburban homes, carrying their knives and axes and guns and garrottes. And I believed also it was only in this underworld that concepts of guilt and evil and justice had any meaning, this world where they were not ridiculed and over-whelmed by sheer weight of numbers. Bundy, Dahmer, Hindley, Chikatilo, Nilsen, the list goes on, an infernal pantheon within which I will now discreetly take my place.

I is for Indolence

After my leaving cert, I signed on as a government artist – I drew the dole. It was an issue of some scandal in the village, after all my father was the possessor of probably the biggest private fortune in the county.

One evening after signing on I sat in a local pub put-ting a sizeable hole in my first payment – I was quietly discovering the joys of solitary drinking. On an over-head TV I listened to the news and heard that the national unemployment figures had topped three hun-dred thousand for the first time. The figure was greeted with equal measures of awe and disgust.

'Christ, it's a shame, all those young people coming out of school and college and no jobs for them. The country is going to hell.'

'In a hand cart,' another added.

A third was not so sure. 'I don't know,' he said, a large straight-talking man. 'Half of those fuckers on the dole have no intention of working, they'd run a mile from it. And it's not as if there isn't plenty of it to do either, look at the state of the roads, or the graveyards for that matter. A crowd of bloody spongers the whole lot of them, if the truth be told.'

It was a brave thesis, particularly so in a townland surrounded by subsistence farms, the owners of which topped up their incomes with government handouts.

But he was right, at least in my case he was. I went home that night and for the first time in my life I knew what I was. I was a sponger, a slacker, a parasite, a leech on the nation's resources. Like most of my generation I had neither the will nor imagination to get up and do something useful with my life. And what was worse I took to my role joyfully, safe in the knowledge that I could fob off any queries by pointing to the statistics or by saying that I was indulging in a period of stocktaking and evaluation before I launched myself on the world with a definite plan. I could loftily declare that I was on sabbatical from life. Only in solitary moments of truth and pitiless insight would I speak the truth to myself: I had no worthwhile ideas and no courage, I was good for nothing.

J is for James

The only shaft of light in my childhood years was the presence of my friend James. Throughout my trial he was the one constant, sitting in the public gallery with his hair pulled back in a tight braid, chewing his bottom lip. I could feel his eyes upon me, placed like branding irons in the centre of my chest. Now he comes to me every week, bringing me my record collection piece by piece and my books, Hesse, Nietzsche and Dostoevsky, a young man's reading, or so I'm told.

James was more than my friend, he was my champion. I would be at the centre of one of those taunting circles, my tormentors wheeling about me, dealing out cuffs to the side of my head and insults. 'Ear we go, ear we go, ear we go,' they would chant. My defence then was to disappear down inside myself, down into that part within me which was clear and painless, a place lit by fantasy, ideas, books and music. Almost inevitably James would round the corner. I would see in his eyes the dark fire that was already igniting his soul.

'Leave him alone, you pack of cunts,' he'd yell. 'Leave him alone.'

Then he would wade into the centre of the circle, shouldering me aside, his Docs and fists flying, working his surprise to the limit by scoring busted noses and bruised balls. Sooner or later however he would find himself at the bottom of a pile of heaving bodies, curling into a tight foetal to ward off the kicks and blows that rained down on him. Just as suddenly my tormentors would scatter, yelling and whooping, leaving James bloodied and bruised on the ground like carrion. In those moments I used to think that James was the victim not of his love for me but of his own rampant imagination. Now I can see him rising from the dust, his face bloodied and running like a clown's make-up and I curse myself for my cynicism.

K is for Kill

The axe swung through the air and cleft my father's skull in two and he lay dead upon the floor.

L is for Lug

When I reached my teens I grew my hair to my shoulders. By then, however, it was already too late to prevent me from being teased mercilessly and earning a succession of nicknames. My peers were never short of cruel puns and covert abuse whenever I was near. 'Ear, ear,' they would yell whenever I opened my mouth to speak or, 'Ear we go, ear we go, ear we go,' whenever we gathered to watch football matches. From national school my name was Lug and in secondary school the more technically minded tried to amend it to Mono. But Lug was the name that stuck and I hated them for it, hated them for their stupid wit and their lack of mercy. But I did not hate them as much as I hated my father on the day he discovered it. He returned from answering the phone in the hallway. It was one of my 'friends'.

'Lug,' he said gleefully. 'Christ, they have you well named there and no doubt about it. We used to have an ass with that name once, Lugs. Mind you, he was twice the creature you are. He could work and he had a full set of ears.'

I burst out crying and ran to my room. I stayed there the rest of the afternoon, weeping and grinding my teeth. I eventually dried my eyes and took a look at myself in the mirror and I resolved then that no one would ever make me cry again.

M is for Music

Because of my impaired hearing my love of music has caused much wonderment. Again this has proved a fertile snuffling ground for those commentators desperate to unearth truffles of reason in this tale of blood and woe.

I am a metal head, a self-confessed lover of bludgeoning rhythms in major chords and rhyming couplets dealing in death and mayhem. My record collection, now numbering in hundreds, reads like a medieval codex of arcana; Ministry, Obituary, Bathroy, Leather Angel, Black Sabbath and so on. My greatest solace now is that I can listen to these records in the privacy of my cell without maddening anyone. If there was anything certain to unleash my father's temper it was the sound of these records throbbing through the house. He would come hammering at my bedroom door.

'Turn that fucking shite off,' he'd roar. 'Christ, you

would think a man of your age should have grown out of that sort of thing long ago.'

But I never did grow out of it and I don't foresee a day when I will. The horror of this music is rooted within me as deep as my very soul and I would no more think of defending it than my father would his own lachrymose renditions of 'Moonlight on the Silvery Rio Grande'.

N is for Never

As in never again. At the bottom of our souls all young men are sick. We do not grow sick or become sick nor is it some easy matter of hormonal determinism. This sickness is our very nature. Having suffered from the disease myself I know what I am talking about. It manifests itself generally as a disorder of the head, a slant of the imagination that preoccupies us with may-hem and blood, slashing and hacking, disease, waste and carnage. There is not a young man of my age who, in the privacy of his own heart, has not thought of killing someone. Many times James and I would sit fantasizing about a kill of our own, our very own corpse. We weighed up the options like assassins and narrowed it down to a single clean strike in an airport terminal bath-room where there is an abundance of unwary victims and suspects. We were armchair psychos, already tasting the blood. Most young men grow out of this sort of thing, taking to heart second-hand lessons in mercy and compassion, turning in wonderment and revulsion from their former selves. Some never learn and continue to stalk the earth with weapons, amassing victims in the darkness. But the truly wretched ones turn away also, not out of principle or humanity but from the antidote at the heart of the disease itself, the terrible soul-harrowing and puke-inducing disgust.

O is for Obituary

QUIRKE (MARY ELIZABETH) died suddenly at her residence, Carron, Co. Mayo, 21 May 1993, in her fifty-ninth year. Deeply regretted by her sorrowing husband, Thomas, her son, Gerard, and a large circle of relatives and friends. Removal to the Church of The Immaculate Conception, Carron this (Wednesday) evening at 7 o'clock. Requiem Mass tomorrow (Thursday) at 12 noon. Funeral afterwards to Cross Cemetery. No flowers. House private.

> Your story on earth will never be told
> The harp and the shamrock
> Green white and gold.

P is for Patrimony

Four months ago James and I stood in a green field behind our county hospital, two unpaid extras witnessing a dedication. There was a small platform bedecked with ribbons, a few local politicians, the diocesan bishop and my father. The field was populated by a motley collection of patricians, merchants and outpatients, a few nurses hung at the fringes. Incredulity hung in the air like a fine mist. We were here to witness the sod-turning on the foundation of The Thomas Quirke Institute for Alcoholic Research, a laboratory annexed to our county hospital and funded in equal measure by European grant aid and the single biggest bequest to the health services in the history of the state, my father's entire Lottery win. I listened as the politicians spoke on the straitened circumstances of the health services and on the pressing need for an institution of this sort in a province ravaged by alcoholism. My father was commended as a man of vision and philanthropy. I saw the bishop sprinkle holy water on the green earth and invoke the saints to guide the work of the institute. Then my father stepped forward to turn the first sod, his public awkwardness belying his easy skill with the spade. The audience whispered and shook their heads and as the earth split and turned I saw my fortune vanish before my eyes. In honour of the occasion James and I left the field for the pub across the road and got sinfully and disastrously drunk.

Q is for Quietus

We sat in the kitchen drinking the last of the whiskey. It was two in the morning and darkness hummed beyond the windows. James was slumped at the table, his head resting in his extended arm, clutching a glass. His speech came thick and slow.

'Every penny,' he was saying, 'every fucking penny gone up in smoke and pissed against the wall. I wouldn't have believed it myself if I hadn't seen it with my own two eyes. And everyone of them bursting their holes laughing at him behind his back. The Thomas Quirke Institute for Alcoholic Research, no less. Sheer bloody madness.'

'Give it a rest, James. I'm fed up hearing it.'

It had been a long day and I badly needed sleep. A monstrous headache had begun to hammer behind my eyes.

'Are you not mad, Ger. Christ, I'd be mad. A whole fortune squandered in one act of vanity. You're his son, for Christ's sake, it wasn't just his to throw away. You're his son and you could have been set up for life.'

'I know, James. It's all over now, though, and there's nothing anyone can do about it. It's all over.'

'I'd kill him,' he said suddenly, rising up and swinging the bottle wildly. 'Stone dead I'd kill him. He hadn't the right, he hadn't the fucking right.'

My father entered at that moment, his face flushed

with drink, the knot of his tie well over his collarbone.

'Hadn't the right to do what, James, hadn't the right to do what? Go on, you young shit, spell it out.'

He was standing with his legs apart inside the door, the cage of his chest rising and falling. He looked like a man who was going to reach for a gun.

'I was just saying it was a real pity that all that money couldn't be put to better use where right people might benefit from it.'

'Is that so? And I suppose if it was your money you'd have known what to do with it.'

James' head was lolling heavily, a wide smirk crawling to his ears.

'I'd have given it to the poor of the parish,' he said, guffawing loudly and gulping from his glass. 'Every last penny. And I'd have put a new roof on the church,' he finished, now giggling helplessly.

'And I suppose you wouldn't have left yourself short either, James. You being one of these poor that prey so heavily on your mind.'

He was leaning with both hands on the table now, towering over James. He wasn't totally drunk, just in that dangerous condition where he could argue forever or lose his temper suddenly.

'Do you know what it is, Mr Quirke, something I saw today? Everyone of those people were there patting you on the back with one hand and smirking behind the other. Telling you what a great man you were and then going away bursting their holes laughing at you. I saw it with my own two eyes.'

James had lost the run of himself now, he didn't care what he said. I stood between them.

'Cut it out both of you. James, it's time you left, I need to get to bed.' I began hauling him to his feet.

'He'll leave when I'm finished with him,' my father

81

hissed, squeezing out the words between his clenched teeth. 'When I'm finished and only then. What about you, James, were you laughing?'

'I didn't know whether to laugh or to cry, Mr Quirke. I was in two minds.' He was swaying drunkenly now, bracing himself between the chair and the table. 'I didn't know whether to laugh or to cry. I was standing there thinking that some people have more money than sense.'

My father lunged at him, his outstretched hands reaching for his throat. James keeled backwards, spilling the chair and my father landed across him, bellowing in rage and surprise. They grappled wildly for an instant. I threw aside the chair and James' boot flicked up as he rolled over, catching me under the chin and knocking me sideways into the table, grabbing the tablecloth and bringing the bottle and glass shattering to the floor. We scuttled to the end of the room and my father came off the floor clutching the neck of the bottle at arm's length.

'I'll cut the fucking head clean off you,' he roared.

He moved towards James slowly, as if walking over broken ground. It was at this instant the axe rose into the air, just off my left shoulder and passed in a slow arc over my head. And it was at this instant also that there was a sound of breaking glass and the light went out. The fluorescent bulb showered down around our shoulders as the axe clipped it and there was a sudden pass of cold air in the darkness, a grim sound of something splitting with a soft crunch. I rushed to the wall and turned on the bulb.

'Oh Jesus, oh fucking Christ.'

My father lay face down on the floor, his head split open and the axe standing upright in it as if marking the spot. He was dead beyond any salvation. James was doing some frantic crazy dance about his head and there was a smell of shit in the room.

'Oh Jesus, what are we going to do, what are we going to do?'

I was stone-cold sober then, hiccuping with fright but perfectly in control. I started dragging James towards the door, hauling him by the collar.

'Go home now, James, there's nothing you can do. Go home.'

I pushed him out into the darkness and slammed the door. My breathing came in jagged bursts and I needed to sit down. I righted the chair and sat at my father's head, a four-hour vigil into the dawn with no thought in my head save that now, for the first time in my life, I had nothing.

When the grey sun rose I stepped into the hall and rang the cops.

R is for Responsibility

Not for the first time James was picking himself up off the tarmac, wiping the blood from his face. I was after telling him rather imperiously that his imagination was running away with him. He was having none of it.

'Those fuckers walk all over you,' he sobbed. 'When are you going to stick up for yourself?' He was near crying.

'I can take care of them in my own time,' I said cryptically.

'Well, it's about time you started. Look at the size of you, you're well able for them, what the hell are you afraid of? And your father too – Christ, you put up with so much shit. You have to be every bit as cruel as they are. You have to meet every blow with a kick and every insult with a curse. You shouldn't take this any more, it's not right.'

'I never asked for your help,' I said coldly.

'Well, this is the last time,' he yelled. 'From now on you can be your own martyr or your own coward. I want nothing more to do with it.'

'No,' I said, 'you'll always be there. You can't help it, you have the imagination for it.'

I walked away, leaving him sobbing on the ground.

S is for Summary

Even now, in the fifth month of my sentence, I still receive weekly visits from my lawyer. There are loose ends still in need of tying up, details to be put to rest. He informs me that public interest in my case has not waned, apparently its notoriety is being seen as indicative of some sort of widespread malaise in the minds of our young people, a kind of national tumour in need of lancing. He tells me that there is much probing of the national psyche in the media.

More recently he has presented me with a sheaf of proposals from publishers and film producers, all of them looking for the complete story, the first-person account. I have refused all of them, returned the documents through the wire mesh. I have no interest in the superfluities that necessarily accrue within the scope of the extended narrative. I have chosen this alphabet for its finitude and narrow compass. It places strictures on my story which confine me to the essential substratum of events and feelings. Within its confines there is no danger of me wandering off like a maddened thing into sloughs of self-pity and righteousness.

T is for Truth

Under oath and on the Bible I swore to tell the truth. I confined myself to the facts, which may or may not be the same thing. I believe now that this preoccupation with the facts is exactly the problem with all kinds of testimony. A clear retelling of the facts, no matter how accurately they record actual events, is a lamentable falling short of the truth. I know now that the true identity of things lie beyond the parameter of the facts. They lie in the treacherous and delusive ground of the fiction writer and the fabulist, those seekers after truth who speak it for no one but themselves with no motive of defence or self-justification. This is the terrain in which someone other than myself will one day stake his ground.

During the days of testimony I saw James leaning forward in his seat, chewing on his bottom lip which had blossomed out in cold sores under the stress. His eyes bored at me from the other end of the courtroom as I confined myself to the facts.

U is for Unravel

The thin bonds of our family unit sundered completely after the death of my mother. On some unspoken agreement my father and I commenced separate lives within the narrow scope of our house and small farm. I rose each day at midmorning when I was sure he was about his business in the fields. I ate alone in the kitchen, staring in mild surprise at the creeping ruin which had taken possession of the house. Now that neither of us seldom bothered to light any fires, paint had begun to peel from several damp patches on the walls. A light fur like a shroud clung to the effigies and icons all about and the windows scaled over.

Yet neither of us would lift a hand to do anything. We were now caught in a game of nerves, each staring the other down, waiting for him to crack. But neither of us did, we were too far gone in stubbornness and pride. The dishes piled up in the sink and cartons and bottles collected everywhere. The house now reeked of decay.

I came down from my room one evening and he was at the table, drinking from a bottle by its neck. I stopped dead inside the door and continued to stare at him. We spoke at the same time.

'This place has gone to hell.'

And still neither of us made a move.

V is for Visit

Now that I have all my records and the last of my books I have begun to sense a distance opening up between myself and James. It gets worse with every visit, a widening fissure into which our words tumble without reaching each other. Most of the last few visits have been spent sitting in silence, staring onto the blank table-top. We have made sudden despairing raids on old memories, seeking frenziedly among old battles and fantasies for warm common ground. But it is hopeless, it is as if we were retelling the plot of some book only one of us has read, and not a very good book at that. I am surprised by the different ways we have come to remember things. I tell him of one of his heroic interventions on my behalf and he grimaces and speaks dismissively of a rush of blood to the head. He tells me a bitter incident of crushed youth and violent temper and I wonder who he is talking about. We are different men now and we hold different memories.

This week he had a real surprise. He sat across from me with his eyes lowered on his hands, the curious air of a lover about to confess some long and on-going infidelity about him.

'This is the last time I'll be here, Gerard,' he mumbled. 'I'm going away – America.' He had developed a twitch along his jawbone since his last visit and I noticed that his nails bled.

'When did you decide?'

'A few months back, seeing you in here and all that. Everything's changed, it's all different now. I've got the medical and a job set up in New York. It's all set up,' he repeated. He continued to stare at his hands.

I was obscurely glad that it was going to end like this. James' days as my protector were at an end and my incarceration was his loss also. I knew our friendship had exhausted itself – consummated might be a better word – and I knew that I was looking at a young man whose mission in life had been completed.

'I hope it goes well for you over there. Make big money and meet lots of women. American women go mad for paddies, I'm told. It's the dirt under the fingernails. Tell them you live in a thatched cottage, I hear it never fails.'

He smiled quietly. 'I don't know what I'm going to do. Probably work for a while and save a bit of money. I'd like to go to college.'

'That's good. It's good to have a plan, if only to have something to diverge from.' I rose from my chair and held out my hand. 'Best of luck, James. I hope it goes well for you.'

'So do I. And thanks, Gerard. You were the only real friend I ever had.'

'It goes both ways.'

'Goodbye.'

'Goodbye.'

I watched him leave and I tried to remember a time when I had ever seen him walking away before. I couldn't.

W is for Wisdom

My father made it clear to me that life wasn't easy. It was his favourite theme, particularly in those drink-sodden days after my mother died. He would fall upon me roaring, snatching the headphones from my ears.

'I suppose you think that it will be easy from now on, ya useless cunt,' he'd roar. 'I suppose you think that it's all there now under your feet and all you have to do is bend down and pick it up. Well, let me tell you here and now that it won't be like that, it won't be like that at all. No son of mine is going to be mollycoddled and pampered and I'll tell you why. Because you'll work for it, like I did when I was your age and every other man of my generation. Because, and make no mistake about it, you young cur, it's work and nothing else that makes a man of you, a real man, not like those fucking long-haired gits I see you hanging around town with.'

He was well into his stride now, pacing the floor and breathing heavily.

'Started work after national school we did, every man jack of us, footing turf at two shillings a floor, nearly a hundred square yards. And damn the bit of harm it did us. It made men out of us, real men who knew the value of money. Now all this country has is young fuckers like you spending all day on your frigging arses, eating and drinking the quarter session with no thought of tomorrow. I'm sick of the fucking sight of you.'

He would grab a hank of my hair then, and lift my face up, his whiskey breath burning my skin.

'But if your mother was alive there'd be a different tune out of you, I'll bet. She'd have put skates under you and not have you sitting here all day like a friggin' imbecile.'

This was the inevitable point of breakdown, the moment at which all his vehemence would drain away, rendering him mawkish and pathetic. He would collapse by the stove, weeping and snuffling into his hands.

'Oh Mary, Mary my love.'

I did not know which was the most terrifying, the honest and direct terror from which there was no escape, or this genuine grief which was his alone.

X is for Xenophobe

We watched the interview on television the following evening. A study in western gothic, it showed the three of us standing in the doorway, my mother staring into her hands, plainly abashed by the attention, my father square-jawed and sullen, glowering darkly at the camera. At their backs I rose up between them, a half-wit's leer covering my face. The bright young interviewer, all smiles and bonhomie, waved a microphone in my father's face.

'Mr Quirke, you are the latest Lotto millionaire, the biggest in its history. It must have come as a complete shock to you.'

Father avoided the bait skilfully. 'No,' he said drily, barely hiding his contempt. 'When you have lived as long as I have it takes more than a few pounds to surprise you. I just checked my numbers on the Nine O'Clock News and when I found out that I had won I went and had a few pints in my local like I always do.'

'You didn't throw a party or buy a drink for the pub?'

'I bought my round as I always do. I've always had money to buy my own drink, anyone will tell you that.'

'Now that you have all this money, surely it will bring some changes to your lives, a new car or a holiday perhaps?'

'The car we have is perfectly good,' he answered bluntly. 'It gets us from A to B and back again. If we wanted to live somewhere else we wouldn't be living here. There'll be no changes.'

The interviewer hurriedly thrust the microphone to my face.

'Gerard, you are the only child of this new millionaire. No doubt you have high hopes of getting your hands on a sizeable share of it,' she said hopefully.

'My father has a sound head on his shoulders; he'll not do anything foolish with it,' I said simply, barely able to keep from laughing.

The interview ended in freeze-frame, catching my father with his jaw struck forward in absurd defiance and the half-wit's leer spreading back to my ears. In the news coverage of my trial it was this image which defined the tone of all articles. The national press barely managed to suppress a tone of there-but-for-the-grace-of-God righteousness. Their articles were consummate exercises in mock anguish and between-the-lines sneering at their dim western cousins. Some day soon I expect to read accounts of sheep shagging and incest purely for tone.

Y is for Yes

Yes, I have my remorse. All that night I sat over my father's corpse and watched the blood drain from his skull over the floor. I was experiencing an object lesson in how death diminishes and destroys not just life, but memories also. All that night I had trouble with my recollection. I could not square this overweight, middle-aged corpse with the towering ogre who had terrorized and destroyed my teenage years. That was a creature from a different era, a prehistory of myth and violent legend. It had nothing to do with this small West of Ireland farmer, this lord of forty acres with his fondness for whiskey and cowboy songs.

There was a clear and horrible disparity in that room, a terrible and universal lack of proportion.

Z is for Zenith

On the first morning of my detention a small deputation of prisoners greeted me in the exercise yard. I was amazed to see that they bore several gifts for me – a ten spot of hash, a quart of whiskey and a list of warders who could be bought off for privileges. I stood bemusedly trying to conceal these gifts in my baggy overalls, watching the bearers retreat diffidently across the yard. Evidently my reputation had preceded me, elevating me on arrival into that élite category of prisoner who were not to be fucked with. I had a secret laugh about that. This of course is on account of the axe. There is no doubt but that the nature of my crime has made it a transgression of a different order, even in here, where there are men doing time for crimes that are barely speakable. Knives or guns are understandable, they are the instruments of run-of-the-mill savageries. But an axe is something else again. It is the stuff of myth, the instrument of the truly sick of soul.

From the beginning I have received fan mail, curious and vaguely imploring missives from faceless well-wishers. Dear Gerard Quirke, Not a day passes when I do not think of you alone in the isolation of your cell. You are in my thoughts every day and I pray for the deliverance of your wounded soul.

Today I received my first proposal of marriage.

I have begun to think again of my future and I have made some tentative plans. Yesterday I signed for an Open University degree in English Literature and History; it will take me four years. Now my days are full, neatly ordered within the precise routine of the penal system, meals and exercise alternating between longer periods of study and my record collection. At night I lie in this bed, plugged into my stereo and smoking the good quality dope that is so plentiful here. The lights go down and peace and quiet reigns all about. I spend the hours before sleep remembering back to the final day of my trial and I acknowledge now without irony the wisdom of that judge when he handed me this life sentence.

THE WELFARE
OF THE PATIENT

Anna McGrail

Anna McGrail was born in Liverpool but now divides her time between London and Brighton. She works both as a freelance editor and a lifetime-contract mother of two. She continues to write short stories but also had a radio play broadcast on LBC this summer and, by staying up late, managed to finish her first novel.

THE WELFARE OF THE PATIENT

She leans against the wall, in the only space of shade in the bright afternoon, and smokes a cigarette while she watches ambulances arrive, families leave. She didn't want to come to the hospital, didn't want to come near him at all, but she had promised. She could turn back now, walk away down the hill, but she is far too aware of convention to ignore it and thinks of the stain her absence would leave upon her reputation. She grinds the cigarette out under the heel of her sandal and brushes her fringe out of her eyes with the back of her hand. She is ready.

The main doors open as you reach out to touch them, inviting. It is cooler inside than out. The light from the ice-cube shaped fluorescent tubes is a mixed blue and pink, brighter, more searching than daylight.

The nurse leads her without a moment's hesitation, once she learns who this is, down the linoleum-tiled corridor and into the right room. It must be the right room because it has his name on the door, official lettering in a small wooden slot, but she does not recognize him, not at all. Not at all, she who knew him better than anyone. She walks in and smells turpentine disinfecting the air.

'I wondered when you'd get here,' he says.

'I didn't bring any flowers,' she says. 'I see you have some anyway.' There are old roses in a glass vase on the window sill.

'What would I want flowers for?' he says. 'You might have brought grapes, though. Isn't that what visitors are supposed to bring patients?'

'Only if they end up eating all the grapes themselves,' she says. 'I don't like grapes.' She places her shopping bag in the corner of the room, takes a can of lemonade from the top and opens it. Very carefully and deliberately she throws the metal tab into the wastepaper basket. She sits down on the moulded plastic chair that is the only concession to visitors, kicks off her sandals and presses the soles of her feet, one by one, against the cold iron frame of the bed.

'You may sit,' he says.

'Thank you.'

'They took nail clippings yesterday,' he tells her. 'What do you suppose they do with them? They've already had blood, urine and my spleen. There'll be nothing left of me.' He lifts his arms, thin as hazel wands, and the tube in the vein in his right wrist moves with him. She is startled. She had not expected him to be able to move by now. He smiles coyly as she stares, on display, the tendons in his limbs visible, strung tight as piano wires.

'Look at this,' he says. He moves his fingers against the light and casts shadows against the white wall, fuzzy at the edges, black in the centre. 'Look. Amazing figures formed by the hand.'

'A rabbit,' she says dutifully. 'A bird, no, an eagle. A Siberian crane. A lesser spotted hedgehog.' At last there is a shape she cannot guess and she grows impatient, shaking her head from side to side.

'It is an angel,' he says, laughing, bending his fingers once again. 'See, here are her wings.'

'What a talent,' she says, pretending to see now, to admire.

'My own invention,' he replies, pleased. 'Sorely missed at parties, I bet.'

'Every night,' she says. 'I don't suppose they allow you to smoke in here.'

'What do you think? You should stop. You'll live longer. Although you'll live longer, anyway, won't you?'

She drinks from the can, the carbonation burning her tongue. Already the lemonade is getting warm, the promising condensation on the cold metal surface disappearing. She tries not to look at the blood, seeping from beneath the bandages. He picks at scabs, idly, short fingernails unhinging the ridged surface. She tries not to look at the marks on his arms. In his wrists, a network of blue veins is clear, as if his skin were becoming steadily more transparent. It is as if he has begun to live in distant oceans, in sunless depths, metamorphosing into a deep-sea creature, the luminous sort, with internal organs visible beneath the skin. The thin arteries beat in the unsteady rhythm of his heart, a display of the mechanics of life that some might consider to be in poor taste.

'It's your turn now,' he tells her. 'Entertain me. Isn't that what you've come for? Do a couple of card tricks or something. Take my mind off things.'

She smiles. 'How are they treating you?' She knows he needs to talk and she can afford to be courteous. She has the time.

'As well as can be expected when they don't know how to treat you. Perhaps they'll name a complication after me. Fame and fortune await. This isn't like Kansas any more, Dorothy.' He laughs. 'Tomorrow I could come down with a whole new range of impressive side-effects. Lycanthropy, for example.'

'I think the full moon is past. I'll consider myself safe.'

'As well you might, Mrs Talbot. They say the innocent

need have no fear.' He grins at her, the striations on his skull becoming darker, and bares his fangs, triumphant as a wolf at the head of his pack. She stays still and waits, watching him stretch taut then subside, aching. Sweat glitters down the side of his face and wets his tongue.

'How are you sleeping?'

He replies that he never shuts his eyes, he cannot, must not. Sleep always takes him to the places at the back of the eyes and he doesn't want to visit those strange countries again. 'There are terrible strange animals here at the end of the world,' he says. 'Nameless and nerveless.' He picks at a piece of loose cotton on the quilt, tracing the remains of a pattern. His hands pluck the covers closer to him with crab-like movements, crustaceans on a journey of their own. He shivers, as if he were cold.

'Lying here under your sheets all the time. Your imagination must be morbid.'

'A car accident,' he says. For a moment, she can see this. Sweat matting his hair, staining his skin, the cold wind on his face, his sore bones scraping along the roadway. There is blood on the tarmac, oily and viscous. 'That's the sort of death I'd like,' he says. 'That's the one for me. Definite. Quick. No hope. Not this.'

'None of us can choose,' she reminds him. She says it quickly and moves on, before he can think through the implications, but she is too late.

'I did choose,' he says. 'I knew the risks. So did you. And I can choose now. Any time. I could leave here for a start.'

'But where would you go?'

'And who would have me?'

'Who will have any of us, once we've come as far as this?'

98

'As far as we can go,' he says.

'Not quite,' she says. 'It isn't over yet.'

She considers a ceremony in a grassy field, his family and friends gathered at last, now there is nothing more to be afraid of. The sun is shining on the fresh soil. The trees stretch endlessly like banners on the green slopes. Beyond that is the desert. The sky turns to white where it touches the white of the land, far at the horizon, beyond colour.

'No,' he says. 'Not yet.'

The shells of conversation are lower and louder. 'Try to think of it as a gift,' she says. 'Most of us ignore the inevitable, bowling along until the bus hits us. Try to think of it as a chance.' Her voice is as gentle as she can possibly make it.

'A chance to do what?' He is angry. 'No matter what I do now, it isn't going to make any difference. I've had all my chances, hundreds of them. Where did they get me? Here.'

Exhausted, he leans forward to throw up in a tin basin. Heat presses. She asks him if he wants a drink of water and reaches for the paper cup. There are two clear bottles on the bedside table. He tells her no. One is gin, the other formaldehyde. They smile, confidentially, friends again.

Sudden quantities of very strong sunlight pour in through the window, illuminating their collusion, making everything incandescent, reflecting off the dust into multiple rainbows. 'Look at that,' she says, dreamily. 'Dust is the most beautiful thing I know.'

'Such words belong to the patient,' says the patient. 'I should be thinking about dust. And I have been. I've thought everything about dust that there possibly is to think. And my conclusion is that one day not only will I be dust, but this room, this building, this country.

Dust. Dust. It's not a new conclusion, I realize, but you can't expect original thinking at my time of life.' He reminds her that a day will come when the entire universe has worn itself out, when there is no further energy available for use, when all is at maximum dissipation and disorder. 'This is known as the heat death of the universe,' he says smugly. He draws her attention to the floor, where there are several cereal flakes, three safety pins and some petals from the fading flowers. 'Things are falling apart already.'

She says she doesn't believe it, although she is accustomed to things dissolving and dying. 'Like those flowers,' she says. 'It's the price of being alive. No one is immune.' The sky outside the window bleaches in the heat, loses all colour and silvers like a mirror, reflecting back the earth. She smiles to think of everything becoming warmer and warmer in the heat death of the universe, all bonds fracturing, all obligations meaningless, until even the separate molecules are broken.

'Visitors are supposed to make small talk,' he complains. 'I'm not here to give lectures. Talk to me about inconsequential trivia. Take my mind off things. Tell me something I don't already know.'

'I may not see you next week,' she says, sitting up straight and pressing her spine against the back of the chair.

'I already knew that,' he says. 'Or, at least, I already guessed it.' He twists his fingers. They are slightly sticky. She cannot tell whether this is from fear or simple sweat.

'Is there anything you still want taking care of?' she asks, brisk now, polite, concerned. 'Letters written? Library books to be taken back?'

'There's lots of things to do,' he says, 'but I can't see

me fitting them all in now. Fulfilling my potential as a violinist, for example, I never got round to that. Then there was being called to the Bar. An exhibition of my oil paintings at the Royal Academy – whatever happened to that idea? Do you know, I once even considered having children.'

She looks at him. 'You'd have made a good father, on the whole,' she says.

'It leaves someone to mourn for you,' he says, 'if nothing else. In my next life I'll start as I mean to go on. Make lists. Never procrastinate. Seize the day. I'll tell you something else I've been thinking about: there isn't enough time left to make amends. Not to everybody. Not to everybody who deserves it.'

'There are still things you can do,' she says, 'that will make a difference. To you. To us. You can die a hero and not a victim, for a start.'

'Want me to go out and kill a monster?' he says. 'You have strange ideas about what a man can do on his deathbed.'

'You don't have to lift a finger,' she says. 'Listen to me. You can be a hero by admitting you're afraid. That's all it takes.'

'I'm not afraid,' he says. 'What do I have to be afraid of now? The worst is over.'

She leans forward, takes his hand. His skin rests lightly against hers, clammy, insistent, and she tightens her grip. 'Think about it.'

He looks at her and looks away. 'I can't think,' he says. 'It's another deficiency I've acquired.'

She sees the shadows beneath his eyes, violet lines. The heat has made him quiet. She releases his hand. 'Aren't you tired?' she says. 'You must be tired by now. I am.'

'You'll be lying here one day,' he says. 'This place or

somewhere like it. You don't know what tiredness is.' His breathing is harsh.

'I know what pain is,' she says. 'It will soon be over.'

'Cassandra.' His voice is so small she hardly hears. 'What do you think will happen? Does anything happen next?' She lets the small voice talk into the silence. 'I've always believed there wasn't anything else. I've lived like there wasn't anything else. No God, no devils, no angels. I don't want to go into the afterlife and come face to face with something I've never believed in. What sort of judgement will there be? If there is no judgement, there will be nothing. Just darkness. Just emptiness. You could tell me, you know. Please, Cassandra, tell me what you think will happen.'

'You know I can't tell you. No one can.'

'I could take out an insurance policy, I suppose. Do you think I've got time for a deathbed conversion? Perhaps you should call the priest. I've got things to tell him, confessions to make.'

'You wouldn't talk to him. I know that much. No more than you would the last time I got him here. I'd be better off arranging the violin lessons, instead.'

'I am so frightened,' he says. 'I never wanted to die alone.'

'I promised you,' she says. 'You won't.'

He wants to hold her hand again. She puts the lemonade on the bedside cabinet. The lines on his palms are ragged and pale, they used to be etched more deeply. He smiles and shrugs his shoulders. His hair is the colour of warm caramel. His eyes are surprisingly blue, as blue as seas should be. 'I shouldn't rely on you like this,' he says.

'Some of us always depend on the kindness of strangers.'

'No,' he says, sharply. 'You are no Blanche to be driven mad by what you see.'

'No,' she says. 'Not that. I could be Florence Nightingale. You could have an injection. A sedative.' She puts her arms around him.

'How about choirs of angels to sing me to my rest?'

'I might manage angels dancing on the head of a pin, given sufficient notice.'

'In formation?'

'If that is what your heart desires, Cinderella.'

'Tell them to start with the paso doble.'

Clouds are beginning to appear, fist-sized on the sky, and it is getting dark outside, now that the sun is hidden.

She sees he might cry. 'Hush, baby,' she says, as softly as she can. 'Hush. Sleep.' She can hardly see his face.

She kisses his forehead, which is white now. His hand against hers, incessant in its movement, seems to weigh nothing at all. There is nothing holding him to the bed. He says goodbye. 'It is,' he tells her, 'a far far better thing I do.'

'Damn right,' she says.

'Tell them,' he says, 'curfew shall not ring tonight.' He closes his eyes.

'My hero,' she says, and smiles and cradles his head. She is patient. She waits. Even as she watches, he stops breathing. The tumult in his hands stills. The shadows remain in the corners of the room, solid bars of darkness. Now all she can hear is the fizz of bubbles from the lemonade, the liquid flattening. She can still taste the sugar on her tongue, leaving a film on her teeth of incipient decay.

She lets go of his hand and lays it on top of the sheet. It is caught in an arch, the last movement in a dance of extremities and terminations. She presses it flat and pushes the fingers together. Her task completed, she gathers up her belongings, puts the can in the yellow container marked 'Clinical Waste', removes his name card from the door and steps out into the air. She is efficient, as well as neat. The city smells of turpentine.

A cold wind starts to blow as she walks down the hill to the train station. Far at the horizon, the sky is grey where it touches the grey of the land. It begins to rain, slow drops the size of coins intermittent against the paving stones. Now she is Azrael, the Angel of Death, who never cries, although she often feels lonely. She walks with all the time in the world through the late afternoon.

PROSPERO'S
OTHER ISLAND

Vivien Gaynor

Vivien Gaynor was born in Australia, educated in Australia and England, now lives in Scotland and is restoring a farmhouse in Italy. Involved in the theatre from an early age, after postgraduate work in London she joined the National Theatre, then ran her own production company. More recently she set up a publishing services business, lectured on small business start-up courses and, among other things, worked as a mural painter. After being shortlisted for these Awards in 1992, she is working towards writing full time. She has published various articles and is currently working on a historical novel.

For my father, who was there.

PROSPERO'S OTHER ISLAND

'So there's this guy lying in his bed, can't sleep, and he hears voices. Looks around, nobody there. Thinks he must be going barmy. Then he looks down at the end of the bed and sees this pair of mozzies standing on the rail. One's holding the mosquito net back, and it says to the other one, "Will we eat him here or take him away?"'

'Ah, pull the other one. Heard that story in Darwin months ago.'

'Darwin? Don't make me laugh. Tiddlers — wait till you see ours. They're so big you can count the rings on their legs across the room!'

Curtis grinned despite himself. Same old stories. They'd done the same to him when he'd first come up, ribbing the new recruit. It seemed a long time ago, but a lot of things can change in a few months. They weren't wrong about the mosquitoes, though. The mozzies, the flies, the heat and the relentless humidity were real features of the place.

He signalled to the boy for a beer. The brown bottle, beaded with condensation, drops trickling down its sides, was the only cool thing in sight. He rolled it against his forehead, sweat and condensation mingling and already warm by the time it dripped off his chin.

'Any of you heroes on for another run?' The station manager leaned in through the door, wiping his face on his hairy forearm.

Curtis leaned back in his chair, looking out under the eaves of the verandah to see the sky. Bright white and streaky, usual midday cloud cover coming up over the horizon.

'Bit late, what's up?'

'Jim Reilly up at the Shamrock's had a spot of bother. Dredge rolled on him, busted his ankle. Wants us to fly him out for the doc to take a look at it.'

Curtis hadn't met Reilly, but all the miners grubbing away up country were as tough as old boots, living in squalid conditions you wouldn't wish on a dog. None of them looked to be making a fortune, but you couldn't tell. Anyway, in this place you could get blood poisoning from a scratch, never mind a broken bone. Better go and get him. If nothing else it would be a chance to get away from the relentless joking of bored young men, the endless card games, too much beer. And the heat, at least for a while.

None of the others had rushed to volunteer.

'Okay, I'll go.' He picked up the wide-brimmed straw hat from the seat beside him, headed for the rack of overalls by the door and pulled his on over his shorts and shirt, leaving it unbuttoned. The very image of the dashing young pilot, he thought. Not quite how he had imagined it, back in Sydney.

'Good on you, Curtis. I'll radio ahead and his boys can bring him down to the strip.'

The crowd at the other table waved casually as he left.

'Look out for Simpson, won't you?'

'Sure.'

The biplane was still on the runway from the last run, the leading edge of the wing and the leather seat scorching as he climbed into the rear cockpit. He left putting on the helmet and goggles until the last possible moment, as the boy swung the propeller and ducked away. The engine sputtered, then roared, and he taxied down the runway. In the distance the jagged mountain ranges stood braced against the clouds piling up behind them; it looked like being a bumpy trip.

Look out for Simpson. They knew he would, but it was becoming a litany, the usual salute every take-off. He put the plane into a long sweeping turn that took him out over the green and white edge of the bay – the palm trees hanging limp, a few canoes on the beach and a couple of launches tied up to the jetty – then round over the mangrove swamps and the bright green of the delta grassland as he turned inland to-wards the mountains. No one was going to find Simpson now.

Joseph was a good singer and the brothers were pleased with him. He had picked up pidgin quickly, and even a little English. He was the first in his district to go to school, and he was very proud of the responsibility. His father hadn't wanted to send him to the white men, but it was the only way he could think of to discover the magic, even if it had meant sending his son away from the village. At the mission they had told Joseph that if he studied well he might become a teacher. He had hung his head and scuffed at the dust with the toe of his shoe, not knowing how to answer. He didn't know what his father would say about that. He had listened carefully to everything they had told him, but it was harder than he had expected to find out the secret. He had asked a few tentative questions, but either they didn't know, which he thought unlikely, or his uncle was right and it was something the white men intended to keep for themselves.

They had told him many stories of the white man's

god, the most powerful in the world. They even said he was the only one. Of course that couldn't be true, but there was no doubt that he was a most potent and generous god, who sent his people great quantities of gifts. They didn't even have to grow their own food, it was all sent to them in boxes and barrels, and most beautifully in bright shining tins. He had collected a couple of the tins to give his father, a great treasure.

Once he was out of sight of the mission and started on the long track back over the mountain to his village he took off his shoes, tied the laces together and hung them round his neck. He curled his toes contentedly in the mud. He would have liked to take off his shirt and tie, but he wanted everyone in the village to see him in his white man's clothes. The brothers had said he could go home for the big sing-sing, and everybody would be there. As he walked he went over the stories he would tell them. He hoped that somewhere in them his father would be able to find the answers he wanted.

As Curtis climbed towards the mountains the sky was whitening with the glare of the tropical noon and clouds gathering faster than he liked. It was a journey he had made many times before, and he was no longer awestruck by the mile upon mile of jungle rolling beneath his wings, the silver flashes of streams and waterfalls showing here and there like slashes in velvet, the mountain peaks vanishing into mist and cloud higher than his plane would take him. He loved flying. He would never have admitted it on the ground, but he never tired of it; alone in the limitless reaches of the sky, him up here and the rest of the world condemned by gravity to crawl on the crust of the world while he soared above it. Maybe they all felt like that, behind the jokes, the interminable cards and beer. Despite the noise, the roar of the engine, the racket of the wind in the wires, the oil that sprayed in their faces and coated the goggles. When they landed they slapped the wings, patted the noses, gave the planes names and called them worse, moaned, complained and treated the job and the life with the elaborate casualness of people who loved what they did and wouldn't have dreamed of doing anything else. There had only ever been one person he could talk to about it, and even between themselves they had treated it all as a joke . . .

Stop daydreaming, Curtis told himself as the mountains loomed closer. There was only one entrance to this valley, and one way out of it at the other end, a cleft like a swordcut. If he missed it he would be walking home, as the station joke had it; there wasn't room to circle in the narrow valley, and no time to climb out of it. The cloud was thickening by the minute; he had to be at the cleft before it filled up and disappeared.

'If he had to break his bloody leg why couldn't he have done it this morning?' Curtis grumbled aloud. He was into the valley now, mountains towering above on either side, flying in shadow, climbing towards the far end, the sun trapped behind the peaks, masked by cloud, the noise of the engine battering back from the walls of rock.

The cleft was coming up ahead; he aimed for dead centre, still climbing, and burst through into the sunlight of the next valley. No time to waste gazing about, an immediate hard right turn took him up the line of the valley towards the little strip at the far end. No one's favourite landing field – mountains closing in abruptly behind, and the strip itself a grassy uphill slope with no margin for error either side. He could just see the group outside the shack, and knew that they would be standing shading their eyes from the glare, looking out for him as they did nearly every day – their lifeline, their food supply, their only contact with the outside world unless they risked the ten-day trek out through unpredictable country.

He brought the plane in, running up the slope, cutting the engine as the local boys ran out and grabbed the wings ready to turn the plane for takeoff. He sat still for a moment, giving himself a few seconds to get used to the sudden cessation of noise. As he did so he saw, over at the far side of the field, a group of 'wild men', their bushy wigs decorated with leaves and feathers, spears twice their height towering over them. He noticed that the local boys were crowding round the plane more than usual, strutting, looking important.

They're showing off, he thought. These new fellas can't ever have seen a plane close to before, and our boys are pulling rank.

He climbed down from the cockpit, taking off his helmet as he reached the ground. He saw the mountain men gasp. One, braver than the others, came cautiously forward and, reaching ahead of himself as far as he could, touched the tip of the wing, snatching back his hand as if he'd been scalded. Curtis knew better than to laugh.

'Want to go for a spin?' he asked genially, knowing they wouldn't understand him.

The leader looked at him and away again, not catching his eye, came carefully forward a few steps, squatted down and looked under the plane. Then, greatly daring, he reached out a hand and ran it down the underside of the fuselage towards the tail. He looked puzzled. The local boys hooted with laughter.

'This bush fella he want see is plane boy or mary!' their leader giggled, a broad grin splitting his face.

The mountain man withdrew to his own group and

they moved away a few yards, talking quietly among themselves, glancing sideways at the plane.

Curtis didn't pay them any more attention. The boys would look after the plane. The local manager came forward out of the group that had been watching the performance.

'Just as well you're here. They've only just got in. Reilly looks crook.'

'Thought he'd broken his ankle.'

'So he has. Come and take a look.'

'I'm no medic, Tom, I'm just the local bus service.'

'Yeah, I know, but you'd better take a look.' His tone was insistent, but he had dropped his voice and was keeping an eye on the visitors.

Inside the shack that served as office and living quarters, Reilly was laid out on an old blanket on top of the bed. A scrawny figure, grey-haired and wiry, trousers held up with rope. Curtis had heard people described as 'grey under the tan', but it didn't prepare him for the ashen look of the grizzled, weatherbeaten face. It was a little cooler and less humid up here, but sweat stood out on Reilly's forehead and filmed his face.

'Tough trip down?'

'You could say that.' The miner's voice rasped in his throat. Being carried jolting in a sling down the steep mountain tracks would have upset anyone, but there was more than pain in it.

'Let's have a look.' The trouser leg had already been split up to the knee. The ankle was broken, no doubt about it, the bruises already blackening and a lot of swelling, but it didn't seem bad enough to account for the man's state. He noticed that Reilly had both arms wrapped across his stomach. Gently he picked one up by the wrist. For a moment the miner resisted, then let Curtis pull the shirt aside. A grubby handkerchief had been wadded up and pressed against the wound just below his ribs, but blood was trickling slowly down his side. Tom sent a boy for water, and together they managed to soak the handkerchief enough to remove it. Tom whistled.

'Hell, that's an arrow wound. What's going on? What happened? Come on, Reilly, wake up, what's been going on?'

'Jumped us. Yesterday? Aye, yesterday. Killed two of the boys, the rest went bush. Had to wait until a couple of them came back this morning before I could get down. Bit far to walk.' He grinned weakly, but quickly gave up, gasping.

'You won't be walking anywhere for a while. What caused it, any idea? We haven't had any trouble up here for months.'

'Dunno.'

'Come on, man, don't clam up on us. Something must have set them off! Were they after the gold?'

'Away wit' you,' he snorted. 'Those fellas aren't interested in gold, wouldn't know what to do with it.'

'What, then?'

He seemed reluctant to speak. 'Dunno, really. These fellas just turned up a few days back, about ten of them. After a handout, I think. Just stood there and made a speech. Then they all put their arms out sideways and made this weird noise. Never heard the like. Don't know what they were on about. Boys couldn't understand them, or so they said. Said they thought it was something to do with tucker. Well, you know how it is, we don't have too much to spare, costs a fortune to get it flown in' – he gave a sideways look at Curtis – 'but we offered them some damper. Not a bit interested. Started making a fuss. We had to give them a bit of hurry-up.'

'What sort of hurry-up?' asked Tom, heavily.

Reilly was evasive. 'Well, you know . . . '

'Yes, I do. Did you kill any of them?'

'Mebbe winged a couple,' he admitted.

The two men said nothing, looking down at him, and waited. The first drops of rain fell heavily, sounding like lead pellets on the corrugated iron roof.

'All right, yeah, we knocked over two of them, wounded maybe three. Their mates just grabbed them and headed for the bush. Then this morning, bang, no warning. Arrows all over the place. I caught this, then trapped my foot in the gear as I tried to get back to the hut. Thought I was a goner. They must have thought so, too – just disappeared.'

Tom looked at Curtis. 'You'd better get him out of here fast. I'll call the District Officer. We may be needing some reinforcements.'

'Right. Can you give me a hand with him?'

Between them they made a reasonable job of bandaging the wound and arranging a makeshift splint for the ankle. Reilly said nothing, but his breathing was hoarse.

They carried him out to the plane, now facing downhill ready for takeoff, and managed, with some difficulty, to get him wedged into the front cockpit.

There had been a dramatic change in the light. As they turned away, Curtis looked back up the hill and saw the sky blue-purple-black, clouds boiling up over the peaks. He had a sudden irrational fear that they would tower up like surf and come crashing over the ranges and down the valley, drowning them all – plane, shack and all tossing like driftwood.

Pull yourself together, stupid, he told himself. You've got enough on your plate without taking fancies. Aloud, he said, 'I don't much like the look of that.'

'Looks like a hell of a storm coming. Perhaps you'd better wait till it blows over.'

'Can't, I'd be stuck here all night. And our hero needs a doctor.'

'Suppose you're right. Rather you than me, though.'

Couldn't agree more, Curtis thought. He went up front to check on Reilly.

'You strapped in?' The miner nodded. 'Better hang on tight, could be a rough ride.'

Even as he taxied to the end of the strip Curtis could feel the wind buffeting the wings. Flurries of raindrops battered at the fabric. Lucky Reilly is such a scrawny little guy, he thought. We're going to need all the help we can get just to get airborne. No second chances in this valley; at best they'd wind up nose down in the kunai grass, stranded until someone else could get up to fly them out. At worst . . .

The valley had never looked narrower. As he left the ground Curtis could see the cloud at the other end rolling towards him, filling the valley. He gritted his teeth; if the cloud reached the cleft that led out of the side of the valley before he did they were in real trouble. He pushed the plane as hard as he dared. There was a tremendous crash, far too close, and sheet lightning lit the sky. He was having trouble keeping control of the plane as the wind caught it and tossed it about, while keeping his eyes strained to the left trying to pick out the cleft in the failing light. It wasn't there.

At the point where it should have been there was nothing but swirling black cloud and more lightning. Suddenly a squall of rain hit him, yawing the plane to the left. 'Get up! Get up!' he shouted as it bucked and twisted, the engine roaring and missing as the rain poured at him. He strained sightlessly to bring the nose up, hardly able to breathe. For a moment it pulled clear of the clouds and he caught a brief glimpse of high streaked blue above the storm, then a downdraught sucked him swirling helplessly back, slipping crazily sideways. He saw the side of a mountain swirl by at his wingtip – trees, rocks, more trees. He knew he was going to hit them, but there wasn't time to do more than shout 'NO!' into a roaring pandemonium, smashing, splintering, louder than the thunder.

Suddenly everything was very quiet. Curtis knew he must be dead. He should be dead, but it was still raining and that didn't seem right. It was pouring down, pattering through the leaves, but quietly, as though far away. He felt as if the left side of his head had been hit with a plank. Not dead, then. He thought his way slowly around the situation, wiggled toes and fingers experimentally. They seemed to respond. His left arm was numb. It occurred to him to wonder where he was, and to wonder why he hadn't thought of it before.

Where am I, he thought, and could almost have laughed except that it hurt too much. Come on, Curtis, you can do better than that.

Still in the plane. How could I have landed the plane? More important, where could I have landed it? Can't see, is it dark already? My God, am I blind?

He brought his right hand carefully up to his face and wiggled the fingers. Five. Not blind then. Why can't I see?

Check immediate surroundings. Still in the seat, still in the cockpit, but the seat seems to have come adrift. I'm wedged in underneath somehow.

He started to struggle out of his hiding place. There was a slow rending, tearing, creaking sound and the plane lurched slightly. He froze, then tried again very gently. More creaking, but no movement. He suddenly remembered Reilly.

'Reilly, where are you?' he called softly. 'Are you there?'

A weak but audible stream of abuse came from the front cockpit.

'Don't move,' Curtis said.

'Don't worry, I'm not planning to.' A slight, mirthless laugh.

Very gingerly Curtis managed to pry himself into something like his normal position and look around. Nothing made sense. They appeared to be sitting in a tree. He looked down. The ground sloped steeply below him, but at the nearest point, below the tree, it was about thirty feet away. Must have come in sideways; the force of the crash had sheared away the propeller and engine, and the wings on the left side. Reilly was sitting with his head six inches from the main lateral branch of the tree.

Got to get help. Can't get him out of there by myself. Can't leave him. But he needs a doctor. What time is it? Late afternoon. They'll know something's wrong, but they can't send anybody out in this. They'll wait till morning. Must make a fire, maybe some of the miners will spot it.

'Reilly? I'm going to get out and make a signal fire.'

'You'll be lucky.'

'Have to give it a go.'

'Guess so.'

Curtis managed to slide out of the cockpit onto a branch. He could see that several branches had been sheared off by the collision, and others that held the plane up were partly stripped away from the trunks. Any movement of the plane made them creak and groan, and he wondered how long they'd hold up their burden.

As he scrambled to the ground he heard Reilly's hoarse whisper. 'Curtis? Whatever happened to that red-headed mate of yours, what was his name, Simpson?'

'Lost him.'
'Oh.'

In the distance Joseph could see the entrance to his village's valley. For anyone else it would have been indistinguishable from the surrounding jungle, but of course he knew every tree. The afternoon storm was rolling up over the mountains, and he quickened his pace. He didn't want to be out on the mountain track when the lightning started. The brothers said it was only superstition and explained to him about electricity in the air, and why thunder made a noise, but though he didn't want to disagree with them he knew they were wrong. Of course it was angry gods making all that light and din – otherwise what was the point of it? They didn't know everything, but of course it wasn't their country. They didn't even know how to make a rainhat out of a palm leaf; he'd had to show them. They had seemed very pleased with their discovery.

The rain started just as he reached the edge of the jungle. Very slowly at first, he could hear every drop as it hit the big leaves and rolled off, but pattering faster and faster until it all made one sound. Then there was another sound, voices; he left the path until he could identify the men. It was either some of his relatives gathering for the sing-sing, or a group from another village whose language he wouldn't understand. As he was unarmed, it would be better not to let them see him.

As they came nearer he saw that it was his uncle and some of his friends; he was tempted to stay in hiding but it would hardly have been polite.

'Why didn't you come to meet us?' his uncle greeted him, slapping him hard on the side of the head. 'It's no use trying to hide in that white man's shirt, we could see you from miles away.'

Joseph thought it safer to say nothing. He joined the group, walking behind them, staying out of arm's reach to be on the safe side. His uncle was obviously very excited about something. They were talking about the magic bird of the white man. Had they really seen one close up, actually sitting on the ground? It has no sex, his uncle said, he had looked; he, his own uncle, had actually gone boldly up to the bird and checked its sex! And later, he said, they had tried to feed it, but it refused the grass it had been offered. So if it didn't eat or reproduce, and yet it flew, and made a terrible noise when it did so, then it must be magic. Or perhaps a god itself, suggested one of the other men, but his uncle scorned the idea.

'It is a servant of the white man's god, and brings his food. If we could just find the magic to command it we could have everything we need, and we could send the white man back where he belongs and live as we please.'

Joseph thought it would be a pity if all the white men went away; he enjoyed his lessons at the mission, even if the brothers wouldn't tell him the secret he wanted and were mistaken in quite a lot of their own beliefs. He had asked them about cargo, as his father had told him, but they were very disapproving. All good things come from Jesus, the Son of God, they said, but as he had never heard them mention that their Jesus had his own aeroplane this seemed unlikely. Still, he at least wanted them to stay until their god came down to earth again; it was obviously what the brothers were most looking forward to, and he would very much like to see such a thing. It sounded as though it would be the greatest sing-sing ever given, with endless food and wonderful presents for everyone. Surely that would make even his fierce uncle happy.

*   *   *

Reilly had been right. The storm had passed, but all Curtis' efforts to light a signal fire had resulted only in a thin trickle of smoke from the wet leaves and sticks. Even the doped fabric rescued from the shattered wings had been useless. He had to make a decision: either stay with the plane and wait for rescue, or set off down the valley and see if he could come on one of the mining camps that dotted the highlands. The first was the text-book thing to do – the plane made the biggest target for a search party. But Reilly wouldn't last long if a doctor didn't get to him soon; and they'd never found Simpson.

In the end it came down to sitting and waiting for help, or trying to find some for himself. He called up to the man still trapped in the plane.

'Reilly! Can you hear me? I'm going to camp down here tonight and leave at first light. If the search party arrives, tell them I've gone downhill and east, would you?'

The voice came faintly from the tree. 'Sure I will. Don't worry now, I'll mind your aeroplane for you.' A wheezy laugh. 'Hang on a minute, there's something you can mind for me in return.' An ominous creak as he squirmed to find whatever it was, then something small and heavy plopped into the moss a few feet away. It was a grubby handsewn bag, tied with string at the neck. 'The week's takings. Hang on to it for me till I get back, or have a decent wake, if I don't.'

'After what you've been through I reckon you're inde-structible, but I'll look after it for you.'

'You do that.'

'Cheers, mate.'

Curtis pulled the pieces of wrecked wings together to provide as much shelter as there was. Night had fallen and the dark was absolute, cloud cover masking any moon or starlight. It was very cold. He buttoned the overall up to the neck; the top buttonholes were so stiff it was obvious they had never been used. He wrapped his hands under his arms and tried to sleep. It was no use. He wished for a blanket, an overcoat, gloves, anything to keep out the cold and the relentless drip, drip, drip through the trees. Crazy, isn't it, he thought. This morning I couldn't have borne even the thought of a blanket, let alone the touch of one. Some people are never satisfied. He dozed, on and off, woken by raindrops that found their way down his neck or into his ears.

A sudden shriek brought him staggering to his feet. A flash of yellow disappeared into the trees away to his right.

'Bloody bird,' he muttered, and took a step in its direction. He was so stiff and cramped that he almost fell, and spent a few minutes rubbing his legs, hampered by the numbness in his left arm. His face was sore, some of his teeth felt loose.

I'll need a doctor myself if I don't get out of here soon, he thought. There seemed to be some lightening in the air around him; in a few minutes more he could dimly see the trunks of the trees, through a mist that permeated everything. It was like being underwater, swimming slowly through the trees, sinking up to his ankles in the moss that covered the ground, the trees, and hung in great swathes through the air. He tripped on a concealed root and fell flat, drowning in the moss, clambered up again and set off downhill, moving as though in slow motion, his brain slowing too as if in a waking dream.

The whine of a mosquito past his ear told Curtis how far down the mountain he had come. He slapped at it automatically and winced as his teeth jarred. He had forgotten he was still wearing the flying helmet, and pulled it off. He had left the misty country behind almost without noticing and was well into the rain forest, the track underfoot easier but ferns and vines everywhere ready to trip him. He looked up; it must be full daylight by now but the canopy above him kept out almost all the light. Huge trees towered above, but he couldn't see the tops of them for the mass of smaller trees and bushes crowding up to reach what light there was. It was remarkably quiet, there didn't seem to be another living creature anywhere in his primeval world. As if to make a liar of him, a large blue butterfly flew slowly out of the wall of green beside the track, almost blundering into him, corrected itself and wandered drunkenly off.

The image made him aware how thirsty he was. The overall was still buttoned to the neck, and he wrestled the stiff top buttons open. Despite the rich green of his world and the warm, dark, dampness he realized that he had seen no pools, no streams. He was suddenly thirstier and started to walk more quickly, sweeping his eyes from side to side to find some source of water. He thought longingly of the brown bottle of beer he'd left on the table the previous morning. Though he knew it would have been warm before he had even finished it, it was the most desirable object he could imagine.

He felt a slight sting on his wrist, looked down and saw that a skinny black leech had attached itself to him. He flicked it off in disgust. It left a trail of blood, and he sucked at it, blood and salt sweat mingling. He wiped a hand across his forehead and saw it was streaked with more blood, felt gingerly across his face and picked off more of them. On the surrounding trees he saw, as though they had just come into focus, that the leaves were alive with leeches, their black, thread-like bodies standing upright, waving their heads to pick up the scent of any likely host. He shuddered, and pulled up the sleeve of the overall. More of them, gorged fat, black against the blackening bruise that covered his arm from the wrist as far up as he could see. The awareness of the damage made him more aware of the pain. He flicked off the leeches, a wave of nausea rising through him. They were everywhere. He ripped open the overall, pulled up his shirt. More of them.

A sob of sheer frustration and nausea shook him and he began to run along the path, squelching through the mud, but the effort exhausted him. He became aware of a distant roaring sound. For a confused moment he thought it might have been a plane, and the frustration of knowing that there was no way it would see him down below his green canopy almost overwhelmed him, but some part of his brain told him that it was no engine note he knew. He thought how lush, green and velvety the jungle looked from above, mile after unbroken mile – of course, the noise, it was a waterfall. He just had to head for the sound, there would be water – drink, wash – and he could follow its course down. Long before it reached the sea he would have found a camp, perhaps a village, and this would all be over.

He set out with more optimism. The noise increased, and ahead there was a little more light. The trees were thinning out. Around the next twist of the track he saw a bridge. A bridge? It seemed so incongruous in this gloomy, deserted world that he thought he must be hallucinating. But it was there, a twisted mass of vines and lianas, and he stumbled gasping towards it. The roar of the water blotted out all thought, spray filled the air, the ground was muddy with it. Curtis reached the bridge, the draught refreshingly cool on his sweaty skin. He closed his eyes and let it blow over him. Then he looked down. Far below, the river crashed through a rocky chasm, spouts and spray flying from a jumble of jagged rocks. It was impossibly out of reach. He couldn't believe it: all the water in the world and he couldn't get to it. He began to laugh, though he felt like crying.

'Get a grip on yourself,' he muttered. 'Don't let go, idiot, or you'll never get out of here.' Part of his brain was telling him that it didn't care, he should just sit down where he was and wait for something to happen. He tried to ignore it, but the temptation simply to give up was strong.

'Must be something.' A lizard ran across the track in front of him, vanishing into the undergrowth. 'He gets water from somewhere. Where? Plants. Must be plants. Maybe water trapped in leaves. Try to find some.' The other part of his brain said, seductively, why bother? It's too much trouble. He pushed the thought aside.

There were orchids in the trees, and vines with big, gaudy flowers. Perhaps they trapped water. He pushed through the brush beside the path towards the nearest, ferns catching at his feet, leeches leaning out towards him as he passed. He raked his hands through his hair and replaced the leather helmet. It was stifling in the damp heat, but it might keep them out of his hair.

Suddenly there was a clearing, a massive fig tree in the middle with huge roots standing like buttresses above the ground. The air was full of the ripe, rotting smell of its fallen fruits that almost covered the ground around it. Curtis tried to eat one but the taste was so disgusting that he spat it out.

There were flowers on the lianas draped round the trunk. He reached for one, tearing it from the vine, his hand covered in the sticky fluid it exuded. He licked at it experimentally but it tasted vile. There were a couple of drops of water in the lip of the flower and he drank it off, gagging as he swallowed a small insect. There wasn't enough water in it to make any difference. He'd have to tear down the whole vine to get even half a cupful.

Too much trouble, said his brain. Don't those big roots look comfortable? Very sheltered. You could tuck yourself in there and have a good rest. You'd feel better for that, wouldn't you? Yes, of course you would.

Yes, he thought, that's a good idea. I'm exhausted. Feel better after a rest. He raked most of the rotten figs out of one of the compartments formed by the roots, lay down and was instantly asleep.

When he woke up he was in bed back at the station. Blue sky outside the window, early morning then, must have slept the night through. Clean, cool white sheets. A dish of fruit on a table by his bed, mangoes, pineapple, rambutan, an apple. He hadn't seen an apple for weeks. He reached for it, anticipating the pleasure of the crisp, juicy flesh.

'Back with us, then. Thought you were going to sleep all day, you lazy so-and-so.'

Someone else in the room, sitting out of sight at the head of the bed. He twisted round to see who it was. Khaki shorts, pale, freckled legs, sunburned thighs. He sat up suddenly and swung round. It was Simpson, red hair flopping over his face, blue eyes creased in a smile.

'You're back! What happened to you, you maniac? We've been wasting good fuel looking for you. Where've you been?'

'Oh, I'm all right, it's you we've been worried about. Got a bad bump on the head there. Still, don't suppose it can have affected your brain.'

They both grinned. Curtis reached for the apple, was about to bite into it when he noticed something odd about his friend. He seemed to be breaking up, rippling in the heat. He reached out to touch him, hit his hand on the table . . .

His hand was throbbing where the leeches had fastened onto it, and the smell of rotting figs surrounded him.

Joseph's uncle had sent the boy on ahead to the village, and he wasn't sorry they'd decided they didn't want him along on their hunt. He was sitting in the ceremonial hut, proud to be in the circle with the men for the first time, instead of at the back in the darkness with the women and children.

He began to tell them some of the stories he had so carefully memorized; of course the brothers had taught him in pidgin, which his people didn't speak, so he had to translate as he went along. Sometimes there wasn't the word, and it was some trouble for him to translate carefully into language they could understand. Sometimes he had to go a long way round the story to explain, but it didn't matter, there was time enough for everything. The sing-sing could go on for days, there was plenty of food, and no one would leave until the last gift had been exchanged and the last pig eaten.

Joseph had decided to start off with the nativity story, and immediately ran into trouble with the archangel Gabriel. He settled for 'chief man with wings, coming out of the sky'. That Joseph's image was of feathers and drapery, from the pictures he had been shown at the mission, and his audience's was bright metallic silver with wings outstretched, mattered not at all – it was a concept they could all accept.

Having established Gabriel, Joseph then skipped over the part about the virgin birth, which the brothers, living in a community without women, must have misunderstood. The problem of accommodation for the woman having the baby was also difficult. It had obviously worried the brothers a lot, but Joseph had never understood why his namesake hadn't just built Mary a little hut of palm branches and kunai grass; his own father could have built one for her in an hour or two.

'And are they truly white all over?' asked one man.

'Yes, truly,' said Joseph. 'They take off all their clothes to wash. I have seen them.'

A woman at the back stifled a giggle. A sigh went round the circle of men. Yes, of course, that would explain a lot. Everyone knew that when somebody died, their spirit went away, turned white and came back again to help those they'd left behind, provided the right sacrifices had been made. So the white men were really there to help them; if they were patient, because, of course, these things had their own time, the spirits would bring them the cargo they so much desired.

Some of the men stood up and put their arms out straight, making the droning noise, but Joseph's father motioned them to stop. Everything in its proper time. Tomorrow they would dance.

Curtis had dozed again, and dreamed, but this time it was of the storm, being thrown helplessly through the sky, falling, falling. Black and purple clouds swirling down at him, rolling like a flood down the valley, the plane tossing like driftwood on the flood. Air demons, wind demons, flew past his face, grinning, big white teeth flashing, long clawed hands reaching out, clutching . . .

He woke again, sweating, shaking, glad to be rid of the dream. But the demons were still there, so close he could see the whites of their eyes. As he stirred they jumped back, but not far. Six or more mountain men, wigs with feathers stuck into them, stone axes and clubs

128

at their belts, light bows over their shoulders, tall spears. A hunting party, Curtis thought, and they certainly look the business. They all had scars on their legs and bodies, the leader a great concave dent in his forehead.

He appeared to be very excited, and was arguing fiercely with the others. Curtis understood none of the language, but obviously the outcome concerned him closely. Probably trying to decide whether to eat me here or take me away, he thought wryly, but he couldn't raise a smile, still groggy from his sudden awakening and troubled sleep. It occurred to him that he was probably carrying enough gold to make these men rich; then that it wouldn't make any difference.

They had come to a decision. The leader came towards him, stopped, reached out and tugged at the chin strap of the flying helmet, but not hard enough to pull it off. Then he touched Curtis' face; lips, eyelids, nose. Apparently satisfied, he stepped back, lowered the spear.

Instinctively, Curtis closed his eyes, but nothing happened. When he opened them again the leader was still there, making pushing movements with the spear. He seemed to want him to move, so, not having much alternative, he did so. Two of them went ahead of him, the others followed, and together the party walked back to the track and turned in the direction of the bridge. Curtis found he was limping, something seemed to have got into his right shoe. He tried to stop to find out what it was, but felt the point of the spear jabbed into his back. There was no sense in arguing.

When they reached the bridge they stopped. One of the advance guard went forward, walked a few steps onto the bridge. Apparently satisfied, he continued across, the bridge swaying above the gorge. The second followed. When they had both crossed, Curtis was pushed forward. With great reluctance, holding firmly to the vine rope edge, he stepped onto the bridge and walked a few steps, slowly, getting used to the swaying. In the middle he stopped, reached down and unlaced his shoe. From the bank the hunters called angrily, but did not attempt to come onto the bridge after him.

The leeches had got into his sock; they must have been there some time, sucking up blood until they were as fat as slugs, three or four of them making a black, slimy ball. Shuddering with disgust, he pulled them away and hurled them into the roaring river. Blood was flowing from the wound they had made but he had nothing to staunch it with. He put the shoe back on with difficulty, the bridge lurching, and continued across the river. The men on the other side shouted at him and shook their spears, but didn't touch him. They seemed not to want to come too close, which suited him very well.

Can't see coming out of this with any prizes, Curtis thought, but while there's life there's hope, and all that stuff. Don't let the bastards get you down. Head up, stiff upper lip, and try not to trip over your feet. He found he couldn't actually confront the possibility of death; that, unknowing, he had assumed it would come in the sky. He was out of his element here.

Suddenly, as they rounded a bend, he could hear singing. A high ululation, accompanied by a lower, louder sound, rising and falling slightly. They moved off the main track onto a smaller one, the sound growing louder. Then came a sight so unexpected, so unreal in the damp green gloom, that Curtis stopped in his tracks.

A windsock – a woven, painted windsock, hanging limp in the heavy humidity. And beyond it a patch of beaten earth laid out like an airstrip, stones ranged carefully down each side.

Through the trees at the other side, a clearing; there must have been a hundred men in it, women and children sitting round the edge except at the far end, where there was some kind of construction. The men were dancing in lines, arms stiffly outstretched, making a loud, low sound, rising and falling. As he watched they broke ranks and began to circle, arms still outstretched, tilted in towards the centre of the circle.

'Planes!' he said aloud, moving unbidden, as if sleep-walking, past the windsock, across the 'strip' until he came to the edge of the dancing area.

Looking down into the clearing, Curtis saw Joseph, sitting in a patch of ground neatly swept, in front of a rough construction of palm branches and packing cases. He could see the stencilled trade names, faded in the damp. The altar was covered with plaited vines, fern fronds and fresh palm leaves, with white and yellow orchids carefully arranged to show off the most prized exhibits.

The blade of a propeller, a handful of wingnuts and screws. Wing struts, still with shreds of fabric attached. Two battered but still shiny tin cans, empty.

And Simpson. Still wearing his flying helmet, the chin strap dangling, wisps of orange hair showing underneath and on his upper lip. Just his head, wizened, the eyes sewn neatly closed with cowrie shells, hanging in a net bag above the altar.

Looking up, Joseph saw with wonder and delight that the brothers had been right after all. Their god had indeed come down to earth again for him, just as they had said he would.

THE DAY THE WOLFMAN ATE MY SISTER

Peter Caley

Peter Caley was born in London and works as a jazz guitarist. He first suspected himself of being a writer at the age of ten; some thirty years later it dawned on him that actually picking up a pen might be a useful means of establishing the necessary proof. Peter lives in Devon with his partner, Polly, and assorted children. He is currently writing his first novel.

THE DAY THE WOLFMAN
ATE MY SISTER

The day Father was pushed to his death from a moving train, and my older sister eaten by a wolfman, was something of a turning point in my life. (And, I suppose, in my mother's, too: it was, after all, the image of her husband's bony body, a lay figure brushed to the gravel by an impatient artist, which triggered her fatal heart attack.)

It was a Tuesday afternoon and rain scratched the windows as we clattered away from the City of the Damned (as Father would have it), and Angela and I were bored.

'Something beginning with F.E.F.G.,' said Angela, panning the lens of a rolled-up teen magazine across the compartment.

'Er, fried eggs and . . . um . . . fish giblets,' I said to annoy her.

'No, stupid,' she said. 'You've got to be able to see it – either in here or out the window. That's why it's called "I Spy".'

All I could see from the window were tumbleweed clouds and the grey-faced, whey-faced factories and housing estates.

'Give up, then?'

On the seat the magazine unfurled like a banner.

'The hieroglyphs of exploitation,' muttered Father and turned his eyes to the horizon. Here were our first fields. 'Corduory patches,' he said, 'stitched to a thread-bare land.' As you can see, Father didn't exactly talk like normal people.

'Never 2 Young 2B Kissed,' said the magazine to my poor, brace-toothed sister. 'How to catch and keep the fella of your dreamz.'

Verity, as our oh-so-modern mother liked us to call her, gave the page the sort of look calculated to turn paper into flame. Too liberal to censor, she was also too passionate, too intense, to resist the opportunity for a lecture. To pre-empt her I said, 'Yeah, okay. I give up.'

Verity sighed. 'And so,' she said, 'do I.'

'F.E.F.G.,' said Angela, the brace throwing the letters slightly out of focus. 'F.E.F.G. Four-eyed Fat Git!' Meaning, of course, me.

And then she clamped her hand over her mouth and giggled, for it was at that moment the wolfman slunk into our carriage and sat panting in the corner, his black overcoat giving off a humid, wet-dog stink.

Another train rattled by, heading towards London. Faces turned to look at us.

'Wave, children,' said Father. So we waved and waved like mad and a few people waved tentatively back, unde-cided, perhaps, whether or not we were taking the you-know-what.

I wondered why Father was always so eager to com-municate with people he'd never ever see again. I re-membered country walks in summer holidays, with Father showering salutations (literally, too: he was never that hot with Ss) on every yokel who crossed our path. Father never really liked people, but I suppose these brief encounters, this friendship without involvement, allowed him to imagine that he did.

'Salt of the earth,' he'd say as we strode off in search of the next village idiot. 'Salt of the earth.'

Suddenly the two trains slowed to a stop; and, grinning, we all tucked our embarrassed hands away. Father didn't know where to look. It was as if one of our holiday bumpkins, instead of restricting himself to meteorological speculation, had invited himself to supper and made a pass at Mother. In his corner the wolf-man smiled and the skin around his lips cracked audibly.

Looking across the track I half expected to see – I don't know – a sort of mirror image, perhaps; a family just like ours: two truculent parents, an overweight, bespectacled eight-year-old boy and an empty-headed girl of thirteen, all headed for the city to take our places. Maybe they'd even have their own wolfman smouldering in the shadows of the wet afternoon. In those days, as you can see, I craved the comfort of symmetry. In those days ...

'Tell us a story, Verity,' said Angela, flashing me a look. We began to move again.

'Yes please,' I said, 'a story. Oh yes, that would be brilliant. Please, Verity, please.'

Mother's attempts at story-telling were usually pathetic, and vastly entertaining for that very reason. But she looked genuinely touched to be asked and I couldn't help feeling a bit guilty, having helped set her up like that, so I gave her what I hoped would come across as an affectionate smile and said 'Please' again, as sincere as you like, and gave Angela a kick for giggling.

'Okay, okay. Well. Ahem. Once upon a time,' said Verity, and suddenly the wolfman sneezed, and none of your discreet handkerchief dabbing or praying hands over the nose stuff, either; he just trumpeted out across the carriage and sat there staring at Mother, an elastic band of mucus dangling from his nose. And then, horribly, he tilted back his head, scooped up the snot with his fingertips and let it slide, oyster-like, down his throat. Had he been the author of 'Never 2 Young 2B Kissed', Verity couldn't have given him a more withering look.

'Once upon a time,' she said again, that edge I knew so well creeping into her voice, 'in Hampstead –'

'Hampstead?' said Father. 'Hampstead? Why on earth does it have to be Hampstead?'

'No doubt you'd prefer me to say once upon a time in Exeter, or Plymouth, or bloody Barnstaple, for Christ's sake. Listen, Alan, you've got your own way in this –'

'For once,' said Father, with a sort of bitter laugh.

'But don't rub it in, all right? Just don't you go rubbing it in – you and your rural bloody bliss . . .'

(The wolfman turned and winked at me and – oh, the disloyalty! – I went and winked right back. He folded one leg over the other; he wore plimsolls and no socks, and where his greasy trouser cuffs rode up no flesh was visible: just long reddish hair that drifted and swayed like weed under water.)

'Anyway,' said Verity, 'in Hampstead – in London NW3 – there lived a woman called . . . called Prudence. She lived there with her two children called, coincidentally, Angela and Neil, and a husband whose name I can't quite remember . . .'

This received a quiet 'Oh God' from Father, who began to suspect, I think, some sort of allegory. (You may, by now, have suspected – even muttered – something similar yourself. But don't lose heart: reading *is* meant to be fun, after all, and there's so much fun to be had – trust me – at other people's expense!)

'Prudence's life was fairly happy,' Verity continued. 'Her children were intelligent and well-behaved and caused her no trouble –'

'Just like us,' said Angela, looking at the wolfman

and slowly crossing her mini-skirted thighs. 'I don't think . . . '

'And her husband, though insensitive to her deepest needs, was at least civilized enough to help her around the house –'

'Oh, she's a *feminist*,' said Angela. 'Now *there's* a surprise.'

Verity's mouth became a narrow slit.

'Angela's only being interested,' I said proleptically. 'She's not taking the you-know-what, are you, Angie?'

'Perish,' said Angela, 'the thought.'

'So what did he do, Verity? This husband, I mean. What sort of things did he do to help her?'

'Well, to begin with, every evening when he got back from the City, he'd make her a nice gin and tonic. And then, let's see, he'd help her prepare the vegetables for their meal and he'd serve the dinner – oh, and wash up afterwards, of course – and he'd always make her a little surprise supper later on in the evening; and then when they went to bed he'd usually have the decency to leave her alone, if you understand me; and on the occasions when he didn't – leave her alone, I mean – he always did his best to ensure that she received the statutory number of orgasms . . . '

(Verity's sense of humour was odd, insofar as you could never really be sure whether or not she had one.)

'So why was she only *fairly* happy? What,' said Angela, 'was missing from her life?' and Father looked up from his newspaper and muttered, 'As if we didn't know.'

'A career,' said Verity, 'to put it bluntly. A job, a vocation, something to bolster up her flagging self-esteem.'

'But –' began Father, and that's when we entered the tunnel.

'What's happened?' squealed Angela, excitedly. 'Where are we?'

'In the dark,' said Father. 'As usual.'

I looked into the corner and two orange circles hung there in the blackness, and then we came out the other side and there was the wolfman with his little slitty eyes and high cheekbones and hair that stuck out in spikes, though not in any fashionable way.

And that's when something went wrong with Time.

High above the wolfman's head a pear-shaped bag of rainwater lost its grip on the window catch and began an impossibly languid descent. The wolfman smiled a smile that made me shiver. He's going to say something, I thought, and I think I reached for Angela's hand.

'Bullshit,' said the wolfman in a sort of slowed down voice, and you could almost see the word, like a gleaming black egg, drop from his lips and roll across the floor and come to rest against the toecaps of Verity's sensible shoes.

I don't know why but the image made me smile and I tapped one sandal on the squeaky linoleum and closed my eyes, and there, sure enough, was the egg, or the idea of the egg, nestling amongst the rubble on the dark floor of my mind's eye.

I could see that the shell's equator was engraved with jagged cracks and I held my breath, thinking sharp thoughts. Suddenly the two halves parted, like a concertina or squeezebox, and all that was left was a glistening hymen which trembled and bulged and – yes! – finally ruptured; and a milk-white bird, a dove I think, climbed unsteadily out and shook off her egg-shell beret.

I remember thinking how lovely she was and then cringing, because I was, after all (as Verity so frequently reminded me), a Typical Male even then. But with her wings tucked into her soft sides the bird looked like a little half-finished snowman with tricky, peppercorn eyes, and 'lovely' just seemed to be the only word for her.

For some reason I began to think then about the sort of women Verity was for ever going on about; women whose husbands drank or swore or lazed about or beat them up or never came home or never went out or smelled bad or grew fat as balloons or went to the football or gambled the housekeeping or never made love or had sex on the brain or went with other women and so on (you know the type); and suddenly I imagined my poor bird eaten by – I don't know – worms, maybe, or maggots or crawling things with tiny half-human faces – things you couldn't even put a name to – and I trembled with the thrill of nascent power.

When I opened my eyes again I had to shake my head to bring myself back to normal because the vision or whatever it was had seemed so clear and real. The wolf-man leaned forward in his seat and the bag of rainwater exploded on the shoulder of his overcoat.

'Bullshit,' he said again. 'Horsecrap. That's the stupidest story I ever heard. A little surprise supper, for Christ's sake! If I was him I'd have gobbed in it. I'd have pissed in it, that's what I would have done.'

(Was it my imagination or did Father look sheepish for an instant? Yes or no, he soon recovered.)

'Now look here,' said Father, adding, for good measure, 'my man.'

The wolfman raised his hand and the shadow of his claw-like nails on the compartment wall was like something from an old horror film.

'*I'll* tell you a story,' he said.

'I really don't think –' began Verity.

'I'll tell you a story about a little girl who loved a dog. The little girl's name isn't important – are they ever? – but the dog was called Adolphus and he was red-haired and massive-headed, and his eyes were bright and cruel.

'Now this little girl had been abandoned as a baby, and one day Adolphus found her, deep in the heart of the woods, and he picked her up in his mouth and carried her to his wonderful home.'

'How was it wonderful?' said Angela. 'Did it have a dishwasher and a bidet and a microwave oven and a video and –'

'It was wonderful,' said the wolfman, 'for this reason: once inside the house Adolphus could walk on his hind legs, and use his paws like human hands, and he slept in a bed – no kennel or basket for him – and he wore suits of velvet and satin, and little shiny shoes on his two back feet.

'An old bitch lived in the house with him, and Adolphus showed the baby girl how to drink the milk from its nipples –'

'Why did it have milk?' asked Angela. 'Had it had puppies? You didn't say anything about any puppies . . .'

'I told you,' said the wolfman, 'that it was a wonderful house.'

'Not so wonderful for the bitch.' (That was Verity, of course.)

'The bitch gradually grew to love the little girl, and it taught her, as time went on, how to serve Adolphus and give him pleasure. The girl soon learned everything there was to know, and then Adolphus realized he had no further need for the bitch and he kicked her to the ground and with his sharpest knife he slit her open from throat to belly. Adolphus cooked the carcase on his little

142

stove, and he and the girl sat down and ate it – with the best cutlery, of course – and toasted their happiness in the bitch's thick red blood.

'Then Adolphus retired to his bed and the little girl went to sleep in her basket on the floor –'

(Looking, then, at Verity, I half expected to see molten lava pouring down her upper slopes.)

'This story,' she spluttered, 'is quite, quite horrible. I think, Mr –'

'Munro,' said the wolfman.

'I think, Mr Munro, that you're a depraved person and I'll thank you to keep your . . . your obscene ravings to yourself. Just keep quiet, for God's sake – keep quiet and leave us alone.'

I couldn't understand the expression in my mother's eyes. There was, it seemed to me, fear beneath the anger and she looked at her fidgety hands instead of the wolf-man's face. The wolfman smiled.

'Too much like the truth?' he said. 'Too much like real life?'

'That's not real life,' said Verity, 'that's not the truth. The truth is, Mr Munro, that the likes of you will soon be nothing but ugly memories. We've got you . . . you *animals* on the run . . . '

(My mother was a surprising creature. A while before, she'd looked up the date those old Suffragette biddies had got themselves underway, and she sent it off with twenty-five pounds to a box number in a magazine. And what was she doing? Only having the Women's Movement's astrological chart done! From this she deduced that sexism and chauvinist piggery and all forms of anti-female behaviour would be banished from the face of the planet by 1999.

Father, as I've said, didn't always *talk* like a normal person; it was Verity, though, who often didn't behave

143

like one. Anyway, this was where I chipped in with my second act of disloyalty.)

'Please, Verity,' I cried, 'please let him go on. I want to see what happens to the little girl.'

'The little girl?' said the wolfman, ignoring Mother's protests. 'Why, the little girl soon became everything a wife should be, and oh, how she loved her beautiful dog! Every morning she made him breakfast and carried it on a tray to his bed. While Adolphus ate she carefully washed him with her tongue and picked the fleas from his coat; and then, having first helped him into his clothes, she would kiss him goodbye for the day and set about her household tasks: polishing and tidying, washing and mending, peeling and cooking, and always remembering to light the little string of candles she had hung above the doorway to welcome him home in the evening.

'Now, each night, when they had eaten and she had cleared away, Adolphus would sit in his favourite arm-chair and allow his wife to undress him. When he was completely naked she would slide down onto his lap and wrap her arms around his neck.

'"I love you, Adolphus," she would say. "You're so handsome and kind and so good to me . . . " And Adolphus would lick her face with his smooth pink tongue and hold her hips in his paws, and he'd pant from the exquisite pleasure her every small movement would give him, until, unable to bear it any longer, he would lift her in his arms and carry her up to his bed and –'

'Enough!' Father had risen from his seat. 'Enough, I say. Desist, sir!'

I noticed that Angela's skirt had ridden up.

'Your knickers,' I whispered. 'He can see your knickers.'

'Shut up!' she hissed and moved along the seat

because Father was blocking her view of the wolfman.
(Or was it, perhaps, the other way around?) Father's
fists were clenched.

'You shut your filthy mouth,' he said. 'You just shut
your filthy mouth . . . '

The wolfman grinned.

'Or?' he said. Father just looked blank. 'If I don't —
shut my mouth, I mean. Just what is it you're going to
do, exactly?'

'Talking like that in front of my wife . . . '

A look passed between the wolfman and Verity.
Verity blushed and turned away; the wolfman went on
grinning.

'Well?' he asked.

'In front of my *daughter*, for pity's sake . . . '

'Ah, your daughter,' said the wolfman. 'Here, let me
tell you what I've got up my sleeve for her.'

Father bent forward in answer to the wolfman's beckoning finger.

'A-lan!' said Verity. Her tone sounded unpleasantly
querulous.

The wolfman pressed his thin lips against Father's ear.
We could see his jaws working but all we could hear
was a strange growling sound. Then Father's face began
to redden. Angela nudged me and giggled. Father's body
twanged with rage and then sprang suddenly upright,
like one of those gardening tools people are always
standing on in comedy programmes.

'You bloody scoundrel!' he spluttered.

'*Scoundrel?*' whispered Angela delightedly. The wolfman stretched indolently and managed somehow to
arrange his features into a parody of innocence.

'But it's only form,' he said, 'and etiquette, too, and
likewise traditional politeness to petition the father of
one's intended in matters as delicate as this.'

'Intended?' roared Father.

'Well, you know what *I* intend doing to her,' the wolfman said, jiggling his eyebrows like Groucho Marx and tapping an imaginary cigar. Angela and I couldn't help ourselves; we both laughed out loud. Father sat down looking bewildered. He couldn't meet my mother's eyes.

The wolfman winked at Angela. 'Come here,' he said in a gentle sort of voice.

'Don't you dare, my girl!' said Verity, but Angela pushed her mother's restraining hand away and clicked across the carriage to the wolfman's side.

'Well?' she said in a voice that implied that this sort of thing happened to her every day. All the playfulness drained from the wolfman's face and he reached out and slid his hand up the inside of Angela's thigh.

I held my breath. Here, suddenly, was real drama, and I quite expected Angie to spit in his eye and flounce out the door like one of those Spirited Women in the cowboy films. Instead, she shifted her weight from one foot to the other which only served to part her legs slightly.

'The old girl must have had pins like these, once upon a time,' said the wolfman, jerking a thumb towards Mother, and it sounded quite common compared with the polite way he'd spoken to Father only a few moments before.

Verity's mouth looked like the slot in a fairy's moneybox as she hauled a sulky Angela back to her seat. Father rose manfully, looking rather impressive, I must admit, but when he spoke he had a bubble in his throat that made him sound like a robot.

'Look,' he bleeped, 'we just want a nice quiet journey – we don't want any trouble. We haven't given *you* any

trouble. Well, have we? I mean, we've left *you* alone.
All we want you to do –'

'For Christ's sake, Alan,' said Verity, 'is this how you
protect your women? Is it? Kick the stinking bastard off
the train. Teach the snot-eating shit some manners.'

'Oh God,' said Angela, turning to me. 'Over the top
or what?'

I shrugged. Why, I wondered, did I have the impression that Verity knew some secret about the wolfman –
something she wanted to keep hidden from the rest of
us?

'Yes, come on, Alan,' said the wolfman, slinking to
his feet and beaming. 'Come on, teach me the sort of
lesson a chap doesn't forget in a hurry. Indulge your
good lady here and kick me orf the jolly old train, why
don't you? Well, I think I deserve it, what?' A sudden
frown visited his face, and his voice changed from posh
to sort of American.

'But listen, do me one favour. Go easy on me, okay?
I mean, have some *pity* willya? I'm a good-looking guy,
for Chrissakes. Can *I* help it if women find me irresistible?' The wolfman threw back his head and howled
with horrible laughter. Verity held out her arms and I
hurled myself into them and buried my face in the whis-
kery folds of her cardigan.

'Look,' said Father in a pale voice, 'I'm sure we can
sort this out. I mean, there's really no need to resort to
fisticuffs or anything like that, you know. Why don't we
just sit down and talk it over like two civilized people?'

I got a bit fed up with Mother hissing in my ear and
digging her nails into my arms so I pulled free of her
and went back to my seat.

The wolfman mulled over Father's proposition for a
while.

'Okay, then, we'll just talk,' he said finally, taking

Father's hand in his. 'But why don't we stroll a little while we chat? That might be nice, don't you think? And anyway, the exercise would do us good for sure.'

So off they set, hand in hand like a pair of young lovers, up and down the tiny carriage, the wolfman sometimes resting his head on Father's shoulder just as if he'd known him for years and was really rather fond of him.

'I say, Alan,' said the wolfman, 'your hands are so wonderfully *soft*. Who would have thought it? I mean, what with all that cooking and dishwashing and scrubbing and so forth, I'd have expected them to be as wrinkly as two little prunes –' he turned to the rest of us, Groucho Marx again –' and I *am* still talking about his hands!' That seemed to break the ice a bit and we all laughed, even Father; but the wolfman pricked his nose up like a dog sniffing fear on the wind. He released Father's hand and shook his head sadly.

'I don't know about you, Alan,' he said, 'but I sense disappointment in the ranks. I believe there may be some amongst us who find your behaviour – and I have to say this – somewhat ineffectual.' He turned to me. 'What say you, little boy? Are you proud of your dear old dad? Is he, would you say, a dangerous customer? A man to be feared when his blood is up? Am I lucky to have survived his fury unscathed?'

'You bet you are,' I lied.

The wolfman smiled and straightened Father's little blue tie.

'Well,' he said, 'we're just going to have to see, aren't we?' He draped a patient arm around Father's shoulder. 'What we're going to do, Alan – and I hope you don't mind – is to put your – um, now what shall we call it? – your masculinity? Um, yes, that'll do. We're going to put your *masculinity* to the test. Do you see?' He

148

sounded like a kindly soul explaining something difficult to a deaf person. Father nodded.

'So let's have some suggestions, shall we?' He looked at Angela. 'You. Girl. Tell me one thing that only *real men* can do.'

'Um, well . . . ' said Angie, wrinkling her nose. The wolfman suddenly snarled, making us all jump. His teeth were long and pointed; they were also, I noticed, the colour of sunflowers.

'Don't waste time!' he hissed. 'Just speak, damn you!' and little bombs of spittle exploded on Angela's cheek.

'Er – they can sing!' she yelled, looking directly into Father's eyes. 'Yes, that's right! They can sing songs and entertain people.' Angela knew, of course, how Father hated making an exhibition of himself.

'Well,' said the wolfman, 'it's a start. I wouldn't have thought of it myself, you understand, but I'm sure it'll do to begin with.' He stepped backwards, extending his arms as if in blessing. 'So, Alan,' he said, 'what more can I add? Your public, as they say, awaits . . . '

Father actually cleared his throat.

'I'm going to fetch someone,' said Verity.

'You shut your mouth and stay put,' said the wolf-man, starting the slow handclap. 'Now, come on, Alan, let's be 'avin' you. Upsy-daisy. Oh yes, well done. Atta-boy. That's the ticket.'

Father climbed gingerly up onto the seat. He had to hold on to the luggage rack with one hand in order to keep his balance.

'This is just like the TV,' said Angie, clapping her hands and jumping up and down. Father cleared his throat again.

'And cue, Alan!' said the wolfman and I held my breath as Father began to sing 'If You Were the Only Girl in the World' in a soft and wobbly baritone. He experimented with various keys and tempi, his voice gradually gaining in volume, and all the time he was looking straight at Mother. Verity's eyes shone with an unfamiliar fondness and she beat time on the seat beside her and then suddenly added her own voice to Father's, taking care, of course, to substitute 'girl' for 'boy' whenever the occasion demanded.

Towards the end Father appeared to get a bit carried away, even throwing in one or two dramatic gestures with his free hand. I thought he seemed quite professional, and we all clapped when he'd finished. The wolfman helped Father down and planted a playful little kiss on his cheek.

'What a performance!' he said. 'A man deserves a drink after a performance like that. Here, let me see . . . ' He patted his overcoat pockets. 'Ah, yes. Here we are. Just what the doctor ordered.'

The doctor, it turned out, had ordered half a bottle of Scotch whisky. The wolfman twisted the cap with a series of tiny snicks and offered the bottle to Father. Father disgracefully declined. The wolfman looked askance.

'Now Alan,' he admonished, 'you're not telling me you're a . . . a *teetotaller*?' He shrank back as if to distance himself from the word. 'You mean you don't drink *at all*?' Father shook his head. 'What? No snifters at the jolly old club? No late night stiff one – and pardon my French – to make the old bedtime duties a little less unpalatable? Alan, you disappoint me. A fellow's *got* to drink, you know. In fact, a fellow has to be rat-arsed, hairy-bollocked, hog-walloping pissed pretty well twenty-four hours a day before he earns the right to enter the door marked "Real Men".' He turned to Verity. 'I exaggerate, of course, but you take my point, I'm sure. I mean, if God had meant us to abstain he

wouldn't have given us hangover cures – am I right?'
He swivelled back to Father.

'Here. Drink,' he said, handing the bottle over. Father just stood there. I remember thinking how gormless he looked. 'I said "Drink!"' boomed the wolfman. He pushed Father backwards onto the seat and knelt astride him, one knee in his chest, and then he forced the bottle between Father's lips and tugged his head back with a fistful of hair. Verity screamed.

There was white foam on the wolfman's jaws as Father gagged, glugged and gurgled, whisky dribbling down his chin and little bladders of snot inflating and subsiding in his nostrils.

Angela started giggling and I slapped her face because that's what you're supposed to do with hysterical girls. She glowered at me.

'You little shit!' she said.

The wolfman scuttled to his feet like a leprechaun and Father slumped sideways onto the seat, his hands clamped onto his head as if he were trying to pull it off.

'I . . . ' he spluttered, 'I . . . I . . . ' And that's when Father's mouth flopped open and began pumping porridgey vomit onto the compartment floor, and all over Verity's feet and legs, too.

'Christ!' Mother wailed, the tears on her face a reflection of the rain on the window. 'Christ, Alan! Jesus!'

The wolfman yanked Father upright. 'Oh, Alan,' he said despairingly, 'are you going to let her get away with that? I mean, getting all steamed up over one little drink. Crawl out from under the thumb, man. You hear me? Yes? Then *tell* her, for Chrissakes! If you wanna go get yourself drunk then that's *your* goddamn business, and she can keep her pointy little nose out of it, right?'

'I . . . ' said Father.

'*Tell her!*'

151

'I . . . I bloody well will, Verity,' sobbed Father. 'If I want to, I mean. If I feel like it. I bloody well will, you know, and you can't stop me.'

Verity turned away in disgust. 'Worm!' she snorted. 'Slimy, disgusting little worm!'

'Oh dear, oh dear, oh dear!' said the wolfman. 'I'm afraid it's time for you to teach the old girl a lesson, Alan. I'm afraid you're going to have to give her a bit of a smack.'

'Wh . . . ?' snivelled Father. 'What?'

'*Hit her!*' screamed the wolfman. 'Hit her, you pathetic little nancy-boy!' And then he leaned forward and whispered something into Father's ear.

'No!' bawled Father and lifted his hand as high as it would go. Verity's face tilted, as if to greet the descending fist, and a bright slug of red blood dropped from her nose.

'You bastard,' she said quietly, and you couldn't really be sure who she was talking to. Father burst into tears.

'Oh, Alan!' said the wolfman. 'My dear, hopeless little Alan! I really think I'd be doing you a favour if I put you out of your misery.' He bent low over my poor, cowering father. 'And you wouldn't stop me, would you, Alan?' His fingers slid between Father's legs and squeezed. 'No. Just as I thought. You wouldn't know how. You don't have what it takes. Isn't that right, Verity darling? Isn't that right?' My mother hung her head.

'Please,' said Father, 'please . . . ' The fingers of the wolfman's other hand closed around Father's throat.

'Please what?'

'Please, sir,' Father said. 'Oh please, sir . . . '

Suddenly the wolfman let him go.

'Open the door,' he said, and Father, doubled up and

clutching his testicles – as Mother always encouraged me to call them – moved to the corridor side of the compartment.

'Don't try my patience,' said the wolfman. Father looked at him uncomprehendingly. 'The other door, man. *The other door.*'

I think, at that moment, we all knew what was going to happen.

'No!' screamed Verity, but Father toddled obediently off and suddenly the door was swinging open and banging against the side of the train and Father was a twisted stickman silhouetted briefly in the doorway.

It was, of course, after Mother had seen Father bite the dust (as they say in the films), and watched his poor leaking body until it had become an anonymous dot, that *she* keeled over and hit the deck. For a while she made the kind of noises I'd heard her make in Father's company on certain nights of the month, and then she was quiet. I think I knew that she was dead.

Stepping over her the wolfman kneeled at Angela's feet. He slipped off her shoes and this-little-piggied her toes.

'You look good enough to eat,' he said. Angela smiled (oh, that brace! I thought) and closed her eyes. The wolfman sank his teeth into her thigh and tore off the flesh in a long ragged strip.

'Mmm . . .' she sighed as he began to chew. I was surprised by her reaction, I must admit, but then I suppose she didn't get much attention from the opposite sex as a rule.

'Take off your clothes,' said the wolfman with his mouth full, and I suddenly realized there was no one there to say 'Manners!' reproachfully to either of us.

Blood – so much of it! – sluiced across the carriage floor and hennaed Mother's naturally blonde hair.

Feeling a bit of a gooseberry I picked up Angie's magazine. 'An All-Consuming Passion', I read and burst out laughing.

By the time I had finished the magazine the wolfman had finished Angela.

'How did all these bones fit inside her?' was all I could say. Angela's jawbone sat on top of the pile and I disconnected her brace and put it in my pocket to remember her by.

'You'd better come with me,' said the wolfman, chewing, finally, on a nipple. 'You've got things to learn.' He lifted me up to pull the communication cord and then, when the train began to slow down, we jumped, hand in hand, through the still-open door.

Something tinkled to the ground beside me: a silver disc, like a dog tag, with 'A. Munro' engraved across it.

'What does the A stand for?' I said. The wolfman just smiled. My eyes widened.

'Will I meet her?'

'Meet her? Oh, that was all a long time ago. She's no longer . . . Listen. Lesson number one: women's uses fade with their looks. Remember that. And this: love exists only in the minds of women, and women, bless their delicious hearts, must always be the willing victims of their own mad invention.'

I realized he was right. After all, I had just lost my entire family, and yet I felt nothing beyond a vague shame that Father hadn't been man enough to stick up for himself.

'What was that you said to him?' I asked. 'You know, to make him hit Mother like that.'

'Oh,' said the wolfman, 'I just told him what your mother and I were doing together in the toilet back there on the train.'

'The toilet?' I said.

The wolfman winked. 'Women like your mother,' he laughed, 'cut off a man's balls and then complain when he's no longer a man. You'll understand one day.'

I recalled my mother's trip to the loo – that would have been some time before you joined us – and the curious expression on her face when she came back into the compartment, and I think I understood a little, even then.

The light was fading fast. In the eastern sky a glowing canopy draped itself over the City of the Damned (as Father would have had it), and the city's heat seemed to be bringing the stars slowly out, like words written in lemon juice. I half expected to see my future up there, scrawled across the sky; but the only hint I had of life's possibilities lay much closer to home – in the wolfman's arrogant stride and the comfort of my hand in his – and, in the end, this suited me just as well . . .

I, too, am a wolfman now, of course, and I devour women and piss in the faces of men like my father. Oh, and if anything happened in 1999 I must have missed it, because here we are, ten years after the deadline, and women are as shrilly disenchanted as ever, and still they try to sell their mad invention to the likes of me.

I think I may have inherited my father's tendency to talk slightly oddly, and certainly Mother's passion (though mine I put to more interesting uses), and from the wolfman, now dead but not forgotten, comes my missionary zeal for converts. I still have poor Angela's brace, and occasionally, whenever I'm on a train and if the company is right, I'll hold it up for all to see, and then, when they're sitting comfortably, I'll begin . . .

MAGDALEN

Alison Armstrong

Alison Armstrong's stories have appeared in a number of periodicals and books, including the 1992 and 1994 *Scottish Short Stories* collections. She is the winner of the 1994 *Cosmopolitan*/Basildon Bond Short Story Competition. She lives in Alloa, near Stirling, and supports her writing habit by supply teaching.

MAGDALEN

If the prisoner has a name she has forgotten it. She is a machine, needing oil. Brodie's piston comes and goes and she feels he is trying to rub her out altogether.

Brodie is so-called because he never takes his clothes off, and when he leans over her, his jacket falls open to reveal the label: 'Brodie & Sons: Tailors of Distinction'. Brodie is over fifty, with pale eyes and a bald head like a long thin egg. His cat's arse mouth tightens when he nears his climax, and he comes like the dregs of talcum powder being squeezed from an exhausted tin. Pfft. His suit is black and ancient – perhaps even older than he. It smells of another person's salty rheum and their last medication on earth. It also smells of eau-de-Cologne, because with there being no running water in the Tower, Brodie insists she saturates herself with eau-de-Cologne before and afterwards. She has to douche with it as well and the stuff stings her unlubricated cunt. It's a kind of burning-out of Brodie, so in a way, the pain is welcome.

Brodie's Tower is square and squat, and it stands on the top of a small tree-covered hill. The prisoner can see above the trees as she lives on the top floor, in a room once occupied by Mary, Queen of Scots. There are no four-poster beds now, though, but there is a sash window – Victorian, and rotting. There is a chaise longue with a split skin; a table, a chair, a bottle of eau-de-Cologne, a can for the necessary, a mirror and a wind-up gramophone. There is also a pile of rugs and blankets, and a print tacked over a damp patch on the plaster. Although there are damp patches everywhere there is only one print. One day the prisoner peels it off the wall for a closer look. It shows a woman in a medieval dress, that falls about her toes like overlong curtains. The dress is low-necked and the woman's breasts look as small and hard as sour apples. The dress is red, and a dragon with a big mouth yawns behind the woman. Brodie says it's ready to swallow her up, but she doesn't seem bothered and she leads the dragon on a long golden chain. She is poker-faced; perhaps because the artist wasn't skilful with faces, but her name or title – 'Magdalen: A Whore(?)' written on the back of the print – suggests an open expression wouldn't suit her.

One more point about Magdalen. She has long bracken-coloured hair, falling loose to below her knees. The prisoner has hair the same colour that falls to her thighs. It is growing fast but Brodie won't let her cut it, even though it gets tangled when she thrashes around in her weird dreams. After every pfft he measures her hair with a metal tape he carries around in his pocket, and every time he finds it has grown about three inches.

Apart from her room, the Tower is derelict. Beneath her feet there are floors of dereliction, ending with the cellar, or dungeon. A rotten door that's been wedged half open for years, lures tramps and children into the dark unpaved region below. One evening Brodie catches a tramp there, who is doing something wrong, something unspeakable. Brodie holds his rifle fastidiously at the man's head and pokes him out of the cellar, but he (Brodie) can't stop the foul thing happening . . .

Brodie is angry when he relates this. Beneath his anger, the prisoner senses his alarm. When Brodie measures her hair, the steel tape becomes a gun against the skull.

Now, she thinks the floor she stands on might collapse and she will fall down and down again into the cellar. The square, squat Tower swallows people, like Magdalen's dragon. The soft earth in the cellar is probably digested people and if her floor gives way she will have a gentle landing. But she doesn't want to land where some smelly old tramp has been.

Perhaps he wasn't very old.

The sunlight, a chute full of mites, falls into the room through the rotting window. It touches the print of Magdalen and seems to make her po-face wink.

Brodie does not wear a watch, so the prisoner has no idea of time. Out of the window, she can see a village which has moving cars, and satellite dishes fixed to the houses, but it's like a village inside a glass dome. One shake and silver snow will fall.

Brodie plays Wagner on the gramophone. He also plays Highland dances and (for light relief) Gilbert and Sullivan. He has read that music is the food of love, and love is what he wants. He doesn't like the sex, because it is dirty. He prays for the strength to desist, but Magdalen gets between him and God.

Some days the prisoner isn't a machine needing oil; she is a foot inside a rubbing shoe. Sometimes Brodie has to stop and get off, in order to wind up the gramophone or change the needle. When the music starts again, the crackles of the old 78s express her own dry skin.

But her dreams have long, soothing fingers. Not only do they rumple her hair, they disturb the bedding and taunt her with sensations. She starts to believe that Magdalen is responsible: Magdalen and that great yawning dragon at her back.

Oh.

Brodie tells her that Magdalen covers a patch of damp. That is her only function, and she does the job very well. Brodie plays *Tristan* very loudly, and sings along to the tenor part. Afterwards, he measures the prisoner's hair, and is cheered to find that it now comes down to her knees. Hair growth, he once read in a reputable magazine, is a fine gauge of amatory fulfilment.

What if I fall pregnant, thinks the prisoner when Brodie has gone. She grimaces as the eau-de-Cologne bites once again. She is being cured, like leather, or ham.

Magdalen grimaces back, sick of being a cover for a patch of damp.

That night, Magdalen sends the prisoner a special dream. The dream's eyes are green, like a witch's, and each iris holds a million fragments of a soul she can't fathom. All she can see are the eyes, but with her hands and her skin she feels the dream's long back, the slight rise of its buttocks, the taut, wiry muscles of its shoulders and arms. She feels it waiting, in a gentle inquisitive way like a poor boy wanting to enter a church. But she can't let it in.

The dream cries, silently. Its tears overflow, fall and wet her skin.

. . . She wakes – thinking, it's not Magdalen's fault things didn't work out. The chaise longue she uses as a bed, now has a sweetish, dirty smell, like honey going bad.

Brodie brings her two presents. The first is a tortoiseshell dressing-table set, once owned by Queen Victoria. The prisoner checks the brush for royal scurf before tugging it through her own hair.

The other present is a pair of amber earrings, each

drop containing a tiny prehistoric fly. Brodie tells her these came from Atlantis, under the sea. He also tells her she is beautiful.

Then he plays *The Mikado* on the gramophone, and afterwards, the tape shows her hair has grown three whole inches. Brodie is pleased, but doesn't show it. The shape of his head gives her an idea of him: he is an eggshell trying to be a whole egg.

Poor Brodie.

But when she walks, she thinks splinters are rubbing together.

Brodie brings her regular meals, packed neatly into sandwich boxes. For washing, she has to stick with the eau-de-Cologne until he brings her new dresses. Then he supplies four large Thermos flasks full of hot water, a bar of ladies' scented soap and a giant fluffy towel.

There are three dresses; one blue silk, one in green velvet and one in ivory satin. They are in the same style as Magdalen's dress, and when the prisoner tries them on, her breasts are pushed high and hard. Brodie laces her up the back, so tightly she can hardly breathe. Her skirts stretch drumskin tight across her hips, then fall wide and loose and crumple at her feet. She can barely move, but she feels beautiful. Her hair is wet from being washed and falls to below mid-calf. It is now as long as Magdalen's.

Brodie leaves her in the blue dress, but unlaces it so she can take it off to sleep. He takes the other two away, for if they stayed in the room, the damp would spoil them. When Brodie has gone, the prisoner lets her hair drape out of the window, to dry in the breeze and the last, intense rays of the evening sun. The breeze ruffles her hair gently, and lulls her almost to sleep. She wants Magdalen to send the dream again, and she wonders if the dream has anything to do with the man in the cellar. Brodie said he would shoot that man if he found him on his property again.

There is no electricity, and Brodie does not allow candles. When the sun is down, darkness is near absolute on a moonless night, and the shapes of things make stolid, sentry-like ghosts. The prisoner sits on the chaise longue and shivers because it is cold. She wonders if the dream will be scared off by her new finery, but she knows he is somewhere in the room.

The nerves in her spine scream as he draws close behind her. She doesn't turn round. His mouth is wet on her neck, and his teeth are sharp. His beard growth rasps slightly and though his hair mingles with her own, she feels its otherness. She wonders if the right thing is happening to her, but Magdalen doesn't care about the right thing. She sends girls and women hot, dirty dreams and watches, grinning and chuckling, until dawn.

He sits behind the prisoner, rocking her back and forth and tunnelling into her bunched-up skirts. He is clothed tonight, and patches of her skin encounter rough material. His smell is all the love juice since Adam and Eve, which has never been washed away, and he is nameless – driftwood, cast up by a dark sea. His arms link across her waist and pull her tighter and tighter until their bones touch through the yards of crumpled silk.

What if he is ugly, she thinks.

But she knows his green eyes are beautiful.

When he comes, it is nothing like Brodie's miserly pfft.

When the prisoner wakes, the room is filled with a grey dusty light. She ought to have taken off her dress before she slept, because now it is stained and crumpled, and it

164

smells bad. She puts eau-de-Cologne on the stain, which leaves a worse mark, but she can say she had an accident with the bottle. She also finds two sore bites on her right shoulder, which (she decides), Brodie did when he forgot himself.

She hangs the dress out of the window, to try to get rid of the creases. She has to greet Brodie wrapped in a blanket, and he is not at all pleased. Yet when he says 'you forgot yourself', his cat's arse stretches in a tight smile, and, accompanied by the wail of the bagpipes, he tries to forget himself again.

Brodie brings her a rope of pearls, once gambled and lost by a mistress of King Charles II. Each pearl is the full moon, and they look cool and magical against her blue dress. But this dress is taken away, to be replaced by the green velvet. For this dress, Brodie brings her kohl and green eye cosmetic and heavy gold bracelets from Imperial Russia, set with topaz and malachite. She wonders if the treasure would turn to dust if the Tower fell down. She wonders, too, what Brodie will do when her hair stops growing.

Then Brodie grows suspicious of the lovebites and she tells him about the other man. She adds, tearfully, that she was forced. So Brodie gets anxious and spends long hours on watch with his gun, and packets of sandwiches. He combs the basement, but prefers to sit on the roof – from where he can see his enemy approach. In his black suit, he resembles a crow. She hears him scuffling from time to time as he changes direction, and she also hears the odd slate crash to the ground below. Silly old sod.

As an extra precaution, he changes all the locks on her door. When he visits he keeps putting the wrong key in the wrong lock, and she has to listen to him fumbling and tutting for an eternity. Magdalen thinks this a huge joke, and the short black dash of her lips occasionally trembles.

The prisoner hopes and fears that *something* will happen, soon.

Brodie removes the prisoner's green dress and brings her the ivory satin. This colour suits the amber earrings and her bracken-coloured hair, but does not suit her jail-pallor. Brodie brings a gift of heavy gold chains – a type (he says) once popular in Germany. He insists that she wears them, but they rasp her as the piston comes and goes; and when he measures her hair, he finds it has not grown a fraction. In fact, it has not grown since she got those bites.

'You're not very good, that's why,' she tells him.

The cat's arse tightens so much, it swallows itself. He looks as though he has been warmed up from the dead; yet even so, he is calculating.

'You hurt,' she adds, bravely. 'You hurt every single time.'

Her head is a chamber of echoes; a shell brought inland and cut off from the real sound of the sea. When Brodie strikes, he will crash her echoing limbo – and there *will* be retaliation because she has blown a man apart.

'Is that so?' he asks quietly.

'Yes.'

The prisoner waits to be struck, but it does not happen. Brodie leaves the room, postponing it. She hears the door clang and several locks slide shut. Not long afterwards, she hears his feet disturbing roofslates; perhaps the same slates that kept the rain off Mary, Queen of Scots.

Then she hears a shot.

Then she hears the tiles clatter off the roof, taking with them an object that falls like a bag of wet cement.

The prisoner rises from the chaise longue and shuffles to the window. She walks sideways so her labia don't rub together. By the time she reaches her window, the dust has settled and she can see the tiles partly covering a heap of old clothes. Poor bastard . . .

Soon Brodie will come back down. He will place his rifle carefully against the wall and say that right has triumphed. Being victorious, he might not punish her for what she said.

A trick of the light makes Magdalen grin, knowingly. But what can she know? She is cardboard, covering a patch of damp.

A late tile falls off the roof – knocked by Brodie's clumsy feet. Brodie wears stout black shoes which he keeps in excellent repair; the man he's just shot went barefoot. His toes were as sensitive as fingers, but they were grimy and were covered in old cuts and bruises. He was after revenge, and Brodie's sandwiches; and he almost got there. But at a calculated moment, Brodie turned and shot.

The story *has* to finish that way, because if Brodie falls, so must his Tower. She can picture the other man clearly now, and he was dirty and ugly, with long matted hair and the beginnings of a straggly beard. If she'd seen him at night, she would not have touched him.

She feels hot; old leather turning back to skin. It is time to do something. It is time to brush her hair . . .

Queen Victoria's hairbrush hits a knot. The prisoner closes her eyes and tugs and tugs, and on the dark screen of her lids she sees two exploding wheels of pain. These are yellowish green, and when she stops brushing they stabilize. In the centre of each a black hole emerges, which pulses gently as the surrounding colour dilates.

Each wheel, each eye, is a sorrowful, microscopic world that she is too big and clumsy to join.

The prisoner opens her eyes. A cape of hair is no protection, when scrutiny comes from within. The man's green eyes *were* beautiful, but they were misplaced, like emeralds hiding in filth. He was not very old.

There is a metallic crash, sounding as though Brodie has dropped his rifle while descending from the roof. Brodie hates carelessness, so this must be irksome, and he will arrive in a bad temper. The prisoner thinks she hears a curse but it is hard to tell because the echo is distorted by the Tower. It makes the stonework tremble, but nothing falls.

It was (she thinks) a bad curse, quite ungodly.

She used to wake, sometimes, with that rotting honey smell on her fingers – but that was before she came to the Tower. Now, the smell competes with the odour of damp, and she is sickened by them both. She leans back on the chaise longue, covered, as far as possible, by her bracken-coloured hair. In preparation for Brodie, her body takes on a doll-like rigidity. Every time she thinks, this is the peak of pain, but there is always a little more.

> Humpty Dumpty sat on wall,
> Humpty Dumpty had a great fall,
> All the King's horses and all the King's men
> Ate scrambled egg for a week.

(He doesn't mean to laugh; he is content staring at the prisoner, who is like a princess to him. But recent events have stressed him, and the recollection of that long thin egg rolling off the roof, is too much to contain.)

She turns sharply, and his instincts make him cower. He is squatting, legs crossed, on the table behind her. Next to him lie Brodie's gun and Brodie's keys. He is bigger, more angular, than in her dreams, and she thinks (stupidly) that his bones are too big for his skin. He is crouched like a broken chair, with soiled and tattered upholstery.

He recovers, and rakes his hair off his face. Then he grins at her. The grin belongs to an urchin. The eyes, with their harrowing lustrous beauty, do not.

She regrets, silently, that she has nothing to offer him, not even a biscuit. It's Brodie's fault, not hers. He kept her short, so she would maintain her figure. The man – who is very young, not much more than a boy – wears a black jacket over his shoulders, like a cape. One pocket bulges with a paper bag that held sandwiches. He pulls out the paper bag, splits it open and picks up the crumbs with his tongue. He does this very seriously, and not a crumb is wasted. His tongue is deep pink against his scruffy black beard, and it has a soft, rounded tip. As he works he looks up through his hair and watches her, almost without blinking, until she wants to freeze, or become *real* china.

He crumples the paper bag and stuffs it back in the pocket. Then he reaches into his shirt pocket and with care, takes out a half-smoked cigarette. He lights it and smokes with his body hunched around it, protectively. His hands are stained and bony but the fingers are graceful; the nails are bitten down to the quick. A pilferer's hands, she surmises. Unlike Brodie, he used the door keys silently, if he used them at all.

'How did you get in?' she asks.

He shrugs, and she does not ask again. Those hands contaminated her – yet he was gentle, and the thought of him could moisten her now if only she were not so tinder dry. She burns like a bush fire. It is Brodie's fault, like the absence of tea and biscuits.

The man uses the tabletop to stub out the cigarette.

He doesn't know any better, and looks anxious when she frowns. The Tower ought to shudder dangerously, but it does nothing, perhaps because the table is unpolished, lumber room stuff. She smiles in forgiveness and complicity, and he grins back. He appears to take her smile as an invitation, because he slides off the table. Standing, he loses some of his angularity, unless it is hidden by his shirt and trousers which belonged, several wearers back, to a fatter person. An old sweater is tied around his middle, and this almost hides the knife dangling on his hip, sheathed. He steps towards her, and excitement threads a string through her belly and starts pulling her where she might not want to go. He stands behind her and, leaning over slightly, trails a fingertip down the centre of her face. When he reaches her mouth, she nibbles gently and glances upward. What she sees is a black jacket lining and a flash of the label: 'Brodie & Sons: Tailors of Distinction'.

The prisoner knows that, if she wanted, she could bite the finger to the bone.

THE HOME-GROWN
BOYS

Tom Smith

Tom Smith was born in Glasgow but grew up in Jamaica. After completing his education in England, he travelled the world: South America, India, Southeast Asia, ending up in Australia and a stint as a farmworker. He returned home to work as a shepherd in the Cotswolds before setting up his own landscaping business. He is now an English Language teacher, and lives with his family near Cirencester.

THE HOME-GROWN BOYS

When Hughie woke up he was still dressed from yesterday. He lay cold and lumpish beneath a winding of
blanket, stiff as a corpse in his only suit which had
twisted and migrated against his night-turnings and now
had him well trussed. With an effort he struggled up
out of the pit, feeling for the light.

In the shock of illumination everything was confused,
unfamiliar. Bare bulb, low brown ceiling, bulging walls.
It took a few moments for the pennies to fall from his
eyes.

The devastation of his bedroom. Like every morning.

Now he was old, sleep was just a black well. No
dreams, no monsters – he remembered nothing. But . . .
had he not already been up, and gone downstairs, and
made tea? Where was it . . . he could do with it. A quart.
So dry he could hardly breathe – if the shallow intake
that rattled his cracked black clapper of a tongue could
be called breath.

Endless life-habits become daydreams. Ravels of routine drawn into the weave of sleep. No tea then. For
that matter, had he been down the passage and found
long, blessed relief . . . or did he just dream he went for
a pee? No wonder his old waterworks were all to hell.

He went to the window and opened the curtain a
crack. Cold, leaking sheet of sky. Bone-grey light of
winter over darkish clumps of land, and the struggling
pipework of trees. Black bronchial tubes!

First cough of the day. Two old bags bursting in unison.

Now he needed that tea. When he could straighten up he shuffled into his shoes, bumbled along to the toilet, clip-clopped downstairs. Endless life-habits. As he went down he met the creeping cold coming up. Cold from the stone, from the earth. Watch it, boy . . . one slip now and you're gone.

The kitchen was small and neat like a larder of ice. The old range had long since ceased to be the warm heart of the house. No improvements to be had now – he'd given up trying. The water system bellowed as he worked the tap open. It spat. Bastard thing. Something in that water was giving him the dithers. He moved about carefully trying to make as little disturbance as possible. Teapot, cup, one spoon. No laying up the table in this house. Now the kitchen was full of steam and blue cigarette smoke, and outside there was fog in the hanging woods.

A familiar. Silvery ribbon of song – the robin was there, waiting. That was good. What was it? The bird is good so long as he don't tap on the window, and then that's your lot. Hughie opened the window a squeak and posted some stale crusts out into the garden. And when he opened up that bit the interference came in.

Sometimes it was like voices. A soft conversation of whispers, always just beyond him, voicing fears. Always there. In the distant sound of the motorway, a steady stirring of the air that never rested, and in closer, continuous things. Insisting, intent on interfering. The alien voices had taken over the village and intended to be heard. What was it? Well, for a start the lies they were spreading were supposed to be for his own good. Lies about him. And the looks they gave him – the interfering

174

scrutiny – added to that. It was spreading into the air-waves now, which hadn't been the same since they went over to FM, and in the satellites springing up. All pointing towards him. The static was very strong on these muggy mornings.

There was that smell again too. A slight smell of sulphur on the damp air, as if the Devil himself might be out there in the murk. Hughie closed the window, tight.

He sat himself down at the old scrubtop table that was deeply scarred with cigarette burns. He made another roll-up – what the hell, he had a thousand diseases. The clock reminded him that the rest of the world had been at work for hours. He pulled the paper over. It was yesterday's but he could read it again. He had mislaid his spectacles but it didn't matter – even with the sharper focus it was a struggle these days. As to what it was about, any of it . . . Things seemed to happen in places he'd never heard of. Spokesmen vying with correspondents, explanations that didn't add up. And offers. Prizes galore, a million to be won, are you destined to make money? Arson, valuable machinery lost, a picture of the blackened shell and insurance men picking through it. More prizes. And here, attacks on horses, bay gelding slashed over a hundred times, next to a smiling girlie. On every page the smiling girlies were invading his paper. Too late – what did he want now with pictures of young women in their pelts? Still, the day would come when they too would wrap up against the encroaching cold. He examined the skinny girl in front of him for signs of goosepimples. There had been times when his work had put him off all that. Seasons of birth and death, obstetric blundering, triumph and disaster. The bloody mess. The lime-pit and the kennel-truck. Sometimes hard to face the wife, do the dutiful thing, after that. Still, she'd never complained. Oh, she'd

175

up and left, found a new man, took the boys . . . but she'd never complained about the job. It was later that she'd given him hell. Such is life.

A very long time ago.

He yawned. The girl in the paper, yesterday's girl, looked up at him with big, soft sheep's eyes as he extinguished his burning nub in her navel. There were others too, of course, they came on every page, pushing in around him like a gather. And it seemed he was among them, he wore the stark red greasy raddle as he worked his way through the struggling, bleating wedge – red, and red again, changing to green, catching them, stopping them, a good stopper this lad, moving on to the blue . . .

He awoke with a fart. Something was tapping on the window. Like a hard bird's claw, wanting in. And there was a face, grinning through the smeared pane. That face. I see you in there. It's me, Stevie.

The boy was soft in the head. He'd been told enough times. It started off as a bit of a game when Hughie kept finding him in the woodshed. That went on until the estate delivered him a load of thinnings for the winter. Now the boy was getting bolder, coming up to the house, peeping in. Sometimes he threw pebbles onto the back roof.

It was no use trying to ignore him now. The face bobbed at the window. Hello in there. It wasn't going to go away. Hughie went slowly to the door and worked the bolts. Stevie was there, waiting. He was soaked through and unravelled, hedge-wild like an escapee. A great gloomy raincoat hung round his shoulders – a dripping tent on the verge of collapse.

'What do you want, Stevie-boy?'

'Can I come in, then?'

'No.'

'For a minute.'

'No. I'm busy.'

'Go on. I'm cold . . . need a dry.'

'What do you think this is – a dog's home? One of your stray centres? You got no right here. You scared off my robin.'

'Please.'

He'd been a nice enough little boy, once. Not what Jesus would want for a sunbeam, but possibly somebody loved him. Now he was afraid to go home. Seen off, and having to rough it. He looked like he'd been a long time lost. But then, that was the look they all had lately. The clothes and the boots and the shaven heads, always a new twist on the culture of desolation – at the moment it seemed to be the Russian Front look. And this . . . head tuft, plaited like some weirdly located umbilicus whereby his head may've been attached to something even uglier. In its starkness it may have been intended to impress, but on Stevie with his carroty hair and long bird skull it looked like a disfigurement only, some unfortunate scalp disorder, and Hughie was moved to pity.

'Come on, then.'

'Cheers, Hughie.'

'But don't bring that wet thing in here, Stevie.'

The coat slumped off.

'No, there's a hook there. Hang it up. It won't dry but at least let it drip.' The boy was helpless. Hughie took the coat and hung it for him. It was a strange voluminous coat, into which an inner lining had been crudely sewn. A lining of pockets.

'What the hell's this?'

But Stevie was gone, already in the kitchen running a check on the place, casting about, touching things. 'God, it's freezing in here. I'd have that old thing going. That burner. I need to warm up, I thought you'd . . . '

'That range? No. Long cold. Well, look at it. Defunct. Used to be a time when it'd be going right through the winter. Heated the boiler too, and you could bake your bread on it. Eh? Imagine. The smell of fresh-baked bread!'

'Can you make bread then, Hughie?'

'No. Anyway I'm on gas. And since you're here I'll put the kettle on, only –'

'Bloody hell! What's that?'

'Air. In the pipes.'

'Sounded like elephants.'

'Look, if you want tea you'd better sit down at the table. And keep still, can't you? Fiddling about . . . can't keep your paws off anything.'

'Hey, I had one of these cups! Diana and Charley Boy. My handle came off, too. Never kept pens in it, though. Any of 'm working?'

'Sit!'

Stevie sat. He seemed smaller, diminished, as if the coat had been a good half of him. Hughie would have said stunted – his stockman's eye, bleared with age as it was, could still spot a poor doer. The tuft didn't help – Hughie knew just where he could put his hands on some old dagging shears.

'What happened to the hair, Stevie-boy?'

'This? Mick done it. Done himself one, too. Not bad, eh – a mate who does hair?'

'Aye. A real teasy-weasy.'

Mick. Another pointless character. So he was at large again. Of all the young in Endcombe, such as there were now, these two specimens were all that remained of the home-grown product. Not much of an advertisement. Except that the Close, sad strip of council roughcast, was not considered part of the village these days. Not in keeping.

'So where's Mick then?'

'Around.'

'I thought they put him away.'

'Yeah.'

Hughie tried to recall. Setting fire to a barn, was it, or a straw-stack . . . something like that. Caught at once – walked into the pub stinking of petrol while the skyline glowed. Heroic stuff. He handed Stevie the tea.

'Magic.'

The boy was thawing. His white claws gripped the mug. A milky dewdrop like a defrosting mistletoe berry started from his beak, and retreated with a sniff. The rough-sleeping smell of him mingled with the earth-burrow smell of the damp kitchen. He was very thin. Hughie thought of all the runty things he'd revived in the past.

'Got any food in, Hughie?'

'No.'

'Not even a biscuit? What about me?'

'There's nothing till I've been to the shop.'

'I'll go for you.'

'No you won't.'

'Well, what can I have then?' Stevie's eye moved at once to the old tobacco tin.

Hughie took it up quickly. 'All right, but I'll make it . . . You're not having a cigar. What do you think I am. Father Christmas?'

'This is better.' Stevie grinned as he lit the pencil-thin smoke, squinted through the little cloud he made. 'I like being here.'

'Well, you're not stopping, you know that. But I'm going to light the fire in the front room, and –'

'Yeah! Let me do that! I'm good at fires.'

'Fine. You can get the wood in. There's the box. You know where the shed is.'

*　　*　　*

Stevie did a good job. He built the fire with the urgent dexterity of someone who has had enough cold. Soon it was hissing purposefully, and offering a miserly heat.

'There. Told you. I'm the business. I can do anything.'

'Well, stop wasting those matches! What are you doing there?'

He was lighting matches, extinguishing them with a flick, and sniffing the trail of smoke.

'I likes it. The smell of sulphur.'

'Give them to me. Now why don't you sit down instead of crouching in the fireplace like a diddycoy? You won't get a wet arse in here.'

'Yeah? I'm not sitting on that sofa. It's got mould.' Stevie perched on a chair, cocky now, enlivened. Jaunty as a crusty robin in what had once been a striking red sweatshirt.

Hughie viewed him afresh, with suspicion.

'What's that . . . on your shirt?'

'This? You mean Penile Dementia?'

'Yes. That. What does it mean?'

'Nothing.' Stevie shrugged. 'Just a group. Official world tour from last year. They were giving them away, because they never went.'

A group. He might have known. Hughie avoided groups of any sort. And as for a group that would exhort its members to display that . . . thing.

The thing collapsed into the folds of Stevie's chest as he leaned forward to scrutinize the contents of Hughie's living room.

'You got a lot of stuff here.' His eyes were moving over every surface, itemizing. Like the bogus valuers that used to call. 'Old stuff, isn't it? But interesting. I like old, dusty things. And you got a lot of books, too.'

'Uh-huh. Books.'

'What's all these books about then?'

'Just . . . books.'

'I never read. Takes too long. I don't rate it.'

'Can you read, Stevie?'

'Course I can.'

Hughie'd never seen the boy in school. The nearest he ever got was lurking round the playground. In the bushes, spying. Looking on. The teachers would tell him to clear off.

'Besides, I'm into computers now.'

'Don't be daft. What would you know?'

'I'm going to have one.'

Well, why not? The world was crackling with satellites and lasers so why shouldn't Stevie creep around the hedge-bottoms with a misappropriated computer under his raincoat? Stevie, who had difficulty using the stub of a pencil. The belief in it all – everyone whizz-kidding themselves. Hughie, for one, was beginning to feel unplugged, like one of those partially restored lunatics with the bare wires sticking out of his head. He knew it was time for a drink – but he would have to get rid of Stevie first.

Stevie was warming up. 'I had one of them electronic cow-collectors. Solar, it was. Didn't work in winter. I chucked it. What I'm after now is a camcorder.'

'A what?'

'Electronic camcorder. I seen one at Tandys.' Suddenly Stevie jumped up, agitated, and started thrusting into the fire with the length of angle iron that served as a poker. 'If . . . if I had it now . . . I'd have it, and I'd be working on that zoom, I can do anything like that! I get things to go, I . . . '

'All right, Stevie, you can put that poker down. There's no use getting excited.' Hughie knew the boy was a bit touched but when he got worked up it was more than that; now his eyes were rolling about. There was a riot going on in there. 'Here, have another smoke. You can make this one.'

'No. No thanks. I've got to go. I'm going to look at it now. I can't touch it but I . . . I looks at it.'

'You mean you're going into town?'

'Yeah. But I'm coming back. I'll get you something. What can I get you, Hughie?'

'You're going pocketing.'

'Course.' The grin was back, and the eyeballs were back in their sockets.

'Nothing, thanks. But look, you're not to cross the motorway. Not in this fog.'

'No chance. I go under . . . through the badger-gulley. Only twenty minutes into town. I'm faster than the bus. I'm a one-off, I am!'

When he was in his coat and shuffling out Stevie turned, as if in two minds.

'I was just thinking. I could bring my stuff here.'

'Eh?'

'Just for a while. I could, uh, do a few things, I could . . . you know . . . '

'What?'

'Well . . . help you.'

'You're the one who needs help, Stevie, not me. You're not dossing here, and that's that. Now off you go!'

'But . . . I can come back, can't I?'

'Maybe. But on one condition. You don't tell anyone you been here.'

'No.'

'You know what I mean, Stevie-boy. I don't want that hairdresser mate of yours here.'

'Course not. No one'll know I been here, honest.'

Then he was gone, round the side of the house and through the hedge gap, into the fog.

Hughie slammed the door and put the bolts back. Going through the house he could smell Stevie like tomcat, but it didn't matter now – he was gone. It was lunch time, he would get out the bottle. That was warmth. As he went to fetch it he was thankful that he had it well out of sight, away from the sweeping gaze of the boy.

Later, Hughie went to the shop. He hadn't been out for days. He disliked walking in the village. Among the hostiles. Nobody spoke to him when he did his bit of shopping.

Coming back was slow. He had to stop and catch his breath – he could no longer make the trip in one go. He had to stop and give his lungs a good clearing out.

Nobody heard. He could've dropped dead and nobody would notice. He'd sometimes entertained the idea of walking out with no trousers on.

Everything looked the same but it wasn't. The old stone cottages, squat and toadlike in the gloom, were now transformed, and changing hands for princely sums. He'd seen them all come, some of them friendly at first, but the kiss of death – whatever it was – got them in the end. Nobody spoke. And there, right in the middle, his own place still with the original thatch. Looking like an ugly relation. How they must want him out! Ah, but he was the life tenant and he wasn't about to be shifted, they'd found that out when the estate changed hands. He had his copy of the agreement, some-where, he kept it safe. If anyone wanted to see.

The air was dead still, prickling with static. In the low winter light everything was filmed with grey as if the colour was washed out. Grey and depressed, and there

was the smell of burning, a sharp smell – more inciner-
ator than bonfire – like someone burning secrets. Black
filaments floated on the air. Here, there was always
someone burning something, and there were always
those people who furiously defended their gardens
against the advancing smoke. Upwind and downwind,
smoking each other out like bees.

Hughie took a small stub of cigarette from under his
cap. As he lit it he was aware of a vague interference of
disapproval, as if striking the match was a crime, as if
doing anything here was a matter for scrutiny. The feeling intensified and he turned round to see a woman
approaching on a horse. That woman, again. He turned
and began walking.

'Hello.'

He ignored her.

'I say. Hello there!'

He stopped. It was no good, he was caught. It was
as if she'd been lying in wait. She drew up beside him,
shifted in the creaking saddle, looked down on him.

'Ah, Hugh.' She smiled carefully, very precisely, and
revealed very white teeth. It wasn't much of a smile.
'Been shopping?'

'Aye.'

'You should get someone to do it for you. Really. I'm
sure it could be arranged.'

'I manage.'

What did the silly creature want now? Shopping. She
had no right to interfere. She was the manager's wife
but as far as he knew she wasn't official in any way.
She had no right to trouble him like this.

'Good. And how are you keeping, Hugh?'

'Fine. Don't you worry about me.'

'Oh, but I do. We all do. It's only right and proper
that we look after you.'

'I look after myself. Always have done.'

'I know.'

'I been in this village long enough. Grew up here. And you wouldn't remember when I was shepherd here. Course, it was a different place then.' That was telling her.

For a second the eyes flashed like bright shrew-buttons but the smile didn't change behind the careful paintwork. She glanced around as if to remind herself of what the village was now. Neat, and cared for. Looked after.

'I just meant,' she continued, airily, 'that it's not easy coping on your own. When you get . . . older. You know, running a house.'

So, it was that.

'Well, its kind of you to take an interest, I suppose. If you want to do something for me, missis, you could get them to come and sort my plumbing. I been waiting over a year for someone to come.'

'Quite. Well I'm sure that could be looked into. In fact I believe the whole property is due for renovation. But I just wonder, Hugh, whether you wouldn't be happier in, well, something more suitable.'

'What d'you mean?'

'You know. In town. Nearer the shops. Maybe with someone around who would help. There are a lot of possibilities we could explore.'

'No.'

'Stand *still*, damn you!'

The horse, a magnificently bred animal, was becoming fidgety. Bored. It's hooves clattered in the road. Hughie stepped back as it raised its tail and urinated copiously.

Horse of a hundred slashes.

'All right. Look, I must get moving. But think about it, will you, Hugh? Oh, and I've asked the people from the council to look in. I'm sure they'll help you sort things out.'

'What?'

But it was her last word. She was off, pushing the horse past him and pricking it into a trot. What did she mean by it, sending someone to look in? What did she want?

Let them come. He'd never let them in because they had no right. He was nothing to do with the council. He knew better. It was nothing to do with her either. The council of all people. She was just out to make trouble. As far as Hughie was concerned she could go . . . shopping. And she thought he was bothered? He wasn't going to give it another . . .

That smoke. It was coming from his house. Thick dirty smoke pouring out. But it couldn't be the neat front fire he'd banked up before he came out. It was the back chimney, that hadn't been swept in years. It was the old range going.

When he got to his front door it was unlocked and he could see that the window had been forced. That bloody boy – he'd been to the shed, too, and half the wood had been dragged out.

Inside the house Hughie could smell the heat and he could smell other things, too.

'Stevie, is that you?'

'In here.'

The kitchen was full of smoke, of course, ancient smoke streaming out of cracks like genii of escaping old cooking grease, mingling with thick coils of wet wood smoke, reluctant to draw. And there was Stevie, and Mick, sitting in front of the range, lounging back with their big boots up on the rail. They'd made a fine mess, between them, breaking up wood on the floor. They'd been in a while, too – must've watched him go out. The table top was littered with empty cans. Strong lager.

'What's this?'

'Hughie – fancy seeing you again.' Mick's breezy, cheeky-bastard manner hadn't changed. 'And I thought you must've popped off!'

'Not just yet, son, as you see.'

Two pairs of eyes surveyed him, unconvinced. Surprised to see him back at all. As if they had inherited the place. Moved in.

'But . . . you are dying.'

'We're all dying.'

'No. I'm young. You're dying, old man . . . I'm living!'

'Same difference, son.'

'No it isn't. And the name's Mick. Remember?'

Hughie remembered. A nasty piece of work. And look at him now. Rat-cunning where Stevie was dim. He was heavier, too, better-fed, with heavy, lugubrious features – offset by a bleached-red tuft that sprouted, stiffer than Stevie's, like a bog-brush. When he smiled his teeth were very rat-like. The smile was one of supreme insolence. I'm here now. This is how it is. Hughie remembered the times he'd fetched him one round the ear, the little bastard; it seemed only a few years ago when he'd come upon him lurking with intent. Wasn't tolerated then. He'd always known the boy had no future. Anyone who would tattoo a dotted line across his throat with the words 'CUT HERE' must be headed for the hopeless pile. He reflected for a moment on all the hopeless cases, all the small bodies he'd cast into the lime pit.

'Okay. Mick. This is my house.'

'Yeah?'

'So. What are you doing here?'

'We like it here. Don't we, Stevie-boy? He invited me. He's a bit of a character, this one. You told me to come, didn't you, Stevie!'

'Eh . . . I suppose . . . '

'Course you did. You said Hughie was on his own. We should get on round. And I thought, fancy seeing him again!'

Stevie looked up furtively. 'I only –'

But Hughie could see how it was.

'And who broke the window frame?'

'Mick.'

'Liar! It was you, Stevie, so don't fuckin' lie!'

'No . . . '

Mick grinned. His eyes were like kitchen knives. 'He's a nutter, see. Do anything.'

Do anything you say, thought Hughie. His head was buzzing – how to see this through, how to deal with it? The unexpected. To think they could slip into his house. He should never . . . His head was full of bees but his face was impassive.

'Yeah. Like lighting this thing. He didn't ask you, did he? You weren't here. Just light it up, he says, light up the range. I know what I'm doing. Well, has to be pissed. Doesn't take much, does it? Do anything now. Mind, this stuff's 8.5 per cent. Anyway, next thing, the chimney's roaring!'

'But –'

'Shut up! I told you, don't lie! Now then. What d'you reckon, Hughie? Look at us. Riders of the rusty range! Not bad, eh?'

'Fine. But you're making a stink outside. It won't be long before they're round to complain. You know what it's like now. What am I going to say?'

Mick laughed unpleasantly. 'What d'you mean, neighbours? Since when did they give a toss? That woman across the road? Little pleaser. I know what she wants, don't we, Stevie. Eh?'

'Yeah.'

'Eh . . . Shagememnon!'

'Yeah! We know what she wants!' Stevie's eyes were beginning to jazz.

'And when Stevie's got his camcorder he's going to get it – on film! In the bathroom, I'd say, all steaming. Isn't that right? In yer face, Stevie-boy. Go on, give her the big zoom, eh, you're going to zooooom . . . ' Mick shoved Stevie's chair from under him and the boy rolled away under the table, arching and kicking and gibbering in rapture. The beer cans rolled on the floor in accompaniment.

Hughie began to back out of the kitchen. He was thinking now about getting out and leaving them to it. They would go soon enough – there seemed little sense in aggravating matters.

'Hey, Hughie. Come back! Don't take any notice of Stevie. I told you, he's a nutter . . . '

'Camcorder!' shouted Stevie from the floor. 'If I-I-had one I-I –'

'Shut up!' Mick jumped to his feet and started thrusting clumsily under the table with his heavy steel-tipped boots. 'Look at him! No better than a fuckin' animal! Come out of there, mawkin!'

But Stevie stayed where he was. 'See? He knows what I'm like. I'm a juggler man. Isn't that right, Stevie? I goes straight for the juggler. Eh? I'm the only one who can handle him.'

Stevie peered out, grinning. Mick leaned on the edge of the table, claiming him. 'Old Stevie! You know his trouble – squirrel loose in the upper branches. Never been any different.'

There was a thump in the chimney and a fall of shiny black clinker.

'Going well now, Hughie.'

'That sounded like the back boiler.'

'Don't worry, you're keeping warm, aren't you? Got to keep warm. Don't want that dicky ticker packing up.'

'Dicky Ticker,' said Stevie.

'Yeah! That's good, isn't it? Like it. All right, so Dicky Ticker's been to the shop. What's in the bag, Dicky Ticker?'

Hughie peered into the bag. 'Just . . . my rations.'

'Come on, let's have a look.'

Hughie placed the items on the table. Tea. Bread. Tin of milk. Cheese slices. A paper.

'That it? You battled all the way up to the shop for that? I wants a bit more than that. Come on – where's the bottle of Scotch?'

'Not a chance, son. Not on my penny-pinching pension.'

'I'm not your son – I'm not anybody's son! I'm Mick. And you're Dick.' His lip curled around the word. 'So, you got any drink here? In this little Dicky house?'

'No.'

'Sure?'

'I expect you've had a look.'

'Stevie said I could have a look round, sess up the place . . . didn't you, Stevie?'

'Well, yes.'

'And I tell you what, it's not very nice. In fact it's fuckin' grimsome. You been missing the bowl, Hughie. And you don't open the curtains. No wonder there's toadstools growing out of the wall. And all the junk. What a state. All those photos up there. Photos of dead people. I bet you know a lot of dead people. And they're all waiting for you to pop off, too.'

'You've had my photos out.'

Kelso. Builth Wells. Pitlochry. The few precious scraps of his life.

'I was only looking. That's what they're for, isn't it?

But who wants to look at a load of old sheep-shaggers at a county show? I don't rate that – useless occupation for a man. Eh? I thought I might find some glossy stuff. You know, bits of fluff. Tucked away. And I know you got the booze stashed somewhere, Dicky-boy, I can smell it. I'm not daft. Perhaps we can have it later, eh?'

Or not. Hughie was aware of the fact, and it hurt him, that if the boys took it into their heads to turn the house upside-down he could not stop them. He wouldn't try. They wouldn't find anything.

'I bet you've got a twelve-bore in the house, too.'

'No.'

'I remember you had one.'

'That was then. I handed it in. Belonged to the estate.'

'H'm . . . in that case . . . I know! Let's make some toast!'

'Toast! Toast!'

Suddenly Mick and Stevie were capering around the kitchen, wildly. Their big boots squashed the cans underfoot as they rummaged in cupboards and pulled open drawers.

'Find me a toasting fork!' shouted Mick. 'I'm having the toasting fork because I'm the Devil. Hughie – Dicky, I mean – I'm going to make you some toast!'

'If you say so.'

'Yes, I do say so. I'm toastmaster. Sit down. Now then, Stevie, give me that toasting fork.'

It was a carving fork, but it was fine. The only problem was that Mick didn't know how to brown a slice of bread.

'Come on. Toast, you bastard!'

The bread was thin, and white, and charred in seconds. Soon most of it was on the floor, blackened to a crisp, but a few slices were deemed edible. 'Butter! Where's the butter?'

'There isn't any.'

'All right. Cheese then.'

The boys made do with fire-damaged cheese sand-wiches. They devoured them savagely, stuffing their mouths, washing it down with the tinned milk. Hughie declined. He watched them falling on the few crumbs he had without the slightest inclination to partake. Any hunger he may have felt was nothing to this.

Mick drove the carving fork into the table. 'That was fuckin' horrible! I'm starving now. You want to get some proper food in this place. No wonder you been scouring everywhere. Dirty Dick!'

It was getting dark. Now Mick started piling wood into the stove. 'Let's rattle it up! It needs more wood already. Stevie, go and look for some more wood. Come on, puzzle-head! Get the wood!'

When Stevie was gone Mick approached Hughie and grabbed his coat. His leering, triumphant face came very close.

'Money.'

'Eh.'

'I said, money. You mean old bastard. Mean as spider's piss! Don't you dare hold out. Not now. I got some shopping to do, too, and I need a few quid. Under-stand me?'

'But . . . I've nothing.'

'Don't give me that crap-trap! You can't hold on to it now. Why d'you think I came here? And if it's not on you we'll give this place a good sorting. Shake it down . . . have the lot. How would you like that?'

He was standing over Hughie, breathing heavily. There was a look of imminent rampage on his face, as if he might explode with rage and frustration, and yet there was also cowardice holding him in check. Hughie was shaking, couldn't help it, he was very angry and his

192

overpowering fear was that he might wet himself. There was a time . . . but that time was long past. Any man would pick this thing up by the tuft and throw him out. He was nothing, why should he have anything? Destined to be nothing and yet determined that he should get something. And he, Hughie, had nothing to give him.

'Well?'

Outside there were sounds of a car stopping, and doors slamming. It was the people from the council.

'Stevie!' Mick pushed Hughie away and ran to the door.

Hughie sat very still in the kitchen. Everything was quiet in the house. He heard a movement in the garden, a light flickered briefly against the window. But nobody came. He got up and looked into the darkness. He could see the car – it was across the road. They were not coming at all. He went to the door and bolted up. When he had done so it occurred to him that the two boys might still be inside, locked in now, maybe hiding upstairs. He stood in the dark, listening.

There. Whispering voices, very low.

A soft conversation. They were his voices, familiar. But now inside the house. Inside voices. The same interference, insistent, they had gained access while the door had stood open, they were telling him so; in a whispering lamentation that seemed to come from the bones of the house itself. A groaning like pain, that was in the creaking joints, the rumbling chimney breast, the shifting, expanding body of the house. Drying out slowly and complainingly as the warm heart began to pump out the heat again. He heard the voices but now they were with him, in here, he had nothing to fear from them. No static. No scrutiny.

When he was sure that there was nobody there he

went upstairs to the toilet. Fingering his way through the usual dark places, he raised the heavy lid of the cistern just enough to take out an unopened bottle of whisky. Then he went into his bedroom, closing the door on the soft counterpoint of voices rising through the house, and put on the light. It was his only light now.

He collected up the scattered photos and put them on the bed. Some of them went back a long way, like he did. He would sort through them – there was a box somewhere, what had they done with the box . . . That was it! He'd go through them all, find himself again. As he was. He could do that, couldn't he? He'd had enough interference for one day.

COTTAGE FIRE: BODY IS FOUND

The body of a man has been found in the burned-out remains of a cottage.

The house near Nailsworth was almost totally destroyed when it was engulfed in flames this morning.

All the emergency services were called to the blaze at Pound Cottage in Endcombe, when the alarm was raised at 3 a.m.

The house in Straight Lane was well ablaze but firemen quickly brought it under control, said a police spokesman.

'The body of a man was found,' said Inspector Neil Robb.

A Home Office pathologist was due to visit the scene today.

Stroud News and Journal, 13/1/90

METROPOLITAN LOVE

Kate Lincoln

Kate Lincoln was born and raised in the north-west of England. After graduating in Economics from the LSE, she embarked on a publishing career but gave it up after fifteen months. She then spent the next few years writing, travelling and working at a variety of part-time jobs. Four years ago she returned to full-time education to study law and will qualify as a solicitor in 1994. She has lived in London for the past twelve years.

METROPOLITAN LOVE

Watch the clock from the corner of my eye, OH GOD, TIME PASS MORE QUICKLY, *PLEASE*. Push back my chair (a fraction too impatiently), stand up and pick up stuff – paper – all colours, all varying degrees of relevance, and drag open a large cabinet drawer. Start filing, quickly, looks busy, looks like I'm trying to order myself, at this time of night. Impressive, eh? Slam shut the drawer, whisk back into my chair, swivel it to the left to retrieve time cards from the dark chaotic recesses of my desk. Check my watch – five twenty-five, okay, take it slow now, don't want to leave too soon, five fortyish looks all right, I reckon, most days, unless I've got a really hot date, in which case it's on the dot – no messing. Then occasionally I'll stay till about ten to, to show willing, and that given the necessary work load, of course I'd be only too happy to stay! Grab a pencil, start jabbing computer cards with a series of scruffy lead dots. In my haste (albeit superficially leisurely) keep making mistakes, try not to curse beneath my breath, sneak a look at my 'partner', who's engrossed in wads of paper, another at my watch – five thirty, okay, step it up a little, jab faster.

Problem is, you see, I've become embroiled in an actual career, training to be an Officer of the English Supreme Court, no less, and it's proving to be a bit of an effort – making the transition, that is, from motiveless and mindless automaton who's *expected* to jump for joy at the donging of the reception clock (and if not, to be quite frank here – why not? Some kind of unpleasant social inadequacy lurking?), to bright and enthusiastic firm member, who's eager to learn and earnestly dedicated to the cause, who's driven relentlessly from within and constantly aspiring for the heights of professional excellence. And to be perfectly honest, some days my offering of effort is pretty paltry.

Calculator out – add up my time for the day – three hours and eighteen minutes. Jesus, I don't believe it, I've not stopped since nine thirty. What in God's name have I been *doing*? Oh yes – stick a chunk of 'unspecified' down on 'The Ainsworth Estate – Tax General' and a couple of extra Ts for telephone on 'Col. Arthur Williamson-Hewitt – Dec'd.' Four forty-two, bit better, oh sod it, it'll have to do. Drag out the Kalamazoo, more paper, more filing, more recording of time for 'the file'. Scratch illegible references on blue carbon zig zags, pile them up beside me. Arrange my desk paraphernalia in rows and stacks, aesthetically pleasing, in shapes square and rectangular, at mutual right angles, corners just in from desk edge. It's required of me by my 'partner', who likes to be neat, and I like to please – oh boy, do I like to please.

'Right,' – say it loud, so he knows I'm off, at an appropriate time, that I've completed all that needed to be, that a natural hiatus has occurred, as my 'right' denotes.

'You off then?' Quick glance, no questioning expression, just a sleepy-eyed look and half smile.

'Yes, I'll see you in the morning.' Answer brightly back, can't afford any show of sluggishness at this stage in the game. Coat on, out the door, down the stairs and slink out into a black back passageway.

Out into the square, dark now, streaked yellow from

office windows. Peer in as I pass, plush decor, smart fittings, eager beavers illumined by lamp light. Evening meetings, consultations, lone graft in file-filled basements. Breathe in the cool night air, glance briefly at silhouetted passers-by. All is hushed, no traffic here ever, no couriers permitted and no heavy goods. Legal sanctum.

Holborn Tube, in the crush. Weave speedily to the escalator down. Stand on the right, no movement, gives me time to organize myself. Time management is the absolute key. Pass in pocket, gloves likewise, purse zipped neatly away; Walkman out, wired up, *Law Weekly* got ready to hand. Perfect – hit the bottom, overtake on the inside, not quite acceptable but who gives a damn? Bottleneck brewing. Corridors and stairs, homeless busker wailing his heart out. Never give money, not on the journey home, would waste valuable minutes. Northbound platform – seething, no train in yet, grab a left. Stride purposefully up the platform adjacent. Empty, always is, some odd kind of route to nowhere special. Gets me to where I want to be more effectively. Check at odd intervals, through linking walkways, that my train hasn't sneakily arrived. Just make it, to the far end, as it whirrs hesitantly into the glare. Zip back to routes north, keep my head down, burrow on and in. Doors crash shut. There's just enough room to flick out *Law Weekly*, and just enough time to consume a column or two – 'Criminal – Autrefois Convict', 'Wills – The Whereabouts', 'Leasehold – Advice Body Mooted'. Read and digested instantly! King's Cross – disembark, at precisely the right spot, whizz into action. Two escalators down, two corridors and another flight of stairs. More weaving, a bit of dodging, the odd shove if it's ever deserved. Platform three – jam-packed. Can I make it to just beneath the indicator before one minute lapses? Edgware it says – one minute. Whisk along the edge, keep my eyes peeled for nutters, who might just decide to knock me over it. Arrive just in time. Check my watch – six ten, making good time. Should be home for six thirty, at the outside, which gives me precisely an hour and twenty minutes, then out again before eight, to be there for eight thirty, provided, that is, the Central Line's running again. Security alert this morning at Bank, no trains, commuters stranded for hours between Oxford Street and Marble Arch. In the filth, with each other. Skim 'Company – Manx Style', take in a word or two, then am spewed off at Hampstead, and lurch up a shaft to the High Street.

Got a date with a mate in the Belsize Tavern. Haven't met for months, in fact it's probably a year. Not an ideal situation. Requires effort and intelligent conversation. About what she's doing, where, how, who with, and after a few, maybe, and more importantly, why? Then on to me. Can I really be bothered to discuss it, again? Let's think, what am I prepared to disclose, discuss and confess? Anything interesting? Well, maybe, depends on how the evening grabs me, how the ambience effects me, how the company does or doesn't inspire me. It's a woman, so no lies, women don't like to be told lies. Mainly by men, as it's men that concern them the most, but by women just the same. They look at you strangely, eyes kind of distant, and say things like 'I see,' and drift away. Whereas men can't even tell the difference, between deceit and honesty, naivety and manipulation, cunning and wide-eyed innocence. Poor buggers, who'd be a man, and have to put up with women?

Meet in the lounge, it's pretty busy, kind of buzzing, but not really alive. Studied, slightly intense, kind of jovial in a Tuesday night kind of way. The middle classes, out drinking. Couples, same sex, conversing vigorously, about the whys, buts and wherefores of their exhausting and angst-ridden lives. Women – the job, the *career*, the flat, public transport, MEN. Men – the match, the beer, work, public transport – tentatively, women. Spot Elaine in a corner with two halves. Rush over.

'Hi, hi, how are you, how are you, good to see you, did you find it alright, I've got lager, is that okay, I couldn't remember what you drank, it's fine, what is it, Skol, yeah that's great, (*Jesus Christ*), sorry I'm a bit late, had to wait EIGHTEEN MINUTES for the tube, couldn't believe it, oh I know, they've been dreadful all week, was stuck on the Circle Line for AN HOUR on Monday, signalling problems, don't tell me about it, I was on time once last week, been working late to catch up, it's too bad, as if I haven't got enough on my plate' garble ... garble ... spout ... spout ...

'Fancy another?' Manage an escape, to the bar, a cheery and superficial nod at the barman, young lad, long hair, pretty, sweet-looking, look again, smile, smiles back, feel lighter, return laden with pints of Tennants Extra. Reluctantly retake my seat in the corner, was somehow manoeuvred there against my better judgement, smile brightly, sup slow, await the bombardment. 'Oh, and this afternoon, at FIVE TWENTY, I was called to con. with counsel.' Nearly choke on my beer – con., what's this – trendy lawspeak? 'As if Rory couldn't have attended, I'm not even supposed to be in lit., what on earth Daryl Hawkinson thinks he's doing dragging me out of a departmental up-date I don't know, as if I haven't got enough on my plate ... '

There's a guy by the bar, good-looking, keeps looking, I'm sure, at who, I wonder. Need to check it out.

'Elaine, I'm just going to pop to the loo.'

'Yeah, okay.'

Squeeze out, from my prison, breathe in, in case he's looking, and witnesses clumsy fumblings. Sidle past, don't look, till I've reached him, then glance up. He looks back. It's quick, but obvious, I'm sure. Pass on and try not to smile. He's nice, very nice. Waltz into the ladies, smirk broadly at myself in the mirror. Brush my hair, re-apply eyeliner, lip gloss, re-emerge into the glare. He's there, his back to me, should I risk a brush? No, definitely not, he's too nice to risk a harlot's brush against, don't want to give the wrong impression, too soon, if at all. Decorum, I believe, is the appropriate theme for this evening.

Ease back to my dark and obscure dug-out, having totally ignored him en route. Reseat myself, and just manage a decorous and kind of shy and sweet, but obviously interested, although decorously so, glance at his beautiful face, before being confronted. He's looking, plunge my Tennants, and try to look interested in that which confronts me – verbally, visually and over-whelmingly.

'. . . Honestly, I just COULDN'T BELIEVE IT, I don't think I'll ever trust him again, but people just don't behave like that, do they? Especially in that type of company. I was so disappointed, but the damage has been done, and there's no going back on it now, abso-lutely not a chance . . . ' Chunter on and on . . .

It's eleven fifteen, the pub is slowly emptying, Elaine still hasn't finished her Skol (the Tennants disagreed with her somewhat), I regard it pointedly, she takes the hint, although subconsciously, and drinks. It gives me a precious moment to breathe, to survey. He's still there, I catch his eye, he sees but without seeing. His glance passes on. The moment has gone. I'm disappointed and pretty irritated. These things need nurturing, careful attention and care, gentle handling and sensitivity. In an evening, in the pub, over three or four pints of beer, there are a certain number of overtures to be made, e.g., surreptitious glances which just happen to be mutual, and the more there are of them, the more blatant, until, very possibly, a smirk may be shared, or alternatively an open sunny smile (depending, of course, very much on the nature of the relationship being contemplated here), so that by the end of the evening, the scene has been set, for a possible verbal exchange, and with any luck, a written one too – e.g., fag packet scrawled with illegible telephone number. But this kind of thing takes time, and as any woman worth her salt will know, reject a good-looking man once, and you've had it. I'd rejected, by showing insufficient interest, through being cornered and fixed eye-to-eye by Elaine.

I bade her farewell. 'It's been lovely, it's really nice to see you again, we must meet again, yeah, we mustn't leave it so long, I've really enjoyed myself, it's good to have a chat, yeah – a real girlie chat, without the men around, ha-ha, so you've got my work number, give me a call, yeah, I'll give you a call next week, we'll sort something out, great, okay, see you soon then, yeah, see you, Elaine.' And felt totally pissed off all the way home.

Wednesday – mid-week. Monday and Tuesday scraped through, just about. On the home straight, or am I? Well, not quite, let's admit it, which is why Wednesday is a bit of a watershed, dividing misery and joyous anticipation, of freedom and things to come. A kind of limbo, with no set pattern, except mood swings and feelings of instability. How does one feel, with two and a half days behind one, yet two and a half to come? Exactly!

Shove on a Wednesday tape – aggressively cheerful and loud, and feel good when I can walk in time to the music across the Inn. Stride purposefully, cheerily, short-sightedly and obliviously, of all that's around me. Dream I am elsewhere, and there, dream I am everywhere. Dream I am all things to all men. Exhilaration.

Dump stuff in a drawer, get a call from a guy who's been hassling me for two weeks, for some stuff, on something. Knot my brow, try to answer, intelligently. Grab a coffee, and a file, and a thick tome called *Hacksaw on Rating*, and open up. Only four hundred pages to wade through in order to confirm what I already know. Called a guy I know, in the business, solved my problem in two seconds flat. But who's 'Arry in 'Ammersmith when there's *Hacksaw on Rating*? 'And your authority for this research, Miss Seeming?' Skim a page or two, then a chapter, another, have digested half the book. Found nothing, skim the index – nothing looks remotely hopeful. Feel stupid and insecure.

Return to chapter one, dismally, painstakingly consume the text, word for word. I've missed something, obviously, something obvious, hidden between words I can't read. Slurp a mouthful of tepid decaff, rearrange the lining of my skirt, that's ridden uncomfortably up, focus for the third time on the opening remarks on 'Liability', *see a beautiful face, and black hair, feel hands on my body, lips on mine*, slurp more, rearrange my anglepoise, so it's perfect, so the beam is ideal for me to deal with the words before me ... Try 'Rating Revisited' on page 354, but there's more, chapter twenty is entitled 'Revisit the Revisit – RATES – The Final Analysis'. Develop a weird kind of headache, take a pill, and another, and the rest of the decaff, pills get stuck in my throat, try to swallow saliva, doesn't work too effectively, try the initial 'Revisit' which I initially revisited the day before, *feel flesh against me, pressing hard, a rough caress, hot sweet breath* ...

'Miss Seeming, I believe Sir John is quite keen to

complete on his purchase of Daleby Woodlands and the Manor House tomorrow. Is everything ready on that?'

Did somebody speak? Peer out from Hacksaw and lust.

'Daleby Manor?'

'Oh yes, of course, I think so, I'll check and get back to you shall I?'

'If you would, preferably by twelve thirty. I've a meeting at one with the accountant. If you could have the draft financial statement ready that would be an enormous help, and the necessary for transferring the money from the appropriate trust funds, details of which *should* be on the file, ha-ha. If they're not I'm sure you can sort it out, and not forgetting, of course, to arrange for the relevant parties to all be on site at ten thirty to complete. Presumably you've already checked that the trustees can be there?' Piercing blue eyes, checking, enquiring, vaguely suspicious.

'Yes, of course.' Smile brightly, ooze reassurance and calm, to ward him off. 'I'll check it right now.'

'If you would.' He hesitates, not sure, so I conclude with a – 'Right then,' and smile worthy of the Goddess Capability herself, and he's gone, albeit reluctantly. Hold my head in my hands – really hurts, veins pulse beneath my fingertips. Blame it on the Tennants Extra.

It's eight-thirty. I'm down the Camden Lock, in a seedy bar, smoking roll-ups because it's cool, and kind of common, and off-beat, and not what an Officer of the English Supreme Court should be doing on a Wednesday night when there's The Law to study, especially when she's draped about some Turk she met in a club in an Islington basement. Rifat and me stand close, and drink Pils out of bottles and lie. To begin with we try to talk, you know, day-to-day conversation. Then we get in more Pils, and get closer and hotter and more deceitful. Then he leans against me, whilst I sit cross-legged at the bar, smoking and smiling deceitfully, flirtatiously, tantalizingly. Then he grabs me and kisses my neck kind of hard. I arch to him and swig more Pils.

'When?' he whispers.

'Soon,' I lie and proffer my pink-painted lips.

Later we're entwined in a black recess, drunk on alcohol and each other. His hands keep creeping to where they shouldn't, especially amidst the public at large, even though we're obscured in a recess. I grab hold of them tight and lower them, raise them, disentangle myself from their grasp, but they get stronger, more persistent. Lips press down and burn my flesh. My insides are boiling, I'm wet. I want him. I press myself into him, pull his hair and kiss him hard, then shift his hands to where they've been shifted from before, many times, teasingly, smilingly, infuriatingly. He kind of wilts, for a moment, his touch is soft and deep, then he straightens and squeezes me so hard I can't breathe. Then he eats me, and I am devoured.

On the way home he drags me up an alleyway, and envelopes me in an urgent embrace. I go with it and peer at my watch, in the gloom, at the back of his neck. It's twelve forty-five. I stiffen and withdraw. He's aghast. He doesn't speak, it's been said all before, but regards me with venom and distaste. I just shrug and want to say, 'Play time over, baby', but instead kind of smile and ease away. His black eyes follow me, all the way up the street, then shut, momentarily, and turn away. Frustration and fury linger. I'm in a black tunnel, wet, and alone. I watch my reflection in the window facing. And wonder what it is that constitutes me. I smell Rifat, and am thankful that my getaway was relatively painless.

*   *   *

206

Thursday, I feel rotten. I'm tired, with a throbbing head. I can't think and am assaulted alternately by nausea and terrible hunger pains. I cram biscuits and down liquid Resolve, then sit and gaze through a window, and imagine Rifat fucking me senseless. My partner returns from a God-given meeting, that was scheduled to last most of the day, and replants himself before me. It's one thirty. My heart plummets, my throbbings throb thunderously. I flash an apparently bright and incredibly normal 'Hi' with a smile, then embed myself in Hassle, Cruttishins and Rustle on *Wayleaves – The Bottom Line*. I don't resurface for the rest of the day, and neither do the wayleaves from the sad and murky depths way beneath the bottom line.

It's seven fifteen, I've got thirty-five minutes to make myself presentable. There are dark shadows beneath my red-streaked eyes, and my skin looks greyish and weary. I am DESPERATE. In my desperate state I recourse to a mud pack, for which, of course, there is absolutely not enough time. I wad it on in uneven wads, then dress while it starts to harden. Then sponge muddy smears off my clothes while it hardens further. Then rinse it from my face and hair and chuck on the make-up. I've five minutes to dry my hair and eat. I manage a banana and couple of 'Jaspers' whilst upturned about ferocious hot air and leave the building two and half minutes behind schedule. I have to run to the station, then miraculously arrive with time to spare. I make the most of my precious extra moments by breathing deeply to rid myself of indigestion. At last I'm aboard and seated. A young boy looks appreciatively, I relax, and prepare myself for the evening.

Thursday night is pub night. A group of us congregate to drink large quantities of lager, smoke Rothmans, Silk

Cut and roll-ups, talk rapidly about love, life and earning money, and get crushed by heaving bodies. Thursday is seething, Thursday is alive, down the Kings Head at the Angel. There's music, noise and heat, energy, vitality, camaraderie, a late licence, and, of course, MEN. And, in fact, one man in particular, around whose head shines a halo of dazzling light. I am transfixed, every Thursday, to a spot where the stage lights beam, to a spot where the energy throbs, to a spot from whence the life-force streams, to a spot where angels make music. Cascading curls of golden hair, pale face, eyes as green and deep as the ocean, lips that smile flirtatiously, delightedly, uncomplicatedly, fingers that fly. Sammy plays soul, from the soul, and croons an accompaniment whilst Frankie serenades amassed masses. Who rock to the rhythm, who dance to the beat, who praise the Lord that the angels have come to make music. Frankie and Sammy are AN EVENT, generating electricity. Our hearts and souls are theirs, for tonight, we sing in adulation.

Sammy is MY EVENT, for the night, for any night he cares to name, for every night, for ever, and ever. Our eyes meet, we gaze, he's lost in the rhapsody, I'm lost in my rhapsody at beholding the rhapsody on his beautiful face. His eyes flit away, for a second, then are back again, resting upon me. I can't acknowledge, all I can do is regard him non-committally, and hope that my passions are not too blatantly obvious. Fascination, maybe, I'll concede, but not this adoration, this adolescent infatuation, this total and all-consuming LOVE. The number draws to a close, it's getting late, quick glances between bar staff and 'entertainment', another? Is there time? The crowd stamps for more, 'MORE, MORE.' Surly nod from head barman, and the music is relaunched – 'Try a little tenderness,' we cheer, we shout, down more lager and light up another cigarette, 'Try a little tenderness, ye-ah, ye-ah . . . '

It's twelve thirty. We congregate in the freezing winter's night – 'So what time is it tomorrow? Eight, did you tell everyone eight? Yeah, eight and not to be late, good night, yeah brilliant, are you coming tomorrow? Yeah I think so, well it's eight in The Elixir. Okay, see you then, do you want a lift? No I'll be fine, I'll call a cab for you, no it's okay, you get off, I'll see you tomorrow, you sure? Yeah I'm fine. Okay, see you later, bye . . . '

I'm finally rid of all my friends, I glance around, crowd thinning, no cabs.

'Katie.'

I turn, nobody calls me Kat*ie*. He's there, beckoning to me, smiling, like an angel, all curls and halo, I waltz over. 'You enjoy it? Yeah, brilliant, yeah? Yeah, it was really good, well I'm pleased about that then.' His eyes delve into mine, momentarily, then he laughs, looks around and requestions me – 'Where are your friends? They've gone. Oh right.' We avoid looking at each other and instead regard the work in progress on the kerb there, i.e., his 'entourage' packing the van. 'You coming or what then, Sammy?' Our eyes meet, we smile, hesitate, and don't move. 'Come on.' There's a woman getting impatient. 'If you want a lift get in.' I touch him lightly on the sleeve of his battered leather jacket. 'Looks like you've been told.' He turns to me, 'Yeah,' and laughs again. 'Sammy, hurry up.' He hails me a cab, instantly there's a black one there, an arm enfolds me. 'Good to see you, Katie,' and a kiss planted firmly upon my lips – so warm, so soft, I can smell him – 'See you later, yeah, bye.' I dart across the street, then turn back, he's waving, a carful beside him is waiting. We smile, a last gaze – happy hesitant, lingering, then the cabbie lowers his window. 'Where to, love? Hampstead, please.' I jump in, we roar off and my butterfly is lost to the night.

One fifteen, I'm in front of the fire and TV, cramming clementines and swigging liberally Highland Spring, I calculate I'll be asleep, with any luck, by one forty-five, which gives me a maximum of five and three-quarter hours, it's not enough, but I don't care, with Sammy's kiss still warm upon me. I wash quickly, deposit clothes with abandon, jewellery ready for the morning. It's one thirty, I'm in bed, I've made it.

When Sammy has kissed me, it's with me all day, like the bird of paradise hovering. I'm dreamy, relaxed, evanescent, in heaven with the angels. I gaze a lot into a hazy middle distance, and fantasize extravagantly about me and Sammy. Nothing sordid, of course, or lustful, God forbid, but thoughts spiritual, pure and sublime. The Law comes as a bit of rude awakening when one's elevated to such a state. It's eleven thirty. *Hacksaw on Rating* has revisited my desk, and is trying very hard to find brain space. But there's not much to spare, I can tell you, what with love, lust and carnal pleasures, taking far more than their regular fair share. Strange words and odd phrases, like 'estoppel' and 'uniform business rate' occasionally surface but are then instantly devoured by a veritable vortex of exotic emotion. I take an early lunch, and a detour to the pub, down an alley and past La Traviata. Renato is in the window, he sees me, I smile and wave, he smiles back and I'm immediately weak. Renato I would do ANYTHING for. He's tall and dark and sexy, and plunges me without fail into a cesspit of priapic desire. We generally wave a couple of times a week, it keeps my blood just simmering. Debbie and I grab a corner, and as it's Friday, rebel and down quickly a couple of halves, and masticate rapidly whilst we gas about the miseries of working for men, being their minions and 'entertainment'. Friday p.m. I waft about the office, being generally elusive and if questioned irritatingly evasive. The hours drag by INTERMINABLY. I am BESET by boredom, cravings for chocolate and sweets, visions of Sammy and me snogging chastely beneath a low pale moon, and dark Renato corrupting my soul. At five thirty I grab out my time sheet, and regard it gloomily, then lie recklessly and chuck it defiantly into my tray. It's Friday and five thirty, and I JUST DON'T GIVE A DAMN.

Six ten, supermarket — bread, water, fruit, tobacco, something cold and pre-prepared to eat instantly without fuss or minutes wasted, bank — cash, newsagent — milk (forgotten at the Eight 'til Twelve-Thirty), home. Stick on some music, loud, stick on the telly to watch pictures whilst I consume my pre-prepared fish, stick whisky on ice to down whilst I bathe and dress, stick on eyelashes and perfume liberally. Ease on down to the West End. Black Lycra leggings, tight, long boots, black leather jacket, sooty black eyes, glowing green, cash in pocket, wiliness to the fore, heart hidden and out of reach. Chew gum, because it's common, and keeps me moving, rapidly, because it's Friday night and I can be ME for two whole days; or rather a common exaggeration of me, to counteract the civilized me, the polite, diplomatic and oh so tolerant me that just about manages to stay intact for five of the week's seven days. Five whole days. How do we do it? *Why* do we do it? Meet in a bar in Soho, busy, high turnover of a manic crowd, talking, laughing, quickly grab stools as a group move out, order shorts, barman's furious and glares — order's not instant, 'and . . . ' Can't remember, chuck in a vodka, 'Haven't got all fucking day, lady.' 'Well, why don't you just fuck off?' Drink, laugh loudly at barman's abuse, discuss who's due, and where, move on.

It's twelve fifteen, we're outside the Barcelona, there's a queue, half way down the street, agree to bribe the doorman, offer ten quid, it's a deal, we're in. Music's loud, so loud it pounds inside me — lambada, salsa, soul.

Am grabbed as I trip the floor — 'Hey, wanna dance?' Question's apparently rhetorical, am gripped tight and spun, garlic, sweat, oiled hair, black eyes and swaying hips. 'You move pretty good, wanna drink?' Question's apparently rhetorical, am steered towards the bar, 'Scotch on the rocks, and for the lady . . . ' he surveys me, up and down, slowly, and smirks, then orders rum and coke.

I'm speechless, aghast, and turned on, fight it, take my drink, casually peruse the scene.

'Hey, you wan' another dance?'

Regard the guy reluctantly, looks Greek, lean physique, black vest revealing smooth brown flesh, 'I'm with some friends.' Return my attention to the crowd, appear cool, indifferent.

'You don't wanna dance with me then?' Body closer, lips smiling and moist.

'Well,' I start to smile, he's up against me, arm draped about my shoulders, 'tell me,' mock serious expression, ear offered for an explanation. 'It's just that I came here with my friends.'

'You wanna go back to your friends?' His bare flesh is soft against mine, his eyes probing, sensual and deep. 'I think I should.'

There's a pause, time offered to change my mind, then a smile, 'Okay,' and an extrication of limbs. 'You wanna give me your number? You wanna go out next week just you and me? Yeah, okay. You like me then?' We laugh. 'Yeah. Oh good.' Pen extracted from barman, beer mat scrawled with 'Chris – 593 0627/5' in return. 'Okay, we'll go out next week, have a real good time,' wink and sexy smirk. 'You sure you don't wanna lambada?' Pose struck, eyes laughing, 'Maybe later.' 'Okay, later.' Quick kiss, eyes upon me, then he's gone. Thank God.

Search the scene, make tracks, find my gang drinking Sol in a corner. Talk's of sex and alienation. Enter the verbal fray, down Scotch and sway to the beat. One or two forays to the floor, then it's time, to stalk my prey. 'Wanna dance?' 'Yeah, okay.'

A friend of a friend has captured my attention, and it's my intention to occupy myself thus tonight. He's mature and terribly civilized. We smile, sweetly, coolly, indifferently, oh so Englishly, no undertones lurking here, of lust or sensuality. We approach the floor. 'You like this music?' 'Yeah, it's fine.'

We dance, to the rhythm, apart, independently, occasionally make a little small talk – the place, the clientele, I dance a little closer, no response, then the beat turns to salsa, I take hold of him. We're pressed close, by the music, other bodies, the heat. 'Come on then, do something!' We dance on, the music gets louder, the pace quicker, the heat more intense, our bodies move evenly, in time. I'm impatient, my mind awash with sweet alcoholic nectar. I reach up, and press my lips against his. Suddenly he grabs me, oh sweet Jesus, fingers grip and bruise, it ends, I stagger, he gathers me up again, I'm reeling, it goes on and on, mouth hard, desire shot through me. It's over, we're back in our corner, swigging Sol and talking clubs, with the gang, as if it hasn't happened. Our eyes don't meet, but we're close.

Later, we're at the Bar Italia, drinking coffee with trendies and heavy-duty mafiosi. There's four of us talking literature; I want him on my own. It's four thirty, the conversation draws to a close, we split, two pairs, and plunge separate and secret nights. His good-bye kiss is chaste and sweet. 'I'll see *you* later,' he whispers. Then my mate and I grab a cab, some fags and a doner kebab, and chatter garbage till dawn. She leaves as the birds start singing.

Saturday, three-thirty, I'm down the gym, pumping iron to Miami funk, sweating toxins, shedding pounds, expurgating my soul.

Nine thirty, I'm in a bar, somewhere in Wardour Street, inhaling toxins, ingurgitating poisoned nectar. I feel good, the scene is cool. Eleven forty-five, I'm cruising south, with this guy in his Mercedes Benz. Got grass and Southern Comfort. Feel better, the scene is serene. Hit the casino, it's 1 a.m., got coke and cash, chuck a wad on number twenty-five, lose, chuck another, lose again, take a trip to the ladies, and another, to paradise. Emerge, feel high and kind of edgy. Grab my guy, feeling sort of hot. Spin again, make a killing, rake it in. Leave quickly and sashay on down to some club in a Knightsbridge basement. Drink vodka, forget to eat, dance slow to real slow beat, up close, feeling's heady.

Four a.m., I'm stretched out, upon a sea of ivory satin. Wet fingers search me, wet lips traverse me, wet desire corrupts my soul. I am taken by the devil, and defiled.

Sunday, I lie very still and try not to breathe. Soft flesh beside me sleeps deeply. My mind skips frantically: faces, conversations, events, all are merged and details blur. I drift off and plunge abstraction. At noon I am woken, for croissant and cappuccino. I eat and soft arms embrace me. Later I am transported, to greenery, and walked, accompanied by love and dulcet tones. Later still I am seated, for late lunch and heavy red wine. The afternoon is spent lazily entwined. Evening – Alessandro and I dine out, on sole and potent Rioja. We talk about life. At midnight he touches me, gently, whispers love then takes me slowly. I submit in ecstasy and with relief. In his brief sleep Alessandro says he loves me, and warns me against infidelity and deceit. Then rises in the dark and whispers, 'I love you,' and 'just one more week, my darling, one more week.'

He thinks his threats and entreaties keep me faithful. That his part-time love is enough, and only he can satisfy the desire he inspires in me. Alessandro has misplaced faith, that when he leaves me I don't partake of the feast that is the city.

Sunday night I sweat guilt and Monday morning I wash it away.

HOOKS

Clare Stephens Girvan

Clare Girvan lives in one of Birmingham's leafier suburbs with her journalist husband and four cats. She has been a member of local writers' groups since 1982, and has written numerous poems and short stories. This is her first successful outside venture. At present she teaches in a primary school, but is planning early retirement so that she can get on with her proposed novel and collection of modern fairy stories.

HOOKS

'Market? You?' Clifford looked up from carefully slicing the top off his boiled egg. 'You never go to markets.'

'Well, I just thought I would.' Mrs Handyside pushed the toast rack towards him. 'It looked rather fun.'

'Not the word I would have chosen. What do you want to buy, anyway?'

'Nothing, really. I just feel like going. I'll see when I get there.'

'I don't know why you want to go. What's wrong with Hannaford's?'

'Nothing's wrong with Hannaford's.' She bit down the rising irritation. Other men, she had heard, muttered over newspapers at breakfast and you couldn't get a civil word out of them. Not so Clifford. Alert from the moment he swung his feet out of bed, the slightest remark was likely to bring forth a torrent of questions and useful advice. Once, she had admired him for it – 'Clifford always takes such an interest' – but there were times nowadays when she wanted to scream that he wasn't in court now, she wasn't some brainless witness, and for God's sake stop hectoring her. Such moments alarmed her. He meant well, and it wouldn't do to become shrewish or a nag.

Clifford saw himself as an indulgent husband, understanding of wifely whims. He smiled nicely and picked up his jacket.

'Well, I should get there early if I were you. It's bound

to get crowded later on. But don't say I didn't warn you.'

He was right, of course. It was indeed terribly crowded. Around her, harsh West Indian ladies pushed each other and crammed their baskets with snappers and salt fish, all knowing exactly what they wanted and cheeking the stallholders. Three hours ago she had felt like Sir Henry Morton Stanley. Now she felt more like Captain Scott.

The whole idea was obviously a mistake. It was all so different from the mouthwateringly vivid markets on the cookery programme last night. They hadn't mentioned the smell, for instance, a rank smell of hundreds of dead fish. Nor was she prepared for the sight of the casual youth behind the counter shoving a knife into their bellies and scraping the guts into a plastic bucket. Or all the chicken parts, legs, breasts and wings, dismembered and neatly rearranged in rows, with necks and livers in separate compartments, blatant as an abattoir.

'Come on, girls! Five lovely breasts a pound! Pick where you like!'

A tray of something pale and raw was thrust in front of her. She backed away nervously.

'Just looking, thank you.'

Markets, like jumble sales, were not things she normally went to. They were not orderly. At home, you bought meat from a butcher, fruit from a greengrocer, cotton from a haberdasher and so on, and the shopkeepers would know you by name and even deliver to your house. That was the way her mother had always done it. It was the best way, and for over twenty years, Mrs Handyside had virtuously done the same.

Until today. This was what came of believing what you saw on TV. It had been breathtaking; smiling,

cheery barrowboys behind munificent piles of aubergines, lemons, oranges, apples, peppers and tomatoes,
banks of cauliflowers and cabbages, spillages of potatoes
and parsnips, bouquets of parsley, buckets of coriander,
rafts of strange fish, cradled in whole shingles of ice.
And such sumptuous colours – reds, oranges, purples,
yellows, olives, emeralds, pinks, whites and golds; the
camera plunged intemperately back and forth, grimy
hands held out huge, voluptuous melons, coins chinked,
customers purchased and were happy.

And then, as if that were not enough, there were the
cooks, chopping, snipping, stirring and shredding kal-
eidoscopes of vegetables and meat into enormous pans
that steamed and sizzled until you could almost smell
them. They tipped in spices and pale liquids and presented exquisitely arranged little platefuls with satisfied
smiles, as well they might. They were masterly.

Mrs Handyside was careful of her figure and it had
been too late in the evening for another meal, but she
made herself a marmalade sandwich and tore ravenously
into it in the kitchen. She had been greatly impressed.

Perhaps she could buy some prawns. Clifford liked
prawns. Unsure, she wandered to the next stall. They
were all so bountiful; how should she choose? She joined
a queue, rested her hands on the counter bar and looked.
Such lovely names – red mullet, silver hake, freshwater
bream, parrotfish. Whatever would Clifford say if she
served him parrotfish? In front of her a woman was
buying mullet, dozens of them, it seemed, slung into a
glowing heap on the scale pan. How did you cook mullet, Mrs Handyside wondered idly, and why so many?

Silver hake, now, that was a possibility. When she
was a child there had been hake, steamed and nasty in
a green-spotted sauce with boiled potatoes, served on
white plates on a white cloth and big trouble to follow

if you didn't eat it. She had avoided it for years as a consequence, and with faint deep-seated memories of utter blandness, became expert at characterful fish of colour; rainbow trout, salmon, scallops and Mr Hannaford's langoustines. Silver hake sounded so beautiful. She had recipes, hundreds of them. She could surely improve on steamed fish in a blot of gluey sauce. Maybe delicately grilled with butter and lemon, or a light mousse Hollandaise? She was good at Hollandaise.

'Yes, love?' The voice shook her abruptly.

'Oh, er, a pound of silver hake, please,' she said triumphantly.

'Want it cut up?'

'Cut? Oh, I think so, please, yes.'

For a moment, she regretted it. Clifford didn't like white fish very much. She should have got prawns after all.

'One pound twenty, love, ta.'

Well, it was done now. Initiated into the sisterhood, Mrs Handyside straightened up a little. It was easy. Inspired, she found more places to buy things; there were fabrics, shoes, hats, Indian rugs, kitchenware, sweets – you could get anything you wanted here. Why had nobody ever told her? And everything was really quite inexpensive, too. She bought modestly, some hooks for the new bedroom door, a bundle of socks for Clifford, a coleus in a pot, a few yards of material to make something, half a dozen tiny ribbon roses for her nightdress. Prepared for battle, she said, 'Excuse *me*,' to a woman who was about to usurp her place in the queue and was pleasantly surprised when the woman meekly backed away.

A handwritten sign caught her eye. 'Ladie's Lignerie. Brief's 3 pairs £2. French £3.'

'Go on, give the old man a treat.'

'I'm sorry?' Mrs Handyside blinked with shock.

'Not you, love, I was talking to me friend.'

The woman behind the counter grinned, revealing a missing tooth, and held a shiny black garment to her waist.

'Nice, aren't they? Three quid, four for ten. Tell you what, Deb,' she leaned forward, wrinkling her eyes confidentially, 'I've got some on meself, and they're a lovely fit. Ever so comfy. You'd hardly know you'd got them on.' She waggled her hips suggestively and winked at Mrs Handyside.

'Doesn't seem much point, then, does there?' remarked the friend.

Mrs Handyside joined in the laugh politely, and her hand strayed out towards the rows of coloured satins. They were certainly very pretty, with little lace edgings and inserts and tiny loops of flowers, especially the black – but no, Clifford would think she had gone mad; French knickers, of all things, at her age.

The plain ones looked excellent value for money. She would get some of those and then go home and have some lunch.

She sang softly around the kitchen as she cooked herself an omelette. This afternoon she would sew the little roses onto her nightdress. The new socks were laid out in Clifford's drawer, the plant was on the window ledge, everything was neatly put away. Except for – she stroked her hips experimentally. The market lady was right – you could hardly tell you had them on.

They were very silly, of course, and she had been a fool to buy them. And yet – they did seem to make her legs look a bit longer, and the strange, airy glide of the satin was giving her a not entirely disagreeable sense of – exposure. Well, she would wear them for a while, then put them away before Clifford saw them. He seemed to like that sort of thing on other women, but she was not that type.

She took her omelette outside to the ornamental garden table and treated herself to a small glass of wine. The sun was high, battening the flowers down into stillness. In the greenhouse, tomatoes and cucumbers slowly grew and ripened. Clifford kept it all clipped and obedient at weekends; it was a well-behaved garden with butterflies nudging at the buddleia as they should. A cat turned and stretched itself comfortably beneath the hydrangea. It lived in the house that backed onto theirs and appeared from time to time in the Handysides' garden. It was a nice cat and Mrs Handyside would have liked to make friends with it, but Clifford always chased it away in case it dug in the flowerbeds.

Next door young Mr Garfield, ankle-deep in rough branches, sawed at the trunk of the tree that had kept out the light for years. It lay at his feet as the chainsaw sliced it like a leek. The Garfields were new; she hardly spoke to them.

But suddenly there was a break in the sawing and a silence that, too, required to be broken. She advanced slightly towards the wall.

'Good afternoon,' she called.

He paused, looked round, and saw her.

'Hi,' he said. 'Warm for it.' His hair stuck to his forehead in wet little curls, and his T-shirt was soaked under the armpits.

'Yes,' she said. She smiled, he smiled. 'I'm glad to see the tree go, really,' she went on. 'It did make our garden rather dark just there. We could never grow much. But Mrs First always liked it, so we never said anything.'

'It'll make a difference,' he agreed.

There should have been more to say; she wanted to

224

say more, something friendly. They were neighbours, after all. Bees buzzed, birds sang.

'Well,' she said.

He nodded at his sawing, they smiled, she went back in.

His industry fired her. She would do a useful thing. She would fix the hooks on the bedroom door herself. It was simple enough; you made a small hole, you put in a screw, you tightened it up, it was done. Clifford, of course, used a proper drill, which she was afraid of, but there would be something in the drawer.

She found a set of screwdrivers, a pointed thing she thought was called a gimlet, and even a pencil to mark where the holes should go, and fetched the kitchen steps. She made pencil marks, she prodded holes, she aligned the hooks, pushed a screw in and even got it started, but then everything failed her. It would not go in properly. She changed the screwdriver for a smaller one, but it was no better and the handle hurt her palm. Perhaps a larger one – but no, it didn't fit the notch, which she noticed to her dismay was now looking slightly damaged. She put a screw in the second hole and began turning. It squealed faintly and stuck. Baffled, she tried the other hook, but her eyes were filling with frustrated tears, and anger against the obstinacy of objects made her push too hard, so that the screw started to go in off-centre and would not come out.

What was wrong? Why were women not taught these necessary things? Was it perhaps something that only men knew, as if by instinct? She could make beautiful satin cushions, she could cook Beef Wellington, acknowledged by all to be difficult, but what were these insignificant skills beside the true usefulness of being able to fix one thing to another? It was somehow diminishing to be unable to manage so simple a task.

Well, she would have to leave it. But she knew how it would be. She would confess to Clifford that she had tried, but the job was faulty, admit her shame. He wouldn't mind. He would smile his nice smile, he might even congratulate her for trying, and then he would put the hooks on properly. He would be happy that she had not been able to do it.

Downstairs, Mr Garfield was nipping off small branches with an axe. He was sure-handed; he knew how to use axes and saws. He was something to do with building, she knew, having seen his van on the drive, his name in huge letters on the side. In the evenings he drilled holes in the walls and put up shelves and Clifford wanted to go round and complain about the noise. Mr Garfield was someone else who would know.

Then she, who rarely performed an unconsidered act, opened the window and called down, 'Mr Garfield, I wonder if I might ask a favour.'

She had not meant to sound so imperious, but he looked up and smiled.

'I'm having trouble putting a hook on the door.' Somehow, she balked at saying 'bedroom door'. 'Do you think you could possibly help me?'

She thought how foolish it must sound to a man so at home with all manner of building tackle, but he said pleasantly, 'Sure, I'll come round. Could do with a break.'

'I thought I would surprise my husband,' she explained, preceding him up the stairs. 'We're having new pine doors and we need to put some hooks in. To hang things on, you know. So I thought I would do it.' She paused, slightly breathless, on the landing. 'But I don't seem to have done it very well. They won't go in properly. I might have spoiled the whole door.'

'Did you drill the holes far enough?' he asked, the expert.

'Oh no, I can't use the drill, you see.'

'Well, that's your trouble,' he said. 'If you get the drill I could do it in a jiffy.'

It was done so quickly. His hands were red-knuckled and bony, scratched from the branches, and easy with the tools he used. She was not familiar with the hands of men, but she liked those hands and their sureness with metal. From the hands, she looked the short distance to arms, dusted red with the sun, from arms to back, an agile butterfly of shoulder blade winging out from the spine. He was tall. He reached up without standing on the steps. His T-shirt lifted over a long pale waist and the beginning of hip-bones.

She sat peacefully on the edge of the bed and watched the ragged edge of the T-shirt cast its faint shadow. Sunlight through the net curtain spattered flower petals onto his back so that the shirt appeared to be made of lace, which was somehow not incongruous. As for lower, no, it was not right to look lower. The buttocks of young men were not to be looked at, not in the way that men looked at those of women. And yet, furtively, dartingly, and more than once, she looked. Goose pimples prickled her arms. She felt quite extraordinarily happy to have him so busy here, in her bedroom.

'There you are.' He had finished. The hooks sat in their places like little upside-down beaks, ready for work.

'How clever of you,' she said admiringly. 'I am so grateful. Have you got time for a cup of tea? Or – I think there is some beer in the fridge.'

'Beer would be fine,' he said.

They sat in Mrs Handyside's pleasant blue and yellow sitting room, French windows open to the garden. Mr

Garfield drank his beer from the can and told her that he had run his building business for eleven years and his name was Tom. Her name, she told him awkwardly, pouring herself another glass of wine, was Prue.

'That's unusual. Is it Prudence?' he asked.

'Yes, it's quite awful. My parents were dreadfully old-fashioned and Church. My sister's called Charity.'

'I suppose it means she has to behave herself.'

'Oh, she can be quite nasty sometimes, you know what sisters are, but we're generally both pretty well-behaved.'

'And prudent?' He was laughing at her, she could tell.

'And prudent, yes,' she answered seriously. It was not by choice, however, but by inbuilt direction. It was something she had always been.

'You have less fun if you're prudent,' he went on. 'It does you good to let your hair down.'

'I expect so,' she said with slight regret. 'But there wasn't much opportunity when I was young. Dad wasn't earning much and we had to be careful.' And then she had married. Clifford was a good catch; everyone had congratulated her. He had provided well, she had kept a good house; both their children were at university. She had everything she had ever thought she wanted. Letting her hair down had never really entered into it.

'Your husband won't mind me using his things, will he?' Foam from the beer gleamed on his lip.

'No. Well, actually he won't know. I shan't tell him.'

'Won't you?' He gave her a mischievous sideways glance, like a parrot, head tilted. 'Why not?'

'I want him to think I did it myself. You won't tell him, will you?'

His chin came up in a laugh, his throat flexed.

'You're safe, I won't. Besides, you can't tell him you've had a man in your bedroom, can you? Aren't you the naughty one, Pru-udence?' He made a mockery of her name, leaning back on the cushion and showing white, regular teeth.

'I suppose I am.'

Naughty – such a friendly word, as if he admired her. A thought struck her and pinkness rose in her face. He was flirting with her. She took another sip of wine and giggled.

'And that's a naughty laugh you've got.'

'Would you like another beer?'

'I wouldn't mind,' he said cheerfully. He seemed quite well settled.

On her way back from the kitchen, she glanced at herself in the hall mirror and pulled her skirt tight, feeling the lace underneath. It was a start. But the rest – the scarcely grey hair that had never been truly let down, the smart dull dress, the shoes whose heels were too low. In front of this sprawled, smiling and rather vulgar young man they simply were not good enough. Before him she should appear in something velvet and uncharacteristically red.

She sat down a little unsteadily. Her stockings rustled as she leaned back and crossed her legs. Her skirt fell away slightly from her knees. Her shoe dangled from a toe. Her glass was empty.

The hake, the silver hake, was good. It was a fine, solid fish, noble in its yellow robe and flanked by tiny peas and new potatoes glossed with butter. Clifford was surprised.

'What's this, then, cod?'

'Silver hake,' she said, busy with the fish slice. 'I thought we'd have a change.'

'I'm not all that keen on fish,' he said.

'I know, but it looked so nice. Eat it up before it gets

229

cold. I want to show you what I did this afternoon.' There was a new firmness to her tone and he raised his pointed eyebrows, but he ate his fish and admitted its excellence.

'So what's this you want to show me?' he said, laying down his fork.

'Come up and see.' She led him to the bedroom and showed him the hooks, dressing-gowns neatly hanging. 'What do you think?'

He praised her cleverness; he pulled and tested the hooks and found they did not budge. He praised her again, smiling his nice smile. Then he warned her about using tools.

'You have to be careful if you don't know what you're doing. They can be dangerous in inexperienced hands. And look, you've scraped a bit of the wood.' The eyebrows came down. 'You'd better let me know next time you want to do a job like this.'

'All right, dear,' said Mrs Handyside. 'By the way, I thought I'd go into town again tomorrow. I forgot something.'

He was rubbing the scratch with his thumb and gave a grunt that might have meant he was listening.

'I want to buy some underwear. And a dress,' she added softly. 'In velvet.'

THE SAVIOUR

Joshua Davidson

Joshua Davidson lives in Brookline, Massachusetts. For eight years he ran his own engine-rebuilding business but decided two years ago to write full time. He is taking a degree in Creative Writing at Emerson College in Boston and has already won a number of awards for writing. He also writes for *Bostonia*.

THE SAVIOUR

Opening his eyes Rudolph Niemann had a fleeting, terrifying sensation of not knowing where he was. So he did what he did every morning when this occurred. Without moving his head he looked about the chamber for the things that were familiar to him: the dusty web of beams supporting the roof, his uniform hanging crisply on the wall and boots aligned below, dutifully awaiting his reoccupation. Then the warm-smelling steam of the shower would find his nose, and reoriented, he would arise.

But the shower was not running this morning, and so he remained slightly unconvinced as he swung his feet to the floor. The planks were familiarly cold, though, and his feet landed precisely where the backed-out nailheads were not. For months he had waged battle against the nails that rose mysteriously out of the floor: with the heels of his boots, with small rocks, with a hammer. The dents around the nails testified to all of them, but the nails still rose up. Some time ago, he had simply learned instinctively where not to step.

Without reflection, Niemann arose and went about his morning business in order to arrive promptly for breakfast at seven thirty. In that half-hour he would clean and shave himself, polish his boots, his insignia, and the beak of his cap, and don his uniform. Just before stepping out to cross the compound to the *Messehalle*, checked the straightness of his cap and tunic in his little mirror. As a final test, he clicked his heels, feeling the snap run hollowly through his body like the ring of crystal. Everything, he knew, was *in Ordnung*; he did not like surprises.

Stepping out of his chamber, Niemann was surprised to see prisoners wandering around the compound. Somehow, they seemed different. They lifted their heads and looked him straight in the eye. They did not approach him, but nor did they shrink away, instead standing like pillars of rags before him. They were not afraid, and despite the fact that none of them threatened or could threaten him, a shiver ran through him.

In a strange sense then, it was some relief when he heard, in English, the words 'Hold it' from behind. He did not turn around because the words were said with the international authority of a gun in hand. But he saw, for the first time ever, these inmates smile. Bony cheeks rose to nearly swallow sunken eyes; difficult smiles exercised remnants of muscles that had not been used in years. It was Niemann's turn to be afraid.

Be as unco-operative as possible. Name and rank only. Volunteer nothing. Niemann reminded himself of his duties as a prisoner. So when the American Major asked tonelessly, 'Who are you?' Niemann answered: 'Lieutenant Rudolph Niemann,' and it was only when he saw the Major smile that he knew he had been tricked into admitting he spoke English. But he determined to give away nothing more; he knew that it would not be he to break the avowed silence amongst his *Gruppe* that ran the camp. No SS man would ever help the enemy; he knew that.

Niemann was confined to his quarters for the day, under guard. All of his texts had been confiscated and he found little to do. He did not like to let his mind wander, and he refused to speak with his guards, so he watched the compound through his window.

He saw the inmates wandering around, through the open gate, and then back again. Wandering in and out of his fellow officers' chambers and the enlisted men's barracks. Wandering right up to his own window and looking in at him, like an animal in a zoo.

He saw the American soldiers and officers wandering too. They looked little relieved that there was no fighting to be done here at Landau. All day long, he watched them cry like babies, or recoil in mortal terror when approached by inmates who could barely walk. He saw them walk around looking at the ground, as if, unable to walk away, they were satisfied just to walk – to not stand in any one place long enough to be a part of it. How could they be winning the war? he wondered. But as the day wore on outside as he watched like a movie on a screen, he felt a strange desire to be outside, on the screen, with them.

It seemed an odd protocol to Niemann that, late in the evening, he should be the first German taken to be interrogated by the Major in the *Kommandant*'s office.

Niemann had prepared himself for the interrogation. He realized that the Major must know he was the camp doctor, that he was a member of the SS and a party member. He might know from the confiscated books, assuming he had translated their titles, that Niemann specialized in eugenics, although his formal training was as an internist. No co-operation. Name and rank. Volunteer nothing. Unity in separation.

'Good evening, Doctor,' said the Major as he settled into the *Kommandant*'s burgundy leather swivelling chair behind the carved desk, a valuable antique that an inmate and his brother, when relocated, had actually carried to the camp. 'Won't you please sit down?'

235

'No thank you. I prefer to stand.' Niemann looked straight ahead, maintaining a rigid German posture. He felt sly in how much of the office he could observe without moving his eyes. He noted the precarious ash on the Major's cigar, concerned that it would fall on the *Kommandant*'s desk.

'Suit yourself,' said the Major. 'Tell me, why are you here?'

Niemann was a bit perplexed by the question. A trick, he decided. 'Because you sent for me.'

The Major smiled. 'Heh, heh. No, I mean, how come you're the only one here?'

'I don't understand. The only what?'

'The only German! How come you didn't screw with the rest of them?' asked the Major incredulously.

Niemann looked at the Major. Not with the contemptuous glare he had prepared, but with genuine puzzlement. He caught himself. This must be a trick; this American was trying to bluff him, crudely. But he wondered – where was everyone else? And how come there had been no fighting?

'Well,' the Major lifted his brow, 'they won't get far. Ain't no place to go.' The Major had Niemann's wallet on the desk in front of him, and was looking through the papers. He came up with Niemann's party card. 'Well, well, look at this. 1936.' He looked menacingly up at Niemann. 'There's a special place in my heart for party members.'

Just then, Niemann realized that the Major had no personnel file, nothing about Niemann except his wallet and personal identification booklet. Like a train erupting suddenly from a tunnel on an apparently long-abandoned rail line, something that had been missing on the movie screen of his barracks window – none of the other quarters or barracks had been guarded like his. He could not help searching for an answer, or a question. 'You mean, I . . . ? *Der Kommandant, die Gruppe . . . ?*'

'Everyone! All your buddies! This place was a ghost town when we got here. Hell, we –'

'They all left? Me –'

'We never would have known you were here if you hadn't walked out of your room this morning like a lost puppy!'

Niemann fell into the chair on his right. The feeling again – not knowing where – or now who, or why – not knowing anything except that he was the prisoner of this chuckling American major. Devastating; but not really a surprise. He had never been more than something tacked on to the officer corps of the camp; never gathered in at meals for the telling of a joke, never invited to play soccer, or go out carousing in town. Never taken into confidence by anyone, never done favours. He had learned to ignore the slights, the lack of rapport, even the tasteless, whispered rumours about him. He had decided that his honour lay in being a loyal party member, a hard worker, a necessary part of the camp structure, and, he had assumed, something worth saving.

The Major allowed Niemann no time to recover from the scald of betrayal. 'What were your duties here, Doctor?'

Niemann had no strength to question the question. He responded as if for the comfort of hearing himself speak: 'I saw to the staff and prisoners.'

The Major swivelled around unfurling his arm towards the large window looking upon the main compound. Niemann's eyes followed the gesture outside. 'Well, I don't see any staff. And the inmates don't look too good.' He swivelled back round and leaned on the desk in one motion, causing the ash finally to snap off his cigar and fall, shattering silently on the desk. Looking Niemann square in his wounded eyes, he asked, 'You're not a very good doctor, are you?'

The Major stood up and slowly walked to the bookcase on Niemann's left, drawing from it a measured tone. 'Doctor, I and my men have been fighting together since Sicily. We've seen things we never thought we would.' He paused to gather. 'But we could never have imagined the things we've seen here. I . . . I'm not even sure what to do here; I'd like to pack up my men and throw them into the Bulge – I bet they wish I would, just to get them the hell out of this place. But we're here, and we can't leave just because there aren't any Germans to shoot at.' He paused for a long, hard look at Niemann.

'You know, you're lucky that you weren't shot dead when you walked out of your quarters, because a lot of my men may have done that . . . I might have, after seeing what you've done to these people. Maybe I should, I don't know.' The Major was getting visibly agitated, and Niemann felt compelled to defend himself before he no longer could.

'Major, I am merely a doctor, I followed my orders – you know what that is like. In the name of justice, I –'

'Justice! Bullshit!' the Major exploded, then settled to a seething calm. 'We have a saying back home, Doc: "Be careful what you ask for, because you just might get it." *Verstehen?* Believe me, Justice wouldn't exactly suit you just now.

'But tell you what, Doctor; I'll make you a bargain. There're a lot of very sick people out there, and you know exactly what's wrong with 'em. I know they're not all going to survive; it seems a lot of 'em would rather just die. But the deal is this: you get those people healthy enough where they can be transported out of here to refugee camps, so that they can walk, and don't get sick when you give 'em something to eat, and I won't let them or my men kill you. It's as simple as that.'

Niemann said nothing.

The Major looked at him, took his silence for agreement, and continued, 'There is a doctor amongst the inmates. They respect him, and he's agreed to work with you. Whatever you need, you tell Lieutenant McDonough, who's outside. The Red Cross is assembling refugee centres in France, and it's my job to get them there; I'm making it yours to see that they're able to make it. Good night, Doctor.'

Niemann did not wake up at seven o'clock the following morning. He had not gotten to sleep until maybe three. The betrayal, his own stupidity, a Jewish doctor, the frightening prisoners, grown men crying, the tenuousness of his own life; all of these things danced around in his mind and his stomach so that he tossed and turned, threw his covers sweatily off, then shivering, drew them on again. When he woke up suddenly at 8:38 a.m., it was from a nightmare. All he could remember of it was being snatched up in the talons of an eagle whose claws dug into his flesh, and just when he felt he was about to die, when he could no longer feel the wounds, the claws were pulled out, causing the wounds to burn again as he plummeted.

He awoke in mid-air, compressed into his mattress, and shot up from his pillow. His eyes groped for his uniform. It hung askew, looking somehow different. It took him a moment to realize that all the insignia and identification patches had been removed, except for the caducei on his collar.

He went about his business, trying to regiment himself as before, but it seemed that his boots were a little duller, and his hat, well, without the insignia, it seemed to Niemann that his hat would look ridiculous. So he left it in his chamber.

Outside, the guard said that the Major would like a word with Niemann, so he escorted the doctor across the compound. An inmate sat in the office, an older man, though all of the inmates appeared so, and he was quite tall, which exaggerated his emaciation. He did not acknowledge Niemann's entrance at once, remaining immersed in what Niemann recognized to be one of his own medical tests. He had on a suit of clothes from somewhere, but they hung on him as though on a hanger. The shirt collar drooped around his chicken-like neck, and the cuffs ran down easily over his withered hands. After a moment he snapped the book shut in mild disgust, tossed it weakly on the desk, looked up at the Major and then at Niemann. As on all inmates, it was difficult to determine any facial features other than the eyes, deep-set and dark brown, full of meaning. They aroused in Niemann not the fear he had felt looking into inmates' eyes for the first time yesterday, but a vague feeling of awe; these eyes seemed already to know Niemann, more so even than he knew himself. Niemann had seen him before, certainly; and struggled to remember his number. The man had been in the camp for at least a year, which now struck Niemann as odd; so few prisoners survived even six months.

The men regarded one another icily as the Major spoke. 'Dr Niemann, this is Dr Berlinger. He will be assisting you in your efforts to consummate our arrangement.' The Major rose from his chair and went to the door, which he opened. 'Why don't you take him to your office and get started? There's not much time to waste. Good day, gentlemen.'

The two men rose, and though Niemann headed directly for the door, in a long, easy stride, Berlinger was the first to go through. Niemann stood back for a moment, as if to register his anger to the Major, who raised his eyebrows in mock impatience and gestured for him to 'scurry along now'.

Berlinger held the outer door for Niemann, and the two crossed the compound to the doctor's office. Despite his obviously poor health, Berlinger took large, graceful, but unhurried strides, forcing Niemann to keep up and arrive, as he felt he should, before the Jew.

'I will enter first,' Niemann felt the need to say.

Berlinger looked down at Niemann for a moment, and, in a deep voice, a voice that gave weight to whatever words it spoke, said in perfect *hochdeutsch*, 'Dr Niemann, we have no time for pettiness any more. Your uniform admits only that you are a physician. It is time to behave as one. It is a difficult enough task to try to save the lives of these people whom you have worked to kill. Having to save yours as well does not make it easier.'

Niemann shrank back, deflated.

Berlinger entered the office, going immediately to the medicine cabinet behind the desk, leaving Niemann no room to get to his chair. Berlinger examined several of the bottles and shook his head. Then he sat down behind the desk in the chair that had been Niemann's for two years, pulled from his pocket some dozen torn and odd-sized scraps of paper, and began to arrange them.

'What on earth are these?' Niemann sneered.

Berlinger looked up, 'A list of your patients by name and condition. I –'

'What, these ridiculous scraps?' Niemann picked one up with scorn.

'Then please be good enough to show me yours,' responded Berlinger. Niemann tried to hide deeper in his disdain.

'I know,' continued Berlinger, unimpressed, 'that the *Kommandant* felt it unnecessary to waste paper on Jews; I used what I could find.' He tossed a pencil stub, whittled down to the metal eraser jacket, onto the desk. Picking out several of the scraps, he continued. 'These are a list of patients in need of immediate care: 137 cases of bacillary dysentery or colitis, approximately 33 of pneumonia. The warmer weather has obviously eased the latter, but will aggravate the former. In addition, all 1,213 inmates, including myself, are severely malnourished, and 190 are effectively starved. Many have individual ailments ranging from heart trouble to skin rashes. Nearly all are suffering from some level of psychological distress. How do you suggest we proceed?'

Niemann was dumbstruck. It took him a little time to fathom the numbers: *137 cases of dysentery, colitis, pneumonia; nearly two hundred at the point of starvation; over a thousand malnourished*. He wanted to ask how such a thing could have occurred, but stopped himself.

He sat down in front of the desk he had sat behind for so long, the numbers rattling hugely in his head. He thought about prescribing cold remedies to soldiers; ointment for the *Kommandant*'s warts; brandy for a junior officer's anxiety. And in all that time, he had not diagnosed one case of pneumonia or checked one case of dysentery.

His chin fell to his chest, and he saw his legs, his hands. They seemed somehow not to belong to him;

they were not, *could not be,* his. If he could have climbed out of his own body right then, he would gladly have done so. The Major was right. He was not a very good doctor.

When finally he raised his head, Niemann found Berlinger gazing at a framed photograph hanging on the wall over the desk. It was of a pair of identical twin adolescent boys, and standing beside them, a pair of men. One of the men was a younger Rudolph Niemann, grinning hugely and standing slightly behind and in the shadow of the other man, who, even in the photograph, seemed in total possession not only of himself, but the others as well.

Niemann looked at it, too – his proudest moment, when he had been selected by Josef Mengele, the other man in the photograph, to assist in that great doctor's genetic research. He looked at his young self; the grin had always struck him as strange, unnaturally large – he could not remember making it – and he always wondered if others noticed this.

Berlinger studied the photo closely for some time, noticing the grin perhaps, but much more as well, in it. And though Niemann had looked at it a thousand times, was, indeed, in it, he waited to find out what.

'What happened to them?' Berlinger asked.

'To whom? The boys?'

'Yes, they are the Dimont twins, no?'

'Did you know them?' asked Niemann, looking across the desk, longing for some common ground, even for this Jew's approval.

Berlinger nodded downward, finally placing his forehead in his big, bony hand. 'I made the tragic mistake of introducing them to your friend there, and I expect they are dead now.' Even closed, his eyes betrayed his anguish.

Niemann asked with the unsure hope of revelation, '*Jakob* Berlinger?' Berlinger rocked his head affirmatively in his hand, eyes still closed. Over a decade of nurtured contempt melted away as Niemann stood up out of his chair, leaned over the desk, and with the first strength in his voice since before his capture, said, 'Sir, I am deeply honoured.'

Berlinger said nothing, did nothing to acknowledge Niemann's tribute. After a pregnant moment Niemann said, '*Herr Doktor*, I have read all of your texts, studied them. *Examination of Heredity in the Treatment of Blood Disorders* inspired me in my advanced studies!'

Berlinger slowly picked his head up and looked sullenly at the wall and made a bitter, abridged laugh. 'You cannot imagine . . . how deeply I wish I had never thought to write it.' He slowly traced his bony brow with his thumb and forefinger. 'How foolish I was not to have imagined that science could be so misused; how theories – really nothing more than postulations and questions – could be amputated from the facts which bore them and given a life of their own by politics and emotion. I am ashamed to say that it marked the death of medicine.' Again his brow sank into his hands. His eyes clenched tightly to force back the tears that he was too dehydrated to produce. Silently, his face turned red.

At last, Berlinger raised his head. Still smarting, he said, 'The Major is right. There is not much time. We must . . . have a plan.' With the last words, his countenance and voice seemed suddenly relieved.

'Yes, a plan,' said Niemann. 'Inmates . . . people are sick, are . . . dying. Dysentery. Pneumonia. Malnourished. These, these must be checked, they will spread.' It suddenly occurred to him upon how many tenuous lives his own depended, and how few auguring deaths could condemn him. He examined himself in the photo on the wall; what had he to smile about?

The plan was first to examine all of the chronics individually, one at a time per doctor, and then to observe the others in small groups. Niemann noticed how at ease patients were with Berlinger, how calmly they put themselves in his hands, and how those hands seemed to know always just where to touch, when to offer support, how much pressure to apply; no one choked when Berlinger depressed their tongue, or flinched as he probed the tender area above the genitals.

Niemann's patients were reluctant even to have him touch them, and he recoiled at first, performing his examinations of the Jewish wastrels as though poking at them with a stick. Only after receiving soothing Yiddish assurances from Berlinger, whom they all seemed to respect tremendously, would they accede to the German's touch, and then only tensely.

Niemann knew that the average weight for an inmate was some two-thirds that of a healthy person of the same proportions. And he knew that, on average, the fat and muscle content of inmates' bodies was less than half of what it should be. He was well-informed as to how the Jewish constitution faltered under the rigours of the camps; he'd read much on the subject, seen it with his own eyes. But the first time he took a pulse, he was struck, sickened even, as he held the wrist – broad as a mop handle, morbidly fluted with tendons, bones, and veins draped in colourless, tissue-like skin – in his own pink, nourished hand. He was repeatedly mortified by the subtle details of emaciation: the pointiness of the bones, the shrivelling of the gums, the looseness of the hair. The patients had perfected extreme economy of movement. If asked to lift an arm, they would allow

245

him to do it for them, and then let it fall, utterly limp. Niemann came to wonder what it was that kept these people alive at all; but alive they were, and people.

A woman he was examining seemed, at 26 kilograms, to be hardly alive. Berlinger had before described to Niemann how some people had for some time simply resigned themselves to death, and were confused, angry even, that they were now to live. He struggled to understand this even as he carried the woman into the room. After placing her listless body on the examination table, he listened for her faint heartbeat. He had gotten nearly through the examination without so much as a word or resistant motion from her, when he lifted her ragged shawl to inspect her genitals. Out of nowhere came a sharp, if not powerful blow to his temple. Niemann staggered back and saw the woman suddenly fiercely alive. Berlinger rushed to her side as she exclaimed in Yiddish, as strongly as her weakened lungs would allow: 'The *Hund* has no respect for a lady!' Niemann watched as Berlinger completed the examination, how he spoke to the woman with a firm kindness, and asked her permission to examine her privates. When Berlinger helped her up, Niemann moved close to help, and receiving back the care of his patient, walked her out. Asking her forgiveness as he guided her towards the helper who would take her back, he tried to relax but not weaken his supportive embrace, to make his hands and arms firm but tender, shaping his strength and lending it to her weakness. As he handed her over to the helper, holding her until sure she was safe in the helper's care, she said, '*Danke*.' Niemann feigned a small cough to conceal the exuberant gasp, and surged slightly to his toes as a tingle rippled up through his body, moistening his eyes and forcing a smile.

* * *

Days and nights and weeks became a single blur to Niemann, who did what he was told – by Berlinger, by
the Major, even by inmates whom he was examining.
Initially, many refused to let him touch them, but Dr
Berlinger would persuade them in Yiddish, and they
would reluctantly bare their bodies and answer the German's questions. Their language was close to German,
Niemann thought – German with melody. It was a sad
language; or perhaps it was the circumstances that made
it so. When, at around eleven o'clock one night, exhausted, Niemann asked, 'When does this happen?' in Yiddish, he was even more surprised than his patient.
Berlinger looked up, and so did the patient he was
examining, and everyone, Niemann, too, shared a
momentary smile.

The doctors worked hard to get ahead of the situation, and each day it seemed to deteriorate slightly less.
Many people were actually relatively well, but only
when that fact was authorized by one of the doctors did
life seem to gain the upper hand in their minds and
bodies, and throughout the camp. But each day, people
died, and Niemann constantly saw the pain of this fact
in his colleague's face.

On Berlinger's suggestion, the Major organized a sani-
tation squad among the inmates. Women laundered,
repaired, and distributed clothes found stored in a barn.
Men buried offal that had festered for months, dug new
latrines, and turned over all the soil in the camp to
sew the rampant bacteria back into the spring earth for
forgiveness. No one complained, in fact some cried at
being given a shovel or a bar of soap, as though the
thing's utility exuded the world's invitation back. Some
refused. From what Niemann had considered human
detritus sprang candlemakers, fine cooks, carpenters,
card sharks; there was talk, gossip, banter – life as there

had never been in the camp before. Tentatively, some people called Niemann 'Doctor'.

By the end of two or so weeks, at once fleeting and endless, there was a noticeable improvement among most of the inmates. Solids were staying down; colour was returning to cheeks and strength to voices; some of the chronic cases seemed to be in remission; people were restless, less exhausted. So it was all the more noticeable that Berlinger didn't seem to improve. If anything, he seemed to have lost weight, and the look of pain still flashed over his face.

'*Herr Doktor*, you must rest,' implored Niemann of the man with whom he had come to feel closer than anyone he could remember. 'Things have improved, yes, but there is still much to do. You must eat and rest! We need for you to be well.'

'Rudolph, you must do something for me tomorrow,' said Berlinger late that night. 'In town there is a man, a German; a chemist. He makes for me a special formula. Ironically, there was a guard I would bribe to get it for me, but now, with the Americans . . . You must go and get it. It's a small vial, nothing.'

Niemann was confused, and not at all sure that he wanted to do anything to anger the Americans. 'How could I go, *Herr Doktor*? I am a prisoner, they –'

'Because you must, Rudolph,' said Berlinger. 'You –'

'They would not trust me,' said Niemann. 'Why should they? They think I will escape, and –'

'Are you going to escape, Rudolph? Do you think about escaping? Do you, do you think you can?' The older man's eyes delivered the question directly to Niemann's soul, but did not push for any more answer than the silence. 'No, I didn't think so. Your place is here; more so than it has ever been. The Major will let you go, and you will return.'

Niemann just looked at the older man. Yes, he decided, he would go if they would let him; he would do this. 'Yes.'

'You will need a small amount of money,' added Berlinger. 'I have none left from the sale of my wife's wedding ring.'

'I have money! An account in town! Tell me how much, and –'

'Not much. Thirty marks or so,' said Berlinger. Just then, his face tightened, and he clenched his bony fist.

'What, *Herr Doktor*? What is it?' pleaded Niemann.

'You must go to town in the morning, see *Herr Apotheker*,' said Berlinger, and he got up and left.

'You remember one thing, Doctor,' said the Major. 'There's no place to go. I'm a man of my word, and I get very upset when people disappoint me. You'll be escorted by Corporal Simon here, who aside from being good company, happens to be the battalion riflery champ. Don't give him a target. I'll see the both of you back here at 1400.'

The two men did not speak on the two-kilometre walk. Spring shadowed them from the woods edging the road, belying its position by chirps and snapping twigs. The air smelled strangely sweet, reminding Niemann of something – he drew in deep lungsfull, trying to inflate the memory, but it remained slippery, unreachable. When they arrived in town, it felt to Niemann much longer than two weeks since he had been there, like he never really had at all. Americans were everywhere. Niemann found the chemist's.

'He is a great man, you know,' said the chemist after Niemann mentioned Berlinger's name, 'but a Jew! Who would think that a Jew – ?'

'How much?' Niemann asked curtly.

'Forty marks,' answered the chemist indignantly.

'I must go draw the money,' said Niemann. 'Go ahead and prepare it.'

As Niemann headed out of the door, the chemist gave a little laugh, and said, 'I'll wait until I see the money.'

Outside, Corporal Simon was nowhere to be found. After waiting for a couple of minutes, Niemann set off.

Walking the two blocks to the bank, in a town he had called his for four years now, he thought for an instant that he saw someone he recognized, but the man turned around the corner without looking at Niemann.

He was not sure what to expect when he saw a pair of American soldiers at the front of the bank.

'Where're you going, pal?' asked one of the soldiers as he moved to block Niemann.

'I'm . . . just going to do some business,' replied the frightened Niemann.

'Uh-uh. Not here you're not,' said the other soldier, pointing to a sign on the door, which read, 'CLOSED BY ORDER OF AMERICAN OCCUPATION FORCE COMMANDER, SECTOR H-16.' Niemann stumbled back, mind reeling in confusion and fear. Where was . . . ? How could it be . . . ?

Niemann shrank into the café seat, desperate for something to find him familiar. Normally at midday, the place was alive with the sounds of eating and drinking: clinking tableware, jutting chairs, the roar of just-concluded jokes, perhaps an accordion; the aroma of hearty German stew would stir the appetite as one entered. But now it was somber. Townspeople ate meagerly and spoke in hushed tones screaming with bitterness. All the noise emanated from one corner where there was a small crowd of American soldiers. Their brash American words and loud American laughter rang out, to be met and subsumed by the resentment and dolour suffocating the room. Niemann had found a small table, apart from either group.

'Just tea,' Niemann indicated to the waiter, who seemed to have asked, though they both knew there had been no coffee for three months. Niemann didn't know what to do. With no money, no formula. With no formula for Berlinger, who knew what would happen? The doctor might denounce him to the Major. Or perhaps it was an American trick; yes, now that the inmates seemed to be getting better . . .

'Niemann. *Wie geht's?*' said a strangely familiar voice from behind Niemann's chair. He turned around to see who —

'Schlussel! What are you — ?' Niemann was shocked to see his former comrade, now dressed in a plain brown suit that seemed a size small on the burly guard.

'Shhh!' warned Schlussel, sitting down at the table. 'There are Americans all over the place.'

'What are you doing here?' Niemann demanded. 'What happened?'

'Most of the *Gruppe* is hiding in a little house just at the edge of town. We got out just in time, barely got all the files. As we were running, two of the dogs got out and attacked us. *Our own dogs!* Can you believe it?' Schlussel looked incredulously at Niemann, who watched him speak but had not heard a word.

'Why didn't —' began Niemann weakly.

'Most of us made it okay,' continued Schlussel, 'but the *Kommandant* . . . one of them nearly took his leg off. He's in terrible shape, Niemann. We have no medicine — we think he may be gangrenous. The smell is terrible.'

'What happened to me? Why didn't you wake me?'

'We tried, Niemann. But they were coming too fast! You must understand!' Schlussel commanded, his whisper edged sharp with duty. Then, placing his hand on Niemann's shoulder, he changed his tone: 'But look, we've all made it, brother! You must help the *Kommandant* – he's been asking for you; he *needs* you. We are going to Switzerland. You, too!'

Walking out with Schlussel, Niemann could not find the sweetness; the air resumed a more familiar taste, which he breathed with shallow rapidity, sifting it for oxygen. The odour of death, the thickness it caused in the air, making everything about life heavier, became discernible as Niemann found himself climbing to the hayloft behind a cottage at the edge of town. He damned his pounding heart for causing him to inhale more than he wanted.

And there were the men who had disappeared from Niemann's life. He remembered how badly it hurt when he found them gone. Now, this hurt more.

'Niemann! I don't believe it!' gushed the *Kommandant*. 'Ah, my boy, it's good to see you. We worried so that night. But I knew you would not let us down!' The stench was terrible.

'You will come with us to Switzerland, yes!' said the *Kommandant*, while Niemann probed the wound. 'These Americans are barbarians, there is talk of SS going on trial for war crimes. War crimes! Can you imagine such rubbish? They declare war on us, and *we* are accused of war crimes!'

'I'm going to have to cut,' said Niemann, after examining the *Kommandant*. It was the first time ever he had looked the man straight in the eyes, feeling suddenly bold. 'I'm going to have to get some things. In the meantime, someone here must boil some bandages. Find a very sharp knife, and a saw. Boil them, too, as well as you are able.' He could almost taste the sweat forming on the *Kommandant*'s brow. 'And get him good and drunk. I need some money for the chemist's.' Nobody moved, and so, looking him straight in the eyes again, Niemann took the *Kommandant*'s wallet out of his jacket pocket and removed forty marks.

'Jesus, am I glad to see you!' said Corporal Simon upon seeing Niemann reapproach the chemist's. 'I thought you'd hightailed on me.'

'When I stepped out of the shop, I didn't find you,' said Niemann. 'I went for a cup of tea.'

'Yeah, well . . . next time you just stay put till *I* find *you*,' said the relieved corporal. 'We'll just keep this mum; between you and me, *okay*?'

Niemann nodded and entered the chemist's. A few minutes later, with the small bottle in his pocket, he and the Corporal started back to the camp.

They did not speak for most of the journey, and Niemann thought how easy it would have been to escape, simply to melt into the town, hide out with the *Gruppe* in the barn. He could have performed some sort of crude operation on the *Kommandant*, and been a hero; received the slaps on the back he'd always hoped for. And then he could have escaped to Switzerland with them . . .

'*Pfennig* for your thoughts,' interrupted Corporal Simon, cheerfully bored.

'What?'

'It's an expression. You know, kind of a conversation starter.'

'Oh, yes. Well, I was just sort of thinking, wondering; hypothetically.' Niemann paused, and decided to continue. 'What is more important to a man, loyalty or moral duty?'

Simon grunted amusedly. 'Loyalty's for saps, Doc.

You put your life on the line for a guy because you know when the time comes, he'll do it for you. That's your duty to you. Loyalty's just a ten-cent word for looking out for number one.'

Niemann didn't respond to this as the two approached the gates of the camp. Before entering the headquarters to check back in, Simon put his finger to his lips and winked at Niemann, 'Remember, Doc, mum's the word.'

'Yes! Yes . . . mum's the word,' replied Niemann.

'Did you get it?' asked Berlinger as Niemann entered the office. He had been writing something, and now hastily stuffed it into his pocket. Niemann sat down but did not respond. He looked up at the photograph of the twins and Mengele, and himself. He thought about what Berlinger had said some days ago: that the spry young boys in the picture were probably dead. Mengele, whom Niemann knew himself to be extraordinarily cunning, was undoubtedly alive; but the other man, grinning absurdly in the shadow – Niemann himself – where was he now?

'Rudolph. Did you get it?' Berlinger repeated anxiously. Niemann nodded, and felt for the vial in his pocket, not removing it.

'I want to know – I want to know why . . . As a physician, I demand to know what this is for,' said Niemann, the relief of having said the words immediately drowned by his apprehension of the answer. But before Berlinger could answer, Niemann added gently, 'I can help you.'

Berlinger looked down at his hands. 'It's not what you think. Please don't –'

'No, doctor! I just risked my life for you! I know that may seem no more than ironic to you, after what you

have been through. But not for me. I could easily have
. . . but I risked my life for *you*.'

Berlinger brought his clasped hands to his lips, and
stared blankly at Niemann's chest, thinking. A wave of
pain swept visibly over him, and when it appeared to
recede he raised his eyes – the eyes which seemed to
understand so much about the world – and said, 'I am
in the terminal stages of stomach cancer.'

Everything stopped. Neither man spoke or moved.
They just sat and stared at one another until Niemann
became aware of his hand, sweating inside his pocket,
clutching the small vial with all his strength. He pulled
it out and went to the cabinet where he chose the newest
needle and assembled it to a syringe.

'How much?'

'Five cc,' replied Berlinger. Niemann carefully drew
the proper amount of liquid into the syringe, balanced it on the desk, and prepared a small wad with
alcohol.

'Where do you prefer, *Herr Doktor*?' he asked.

'The basilic vein should be fine, either arm.'

Niemann unbuttoned Berlinger's cuff and rolled his
shirtsleeves up the long, shrivelled arm. He tied a length
of bandage snugly around the upper arm, pressed tenderly around the deep, hollow elbow pocket and found
the vein, smoothly stroked it with the alcohol pad, and
injected the preparation. He had done this procedure
thousands of times before, but for the first time he felt
assured in his actions. The needle pierced the skin without the slight spring of resistance then subtle 'pop' that
indicated misapplication. He was doing it right; he had,
finally, the 'touch' that all of the medical knowledge in
the world could not teach.

'Thank you, Doctor,' said Berlinger as relief washed
over his face.

As he cleaned the wound and the apparatus, Niemann spoke tentatively. 'Surely there is something we can do? I can operate, excise the malignancy; at least give you some time.'

'No, Rudolph, there is nothing to do.'

Niemann sat for a moment, knowing what he wanted to say, just not how to say it. He looked at the photograph on the wall.

'There were operations . . . I participated in some of them, with Dr Mengele,' said Niemann, at once repulsed by what he had done and hopeful that it might now bear some fruit. 'We removed organs, replaced them . . . ' He felt sick to his stomach but forced himself to continue. 'Eventually, they all died, mostly from infection. But with the new drugs, the penicillin, we may be able to make it work.'

'No, Rudolph. I am not interested in living any longer than I must. Nothing is left for me,' Berlinger said, his eyes meeting Niemann's. For the first time Niemann found that, for all their vast knowledge, their deep understanding, these eyes contained no hope. 'My work has been thoroughly perverted, my family destroyed.'

'But you can teach us again, make us understand again –'

'I cannot teach them to unlearn, Rudolph. And you know, I watched my own son die, and I no longer understand myself . . . '

Niemann wanted to say something to convince him. But he could not. He took the old doctor's trembling hands and held them in his own.

'We must get back to work,' said Berlinger. 'No time.' Niemann did as he was told.

Berlinger betrayed none of his sadness to the patients, and out of respect and professionalism, neither did Niemann. The rest of the day was spent as those before, examining small groups, individual chronics, a man that had, in his fervour, worked too hard that day and collapsed. Niemann was quietly grateful that people no longer recoiled from him as they had in the first several days. Some began to ask him questions as though they considered him their doctor. One woman told him what beautiful hair she once had, and wondered if there was any way she would ever get it back. He nearly told her he did not know, but caught himself and assured her it would; her face lit up at the thought, and his at having prescribed a happiness.

But throughout the afternoon, he was reminded of Schlussel, and the *Gruppe*, and the *Kommandant* lying there, waiting for Niemann to return. Looking out the window, he tried to picture the camp as before, only a few weeks ago, with captains and lieutenants strutting about pridefully. But he could not conjure the memory; despite having seen all of them only hours ago, they were completely gone from the camp, which, while physically unchanged, was utterly transformed.

Just as Niemann accepted that they had been forever cut away from him, he remembered the *Kommandant* lying there, slowly but surely dying. For a moment he savoured the vicious joy of vindictive justice, but in the next moment, he thought about Berlinger's condition, and wondered what justice there was in that. He had been convinced once that he joined the party for justice; that, in struggling to establish a practice after leaving medical school, he was just in denouncing the old Jewish doctor in his own hometown; and that justice had prevailed when the old doctor's patients turned to Niemann. He puzzled over how easily he had dispensed a commodity of which he now realized he had no grasp.

No, justice was no longer, indeed had never truly

been, Niemann's to mete out. The best he could do was try to nurture it in his way, as a physician. He could not condemn the *Kommandant* to death, nor Berlinger to life.

'Yes, Doctor, what can I do for you?' asked the Major, not looking up from the papers on his desk.

'May I sit down?' asked Niemann.

Still without looking up, the Major extended his hand cursorily towards the chair.

'There is a man in town, I saw him there yesterday,' said Niemann, 'who needs my help very badly. I would like –'

'Who is it? What does he want?'

'He has a medical ailment,' answered Niemann vaguely. 'A shopkeeper from the town. I attended him once before, and he feels I know his ailment, and so would like –'

'– You to go and have another look at him, h'm?' said the Major, interested enough now to look at Niemann. 'Where does he live?'

'In a small farmhouse at the edge of town,' answered Niemann. 'I could go with several of your men, though he may want them to wait outside. But you have my word –'

'– That you'll fix him right up and come back here, right?'

'Well, yes, exactly. Two or three hours, at the maximum,' said Niemann.

'And after that, will you have to attend to him again?' asked the Major.

'No, he is planning to leave the area with his family. As soon as he is recovered.' Niemann felt the Major was going to consent.

'His name wouldn't happen to be Colonel Pfluger, would it?'

258

Niemann's jaw dropped, he gasped for air.

The Major stood up, walked around the desk and behind Niemann.

'See, I only look stupid, Doc. It works pretty well,' said the Major, in a jovial tone that terrified Niemann. 'Corporal Simon didn't lose you yesterday, but your friends found you . . . '

'They are not my friends! I was only –'

'I know, you were only going to operate on the Colonel.'

'But it's the truth! Look, I came back,' pleaded Niemann, his heart pounding. The Major came right up close behind Niemann, and put his hand on Niemann's shoulder. Niemann broke into a cold sweat. His throat tightened.

'You know, Doc,' continued the Major in the smiling tone that seemed to Niemann to be the American's ultimate sarcasm. 'I believe you. Simon told me about your little conversation on the way back. I don't think you're stupid enough to cross me.'

The breath that Niemann had held tightly as possibly his last, escaped, and he turned around, incredulous. 'You believe me?'

'If a man's earned the benefit of the doubt, I give it to him,' shrugged the Major. 'Like I said, I only look stupid.'

'What about the Colonel's leg?'

'Chopped above the knee, at a field hospital.'

'Do they know about me?' asked Niemann furtively.

'Don't see why they would. A pacification unit took them. Intelligence just told them where to go,' replied the Major matter-of-factly. 'Why, you want to visit them now? I can't allow –'

'No! No,' replied Niemann, 'not at all.'

*   *   *

Niemann stayed up late that night with Berlinger in their office. On Berlinger's insistence, they had kept detailed records regarding each of the patients, and had scientifically tracked the primary infectious and nutritional ailments, which he felt might be useful in the future. The two were up later than usual, collating and arranging the information in files. Niemann felt this night was different than the previous late nights.

'Are we finished, Doctor?' he asked Berlinger.

'The Major asked if he could start transporting tomorrow,' said Berlinger, not looking up from his work. 'I feel they can travel; the care will be better in France. Unless you have objections?'

'No. No objections,' said Niemann nervously. 'It is time for them to move on. To start anew.' For the first time in weeks, he fretted for himself. 'I have tried as best I could.'

'Yes, you have.' Berlinger lifted his pencil and looked up at the younger man. 'I am deeply grateful. So are they.'

'Thank you. But . . . what about the Major? I am still his prisoner. Does he think that I . . . ?' asked Niemann, trying to disguise the fear that gripped him.

'I don't see how he could not,' responded Berlinger with an assurance that soothed Niemann, but could not convince him. He tried to think of something else.

'How old was your son?'

Berlinger sat back in his chair and drew a deep breath. 'Josef was about your age. He would be thirty-four.'

'Was he also a physician?'

'Yes. I was very proud of him,' said Berlinger, staring at nothing. 'I wanted to practise with him, but he wanted to try on his own, to get out of my shadow.'

'A shadow to some is a beacon to others.'

Berlinger looked up at Niemann, and a faint smile

curled his lips. 'Yes, I suppose it is.' The two men sat looking at one another for a few more moments until Berlinger rose and said, 'Good night, Doctor.' As he passed by Niemann, he stopped and put his bony hand on Niemann's shoulder. 'I will make sure he knows.'

Niemann raised his hand across his chest, placing it tenderly atop the old man's. After a moment, Berlinger withdrew his, and left, leaving Niemann to sit for a few moments by himself. Then he got up to leave as well. On his way out the door, something caught his eye: the picture on the wall. He drew close to it. Yes, the boys were dead. Yes, Mengele was still alive. And yes, the Rudolph Niemann who had been born that day, in the shadows, screaming silently through his clenched teeth just to keep from disappearing completely, no longer existed. He took the picture off the wall, removed it from its frame and tore it into pieces, which he placed in a dish and burned.

Niemann was anxious, but exhausted, and fell asleep quickly that night. He dreamed he was in a courtroom, bound by chains. Facing him were six gaunt pairs of identical twins. The clothes fell off each pair in turn to reveal identical, gruesome scars coursing and stretching over their bodies, then each pair pointed in tandem at Niemann. The American Major stood, waiting for a decision, a noose in one hand, and chaincutters in the other. In the back of the courtroom, Niemann saw Mengele, free, in disguise; he struggled against his chains to point to Mengele, and some people looked where he was pointing, but Mengele had vanished.

Niemann awoke. Outside were dozens of trucks, and inmates swarming around them, hugging, laughing, crying, even dancing; bursting with life like the buds on the trees. Niemann stepped outside, looking for Berlinger. He was surprised not to see him with the inmates; he wondered where he was, if he felt all right. Niemann started towards his office. But halfway across the compound, a soldier stopped him.

'The Major would like a word with you.'

'Where is Dr Berlinger?'

'The Major wants to see you now,' replied the soldier.

In the office the Major was standing beside the window, looking out at the activity in the compound. 'It's really quite something, what you and the doctor have done here. I'd like to thank you.'

'Have you seen Dr Berlinger?' enquired Niemann anxiously. 'Is he to leave with the others?'

The Major paused before answering, 'No. Dr Berlinger has – already left.'

'What do you mean? Without telling me?' Niemann was puzzled by the look on the Major's face; he read the sadness, yet continued weakly, half hoping against what he half knew. 'Without saying goodbye?' Niemann sat down.

'He injected himself with a fatal dose of morphine, late last night.' The Major turned to Niemann, and pleaded, 'Do you know why he would do that, Doctor?'

Niemann tried to choke back tears. 'I wanted to save him,' he sobbed. 'But there is no cure.' And then he chose to not fight the tears, to just let them come. The Major was silent as the doctor cried, for Berlinger, for the people, for the Americans, and for himself; tears of loneliness and shame.

But a man soon runs out of tears which are futile. From outside, the yelling, laughter, and crying reached in to Niemann, and lent him the strength to retake his composure. This, and his own pride, a little bit somehow saved, straightened his back, and lifted his head again to face the Major.

'He left this for you.' The Major pulled an envelope

out of his drawer, tossed it on the desk in front of Niemann, and sat down expectantly.

Tentatively, Niemann picked it up, opened it and carefully removed the contents: some documents, and a passport belonging to 'Josef Berlinger'.

He flipped through the passport to find that the picture had been removed, but the identifying features — blue eyes, dark hair, six feet, age thirty-four — seemed strangely to describe Niemann himself. With it were several wartime identification papers, all for Josef Berlinger, stamped '*Jude*'.

Niemann looked up at the Major and placed them on the desk. The Major slowly picked each document up, studied it, then folded it. After examining them all, he took the passport, studied each page, and set it on the desk with the documents. The two men sat silently, focusing on Berlinger's legacy.

At last, the Major pulled Niemann's wallet and identification out of the desk, opening to the page with Niemann's photograph. Looking up at Niemann, he said, 'It's a very good likeness.' After regarding it for a moment, he tore the picture carefully out, and inserted it into the younger Berlinger's passport. Then he gathered up the documents, and with the passport, slid them back into the envelope. Arising from behind the desk, he circled it and stood before Niemann. After a moment, he tucked the envelope into Niemann's breast pocket.

WHITE CHRYSANTHEMUMS

Bronia Kita

Born in 1959 to an English mother and a Polish father, Bronia Kita read English at York University, intending to write novels and live in the South of France. Instead she found herself working as a law librarian and living in South London. She took a solicitor home for reference purposes and now they have a daughter, Ilona, aged one, who provides Bronia with her best excuse yet for not writing.

WHITE CHRYSANTHEMUMS

They had been married for fifteen years, almost exactly: fifteen years, two weeks and three days. It had never occurred to him that anything might happen to her, why should it? If he'd thought about it he would have realized that, barring a suicide pact or a motorway smash-up, one of them was bound to outlive the other, but he hadn't thought about it. It was too early to consider such things, and besides, women live longer than men; if one of them were to be widowed it would be her. That word said it all: it wasn't possible to be 'widowered'.

She never seemed to be ill, he hadn't yet been made to realize that she was mortal.

He was pruning the roses when the doorbell rang. At first he ignored it, thinking she might already be back, but when the ringing persisted he put down the shears and went to answer. If he looked out of the window he could see how far he had got: all around the borders and about halfway across the island bed in the middle. The two bushes on the left were a foot taller than the three on the right.

For several days the shears had lain on the grass until his next-door neighbour, a keen gardener, able to bear it no longer, had taken them inside.

His first thought when he saw them was they they must be conducting house-to-house enquiries of some kind, but when he realized that one of them was a woman he felt a surge of panic: don't they always send a woman when there's bad news, to do the comforting and the mopping up? Then they told him that his wife had been 'involved in an accident'. (Such wonderful euphemisms they use: as if an accident 'involves' you rather than shakes you, twists you, disfigures you, maims you, kills you.)

They must have made a mistake: she had scarcely been gone an hour. She had a few things to do in the village; it was so close, surely he'd have heard the sound of a crash?

It wasn't a crash, they said. She was crossing the road at the time and was hit by a car. (But that wasn't possible either, traffic moved too slowly through the village.) He didn't ask: probably he could tell from looking at their faces. And how he had stared: he could feel his eyelids drawing back into their sockets as he stared at those two faces, although God alone knew what he was looking for. Did he expect them suddenly to smile and admit that it was all a practical joke?

In the back of the car the policewoman took his hand, and he realized that he was still wearing one of his gardening gloves. He took it off, and not knowing what to do with it, dropped it on his lap so that it fell onto the kerb as he got out.

Apparently she had just left the dry-cleaners and was standing waiting to cross the road, her clothes in their plastic wrappers over her arm, when a driver had signalled her across. She had smiled at him and stepped off the kerb. He had bent to change the tape he was playing, somehow lost concentration, and the car had moved forward. They knew all this because the driver had told them. He kept repeating that he'd just wanted to change the tape. Something about her had reminded him of an ex-girlfriend and he was looking for the Billy Joel number that had been their special song.

The accident had been witnessed by a girl who had just served his wife in the shop, which explained why they had been able to identify her so quickly. As there were no other customers at the time she had been watching Annie go, had run out and knelt beside her, been the one who went with her in the ambulance, the one who was with her when she died.

The girl was still at the hospital when he got there, crushed into the corner of a chair in casualty, a shredded paper tissue in her hand.

He recognized her: he had always thought her surly, and her podgy face with spots around the mouth disgusted him rather. Annie had said that if he were sixteen and had a podgy face with spots around the mouth he'd be surly too, and anyway, surliness was usually a mask for shyness. Now he took the girl's hand, not because he wanted to comfort or to thank her, but because he wanted to touch the last thing that his wife had touched. Looking at those bitten nails with vestiges of ugly pink polish clinging to them he imagined Annie's elegant white fingers, like candles guttering as the flame died. He thought how strange it was that his wife and this girl should have met so many times in such a mundane situation, neither having any idea that their lives would fuse together like this. He resented her for taking a role that she had no right to play. He closed his hand over hers and lowered it.

Soon afterwards the girl's mother had arrived and he'd had to listen to her expressions of sympathy, realizing that they were just the first of many, a little easier to deal with perhaps, because they came from a stranger who would not expect much in response.

Then he had to go through the business of formally identifying the body. He hadn't been sure what to expect: whether there would be much blood, whether she would even be recognizable. He was half desperate to see her, half repelled at the thought.

There wasn't much blood, nor any real sign that she'd been the victim of a violent death save for a large bruise on her temple with a graze at its centre. It wasn't true, though, what they said about the dead looking as though they slept. This looked like her but it wasn't her, like a waxwork. If the eyes were to open he felt sure they'd be made of blue glass.

She had a thin skull, so the doctor said. It was unlucky, but some people's skulls are thinner than others, some spots on the skull are weaker than others. If the same thing had happened to somebody else, they might have survived. It's not something you can foresee, not something we're tested for, and even if we were what could one do – walk around with a crash helmet on all the time?

So many things that had added up against her: if she hadn't gone to the village at that particular time; if she had visited another shop before trying to cross the road; if that man hadn't stopped for her; if she hadn't reminded him of someone; if he hadn't decided to play that song; if she hadn't had a skull like an eggshell . . . All these 'ifs' could send you mad.

Was there anyone else they should inform, they'd asked him. 'Her sister,' he'd said, jolted out of his reverie, 'I'd better call her sister.'

'Jane? Something terrible's happened.' That was all he'd needed to say. He was surprised at how few words were necessary in such a situation. Perhaps people were always unconsciously waiting for something like this, attuned to the break in the voice, alerted by the call at an unusual time?

As she'd answered the phone, Jane had been shouting to her children to stop squabbling. How cruel he felt to be interrupting the precious banality of their lives like this.

While he waited for them to come he sat with the body. He already regarded it as that, and was shocked by his acceptance. He felt terribly claustrophobic in that little cubicle but at the same time he did not dare get up and walk around out of some obscure fear that she might disappear if he left her. These were his last moments with the body that had been so precious to him and he didn't want them to think that he was finished. How ironic it was that when he'd first met her he'd been obsessed with her body, wanted to become familiar with every inch of it. Now it was all that he was left with, and he didn't really want to look at it.

He felt that he should do something, so he reached out a hand and touched her hair. It was a rich auburn colour, the first thing he'd noticed about her. On impulse he felt in his pocket for his gardening knife and before he'd thought about what he was doing, hacked off a lock. He curled his fingers that, despite the gloves, were stained with soil, around the hair and lifted it away, then felt guilty. It looked so obvious. What would the hospital staff say? She was his wife, wasn't she? But she wasn't, not any more. She was a 'body', not his to do as he liked with: he'd have to bury her.

He recalled that she'd told him once about a mad Spanish queen who was so grief-stricken at the death of her handsome husband that she'd taken his corpse around with her for years, everywhere she went. He hadn't been able to understand that: 'If all she was attached to was his body surely she could have found someone else who looked like him – she was queen, after all.'

'But it wouldn't have been the same: there would be so many little differences – in the way he moved, his voice, which side of the bed he liked to sleep on . . . all the insignificant things that add up to the person you love.'

He remembered her words now, as he looped the hair in a circle and put it carefully in his wallet.

Jane and Malcolm arrived then. In all the years he had known Jane he had never seen her after she'd been crying – maybe a few tears after the moving final scene of a play or a film, but not after she'd really been crying. She was barely recognizable: not only her eyes but her lips seemed swollen, and her face looked as though she'd been flayed.

'I'm sorry we took so long, I had to find someone who could take the kids. Oh, God.' She moved towards the body, took hold of both its hands, and leaned forward, looking at the face. He saw the stains made by her tears falling on the white sheet. Suddenly she stretched out her arm and touched the forehead, then let go, and raising both hands to her mouth, ran out of the room.

Malcolm, who had touched her shoulder as she passed him, said, 'She keeps being sick – once at home, twice on the way here. Had to stop the car. Can't be anything left by now.'

He felt inadequate in the face of such grief, like an under-rehearsed actor in a tragedy. He looked at Malcolm, Malcolm looked away.

They had told him that she died almost immediately. He hadn't realized until then what a cruel little word 'almost' could be: 'almost enough', 'almost there', 'almost made it', 'almost immediately'. How much suffering might those six letters represent? What happened to your brain when your skull cracked like that? Had she been aware of what had happened to her, of the girl leaning over her, of the man who had killed her crying hysterically? Try as he might, he couldn't imagine it; tragedies are supposed to happen on motorways, during storms or thick fog. The conditions have to be right.

He was a photographer, trained to capture dramatic situations in appropriate settings – although in his work for a local paper there was little scope to use his training – and a dead woman in a gutter should be lit by a streetlamp or drenched by driving rain. It made him realize how cliché-ridden people's imaginations were, and how he and others like him had contributed to that. The staff at this hospital could tell you that 'freak accident' was a tautology: there was no such thing as a normal accident, one that occurred on time and to specification.

He hadn't wanted to go home with them, but Jane had insisted. As they left a nurse had handed her Annie's handbag and the clothes, still in their plastic shrouds. They bore no mark of what had happened. Watching Jane as she stumbled almost blinded by tears along the corridor, he was struck by how deeply conditioned people are to carry out everyday tasks: she had put the strap of the bag over her shoulder and folded the clothes over her arm in the way she would have done if she were just leaving the shop with them.

As they were about to get into the car she had suddenly turned to him: 'How am I going to tell the kids?'

He hadn't known what to say, so he had touched her hair which, although she was younger than Annie, was already fading.

Of course the children knew that something was wrong, he could see the anxiety in their eyes when the neighbour opened the door. As soon as they got home Susan had asked, 'Has something happened to Granny or Grandpa?'

'No, sweetheart,' Jane had said. 'It's your Auntie Annie.' For a long unbearable moment his niece had looked towards him and then back at her mother.

'Is she dead?' she asked in a quiet, controlled voice. Unable to answer, Jane hugged her and began to cry again, and over her shoulder he saw Susan's face before she turned and ran upstairs.

That night he lay awake listening to his niece crying. It was a terrible sound – a wail that suddenly cut off and resumed, over and over again, always the same note. Occasionally he heard the low murmur of Jane's voice as she tried to comfort her, as he writhed on the bed, drawing up his knees, turning over onto his back, to his left, to his right. He felt inexplicably guilty, as if it were he who had brought this upon them, all his fault.

Eventually he sat on the edge of the bed with his head in his hands, then went to the bathroom to splash his face with water. On the way back his nephew's bedroom door opened and Michael stood looking up at him.

'Can't sleep either?' he asked him.

'I'm frightened,' the little boy said. He took him back to bed with him and they had both fallen asleep. He awoke long before Michael did, but lay still so as not to disturb him, waiting for sounds of movement elsewhere in the house. Susan had fallen silent eventually and was presumably asleep now, too. His first thought, even before he had opened his eyes, had been: she's dead. Once again he was struck by the inadequacy of his reaction: his wife was dead and he lay there watching the familiar objects emerge from the darkness and gradually take on substance as dawn broke. He was shocked to realize that he even felt slightly hungry.

Michael became increasingly restless and eventually opened his eyes. He lay still for a minute, blinking.

'I had a nightmare that Auntie Annie had died,' he

said. 'Then when I woke up I realized it was true. Why did she die?'

'It was an accident,' he said, hoping Michael wouldn't realize that he was telling him how, not why. 'It could have happened to anybody.'

'Does that mean it could happen to you, or to Mummy or Daddy, or Susan – or me?'

'I suppose so, but it doesn't happen very often. Most people – at least in this part of the world – die because they grow old.' He was hoping against hope that Michael wouldn't ask him whether Annie was in heaven, as he wouldn't have any idea of how to answer, but after a pause he said, 'I don't want to grow old, but I don't want to have an accident, either.' Unable to cope any longer he had taken him downstairs.

Although Jane had tried to persuade him to stay he'd insisted on going home. He had to face it sooner or later, and he preferred to do it now, before the truth sunk in, or he might never be able to bear it.

It seemed strange as they drove up to see that the house was still there, just an ordinary small house in the middle of a street, with nothing to mark it apart from all the others.

Once inside, he experienced the sensation he always had when returning from a holiday: although he believed he had a clear picture of each room in his head something was subtly different, as if he'd suddenly stepped through the looking-glass.

Jane walked around touching things. Perhaps she couldn't believe everything was still there, either. Then she went over to the vase of white chrysanthemums on the table in the bay window, lifted them up and let them drop again, and he realized what she was doing: trying to make a final connection with her sister by touching the things she had so recently touched, as if attempting to absorb any latent energy left behind, as he had with the girl's hand.

She didn't want to leave him there, didn't want to leave the house, but she had to get back to her own family, so she went at last, letting the silence fold in on him.

He was completely at a loss. Jane and Malcolm had taken on the responsibility of telling people and making the funeral arrangements. He knew there must be other things that one had to do in this situation, but his mind was too numb to think of any. On the other hand he could hardly just read a book. He sat at the dining-table and stared at the garden. He should have been thinking of her, but he wasn't consciously thinking of anything. He felt paralysed, physically incapable of getting up and walking away.

He didn't know how long he'd been sitting there when his mother arrived. He had thought that he wanted to be alone, but it was a good deal easier having someone else in the house, as it meant he had to fight the feeling of creeping inertia that threatened to overpower him. Although he wasn't particularly close to his mother their relationship meant that he didn't have to make much effort to speak to her, while at the same time she was able to take over his life, impose some form of structure.

It soon became evident that she had agreed with Annie's mother that he mustn't ever be left, so they took it in turns to mind him. Whereas he could overrule Jane he couldn't do the same with them, and besides he could tell that it was necessary for Annie's mother to believe that his grief was greater than hers, so that she felt bound to look after him. He couldn't decide whether it was unfair to women that they were expected to do so much caring, or to men that they should be made to feel redundant at such times.

His first feeling on seeing her mother had been one of repulsion: she looked so much older with her eyes rimmed with red and her mouth sagging. He was almost affronted that she should still be alive. When he realized that she felt the same, he stopped hating her.

The two mothers didn't really like each other: it was bizarre, watching them trying to be civil to each other.

Whereas his own mother prattled on about the doings of people he didn't know or scarcely remembered, Annie's mother couldn't help but talk about her daughter, but he didn't mind. He didn't want people to behave as though she didn't exist, even though she didn't, any more.

'She was a lovely baby,' she told him, sitting opposite him at the table (he noticed that she, too, held a handkerchief screwed up in one hand like the girl from the cleaners, although hers was cotton, embroidered in one corner with violets). 'Jane always seemed to be crying, but Anne was so good it was like having a baby doll.'

On and on she went, telling him tales of Annie's virtue, her looks, her intelligence. She's fixed now, he thought. She'll never be able to change her mother's picture of her by running away and leaving me for another man or cutting off from her, or anything else she might have done to blot her copybook.

Her traumatized mind was confused, so that she assumed he knew people from Annie's past with whom she'd lost contact long before he met her, but he didn't mind her rambling: she needed to talk, to hone the image of her daughter as if she were cutting a diamond, exposing the facets that would reflect the light, and he needed to listen.

Occasionally she would use some quaint phrase: 'She gave me an old-fashioned look', or 'I never saw the going of it', that Annie must have got from her, and he would start, almost as if he heard her voice again.

On the day of the funeral he came downstairs to find his own mother applying make-up to the face of Annie's mother, who sat, as unresponsive as a stroke victim, staring ahead of her. He stood and watched as she painstakingly rouged the lined cheeks, applied lipstick to the slack mouth.

'I had the devil of a job getting her dressed,' she said, without looking round. 'She wears one of those corsets with dozens of hooks and eyes and I couldn't get it lined up properly. Kept having to start again.'

'You could have asked me for a hand.'

'Don't be daft,' she said, shooting him a sharp glance. 'Hasn't she got enough to put up with, without having to endure a man seeing her in her foundation garments? Now, Dorothy,' she went on, taking her hand, 'you've got to make an effort. I know how you feel, it was the same for me when I lost my Timothy: I felt like climbing into that grave with him, but I had my husband to think of, so I got on with life, and it gradually got easier.'

His brother had died a cot death before he was born, but she'd never told him that she'd felt like that; he'd never really considered it.

Annie's mother was looking at her now, showing signs of life. Her eyes filled with tears and his mother took her handkerchief and dried them carefully.

'Not yet, love,' she said.

He went through the funeral as though he were a visitor from another planet who had slipped unnoticed among the mourners. There were a lot of people there, some of whom he didn't recognize and who must have been colleagues from her work. In particular he noticed a tall thin young man with glasses who sobbed continuously.

His niece insisted on sitting next to him and holding

278

his hand, and it was only halfway through the service, when he noticed her casting a surreptitious glance at him, that he realized she had done it to comfort him, not herself.

The church setting only made the whole proceedings seem more surreal: she hadn't believed in God any more than he did. He should have thought of something else, but there had been no time. It was going to be a cremation, but Jane had suddenly been repelled by the thought of burning her.

'It's not *her* any more, Janie. She's gone.'

'I know that. I know that rationally, but if we burned her there'd be nothing left. If she's buried at least there'll be a grave we can visit.'

He'd let Jane have her way, insisting on only one thing: that people be asked to make a donation to charity, rather than waste money on flowers. Now, seeing how stark the unadorned coffin looked, he wasn't sure he'd made the right decision. It was lowered bare into the ground, until Jane and the two children threw some blooms from the garden onto its lid. They were white chrysanthemums, like the ones still in the vase at home. They'd lasted a long time, longer than she had.

They'd wanted him to throw the first handful of soil, but the thought appalled him, so Jane had done it. She'd gone to the doctor for tranquillizers and had tried to persuade him to do the same, but he didn't need to, he felt like a sleep-walker anyway. They made her clumsy, so that she couldn't co-ordinate, and she'd dropped her bag. It narrowly missed toppling into the grave. His nephew had picked it up and tried to hand it back to her, but realizing that she was oblivious, he'd kept hold of it. The whole affair had seemed so bizarre that he'd found himself looking around for Annie so that he could catch her eye and exchange smiles.

Back at Jane's he had surprised himself by the way he'd walked around, talking to people. It was just as well everyone wore black for funerals, or he might have forgotten that this wasn't just an ordinary party. He wondered when it became acceptable to talk about other things again. Was there a point when you crossed the Rubicon and life could continue, or did it just happen gradually, without your noticing?

The tall thin young man was still having difficulty controlling himself. Somebody told him that his name was Jonathan and that he had been a member of Annie's 'team'.

'He's taken it hard, poor chap. He really admired her.'

It was more than that, he thought, as Jonathan was brought over to him. He loved her. He loved her, and I never even knew he existed.

After the guests had left and Jane had gone to lie down, he went to the kitchen and loaded the dishwasher while his mother moved around covering bowls with clingfilm and fitting them into the fridge.

'Funny, isn't it — how people always feel obliged to provide food after funerals when nobody wants to eat, or at least they don't want to be seen to eat, in case they seem callous?' Changing the subject, she said without looking at him, 'You should have had children, you know. They would have been a comfort to you now.'

'You can't have children just so that one day they'll be a comfort to you.' He felt quite angry. 'They'd be *motherless* children. It's had a bad enough effect on Susan and Michael; imagine how hard it would be for her own kids to deal with.'

His mother had a talent for hitting raw nerves: the same thought had occurred to him and he'd dismissed it. They had never decided for certain that they didn't want children, but it had been deferred and deferred until they would have had to do something about it soon if they were going to. And now it was too late.

He had been vaguely in favour of the idea, but Annie had seen so many abused and unloved kids that she didn't want to bring more into the world, and ultimately it was her decision. Now he'd never see a child with her eyes, her hair, playing in the garden . . .

It was better this way, he told himself. How would he cope with his job if he had a family to take care of? The paper wouldn't take kindly to kids tagging along on assignments, even if they did carry some of the gear.

Anyway, Susan's reaction had frightened him somewhat: she wasn't yet eleven, but after her first outburst of grief she had appeared so adult in the way she kept checking on him that it seemed wrong. She shouldn't understand so much at that age, kids nowadays seemed to grow up too fast.

But when he went back to his empty house he felt less sure: if he had someone else to look after it would be easier to force himself to carry on with life. Meals would have to be prepared at regular times, some sort of routine would be necessary, and gradually, as time passed, it would regain a semblance of normality.

It was so unfair to be expected to continue like this; you need time to learn to be a single person again, just as it takes time to learn to be two people, to replace 'I' with 'we'.

He couldn't bring himself to cook, not just for himself, but that evening just before seven, the doorbell rang. When he went to answer it there was no one there, but somebody had left a tray on the doorstep with a plate of stew and a dish of apple pie. There was no sign of anyone, so he'd taken it inside and sat down in an armchair with the tray on his knees. It was then that he had cried at last. Looking at the stodgy food that he couldn't eat he had finally realized that he was alone, and he'd cried for his loneliness and for another reason, too: he'd cried because this gesture was exactly the sort that she would have made.

He did in the end eat some of the food, and more the next night when the same thing happened, until by the end of the week he was eating everything on his plate and leaving the washed dishes on the tray on the doorstep as if they were empty milk bottles. Although naturally he was curious, he respected the wishes of his anonymous well-wisher and never tried to spy on her — he was sure it was a woman. After two weeks the deliveries stopped, but by then his appetite had returned, and besides he had realized how much time he could fill by chopping and preparing food. He began to treat himself like the child he didn't have and ate deliberately slowly, in front of the television, never letting the dishes pile up, but washing and drying everything after each meal before putting them away in the cupboards.

They had rarely watched television before, preferring to read or listen to music. Annie had often had reports to write and he liked to mess around in his darkroom, so they didn't really need it. He had never minded silence when he knew she was there, or would be coming home soon from her Spanish class or an evening with friends; now it was unbearable, and he would rather have any noise in the background to fill it. He half watched programmes he had never before known existed: daytime soap operas, inane quiz shows, documentaries about threatened wildlife. He fell asleep in the second bedroom listening to the soporific tones of late-night disc jockeys.

He had moved most of his clothes out of their room so that he wouldn't have to keep seeing her things, but one day, after he'd started working again, he needed a particular jacket, and as he reached into the wardrobe his hand had brushed against one of her dresses. He took it out and laid it on the bed. Lying there, two-dimensional, it didn't seem to bear any relation to her shape. He brought out another, then another, but none of them looked quite right. They were like the sloughed skins of lizards, he couldn't expect them to look as though the body were still in them. Once he had started he couldn't stop: he took her underwear from its drawer, emptied her make-up bag onto the dressing-table, held earrings up to the light. But he wasn't a magician: he couldn't conjure her up from these elements as she had conjured herself. He tried to pull on one of her skirts, but it was too small.

That night, as the canned laughter of some comedy blared out from the television, he slowly painted his nails with some of her nailpolish.

He was continually finding things that made him think of her: one day he decided that he must hoover the floors, and as he knelt to clean under the bed he saw a single stocking. He lay down and reached out for it. It was covered with small balls of dust, but he put his hand inside, stretched out his fingers, and smelled it. Then as he lay there he noticed something else: the entire carpet was covered with a filigree of human hair. If he rubbed with the heel of his hand it would form a clump. The whole house was like this, her hair spreading and filling it secretly, like ectoplasm. He abandoned his attempts to clean after that, as it would be like ridding himself of her.

He became aware as time went on that the precise lineaments of her face were growing less sharp in his memory. He realized that he hadn't looked at her much, not properly, there had been no need: she was always there, somewhere in the corner of his vision, bending over her work while he read the paper, sitting on the other side of the table, walking beside him. Virtually the only occasions when he had looked at her squarely had been when he was photographing her. Then he remembered: there was a half-used film in one of his cameras. It was black and white, but it carried his last pictures of her.

He took it to his darkroom and closed the door. He felt sick from anticipation and the smell of chemicals as one by one the final six portraits of her swam into focus. In five she was smiling, but in the last her head was slightly bowed and she was looking up at the camera, her face pensive. He remembered taking it late one evening when they had just come in and she was tired.

He leaned forward, trying to take in every detail, every nuance of expression. Her name was Anne Elizabeth Walsh, she was thirty-nine years old. She was a social worker. She enjoyed Dickens and loved Emily Brontë. She was allergic to penicillin and liked Mozart and Chopin. Her hair was red, her eyes were blue. She was killed by a man who was changing a tape. She had no children. She had a small scar beneath her chin. She wanted to make a better world. He had loved her.

He lifted the prints one by one and pegged them up to dry.

THE FOOL

Kirk O'Connor

Kirk Patrick O'Connor was born in 1968 in Manchester. Brought up in Sussex, he attended Brighton University and East London University where he received his degree in European Finance. For the last four years he has worked at a puzzle magazine publisher in Redhill. He has written poetry since childhood and was published last year in an anthology of modern poetry. Other interests include literature, travel, martial arts and psychology. *The Fool* is his first short story.

THE FOOL

Perched in the knotty hair of this oak, I warble and twitter about insoluble things; games perhaps, or the last days of a man who had long forgotten who he was and what he was.

The hours prior to its first manifestation had been quiet. After dinner with the minister I retired to my ante-chamber; a circular room with pale walls upon which hung ancient statutes. The marble floor was polished to perfection and amplified the dignity of the room through the few pieces of furniture that I had sanctioned.

While resting in my favourite chair I allowed myself the luxury of pondering upon my life and its many achievements: the party of rule that I moulded out of the chaos of the early years, the complete revision of a bankrupt legal system, the careers of my sons, the marriages of my daughters, the modest wealth that I had accepted from an ever-grateful people – which I subsequently lavished upon them in the form of public works of art.

The flutter of wings from outside the large open window intruded upon my thoughts. I was irritated and made a mental note for the gamekeeper to investigate this disturbance in the morning. Birds were not allowed near my properties.

The fluttering started again, louder. I ignored it. Its tempo increased. I muttered a curse and brusquely got to my feet. 'Damn you crows!' I shouted. 'I'll have your beaks for this!' And thumped my way to the window.

Then it appeared, man-like, crouched on the window ledge.

It looked like a harlequin, or some kind of jester. Its livery was quartered in lurid green and pink. Little silver bells hung from its cockscomb and jarred like loose fillings. Its face was pure murderous Punch with the hooked nose, goggle eyes and thin lips. Its chest protruded like a chicken's and its legs were spindly coils of wiry muscle moving under purple tights. Taloned hands dug into the window frame on either side.

I stood absolutely still some five feet from the monster, appalled and fascinated in equal measure.

It cocked its head and shifted one pace to the left, muttering to itself. I strained to hear.

'What goes on four legs in the morning, two legs at noon, and three legs in the evening?' it croaked.

'Hardly original,' I replied.

'Well, fuck you!' it screamed, and disappeared in a jangle of bells.

I remained motionless for some minutes. Eventually, I summoned a servant, and no, nothing had been heard, and yes, those were very peculiar scratch-marks on the window. Was master feeling well? Would he require the carpenter tomorrow? I shook my head, increasingly puzzled by this discrepancy in phenomena.

You may wonder that mine was not an ordinary reaction to such an apparition; I did not measure myself by such prosaic criteria.

My life must be measured in metre, like poetry. In my own way I have taken the golden unbending laws of life and laid them across the backs of a once undisciplined and desperate nation. And in that I paid the ultimate price with my first son. Whatever the present, even as the nation slips into ruin at the hands of its current leaders, I know that my deeds and reputation are writ in marble.

The phantasms of the past will seek to return and suck out all the glory of the present. I looked upon that vivid thing, perched on my window ledge as nothing more than my personal Banquo. Frightful, but harmless.

It appeared again in the window the following night. For a few moments it remained silent, swivelling its head around the room like a baleful searchlight. Then it began to pant. The panting grew heavier, reminding me of a massive black dog I had freed from my father's coal cellar one pitiless summer's day many years ago.

Then it spoke. 'The man who made it did not want it; the man who bought it did not use it; the man who used it did not know it. What is it?' This riddle was delivered in the same unhuman voice as the previous night; a kind of sing-song squeal.

Fortunately, word-games were a private passion of mine and I already knew this one. 'A coffin,' I answered. 'Now, my turn.'

The thing shifted, seemed more interested, slightly expectant.

'We have a horse without any head, and all dressed up, not living or dead.'

'A clothes-horse!' With a satisfied squawk, it was gone.

These word-duels carried on night after night. At some random point in the evening the thing or 'Punch', as I had named it, would appear and challenge me to a contest of wits. My daylight hours were spent constructing tactics of attack and defence; researching and creating new riddles to trick Punch, while attempting to cover every possible angle of its offence.

I had little time to reflect upon the nature of the beast, the consummate ease in which it answered my riddles was both astounding and alarming. I had my servants scour the libraries both public and private, for any information concerning my adversary. And while it seemed an amalgam of many things it clearly was not one or the other.

Absorbed in this bizarre contest, it came as a shock to be informed that my movements beyond the perimeter of the estate were suddenly barred by court order. My monthly excursions were now denied to me, as were all visitors except those sanctioned by the government.

While I was recovering from this latest setback, Punch appeared with its usual supernatural efficiency at just past eleven and invited me to start proceedings. I cleared my throat.

'There's a man in a room without doors or windows. The only furniture is a wooden table. How does the man get out?'

The answer was scornfully flung back: 'He bangs his head against the wall until it's sore and takes the saw and cuts the table in half and puts the two halves together to make a whole and gets through the hole and shouts until he's hoarse and gets on the horse and rides away.'

Silence. It licked its lips. 'What did the man do when he thought he was dying?' As I feverishly searched for a solution an evil grin slid across Punch's face. I sensed imminent violence. My eyes flickered towards the door, and I had it!

'A living room! He goes to the living room.'

Punch's smile broadened, but was colder. It nodded towards me. I rubbed the sweat out of my eyes and recited my next conundrum.

'Why is I the luckiest of vowels?' For a moment I

thought I had it confounded. Then its whole frame convulsed with a series of cackles and wheezes. I blushed madly and was incensed, the thing was mocking me! 'Well? At a loss for words? Met your match? Eh? Eh?'

Its face dropped like a guillotine. Hooded eyes unpeeled me layer by layer.

'Because it is in the centre of happiness, while E is in hell, and all the others are in purgatory.'

I stumbled back towards the door. Yet I knew that if I turned to run the thing would be on me. Punch's eyes momentarily shifted to my hopeless goal. It leaned forward into the room.

'Long slim and slender, dark as home-made thunder, keen eyes and peaked nose, scares the Devil wherever it goes.'

'A shotgun,' I replied.

Punch whooped and hopped into the room. 'No! A snake!' My knees gave way and I half fell, half scrambled towards the door. In an instant it was there.

'Next time,' it smiled and slunk out through the door, leaving me shivering and sweating in the dark.

I did not sleep or rest that last night. I felt its presence all around me. I somehow comprehended that fleeing, in the physical sense of the word, was useless. Why I should have been singled out in this monstrous manner I did not know. I had committed no singular crime that could warrant such diabolical attention. I had merely lived my life to the best of my abilities just as anyone else might do theirs.

If I was guilty of anything, then it is to have ruled with my eyes open to the consequences of my actions. All that I have done weighs like shining gold upon my shoulders. Not even this government can understand that the garments of greatness are weaved from gold and marble and must be worn with dignity, though the burden is agony.

That morning a state official with a squad of investigators arrived at my house and informed me that the file on my first son's mysterious death was to be reopened in the light of new evidence. He demanded access to all my private papers and had the mansion summarily strip-searched by his thieves.

Why all the sudden interest from the state after so many years? The answer was obvious, Punch had opened up a second front! How naïve of me to think it would fight fair. The creature was obviously an embodiment of all that is foul and base in today's society. I had to destroy it!

I was allowed to summon my solicitor, accountant and physician, instructing them in their various duties. I sent for the local priest and commanded him to perform an exorcism. After dismissing my bewildered servants I returned to the antechamber loaded with religious gewgaws, and opened a priceless claret.

Just after midnight, it appeared in the room. I flinched, knocking a bottle over. The liquid rinsed across the marble.

Punch peered at me and tittered, its bells tinkling like broken glass.

'When I first appear I seem mysterious, but when I'm explained, I'm nothing serious.' This was a well-known poser and I knew Punch was toying with me.

'The answer is riddle,' I replied. It scuttled back towards the wall and waited with crab-like patience.

'What is it, a rich man has and wants more of, a fat man has and doesn't want, and a poor man wants and can't get?'

'Pounds.' It sneered as it picked its nose and nonchalantly flicked the mucus onto my Louis XVI chaise longue. 'I move without wings between silken strings, I leave as you find, my substance behind.'

My mind went blank as I panicked. Punch clucked impatiently. The chaise longue was my inspiration.

'Spider,' I mumbled.

Nauseated and frightened I found that I could only think of one riddle in return.

'Two brothers we are, great burdens we bear, all day we are bitterly pressed; yet this I will say – we are full all the day, and empty when we go to rest.'

Did I detect something else in its eyes as it slowly enunciated its answer, perhaps an acknowledgement of truth? As 'shoe' echoed around the room I started to cry.

Punch's voice compressed to a steely hiss. 'I'll give the answer and you work out the question.' It paused, letting the horror and injustice of its trick sink in. Outside, the wind had dropped and the trees had stopped shuffling their leaves. Only my pathetic snuffles could be heard. It leaned forward and whispered with extreme malevolence: 'Office desk.'

The words seemed to close like tree roots around my chest. I felt faint and shallow; my eyes stung and my nose ran. I whimpered something idiotic and hopeless. Punch leaped to its feet and howled triumphantly.

'A man took a train on Monday morning – walked to the City and went calmly into his office, then suddenly leaped into the air and took a running jump towards the window. Where did he go then?'

It was upon me.

Dead. All dead, Judy. What can a pretty boy do? Judy? Where are you? I'm coming to get you. Hush, my baby, or I'll cut you up into little pieces. Pieces of hate, pieces of hate! He's behind you. Oh no he isn't! Take that!

Long and slinky like a colt, its guts spew out when it tries to bolt.

I sucked up the last gobs of flesh and flew out into the trees.

A POETRY READING ON RIVERSIDE

David Evans

David Evans was born in South Africa but left after a period of imprisonment for anti-apartheid activities. Since then he has lived and taught on Merseyside. He writes poetry and plays and has just completed a novel set in the Languedoc region of France.

A POETRY READING ON RIVERSIDE

Now that word about the poetry reading has got around it's hard to convince anyone that we were just looking for a quiet night out. For one thing, nobody believes I'm the sort usually to be found on a cold March night sitting in a side room of the Arcadia, one of Riverside's arty bistros, with a guitar between my legs and a sheaf of songs in my lap while some old guy drills on about injustice somewhere in Southern Africa.

This is partly because I was a bit of a tearaway at school, sagging regularly, and determined to leave as early as I could to earn the money to buy myself a good time – a good time being clubbing and pubbing. My mother says I take after my dad, not her. *She* believes in the magic of words and the talent of Riversiders, pointing proudly to all the writers and musicians and actors the city has given to the world – all descendants of the rich mixture of people brought in by the sea. What she forgets is that they came here to escape poverty and now leave for the same reason – which I'll do as soon as I can scratch together the money to get away to London or New York, or wherever people have more to live on than giros and tales of how hard it used to be. On what I earn as a checkout girl at Woolie's this won't be for a while.

I must have been quite a disappointment to my mam from the start; her only girl and skiving literature lessons whenever I could. She's always been good about it, though, trying to see talent in my liking for pop and my amateurish plucking at the guitar inherited from my brother Pat, and not talking about my friend Julie more than once or twice a day. Julie's the daughter she should have had, shining at school while I barely glimmered.

The poetry reading was Julie's idea, of course.

When we left the comprehensive school, Julie and I swore that whatever happened we would keep seeing each other, even though she was going on to university and I was fated for Woolie's. And we have. What has kept us going has been a bit of a mystery to some people in spite of our having been born in the same street, having dads more or less permanently on the dole and the ale, mothers who meet regularly at the same pawn-shop and enough brothers and their loutish mates to make female solidarity part of the survival kit. I put it down to us both being determined that whatever we did we weren't going to settle for marriage and kids – the style around our way – until we'd tried everything else.

So we made this pact. Once a week we'd do something together, taking it in turns to decide what. Julie usually chose items from the culture menu – plays, foreign films, concerts, operas when she was really in funds – while I dragged us off to the ABC or the Odeon, gigs by the usual loud local groups making a name or trying to live one down, and a succession of discos. Funnily enough we often liked each other's choices best. I really got off on theatre, especially when there was something on by Willy Russell or Alan Bleasdale. Julie, on the other hand, seemed to enjoy discoing most, perhaps because with her figure and tumbling black hair she looks and moves like one of those movie waifs – you know, the starving but sexy kind.

Our best night out together, though, was when I made her come with me to the wrestling and she forgot that she was a third-year student sure to get a first-class degree and became so worked up over what Ugly Ulrich was doing to The Blackball Kid that she was up next to the ring with a whole lot of old ones, effing and blinding and trying to swat the big German with her handbag. He wanted to date her afterwards but she couldn't be arsed.

'Your little finger would split me in half, big boy,' she said, smiling up at his six and a half feet from her five foot two. You'll gather from this that Julie hasn't been totally wrecked by higher education.

Another reason for going to the bistro was that a fortnight after the wrestling I yanked Julie along to the Cuckoo's Nest because I'd heard Tom Fry sometimes turned up there, sang a few songs and played a bit of pool. Tom Fry is a kind of British Leonard Cohen, only much younger. We were waiting for the band and having what was meant to be a quiet drink when some lads got into dispute over a recent football game and began heaving pool balls around, first at each other and then at everyone in sight; pool balls being the local answer to the Exocet missile. Julie got us both down under the table just as a ball shattered the half-glass of Guinness I had put down in front of her, then ricocheted on and up to smash the bartender in the middle of the forehead before starring the mirror behind him. We crawled out through the door, not caring to see the rest.

We learned later that the score of casualties by the end of the evening was Everton 4, Liverpool 3, excluding a neutral bystander and the barman.

After that I suggested Julie choose the entertainment for a time until I got my nerve back.

Which is how the poetry reading came up.

We were sitting in the relative peace of Effing Nellie's, so named because the manageress had never in living memory made it through an expletive-free sentence, when Julie produced this poster she'd taken down from a wall in the university.

'It's time for a change,' she said, 'something quiet and improving.'

I looked at the poster. 'Songs of Politics and Passion: Guest Poet: Simon Verster – veteran of the South African struggle.'

'You know I'm not the poetry type,' I objected.

'Nonsense. You scribbled away with the best of us when they allowed creativity sessions at school – and what about your songs?'

'They're just for laughs.'

I was lying, of course. Like every other girl in Riverside I've been trying to write songs ever since I was old enough to listen to Joan Armatrading and finger a guitar.

'Look,' Julie jabbed a finger at the small type and grinned at me, 'they're encouraging performers from the floor. You could try out some songs there – might even catch some useful person's eye.'

'Like the time I got hissed off in Smoky Joe's? Besides . . .' taking my turn to jab the poster '. . . it says Politics and Passion and you know politics piss me off.'

'But what about the passion, eh? I'm told that Tom Fry said he might look in and sing a song or two. What's more, it's only 50p at the door and we get a happy hour.'

Shrewd Julie! We were both pretty near skint. Also, as she well knew, I'd fancied Tom Fry rotten ever since he'd done a Musicians-in-Education gig at our school, looked over some of us kids' stuff and said mine had promise. And, on top of that, a chance to sing my stuff in a place with a bit of class – all for only 50p! How could I resist?

'They wouldn't let me perform,' I objected, trying not to sound too keen. 'Not in the Arcadia Bistro.'

'That's where you're wrong, Sharon. They let anyone – even Nigel Parkinson.'

'Never Nigel Parkinson.'

'Nigel Parkinson. It was Nigel who first told me about it. He knows one of the organizers.'

'Or pretends he does.'

'He introduced me. A prat called Paul Curran.'

Mention of Nigel nearly put me off. He grew up in our street and went to our school until his parents made a bob or two, moved and sent Nigel to one of those fee-paying schools, which was a happy event for the rest of us, except that he burned for Julie and kept re-appearing, first on one of those bikes that costs as much as a small car and then in a VW cabriolet, trying to get Julie to go out with him. She wouldn't but he hung around a lot trying not to take no for an answer. When Julie went to university, it turned out he was there too, and as hot for her as ever.

But Nigel was Julie's problem. And perhaps she was right: we were getting into a rut and a quiet, improving poetry night was the answer.

I continued to moan. But as the date approached I got more and more excited. Usually, I tog up in the kind of gear that pulls a man – around our way, that is – not because I'm mad to have one but because it's the style. This time, though, I cut out the heavy make-up, dangling earrings, clingy dress and fishnet tights, whacked on a Save-the-Whale T-shirt, dungarees and Doc Martens and stuffed my mop of ringlets into a sea-man's cap; almost exactly the kind of outfit Julie – who normally prefers the Greenham Common look – could be expected to approve. Perversely, she arrived at our front door in a slinky black top under a smart leather jacket, a short skirt, silk stockings and heels, explaining that she'd been too busy writing essays to visit the laundrette and so was stuck with clothes from her pre-femmo period. Luckily, they still fitted. And, of course, she looked gorgeous.

My mam, who almost always has a bit to say about our gear, didn't comment this time, except to predict 'a night of magic'. I put this restraint down to her being made up that we were getting into high culture; 'pawtry', according to her, being a gift of the gods.

We were grinding along to the bistro in Julie's old Mini, past the row of Georgian terraces behind the Cathedral, when Julie said, 'There's Phyllie,' and swung into the kerb.

It was Phyllie sure enough, shivering on the pavement in a skirt that barely covered her arse, a thin blouse with the three top buttons undone and a pair of skyscraper heels: Phyllis Dunn, twenty-two, a former schoolmate and on the game to finance a habit picked up from the guy she took up with in fourth form and who stayed around just long enough to give her a kid. She works her patch so hard they call her Road Runner. Not much magic in her nights.

There's a motherly side to Julie. 'You can't stand around like that in this weather,' she said to Phyllie. 'Get in and come for a drink in the bistro with us or let me drop you off home.'

'Can't,' Phyllie got out through chattering teeth, 'I'm in dead trouble – months behind with the rent. Tell you what, though, you could lend me your jacket. I'm frigging antarctic out here.'

Julie went on a bit, trying to persuade her to get in

the car. But after a while she took off her leather jacket and handed it out of the car window.

'You're mad, you,' I said as we drove off. 'She'll sell it for dope or worse.'

'Better that than selling herself.'

Because I was feeling bad about Phyllis, I said, 'If you're giving clothes away, you should at least have worn a bra. You're showing nearly as much as she is.'

It wasn't true. But Julie has quite large boobs for her size and cheeky nipples that prick out at you. This never bothers her, but it doesn't half unsettle some men, who don't seem to have been properly weaned.

'Wave when we turn the corner,' was the reply.

I looked back. There was no Phyllie – only a big Granada pulling away from the corner where she'd been standing.

Inside the bistro we barged through a main part full of the types you might expect to see drinking and eating just before a show in the nearby theatre – gents in suits and their furred and trinketed women, pretenders looking like actors and actors looking like factory workers taking a break – straight into a side room. This had a bar tended by a girl who looked like an exile from the real scene in the main section. Not surprisingly; after the bustle and heat there this room seemed desolate with its scattering of empty tables and chairs, dim lighting and droopy pot plants. The only other inmates were a woman with pale yellow hair wearing a high-collared white blouse and the kind of long black skirt popular with women in orchestras, a wimpish-looking man in cardy, flannels and sandals and an older couple, all talking at the bar.

They looked around as we came in, and, realizing we weren't important, carried on their conversation. I'd have left then, but Julie had got to the bar and ordered a half of Guinness each. We sat down at an empty table and I began to feel all right, even if I was scared witless at the possibility of having to sing.

After a while a man came over with a book of tickets.

'Hello, Julie,' he said. 'Nice to see you again. Nigel will be in later.'

'The later the better,' Julie said. 'Never would be better still.'

He went lemon-gobbed at that, but smiled. 'I suppose you'd like to read some of your immortal work?' he said.

'No, but Sharon has a song or two worth listening to.'

He ran a look over me, like some guys inspect the underwear in Woolie's, and clearly wasn't thrilled by what he saw.

I didn't like what I saw either. He was a short, red-faced man whose plump body was crammed into a blue linen suit. He had on a blue-striped shirt with a white collar open at the neck and had given himself extra height by wearing black boots with thick heels. On his wrist was an expensive gold watch and next to it a silver bangle.

'Ah, we'll see after the interval,' he said, ripping two tickets out of the book and dropping them on the table before clopping off on his heels.

'Arsehole,' Julie said. 'That's Paul Curran. He's in Public Relations. Emma Porter – the yellow-haired woman at the bar – got him to help promote the group, but he mainly promotes himself while she does the real work. He fancies himself as a performer, too.'

'Takes all kinds.'

'I've never seen why.'

The place was filling up now as small groups of people banged in through the swing door and headed for the

304

bar or sat down at the tables. Most of them were young, with the Oxfam sale look that marks out university students' clothes but there were a few older people, including a really posh-looking middle-aged woman in Jaeger coat and her meek and mousey companion in a Windsmoor job with a chiffon scarf around her neck. No sign yet of Tom Fry or, thank God, the lovely Nigel. The Curran one clopped about selling tickets before heading for the bar and the couple who were in conversation with Emma Porter and the wimpish guy.

'That'll be Simon Verster,' Julie said.

He was quite old, with lots of thinning grey hair and a dark thin face with a hooked nose and hooded eyes, the lot balanced on a skinny neck so that he looked a bit like a good-natured vulture. The woman was younger, about forty to his sixty. She had a fantastic face, nearly as dark as his, with slightly slanted eyes, a wide mouth and a strong chin, and cropped hair of such a fierce red that you could have sworn it was on fire.

'And her?'

'Jeanne Cartier. She's his agent, pushes his work about, and, they say, keeps his bed warm. A writer, too – Anglo-French crime novels, most of them about a woman detective called Sappho.'

'Sounds kinky.'

'They're damn good. Anyway, she's used her connections to make him a bit of a cult across the channel.'

'May we join you?' The couple we'd been discussing were suddenly at our table. I prayed they hadn't overheard us.

'Sure,' Julie said, blushing in a way I thought she'd left behind with schoolbooks and pimples.

'We're escaping that man Curran,' Jeanne Cartier explained pleasantly in an accent that had just a rub of foreign spice. 'He's trying to talk down Simon's fee –

which was too low in the first place. On top of which he's a bore.'

'She means that he's never read a thing we've written,' Simon Verster grinned.

'That, too,' she replied. 'Simon's visit was Emma Porter's idea.'

'Time to begin, friends.' Curran was standing at a table near the swing door, pint in one hand, cyclostyled programme in the other. 'Welcome to another evening of Poetry Now. We'll be hearing soon from our distinguished guest writer, Simon Vorster . . . '

'Verster, Paul.' This from the wimpish young man.

'Of course, Verster. But first a quick warm-up song from my co-organizer, the brilliant and beautiful Emma Porter, to be followed by Simon, then some local poets and last but not least in the first half, the great white hope of self-accompanied song, Nigel Parkinson.'

'Shit,' breathed Julie.

'Bad as that, is he?' Simon Verster grinned again. 'Worse.'

The song Emma Porter chose was one of her own, a long wail about trees unleafing and love lost.

'She's ripped off Gerard Manley Hopkins,' Julie whispered. 'We did that poem at school, remember?'

'You're absolutely right,' Jeanne Cartier said approvingly, 'and the original is better.'

She gave Verster a small push. 'Get up there, Simon, before she sings an encore.'

He lumbered off willingly enough.

'It's my honour now, friends, to introduce Simon Verster, political poet and activist, who spent five years in a South African jail . . . ' began Curran.

'Eight,' the old writer said mildly.

'Sorry, eight.' Curran peered at his programme. 'Apart from which he is the author of several books of poetry, including the Mandela Trophy winner for the best political verse of 1989, published by Faber.'

'Heinemann, 1986,' Jeanne Cartier murmured murderously. 'Faber turned it down.'

'The title being –' he waved the programme – '*On the Crag*.'

'*Under the Krantz*,' Julie put in.

Jeanne Cartier looked at her keenly. 'You know it?'

'We got it out of the library,' Julie said. It was almost true. *She* had.

An elegantly plucked eyebrow arched. 'Amazing.' Then she turned away slightly to listen to Verster.

His stuff wasn't bad and he read it quite well in a low nasal voice which went with words like *sjambok, boer, donga* and *vrek*. But I couldn't really concentrate; at that point the swing door coughed open and Nigel Parkinson was among us, bumping his guitar case past the distinguished writer and sweating over to the bar where he loudly demanded a pint of bitter. Once he had it in his fist, he lay back against the counter and gave the room one of those scrolling glances that they seem to teach at universities along with all the other poses. Eventually he allowed himself to notice Julie and me and lifted his glass in what he believed was a casual salute.

'He's seen us,' I reported unnecessarily. 'He'll be over here any minute.'

'Not until he's had a few at the bar. He's too mean to get a big round in.'

Julie was right. Nigel stayed where he was. He stayed there even when Verster finished his spell and was followed first by an earnest young woman in a dirndl and one of those lank old-fashioned hairstyles, who read a yard-long poem against pollution and the plastic society, then by a lively butch character in leathers who banged out a song about women biking and a funnier one about the sexual inferiority of men who had to compensate by buying big cars and aircraft and guns.

These seemed to unsettle Curran. He clopped noisily up to the bar and ordered a drink, taking care to say 'love' and 'dear' loudly and patronizingly to the bar attendant before launching into animated chat with Nigel, whose greasepaper face reflected what he hoped was contemptuous amusement. Next a man came on to read a poem defending smoking, waving a lighted roll-up around to emphasize his arguments. It would have gone down better if he hadn't coughed and spluttered at several points and kept throwing furtive glances towards the swing doors every time someone pushed in through them, as though he was expecting to be arrested any moment. Maybe he was: I wouldn't like to bet that there was only tobacco in that spliff.

Next, just before the interval, came Nigel.

Curran made a meal of the preliminaries, telling us all that Nigel was the ideal three-in-one combination: a lyric writer, a singer and a player, brilliant in all departments. His work was muscular and masculine without being brutal and macho, sensitive without being sentimental. While this praise was being heaped Nigel was lugging his guitar to the centre of the room, fiddling with his calf-length boots, pushing his dingy T-shirt into his over-tight jeans and trying unsuccessfully to keep a glow of self-approval off his face. After some tuning-up while he looked around the company as though expecting to find a West End impresario hiding there, he began his routine.

But before he could get going there was a fuss at the door where Emma Porter had positioned herself. I could hear a voice as familiar as trouble in our street saying, 'But she said to join her here,' and Emma Porter's posher tones loaded with quiet reluctance. Then Emma Porter stood aside and a figure like a wet floor-mop in a dripping leather coat was inside the door and heading for our table: Phyllie.

'It's pissing down outside,' she said, helping herself to my Guinness as she sat down. 'A mush pushed me out at the top of the street because he couldn't get a hard-on and said it was my fault so I came on in.' She leaned across me and touched Julie's arm. 'I'll give you your jacket back when I've dried out, kid.'

'Fine, and I'll get you a drink,' Julie said. 'But first meet two famous writers.'

I'll say for the pair that they took it well, not looking sideways the way I might have done if I hadn't been at school with Phyllie. Simon Verster shook hands, then insisted he get the round and Jeanne Cartier produced an expensive-looking handkerchief from her bag so that Phyllie could dry her hair.

By this time Nigel had got going.

It was last, as we say round here. He started with some song about Empire. I could hear words like 'greed' and 'exploitation' and phrases like 'fetid foot-soldiers' and 'conscripted proles' croaked out in a hoarse whisper while he lurched and wriggled between the tables, the neck of his guitar waving about like a fairground donkey's dong, threatening to crack elbows and sweep glasses off the tables. Now and again he would raise his head and howl a word or two, then revert to his croaking or run out of breath altogether and and stand writhing in front of his gob-smacked listeners, sweat dripping like grease off a Christmas turkey.

When Nigel had finished the first song and had fetched up in front of our table, either because Julie was there or because he thought the distinguished poet had to be deeply impressed or simply because he was out of puff, the wimp stood up hopefully for *his* turn, crumpled bundle of poems in his hand. But before he could move, Nigel was off again, singing a number which he interrupted himself to announce was titled 'Look for the woman' or – probably auditioning Jeanne Cartier this time – '*Cherchez la femme*'. This he rendered with the familiar mixture of howls, growls and moans, in between raking his fingers across any strings they happened to encounter.

'Sweet Jesus,' groaned Jeanne Cartier. '*Quelle horreur.*'

Simon Verster was staring at Nigel in fascination. 'He can't write, he can't sing, he can't play and he's unintelligible,' he said in awe. 'What can he do?'

'Get pissed and pester people,' I said, and got a nod of agreement from Jeanne Cartier.

'I'm not even sure who he thinks he's imitating,' she said. 'He could be trying to be the white Jimi Hendrix or perhaps a born-again Elvis.'

'Perhaps he's just being himself?' Verster ventured.

'In that case, there's no hope at all.'

Nigel had finished his song to polite applause and was holding up a plump hand. 'My final song,' he announced a little thickly, 'was created in the belief that feminism has gone too far. Women aren't asking for equality any more. They want to dominate.'

'Lezzies,' shouted some guy from the middle of a small group, all got up in trench coats, who had filtered in once Nigel began singing.

'*Merdeur*,' Jeanne Cartier said with quiet venom.

Nigel smirked and added, 'It's called "Men Back on Top".'

Curran applauded loudly, followed by the trench-coated young men.

There was hissing from a surprising quarter: the woman in the Jaeger coat.

What was audible of the song was predictable after the title. The couple of lines I did hear went something like:

> Women want lovers who are really cocksmen
> Who'll give them orgasms again and again.

'Not one after the other,' Phyllie said, just loud enough to be heard. 'It's all ale-house talk.'

'Let women be women and males be males,' Nigel moaned on.

'Ale-house talk and brewer's droop,' said Phyllie.

Verster chuckled. He, at any rate, was enjoying himself.

I wasn't. 'I can't perform after this clown,' I said. My sheaf of songs was rustling in my hand like leaves in a wind.

'Of course you can,' Jeanne Cartier said, laying a hand on my wrist. '*Courage*.'

'Get on,' Julie said. 'We'll back you up.' She looked at the others. 'Won't we?' They nodded and before I knew what was happening they were crying out 'Sharon's turn!' and pushing me forward past Nigel who, after a defiant moment when he just stood there, sulkily dragged his guitar back to the bar.

'Sharon,' Julie shouted, echoed by Phyllie's squawk, Jeanne Cartier's contralto, Verster's nasal croak and, I thought, though I couldn't be sure, the voice of Jaeger coat. The wimp stood up, waving his own sheaf, then sat down.

I thought my legs were going to melt and dump me on the floor. Over by the bar I could see Emma Porter frowning slightly, then as I began to sing 'Shop Assistant Blues', a bit choky at first, but picking up strength, she shrugged in resignation.

I sang another song, joky and a bit rude, called 'Men's

Underwear' and had a bad moment when Curran came off the bar towards me, scowling. But he walked on and out of the door.

I wasn't brilliant, but when I sat down there was a fair amount of clapping and a bit of stamping and one or two cries of encore. Julie gripped my hand and told me I'd been a star and both Verster and the Cartier woman smiled at me. I felt shaky and quite weepy, but pleased, too. Nigel was glaring slivers of glass, but I wasn't going to let that worry me.

Meanwhile the wimpish young guy was finally up at the front. He read two thin little poems and got some thin applause. Then Emma Porter announced Verster would read a second time, followed by Curran and, to wind up, Verster again.

After announcing that these were the 'rashly promised' poems of passion, the old bird began with one about missing his wife in prison, which Phyllie liked, whispering loudly to Jeanne Cartier that it was dead sad. He followed it up with one about wanking in his cell which was a bit embarrassing but was respectfully received and got a sympathetic 'Poor old sod' from Phyllie – which confirms my suspicion that she's too soft to make a living on the game. Then he read a poem, quite funny really, about hopelessly fancying Joan Bakewell, who'd apparently interviewed him on some arts programme.

Suddenly Nigel, mumbling something I couldn't catch, was forcing his way past Phyllie and in between Julie and me, almost pushing her off her seat.

'Oh, get off,' Julie said, not looking at him.

'Jus' wanna be with . . . ' he muttered, plonking himself down.

Now the old poet was beginning a piece about two tipsy middle-aged lovers at the back of a bus. Nigel was wriggling about and trying some unintelligible chat out on Julie.

'Listen, you,' I said, 'I want to hear this, so why don't you shove off?'

'That's right, Nigel,' Julie said, 'you're not wanted here.'

Nigel stayed where he was and went on wriggling and mumbling.

'Oh, piss off, Nigel,' Julie said, losing patience.

Jeanne Cartier was watching us sharp-eyed, half amused, half irritated. From behind, the Jaeger coat leaned over and said, 'Shush.'

Simon Verster read on:

> 'This hot and hungry mouth to mouth
> the travelling hands
> the warmsweet reek of drink and lust
> must surely scandalize . . . '

Nigel dropped his greasy head onto Julie's shoulder.

'Oh, fuck off,' she snapped. He mumbled something but didn't budge.

Meanwhile Verster's bevvied pair snogged away:

> 'Those wrinkles, these lines, those marks of time
> are mortality inscribing his irresistible claim
> but under my hands your breasts throb with life
> if it isn't quite mate nor is it endgame.'

Perhaps it was the power of poetry. Perhaps it was just coincidence. Perhaps those cheeky nipples were too much for the silly sod on top of all the drink. But Nigel gave out a noise somewhere between a moan and whimper and groped Julie's breasts.

She didn't hesitate. Grabbing his pint from the table she tipped the contents into his lap.

He swore and jumped up, half knocking me from my

313

seat. The woman behind made a few remarks which weren't normally associated with Jaeger coats; nor was the accent, which was pure dockside. Then Emma Porter, and, surprisingly, the wimp, had hold of Nigel and were wangling him gently but firmly off to the bar.

Unaware of all this, the old writer read to the end of his poem, acknowledged the rather ragged applause and came over to us.

Someone must have called Curran because he came clopping back into the room brandishing his glass and shouting furiously. The reason wasn't at all clear but the target was – Julie. From his babble it emerged that if anyone was going to pour beer over Nigel, he was the one to do it because apparently that kind of thing was 'a chap's business'.

To emphasize his argument he raised his pint and poured it over Julie's head.

In the uproar that followed Curran yelled something about Julie and me being barred from the rest of the reading – and any future readings. I protested loudly. Emma Porter protested mildly. Jaeger coat, who was rising up my popularity chart fast, called Curran 'a stupid middle-class git who couldn't run a piss-up in a brewery'. Her meek mate said nothing – just looked misted up. Julie sat stunned, beer running down her face and neck.

The trench coat brigade gathered round us shouting, 'Gerroff' and when the wimp appeared protestingly at the centre of this merry throng someone swung a fist at him – landing mysteriously on his back on the floor. The exile rattled down the steel shutter at the bar. It was all beginning to look like a posher replay of the Cuckoo's Nest bother. At this point Simon Verster and Jeanne Cartier made it known firmly that if we had to go they would go, too.

Curran looked ugly and in a mood to try to have us all thrown out when, suddenly, Phyllie, hair still soaking, mascara spread all over her cheeks so that she looked like a half-drowned panda, was pointing at him accusingly.

'You there, soft dick,' she shrieked. 'You owe me money. I didn't recognize you at first because you look different with a man's clothes on. But I've been frigging chasing around looking for you for weeks. Now you pay up or I'll tell all of these –' her narrow hand gestured to include us all – 'what you made me do.'

He stared at her unbelievingly, the red face in spasm. You could have heard a tissue drop. Phyllie had the floor and was enjoying it.

'He's a real bastard,' she said. 'Kinky and mean with it. A cross between Scrooge and the Marquis de Sade.'

Curran opened his gob but no words came. Turning round he clip-clopped fast out of the door.

Verster was studying Phyllie admiringly. 'A cross between Scrooge and de Sade,' he murmured. 'The judgment of the hold-door trade has been delivered.'

'Was that true?' I asked Phyllie. 'Was he really your client?'

'No chance.' She laughed and shook her head. 'He's a mush, though. I've seen him around. Anyway, he was going to throw us out, wasn't he?'

It was then that Nigel chose to make his comeback from the bar. He had his guitar slung round his neck and was clutching a pint in his hand, half of which he heaved over Julie, the other over me. Before we could react he had clambered onto our table, helped by a trench coat, and stood there swaying in unsteady triumph. 'I'm gonna shing a shong that'll really pleashe you,' he slurred. 'It putsch the relationsh between men and women in pershpective: "Eshkimo Nell"!'

The trench coats roared their appreciation. Several women began to hiss and shout 'Sexist' and 'Pig' and even 'Shitmouth'. Nigel handed down his empty glass and began to strum, leering at us all.

He got through the first verse, actually managing to be audible *and* keep to the tune. But as he was moving into the second verse, the meek-looking woman who had come with Jaeger coat got up, excusing herself politely, and walked quietly behind Nigel, who was enjoying himself, spreading his legs and making bonking movements with the neck of his guitar. It was difficult to see what happened next, just that suddenly Nigel gave a squawk and, flinging his arms in the air, fell from the table with a crash and a violent twanging.

Confusion again. Trench coats rushed forward to pick up Nigel and his shattered guitar. There was a lot of shouting and some swearing. The bar shutter came rattling down for a second time. The meek woman began to sob and Jaeger coat moved quickly to comfort her.

'I'm so ashamed,' the mousey one wept. 'But I had to do it, love. He was so vile.'

'What did she do?' I demanded. Julie, still stupefied, shook her head, but Phyllie had the answer.

'Squeezed his balls,' she said. 'Good one.'

'So this is your quiet, improving poetry night,' I said to Julie, who, though looking pretty sick, managed a wan smile.

Emma Porter had me by the elbow. 'Would you mind singing again? Phil –' she nodded towards the wimp – 'thinks you have the right kind of robust approach.'

'He's right,' Jeanne Cartier said encouragingly as I dithered, trying to decide whether I'd been insulted or complimented, 'and *I* would very much like to see you sing again.'

So I did. I sang some of my own stuff, then a few numbers from the Joan Armatrading repertoire and even a Michelle Shocked number. The women showed their support by applauding loudly at the end of each song and the trench coats, after a few boos and catcalls, more or less quietened down. The exile reopened the bar.

Tom Fry didn't show up and I was sorry about that. On the other hand Nigel and Paul Curran didn't come back that night and, according to Emma Porter and the wimp over drinks afterwards, won't ever be coming back.

In a night of surprises there were two more to come. When I found myself in the women's room with Jeanne Cartier she gave me her card and took my address and said that she wasn't in the music agency business herself but she knew some women interested in new talent who would probably get in touch with me.

They haven't so far, but my mam is convinced they will.

'These things take time,' she said when I told her about the evening and added smugly: 'I told you it would be magic, didn't I?'

Meanwhile I've had one or two invitations to sing: nowhere much, but an invitation is an invitation and I might yet get paid.

That's almost all. Julie got her first and a part-time lectureship. We see a bit of Emma Porter and the wimp – who turns out to be not so wimpish and an expert on street defence – and like them quite a lot. I may sing at their wedding, though Julie says it would be prostituting my talents to use them at what she calls 'the tragi-comedy'. Phyllie is off drugs at the moment but still on the game. Nigel avoids us now and I've never seen Curran again.

I've never seen Tom Fry either, but somehow I don't mind too much. I didn't tell my mother about the second surprise – how, after the bit of chat, Jeanne Cartier kissed me, taking hold of me very gently and bringing her mouth down on mine very slowly, I think to give me plenty of time to escape if I didn't like the idea. I'd never been held and kissed that way by a woman before, but I liked it enough to take up Jeanne Cartier's offer to stay with her if I visit London.

So maybe my mother was right after all. There was magic of a sort that night. Just how strong I hope to find out when I get to London.

THE POSSIBILITY
OF JACK

A. S. Penne

Born and raised in Vancouver, A. S. Penne
has also lived in Montpellier, Montreal,
London and Sacramento. She currently
lives on the North Vancouver mountainside
with her daughter, cat and dog, and is
working towards an MFA degree at the
University of British Columbia. Ms Penne
writes non-fiction, short fiction and
screenplays.

THE POSSIBILITY OF JACK

Marie turns sideways to the mirror and looks at her profile. She pushes the gentle bulge that is her abdomen, shoving at either side of the slackness, bunching the fat into a doughnut shape with the bellybutton at centre. She shakes her head. Where had it come from?

Disgusting. Last year I looked all right in a bathing suit, but not now. Not any more.

Her eyes move upwards and she leans into the mirror, checking for new wrinkles around the eyes and mouth. Even her face betrays her, sagging into blobs around the eyes and the jawline.

Forty-four and my sex life is over.

Marie sighs, turns from the bleak vision in her mirror and slumps into a favourite armchair. Her right hand instinctively covers her eyes, closing them on the dull afternoon. When they open again, she is looking at the phone. She stares at it, wills the sound of its ring, then gets up. She crosses the room, dials a number she has known for years.

Jack isn't foldout material either. Maybe it could work . . .

Jack had been trying to seduce Marie, doing things that made his intentions entirely clear. It had been going on for a long time now. Almost a year, Marie realized. Ever since last summer.

Jack liked to give things, bring things to Marie. He

seemed to want to fulfil some archaic image of man-as-provider and it made her feel as if she was supposed to play a role too, to blush at his ardour or to swoon at his mere glance. It annoyed Marie that she gave Jack her full attention for his unwarranted gifts.

Sometimes Marie wished that she could just dismiss him with a sharp warning: 'Piss off, Jack – I'm not interested!' But they'd grown up together, gone to school and university together, and, when eventually they commiserated over their individually failed marriages together, Marie discovered a kind of intellectual kinship that she hadn't been aware of before. When they talked – when he didn't want something from her that she couldn't give – Marie felt aligned with Jack, attuned to his way of thinking. At those times she found herself re-evaluating his presence in her life and then she grew confused about whether she wanted to be more than just old friends.

If they'd been lovers, it might have been easy to accept his repeated attempts to woo her, but Marie had difficulty seeing Jack in a sexual light. It was like trying to imagine bedding Santa Claus, his fatherly beard, the crinkles around his eyes, a well-rounded belly. There was no stir in her nether regions, no hot rush between her legs or her ribs when she considered Jack. But Marie wasn't stupid: she knew that thirty-five years of friendship was worth more than most marriages these days.

And so Marie had a special relationship with Jack. They did the kind of things that married couples do, or at least the kind of things that Marie thought married couples should do together. They hiked, sailed, skiied, went dancing and made dinners together.

Last summer they'd gone on a canoe trip of the Powell Lakes. In Vancouver, before they left, Marie had been scared – going away with a lonely man – but also yearning to go. To be in the wilderness again.

They'd taken the dogs, his and hers, and gone into the pristine quiet of the forest with their world on their backs. Marie's terrier raced ahead of them while Jack's Labrador padded along behind.

'Mutt and Jeff,' Jack had remarked. Marie had thought he was referring to him and her.

'Aw, you're not a mutt! You're just a purebred in disguise!' she'd jibed.

The August heat blazed and each day Jack came off the lake with a deeper shade of tan. As his pallid city exterior receded Marie found herself looking at Jack in a different light. He was fit and healthy, despite his beefy figure, and she liked the fact that he was outdoorsy, contemplative, financially secure – all traits of her own. For a brief afternoon, Marie closed her eyes against the summer sun and imagined changing her friendship with Jack into something else. What she dreamed of, though, was something bigger, more consuming than an easy companionship. Marie wanted a challenge and so, when the face in her dream was not Jack's, she opened her eyes and dismissed her imaginings with a grim smile. She and Jack were good friends and she didn't want to complicate things with unrealistic expectations.

The trip took on a rhythm and a life of its own, whole days of visual splendour unfolding one after another. They rose early, while the air was still mild, swam in the warm, mirror-still water, eating breakfast between the tall cedars and the dark shore, waiting for the sun to burst above the black hills around them. During their paddle to the next portage, periods of quiet strokes were interrupted with serious philosophical discussion or, sometimes, jokes that filled the emptiness with their startling laughter. Marie felt swollen with happiness, freed by the knowledge that their common history made such a trip possible, without suggestive overtones.

Sometimes they stopped early in the day to swim or fish all afternoon, or lie on the rocks and read. At night by the fire, they'd relive old events or discuss new directions in their lives, and in the silences they'd listen to the plaintive loons on the lake. Looking at the horizon, Marie was content to see all the years she and Jack had spent together melted into one long memory.

But that memory was scarred now, like a photograph folded in half. Jack had said something that changed everything between them. On the canoe trip, the fourth day out, they'd gone for an evening walk along the trail from their campsite, found a hewn-out log facing the sunset. They sat together enjoying the feeling of being in a painting, small figures at the corner of a large canvas.

And then 'I'm really interested in you, Marie,' spilled into the quiet dusk and Marie's neck seized. She fought her impulse to run into the fading day, stayed and felt the gigantic silence between them. A loon crying out to some lost mate, noisy and alone in the middle of the lake, swam circles in the dying light. Marie focused on the loon, the bird's need so loud he couldn't hear the silence all around.

The daylight ended steadily and Jack spoke again: 'What are you thinking?'

'I wish you hadn't said that.'

From the periphery of her view, Marie saw Jack's head turn away, bow and look at his hands clasped between his legs, foot tracing patterns in the dirt.

'Look, Marie – we've known each other since kindergarten . . . we have a lot of history together and the last few days we've shared a lot of fun. It's easy to be with you and I just thought . . . I guess I just wanted to let you know that.' He picked up a rock and flung it into the distance. It was too dark to see where it landed, but Marie heard the *plock* of rock entering water.

Then she felt Jack's hand reaching for hers. She squeezed it quickly and let go, stood up.

'Let's go back and light a fire – it's getting cold.'

'Okay. But don't be upset about this, all right?'

'I'm not,' she lied.

Marie didn't know she had lied until she felt the knot growing in her neck on the way back to camp. She didn't know how to dissolve her fear and for a moment she wished she could make Jack disappear like the rock in the water, covered over by darkness.

Marie hung over the edge of the canoe, peering into the depths of the lake. Near the shore she'd been able to see the bottom, but out here in the middle of the water there was nothing more than her imagination at work. Marie couldn't tell if the eerie hint of dark floating shapes was her paranoia or the rays of sharp sunlight making images of floating particles in the water. Every so often a deadhead covered in slimy algae would appear, poking up out of the dusty depths, pointing at her like a finger. She was supposed to warn Jack if any of the deadheads were sharp enough or close enough to the surface that they needed to paddle around them. But he was paddling so slowly this morning that she didn't worry too much.

'Marie?' Something about Jack's tone.

'Mm-h'm?' she responded, hoping her warm laziness would influence whatever he had to say.

'Can we talk some more about last night?'

Marie closed her eyes. Water, water everywhere. Over her head.

'I'm not sure I have much to say about it, Jack.'

'I'd just like to know how you're feeling.'

Marie picked up her paddle, began stroking the smooth water, stirring it into black ridges. 'You're my friend, Jack. I like you for my friend. I don't want to change anything.'

'I don't either, Marie. I just want us to be closer if we can.'

'That's what I'm saying, Jack. I don't think we can be closer without being physical and I don't want that.'

'Is there a particular reason you aren't interested?'

Marie let the silence build around the sound of the paddles dipping and sifting through the water. She bit her lip, trying for the words that would tell Jack she wasn't attracted to him that way. She wanted to end this trip, get out of this canoe and still have Jack for a friend.

'I don't want a lover, Jack. I'm happy being single and having lots of solitary time. My life is very full, even hectic. There's no room for someone else in it.'

'Even one night a week?'

'Yes! I mean no! I mean there are lots of weeks where one night a week is too much – I don't always have the time!'

'Well, on those weeks you could just tell me you're too busy and I could do something else . . . '

Marie could feel the ridges of tension building along her shoulders, the dampness under her arms, the exertion of all her energy. And now her eyes burning too.

'I don't want to be committed to anything or anybody, Jack. I just want to concentrate on pulling back and focusing on my life now, Jack.'

'Does that mean we could try again later?'

'Let me think about it, okay?'

'I understand – okay.'

The tears stung Marie's sunburned cheeks and she stopped her furious paddling to wipe her nose. She was glad she had her back to Jack, glad she couldn't see his good intentions.

She dosed her coffee with an extra shot of Southern Comfort that night. It helped her get to sleep, but she still found herself awake and claustrophobic later. She climbed over the two dogs to unzip the tent door.

'You okay?' Jack mumbled from inside his sleeping bag.

'Fine – I'm fine. Just have to pee,' Marie whispered into the opening as she closed the fly behind her. Outside the dark was so complete that she froze, listening to small scufflings in the bush. After a minute, the night noises and the blackness grew familiar and the lunging shapes on the trees became towels swinging in the night. Marie curled her blanket around her shoulders and hunched up against a trunk to stare at the lake.

A loon paraded close to shore, erratic zigzags of head and wake. Marie watched the bird, admiring the reflection of moonlight on its spotted back, imagining she could see the glint of its black eye looking at her. She remembered reading about native youths sent into the forest to find their spirit guides and momentarily wondered about this loon's presence, waiting for it to give her a sign.

Marie watched the dark bird swim a zigzag pattern across the still lake, hunting for something. When it dove, Marie closed her eyes, listening for the underwater sounds of fish and insects, trying to feel the pulse of dark water against her face and in her ears. When the loon surfaced, Marie could see nothing in its beak, could only guess where it had been. Not even a sheen of wetness remained on its back, as if the water had not touched the bird streaking through blackness.

It made her think about how wanting something too much can obsess a person, about how Jack wanted something she didn't want. She didn't see how Jack's obsession could be forgotten or even allowed to fade without affecting their friendship. It felt like his need was always going to hang over her so that, whenever she looked at him, Marie would remember the stifling feeling of being in the canoe, the tent, the water.

At dawn, Marie uncurled herself from the blanket to swim in the coloured water. The envelope of warm waves against her nakedness soothed the rawness of the night. She swam away from the shore, into the middle of the lake, and when she turned to look back at the campsite, she felt the caress of the hot sun on her head out of water. Removed from Jack's shadow, Marie felt less disposed to be angry with him. She wanted to be kind, not hurtful. After all, he was her friend, her old friend.

She saw Jack's bulky shape moving about the campsite, saw him setting up the camp stove to make coffee. He flung the remains of last night's brew into the campfire ashes, then trudged down to the water's edge to fill the pot. Marie was treading water, waiting for him to notice her. Jack rose from squatting by the water's edge, turned and walked back up the slope to the picnic table. Marie put her face into the water and swam slowly, definitely towards the rock where her clothes lay.

'Hey!' Jack's voice, fuzzy from sleep, croaked when he saw her come up the slope. 'Where were you?'

Marie was towelling her hair as she walked towards him. She sat down at the table, a spot in the sun. 'Out there. I waved at you when you were peeing . . . didn't you see me?'

Jack's eyes widened in surprise, a reaction that intrigued Marie. She bent over, let her hair fall forward, rubbed the wet undersides of her head, waiting for him to call her bluff. But Jack said nothing, busying himself instead with the knotted food bag. Marie looked at him

328

through the curtain of hair over her eyes, watched as he buried his arm in the canvas bag, groping about in fierce concentration. She could feel his tight silence and realized, without understanding, that she had made him uncomfortable.

'Jack.' She sat up and flung her hair back, intending to put him at ease.

'Yeah?'

Jack's shirt stretched across his broad back and Marie waited for his shoulders to turn. When they didn't, Marie changed her mind. 'Do you want porridge for breakfast?' she asked quickly.

'I guess. Yeah, sure.'

They listened to the coffee bubble and hiss while they ate. The lake – and Marie – shimmered, calm under the glare of the morning sun.

It was well after the summer, the air deepening into autumn sharpness, when Marie felt enough distance to think about the canoe trip with any pleasure. The end of the trip had been irritating, a long, drawn-out summary to a foregone conclusion. Jack's neurotic idiosyncracies about packing and his insistence on being the leader had forced Marie to relinquish the calm she'd found after her long night in the presence of the loon. During the last two days of the trip, whenever Jack had spoken to her, the sight of gentle longing in his eyes had caused a sharp edge to creep into Marie voice. In the evenings, to have some time to relinquish the constant vigilance she kept, Marie had encouraged Jack to go fishing, leaving her alone with the dogs and the sunset and giving her time to plan just how, when they rested along a portage, she could keep him from massaging her tired back muscles.

Of course she'd had to hug him goodbye at the end

of the trip, but she'd done it without care, untangling herself quickly from Jack's stubby arms. Now, though, standing at her bedroom window, feeling the Arctic air drift down from the mountains like a long whistle of ice, Marie considered the long, west coast winter, the grey afternoons and the black nights to come. She thought about Jack's invitation to call him any time and she wondered if she'd been wrong, too hasty, to push him away. The possibility of Jack – of any man – being in her bed was enticing and Marie didn't want to think about possible repercussions.

After phoning Jack, Marie lies down, remembers images from that hot summer far away, wonders if she'll ever get to do it again. Later she spends an hour putting on make-up. Not that she has to look a certain way for Jack, but so that she feels a certain way about herself. For a while it works: Marie feels calm and capable when Jack arrives. But later, at a singles bar, Jack starts talking about the two of them again, resurrecting the possibility of being a couple in a relationship.

'I think it's important to know what turns your partner on, don't you?' he says from across the table.

'I think that's the kind of thing you discover about someone as you get to know them,' she answers.

'What about asking, though, so you can experiment together?'

'Feels too cold and calculated to me.'

'You wouldn't like to be asked?'

'I guess that would depend who was asking, Jack.'

'If it was me? If we were ever to get together?'

Marie feels her anxiety – his stubbornness – slam into her brain like a cell door. She pleads allergies to the cigarette smoke in the air and goes to the ladies' room. She knows that Jack will call for the bill while she's gone. He will hurry to pay before she gets back, holding his wallet close to his chest as if to protect it from muggers. Marie is glad to avoid that scene. She would have to look down, away, to hide her embarrassment at his lack of finesse. She is uncomfortable that she costs him anything at all, that he never lets her pay. Marie feels she is providing a kind of service, prostitution of a lesser degree.

They go to Jack's place. He wants to play her his new CD of Gaelic jigs. Marie hopes the music will break the funk she has slipped into. But Jack's apartment is like an animal's den, grease spatters all over the stove, dust as thick as a layer of topsoil so that mess seems to sprout from it – Marie squeezes herself into a corner of the couch, sits with her legs tightly crossed, her back stiff. Now everything crowds her – the way Jack is dressed, his clothes as if they have lain in a wrinkled heap all night; his portly body; his annoyingly easy-going nature. Suddenly she must go home. Not feeling well, she tells him. Jack helps her on with her coat.

In the car Marie takes deep breaths of air like stiff snorts of brandy. To calm herself. She feels a reckless anger building inside. She wants to force Jack to look in a mirror, see himself.

'Even semi-greatness requires attention to details,' Marie wants to say. 'You could be great at something. You've just got to find it. A career, an interest – find something other than me to devote yourself to.'

Eventually she asks, 'How was your interview last week?' and Jack answers in the way she expects.

'Oh fine. But the guy I talked with seemed unclear about what he was looking for and whether they could use my expertise or not.'

'So when do you expect to hear back from them?'

'Well actually I thought I'd've heard something by now.'

'Are you going to call them back, check it out?'

'No. I figure if they don't call me it means they're not interested.'

Marie glares out her window. The rain begins as Jack's car turns into her street. Marie tries to imagine the two of them, she and Jack, lumped under the covers, her sagging stomach against another bulge of unfamiliar origin. If she gave in to her physical desires, if the experience turned out to be like a stuttering teenage foray into the world of passion – slobbering, perspiring, unfulfilling sex, insubstantial and immemorable or, worse, all too memorable – how would she dismiss him then? Jack, she knew, would want to stay for breakfast the next morning, would want to talk about how wonderful last night had been.

And he might suggest moving in, making pancakes and eggs for her in the morning. The quiet calm of mornings filled with coffee and muted barking in the distance would have to end. Instead there would be Jack, too attentive for her to slip away, so earnest that she must listen, wanting her full concentration. He would bury her with his blatant desire; she would become invisible, even to him.

Marie slips out of the car when it stops at the kerb. 'Good night, Jack,' she leans down to say. 'Thanks.'

Marie digs for her keys while Jack's car coughs at the side of the road. She stands in darkness, the outdoor light left off when she went out, hoping that Jack will not get out to help her. When she unlocks the door, Marie stands in the flood of light spilling out from the opening and waves goodbye. As Jack's car pulls away, the headlights catch a dark shape approaching Marie's walkway.

Marie recognizes the heavy, rolling movement of old Mrs Grapelli from next door and she turns on the porch light to help the nearly blind woman. For a long minute the night air is filled with Mrs Grapelli's ferocious wheezing and the sound of her cane scraping the walkway to Marie's house. Near the bottom of Marie's stairs, Mrs Grapelli stops, tips her head up sideways to the light. Like a robin, Marie thinks.

'Is ... this ... ' the old woman's voice is thin, so sparse that Marie leans forward to listen.

'It's Marie, Mrs Grapelli. You've got the wrong house. Shall I take you home?'

'Please ... ' the woman wheezes.

Marie descends the uneven wooden stairs, takes old Mrs Grapelli's arm and turns her gently, slowly, heading back up the walkway.

The old woman moves with small shuffling steps and Marie pauses several times to encourage her. She studies the bent crone, simultaneously amazed and repulsed by her advanced age. Marie stares at the blue wateriness of the skin on the back of Mrs Grapelli's hand, the pronounced curve of her shoulders hunched beneath a loose shawl, the painstaking effort of her breath, coming so slowly and with such gasping sounds.

At the Grapellis' house, Marie hands the old woman to her granddaughter, a tired young mother, harassed by the non-stop duties of caring for others.

Back home, Marie closes the door and sighs. There was, after all, the matter of companionship. Who would check on her when she was old? She had no one, no husband or child. What if she became like old Mrs Grapelli, bent and blind, wandering city streets at night, dependent on horrified strangers to pick her up when she slipped and fell on old, splintery bones ...

The city lay beneath the pressure of steel-grey skies. A wet snow had begun to fall and Marie's eyes were drawn to the sleepy dance of the flakes outside. She got up from her desk and the half-marked pile of student exams to stare out the window.

When the phone rang, Marie leaped to answer it. The thought of human contact, if only at the end of a telephone line, was reassuring.

'Guess who,' said Jack.

'Hi, Jack. I was just sitting down to work.'

'Okay – I won't take long. I forgot to tell you the other night that I finally took the film from our trip in to be developed and I just got it back. Thought you might like to see the prints?'

'Yes – yes I would. Are they any good?'

'Well the ones of the dogs are the best!'

'Figures!'

'What about tomorrow ... what are you doing in the morning?'

'Tomorrow's good. About ten?'

'Sounds great.'

'Come in – you want coffee? I just made some.' Marie opened the door wider to Jack.

'Sure,' he beamed at her. 'Love some. Here –' he held out an envelope – 'I brought you a Christmas card.'

It was a rude one. 'Is that a candy cane in your pocket,' it asked on the outside, 'or are you just glad to see me?' inside.

'Nice taste!' Marie remarked without looking at him.

'I found it at my dad's place.' Jack's father had died

six months before and he was still cleaning out the house to sell it.

There was a handwritten inscription inside the card:

Roses are red
Violets are blue
Why don't you come for dinner Saturday night
for some lamb vindaloo?
Then we can take all our clothes off
And I'll kiss, nibble and lick you!

Marie turned aside as the panic rose in her chest. She felt Jack's eyes watching her. Marie held onto the counter with her empty hand and laughed, hoping it didn't sound too hollow. She turned around. 'I'll have to censor these last two lines in case anyone else reads the card!'

'You like my proposition?'

Into the blur of her thoughts swam the crying loon of last summer. Marie heard again the bird's loud need, the lake's waiting silence. She saw the loon dive and traced its body streaking like a dark rock, beak pointed at the lake's bottom, weaving to miss the deadheads. She held her breath, waiting for the solitary bird to surface, to see if he'd found anything. Anything at all.

The silence was drowning Marie, choking any possibility of words in the small passage of air from her chest. She stood next to Jack, her willing mate, trying to think. Trying to try. Maybe she should . . . If it didn't work, she could tell him later . . .

He put his arm around her shoulder, stood next to her against the kitchen counter. It was the *good night* and *thank you* which always seemed to mean something else at the end of an evening. At least that would stop . . . If she did . . .

'Earth to Marie,' Jack spoke into her ear.

The intensity which permeated anything Jack did or

said. It depleted her and left her wanting to hide. The rocks, the water.

'What's going on in there, Marie? Don't shut me out.' The arm on her shoulder held her against his body. Marie felt herself being pulled under; she struggled to keep her head out of the water, mustered a smile.

'Sorry, Jack. Not all here I guess.'

'That's okay.' The cupped palm around her shoulders, gripping. 'I'm here for you, you know.'

Jack bent his face over Marie's, his eyes so close that she shut hers against them and Jack reached his mouth to hers. Her neck tensed at the first tickle of moustache. Jack's other arm pulled her round and into him. Marie tried to steer her way through the deadheads with her eyes closed. The rush of water against her ears.

The winners of the 1994 Ian St James Awards

In category A – 2,000 to 5,000 words

Alison Armstrong
Stephanie Ellyne
Clare Stephens Girvan
Anna McGrail
Kirk O'Connor
A. S. Penne

In category B – 5,000 to 10,000 words

Peter Caley
Sue Camarados
Joshua Davidson
David Evans
Vivien Gaynor
Bronia Kita
Jackie Kohnstamm
Kate Lincoln
Mike McCormack
Tom Smith

The Killing Anniversary
Ian St James

'Ian St James has the gift of storytelling.'
THE TIMES

Two men and a country born in blood. Generations of hatred erupted in their final confrontation . . .

Their families had fought side by side in the savage days of Ireland's birth. But the love that bore them also spawned in one of them a bitter jealousy, a burning hatred and a perverted lust for vengeance. For he was consumed by the blind fanaticism of class war and an insatiable hunger for personal vendetta. The time to celebrate the killing anniversary was close at hand . . .

'Irresistible.'
NEW YORK TIMES

ISBN 0 00 617178 8

The Herb Gatherers
Elizabeth Harris

A powerful and obsessive love echoes across the ages . . .

All his life, Rafe has been haunted. The tormented spirit of mysterious Alienor, abandoned by her Crusader lover centuries ago, will not leave him alone. Who is she? What does she want?

Despite a growing sense of danger, Rafe follows a trail to the quiet Kent countryside and there, as if waiting for him, is Nell. Her resemblance to Alienor is uncanny . . .

'Enormously enjoyable . . . hard to put down. Elizabeth Harris writes with sensitivity and skill and a spine-chilling eye for the sinister'   Barbara Erskine, author of *Lady of Hay*

ISBN 0 00 617986 X

The Egyptian Years
Elizabeth Harris

The mysterious disappearance of Genevieve Mountsorrel in the Egyptian desert in 1892 was a longstanding family puzzle. Newly married, the young and vivacious Genevieve had sailed for Egypt, happy at the prospect of a new life. No one could explain the tragic turn of events. Only her parasol had been found, hastily discarded in the hot and dusty sand.

A century later, Willa, a distant relative, discovers Genevieve's diary. Drawn immediately into an astonishing story, she learns of Genevieve's secret life and the child she was forced to abandon, the truth about her sinister husband, Leonard, and the extraordinary drama of what really happened to Genevieve Mountsorrel . . .

Acclaim for *The Herb Gatherers*:

'Enormously enjoyable. Elizabeth Harris writes with sensitivity and skill.'
Barbara Erskine

ISBN 0 00 647191 9

☐	CROCODILE TRAPP Brian Callison	0-00-617997-5	£4.99
☐	GREEN SHADOWS, WHITE WHALE Ray Bradbury	0-00-647634-1	£4.99
☐	AN OLDER WOMAN Alison Scott Skelton	0-586-21508-5	£5.99
☐	THE RED SHAWL Jessica Blair	0-586-21857-0	£4.99
☐	LET NOT THE DEEP Mike Lunnon-Wood	0-00-647590-6	£4.99
☐	DOLL'S EYES Bari Wood	0-586-21862-9	£4.99

These books are available from your local bookseller or can be ordered direct from the publishers.

To order direct just tick the titles you want and fill in the form below:

Name: _____

Address: _____

_____

Postcode: _____

Send to: HarperCollins Mail Order, Dept 8, HarperCollins *Publishers*, Westerhill Road, Bishopbriggs, Glasgow G64 2QT.

Please enclose a cheque or postal order or your authority to debit your Visa/Access account –

Credit card no: _____

Expiry date: _____

Signature: _____

– to the value of the cover price plus:

UK & BFPO: Add £1.00 for the first and 25p for each additional book ordered.

Overseas orders including Eire, please add £2.95 service charge.

Books will be sent by surface mail but quotes for airmail despatches will be given on request.

24 HOUR TELEPHONE ORDERING SERVICE FOR
ACCESS/VISA CARDHOLDERS –
TEL: GLASGOW 041-772 2281 or LONDON 081-307 4052